Blaze & Skyfire

The Root of Glory: Book Two

By Robert Digitale

Franklin Park Press
2015

Franklin Park Press
Santa Rosa, California
Email: rdigit9@yahoo.com

Blaze & Skyfire
The Root of Glory, Book Two
By Robert Digitale

Library of Congress Control Number: 2015953722

ISBN: 978-0-9832435-1-9

Fiction/Fantasy

Printed in the United States of America

To:
Tim, Dean and Paul,
three friends who have challenged me
to be a better writer and a better human being.

Blaze & Skyfire Characters

The MuKierin (Clan of the Horse)
Roj: the Horse Stalker
Blaze: his son
Remy: Roj's sister
Noli: Remy's husband
Roff: Noli & Remy's son, Blaze's cousin
Stannis, Kick, Harney & Quirt: Roff's cousins
The White Beard: the King's Steward
Tustin: a slave rescued by Blaze
Cisly: a courtesan
Lowi & brother Sunny: insurrectionists
Darnelle: Lowi and Sunny's sister
Chakka Ri: the GrandElder
Morros: the Elder of Orres
Shutoo: counsel to Morros
Bar MuBarishta: a cadet at the Academy

The King's People
Healdin: The King's daughter, Roj's wife
Mirri: Healdin's servant
Tor: Commander of the King's army
Aidyn: Sorenth's rescuer
Burl: Tustin's guide

The Rebels
Pibbibib: known as Backstabber
Weakling
Zoirra: the rebel Master
Lord Mackadoo: Zoirra's key envoy
Mackadoo's sergeant
Rakmah: an underling of Mackadoo
Zhaggee: a Red Brigade warrior

The Pappi (The Clan of the Lake)
Bairn: a trader and Pappi council member
Sorenth: a cadet at the Academy.
Lon: a cadet
Tie: a MuKierin and former slave
Bo: Sorenth's brother & chief cadet at the Academy

The Quolli (Clan of Thieves)
Yawnna: a Quolli maiden
Ciga: Yawnna's father
Kitar: Yawnna's servant

The Academy: School for the Clans
Aeres: the headmaster

From Book One in The Root of Glory:
HORSE STALKER

HORSE STALKER told of a young man who changed the future for his people. To do so, he had to ride a great horse, trust a mysterious woman and survive the attack of ageless enemies who feared he was about to discover an awesome power.

The story began when Roj, a young horse hunter, chased a Spotted Stallion into high desert mountains. There, Roj and his brother-in-law, Noli, met an old hermit, who warned them they were in great danger from strange warriors who were "old as stone and fierce as wolves." The hermit took the two young men for protection to a foreign woman named Healdin. She told Roj the forgotten history of the Seven Clans of the Dry Lands, including his own people, the MuKierin.

Long ago, a King rescued Roj's ancestors from starvation and thirst in the desert. In return, they stole the King's power, the Root of Glory, and ran off with it. For months after, the people fought and killed each other in their attempts to control the power. Eventually it disappeared, but not before its light had pierced the hearts of all mortals and left them with an unquenchable longing, a yearning that has been passed down to all their descendants. That longing cannot be satisfied until the same King sends a champion to recover the Root of Glory and bring the people to his home in the Green Lands.

For generations, the people of the Dry Lands have been terrorized by giant, ageless warriors who long ago rebelled from the King after failing in their own attempt to steal the Root of Glory. The rebels are known as the Realm, and their master Zoirra was blinded when he tried to steal the great power. Nearly all the rebels fear to touch the Root of

Glory, but Zoirra has vowed to somehow take control of it and use it to vanquish the King.

Among the evil ones are two lowly warriors, Pibbibib, known as Backstabber, and Weakling. In an early battle with Healdin's allies, Pibbibib and Weakling killed the hermit but failed to murder Roj and Noli. From that encounter, the two warriors became valuable to the Realm because they are the only rebels who can recognize Roj.

Healdin safely returned Roj and Noli to their home in the low country. She later told Roj that he could change the future and help his people if he would become the Horse Stalker, the man who could ride a Spotted Stallion at the Challenge of Orres. At this challenge, many MuKierin tried and failed to stay atop the great horse. But Roj succeeded and was named the Horse Stalker. Immediately he became wanted both by the Realm's warriors and by a conspiracy of humans who had long been seeking the Root of Glory. Both groups suspected that Roj might be the King's champion and might know the whereabouts of the great power.

With Healdin's help, Roj escaped to the Pappi, a clan that lives beside a great freshwater lake in the west. There he stayed at the estate of a trader named Bairn. Healdin eventually joined him there. Meanwhile, the human conspirators kidnapped Roj's brother-in-law, Noli, and took him to the lake country to use him as bait to capture Roj. In order to save Noli and himself, Roj falsely told the kidnappers that he could take them to the Root of Glory. Meanwhile, Pibbibib and Weakling learned the kidnappers had taken Roj. The two warriors gave chase in the hopes that Roj was headed to retrieve the great power. On a darkened hilltop, Roj and Noli managed to foil and escape their kidnappers. In a confrontation with the rebel warriors, Roj wounded Weakling with a stone blade that had been given special powers by Healdin. Weakling survived the stabbing and discovered that power from the blade now lived inside him. With them, he could sense the approach of the King's warriors. Pibbibib vowed to use Weakling's "gift" to help him take control of the Root of Glory.

After the battle, the King's warriors rescued Roj and Noli, and Roj finally professed his love for Healdin. She agreed to marry him and told him that she is the daughter of the King. Roj then learned exactly how he would change the future: He would father a son, the King's grandson, who one day would become the champion.

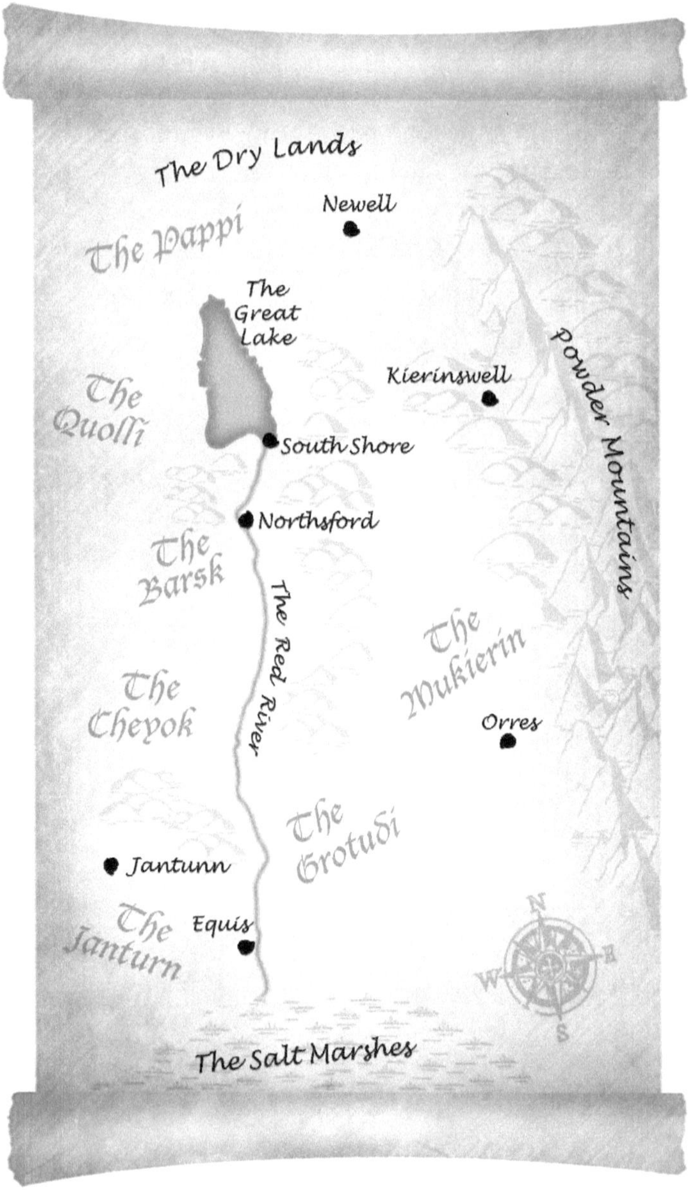

The Dry Lands
Newell
The Pappi
The Great Lake
Kierinswell
The Quolli
South Shore
Powder Mountains
Northsford
The Barsk
The Red River
The Mukierin
The Cheyok
Orres
The Grotudi
Jantunn
The Janturn
Equis
N
E
W
S
The Salt Marshes

Introduction

Alpine flowers bloomed blue and white when Roj and Healdin returned to the Powder Mountains. It was high summer, and Healdin was great with child. Even so, she was determined to give birth in Roj's homeland. As a result, the couple left the great freshwater lake of the Pappi and journeyed east to the land of the MuKierin, the Clan of the Horse. After a week's journey they returned to the same high country where they had first met, a land of scarred peaks and desolate ridges. There in a cave in a treeless canyon, Healdin gave birth to a son. And they named him Blaze.

The White Beard, the King's steward to the MuKierin, immediately sent messages to a select group of old horse hunters. He urged them to gather for a special journey into the high country. He also sent word to a young man of a prominent family in the capital of Kierinswell.

A week later, the White Beard arrived at the base of Fire Mountain, the sacred meeting place of his people. The mount stood about an hour's ride east of Kierinswell at the end of a long valley. It was a great, exposed hill with its top as flat as a table. There, on a late summer morning, the old horsemen gathered. Two strings of packhorses stood loaded nearby. And off to one side waited a stout, young man in his twenties. His name was Chakka Ri, and his late father had been an Elder. He stood tall, with an ample belly, a groomed brown beard and a close-cropped head of hair. His costly grey tunic stood out from the worn cloaks of the horse hunters. The old men, who cut neither their grey hair nor their beards, greeted each other with knowing smiles. They had waited so long for this day. The young man stared silently at them.

At last, the White Beard gave a signal and the party set off, turning east into crooked ravines and over the rounded hilltops of the eastern foothills. All day they passed massive boulders and great thickets of prickly brush clinging to parched slopes. By evening, they had climbed high into the wild lands above Kierinswell. The group kept traveling until the sun dipped beneath the western hills, perhaps to show

Chakka Ri that these old men weren't yet past their prime. That night they camped in a spot with poor feed for their horses but a little water. They ate dried meat and flat bread and washed it down with desert tea. Few of the old men did more than nod at the Elder's son. Chakka Ri went to bed early and had a fitful night sleep on the unmercifully hard ground.

At dawn the packers once more made two long strings of their beasts of burden—the tail of the lead horse tied to the head of the one behind it, and so on. When the party set off, Chakka Ri rode near the rear of the procession. But later in the morning he nudged his mount ahead, making his way into line behind the White Beard. They rode in silence until they reached a promontory that provided an expansive view of the brown ridgetops around them. A few peaks stood out from the rest in the morning sun. The highest were dappled with snow from the previous spring. The old man pulled his horse aside and motioned to his young guest. "Very few MuKierin have come up here and lived to tell the tale, Chakka Ri. For years, the high places were a graveyard for those who rode up here. Even now the land holds much danger."

"Do your companions want me to come up here?" Chakka Ri asked. "I don't think so."

"They know that you must come with me. That is all that matters."

"I have come as you asked. In return, you must tell me about the old days with my parents. I want to know why my mother married my father and not you.

The old man nodded. "Yes, I promise to tell you what you want to know. And I want you to meet someone up in these mountains. We should find him tomorrow. In the meantime, let me remind you that we have crossed into dangerous country. Up here I urge you to watch who you trust. For the sake of your mother and your late father, I will say it again. Watch yourself."

That day the riders moved beyond the foothills and entered great mountains. On rocky trails they passed scattered bunches of blue wildflowers and spied white goats bounding along the cliffs above them. That night they camped on the edge of a green meadow. A small stream trickled nearby, fed by a glistening snowfield from a northern slope. As the sun set, Chakka Ri sat on his blanket and gazed silently at the vast wilderness all around him.

On the third morning, they passed along a narrow trace to the top of a great ridge. From there, they descended far into a treeless canyon. An hour later they turned a bend and spied a young man in a dark brown cloak, standing by the mouth of a cave. The horsemen rode up and formed a semi-circle around the stranger. Chakka Ri held back and studied the surrounding hills. The land seemed empty.

The White Beard announced, "Brothers, here is the man. This is the Horse Stalker."

"Welcome, friends," said Roj. "Please come inside. My wife and I have been waiting for you."

The men dismounted and tied up their horses. A few grabbed leather pouches from their packhorses before entering the cave. Chakka Ri came last. Immediately he caught the scent of fire and let his eyes adjust to the dim light from a few tapered candles. Before him a tall woman sat on a great cushion by a small fire. Her face was veiled and she wore a black shawl. In her lap she held a small babe wrapped in a gray blanket. And beside her lay a golden-haired hound with bent ears and a dark, wolf-like snout. The dog's head perked up at the sight of the strangers. He seemed ever watchful, but he never barked nor growled.

Roj proceeded to light more candles and place them on small rock ledges along the cave walls. The old horsemen stood dumb and awkward, trying not to stare too long at the woman and her infant. Finally the Horse Stalker took his seat beside his wife. As he did, the White Beard stepped forward and leaned on his staff.

"This is the child," he declared. "This is the one the Stone Woman promised us long ago. After all these years, her words have been fulfilled. The child has come. And we are the first MuKierin to behold him."

Some of the old men began to kneel. Others wept. Two men reached out and hugged one another. The White Beard bent down and took the child in his arms. "Bring me the oil," he said. Another man pulled a small clay vial from a pouch and removed its wooden plug. Holding the child, the White Beard dipped a finger in the oil and placed it on the babe's meager crop of brown hair. "I am the King's steward to the MuKierin," he said. "I am the first to give my allegiance to this child. My hope is that he will become a man after the King's heart. And may I never fail him."

He returned the babe to his mother and stepped back among the men.

A horse hunter with reddish cheeks and a thin gray beard stepped forward. In his right hand, he held a leather thong with a black volcanic stone, the sacred stone of the clan. It was nearly circular with a hole in it. The man said to Roj, "We give this stone to the child. When he wears it, may he remember all the children of the Stone Woman."

As the man stepped away, he turned and locked eyes on Chakka Ri, who returned the stare. After a long gaze at each other, the two men looked away. As they did, the White Beard raised a hand and spoke: "Let us drink to the health of the child."

At those words, Roj rose and took up a wineskin. He began to pour out its dark red contents into a collection of clay goblets. Chakka Ri inched forward, seeking to catch a better look at the veiled woman. Their eyes met and she stared at him without flinching. He noted the hound also had fixed its eyes on him. After a few moments, Chakka Ri withdrew to his place in the shadows. Meanwhile, each man received a goblet. The White Beard raised his drink and declared: "To the child of the King!"

"To the child of the King!" the others replied. Chakka Ri glanced down uncomfortably at the wine in his goblet. He could imagine the clan's Elders watching him. To them, this whole affair likely would verge on treason, declaring allegiance to the offspring of some dirt-poor horse hunter. He watched the man who had given the gift of the black stone.

The fellow raised his goblet high and drained it. Chakka Ri, however, set down his own wine untouched along the base of the wall.

A moment later the old horsemen turned and began to exit the cave. Chakka Ri found himself caught up among the others as they shuffled slowly back through the narrow, stone passageway and into the light of a bright summer day. After a minute, the White Beard strode outside and mounted his black mare. Chakka Ri ran to him. "White Beard, please wait," he called. "What just happened?"

"I cannot talk now, Chakka Ri. Come to me with the others tonight. Then I will try to answer all your questions." He spurred his horse up a steep section of trail near the cave.

The other old men grabbed the reins of their animals and led them over to a clearing, where they began to unpack. Chakka Ri turned back toward the cave. The Horse Stalker and his family must still be inside, he thought. The young man strode alone back through the entrance. Inside, the candles had been extinguished, but the fire still burned. Chakka Ri found a candle and lit it at the fire. He held the small light high and spun slowly around. There was no one there.

"They aren't here," called a voice from the cave's opening. "There must be some way out through the back end." Chakka Ri turned to behold the speaker. Before him stood the red-haired man who had given the gift of the black stone.

"I wanted to talk to them," Chakka Ri said.

"You can do that after they are taken to Kierinswell. Right now I need your help."

"My help?"

"Yes, Red Pony. That is the code name the GrandElder gave you, isn't it. And mine is Pinto. Yes, you know that name. That's enough of the formalities. We have work to do, boy.

"The GrandElder sent me here as an observer, not a fighter."

"I don't need a fighter, Red Pony. Just a boy who will obey me like the GrandElder told him to. You have quite a future ahead of you, or so I'm told. But it will reflect badly on you if our leader should learn that you failed to help me apprehend the Horse Stalker."

Chakka Ri's shoulders slumped. "What do you want me to do?"

The old man pulled out a small vial and handed it to him. "Drink this. It will make your stomach a little sick, nothing too serious. But it will provide us with an excuse. This evening the others are going to join the White Beard and the Horse Stalker farther up the mountain. They are going to hear special songs in a secret place—the King's own people singing, they claim. You and I will be staying behind. You will seem too sick to ride, and I will stay behind to help take care of you. Of course, the others will refuse to leave us alone. Surely one of them will stay with us. Even so, I'll find an opportunity to get away. We had a troop of soldiers following us into these mountains. I intend to find them and bring them back here by morning. That should be in plenty of time to arrest all these traitors, including the White Beard. Now drink your medicine. We need to get on with this."

Curse the GrandElder, Chakka Ri thought. *And curse this spy.* Even so, he obeyed, downing the small vial's contents. It tasted sickeningly sweet. The two had barely exited the cave when Chakka Ri's midsection contracted as if he'd been kicked. He fell to his knees and let loose his breakfast. When the first bout of nausea passed, he collapsed on his back and fought to catch his breath. Soon he succumbed to a second round of vomiting.

The old horsemen congregated in small bands by their horses. From there they silently watched the young man's prolonged sickness. Chakka Ri couldn't hear what the spy was telling them and he didn't care. He had nothing left in his stomach and still the nausea attacked him. Eventually one man edged up with a small brown jar in his hand. Carefully he poured out a thimbleful of its contents into a great wooden spoon and knelt down. "This be for what ails you," he said in the broken dialect of the old horse hunters. "So says the White Beard."

Chakka Ri stared hard into the old man's dark eyes, looking for any trace of trickery. The man peered back straight and steady. Chakka Ri took the spoon, sipped its plain-tasting contents, and lay back down, too weak to move.

The old men napped until suppertime. After a brief meal, they rose and saddled their horses. Leaving behind their pack animals and most of their gear, they rode off while the sun was still an hour from setting. Chakka Ri remained too weak to move. He took in nothing but water. When the main group left, he noted that the spy had remained in camp, as had the old horse hunter who had given him the medicine to soothe his stomach. The latter one helped move Chakka Ri to flat ground and brought over the young man's bedroll, saddle and gear. As his strength returned, Chakka Ri fumed. *A little sick? That blasted spy poisoned me. I don't care what the GrandElder said. I'm not going to trust that man, and I certainly won't offer him any more help.* He rolled over to a pouch on his saddle, pulled out a sheathed knife and set it beneath his head. Whatever was to come, he wanted to be ready.

No one bothered him until well after sunset. In the fading light of dusk, the spy sauntered over, looking back to carefully note the position of the remaining old horseman. "Well, that one is a bit of a problem," the spy chattered, consciously not looking at Chakka Ri. "He just keeps tending to his horse. He refuses to come here, even though I keep asking him to have a look at you. Imagine that."

"He must realize what a snake you are. You should know that I have allies on the Council. I am the son of an Elder. Do you think the GrandElder can spare you after what you did to me? You're going to regret this, I promise you."

"Ah, boy, you must understand how sorry I am. Here I've made you puke all afternoon and now the time has come for you to do it all over again. It truly saddens my heart. Believe me, boy, when I say that it's nothing personal. I just need a little help in getting away."

The thought of another round of sickness caused Chakka Ri's eyes to bulge in defiance. From his bedroll he reached for his knife. But before he could unsheathe it, the spy kicked him fiercely in the ribs. The young man clutched his sides and dropped the blade. The spy smoothly kicked it away, grabbed Chakka Ri by the ear, snapped back the young man's head and poured down another dose of the nauseous potion. After forcing it down, the older man released his victim.

"Rich boys like you ought to have more sense than to come up here and play such dangerous games," the man said. "Now, Red Pony, you lie down and keep quiet or I'll slit your throat. Don't test me, boy."

Chakka Ri felt his stomach tighten again. He vomited and cried and vomited again. *Where is the White Beard?* he wondered. *Where is someone who will help me?*

Soon he heard the spy and the old horse hunter coming toward him. He turned to note that the latter was leading his own mount—possibly using it as a shield against the secret agent. Chakka Ri considered whether he should try to warn the old man, but the nausea struck again and it was all he could do to keep his head off the ground. When it stopped, he lay down his head and wept.

After a few minutes of silence, a hand touched his shoulder. "Lean over, child," the old horseman said. "He must have put another dose of bad medicine in you. I be sorry, boy. The others say, 'Keep the trickster here until nightfall.' So I try. But here he goes and makes you sick again. And it works. He be gone and I be here alone with you."

The old man again pulled out the spoon and jar. Chakka Ri took another small dose of the good medicine. The nausea stopped, but soon his body began to shake with chills. The horse hunter built a fire beside the young man as night descended on the mountains. From time to time, the elder threw new wood chips and brush on the blaze. A quarter moon rose slowly above the ridge. But Chakka Ri was too tired to take notice.

The night grew cold but the young man slept soundly. He woke at dawn to find extra blankets piled atop him. Weakly he raised himself in the early light to see if the other horsemen had returned. To his surprise, the camp lay empty. All the gear around him had vanished. Worried, he sat up and looked to where the string of extra horses had been tied last night. Only his saddle horse and packhorse remained. All the other animals had vanished. Chakka Ri's head slumped back to the ground. The old horse hunters must have run off in fear. Who could blame them? The spy might return with troops at any moment. Even so, it saddened Chakka Ri to think that he had been abandoned in this great wilderness.

Well, if they're caught, they can't look to me to stop them from being hanged, he thought. *Except perhaps the old man who gave me the good medicine. I suppose I should try to help him. Perhaps I can see that he gets the debtors' chains rather than the gallows.*

Out from the cave stepped the White Beard. "Come over, son, when you're ready," he called. Chakka Ri perked up in wonder to see the old man. He immediately stood up, but his legs wobbled as he started forward. Clutching his midsection, he strode slowly to the cave. Inside he drew near the fire to warm his chilled hands. He smelled bacon frying in a pan on the nearby coals. He spied broth steaming in a pot hung above the flames.

"I thought everyone had abandoned me," Chakka Ri said, slowly rubbing his hands. "Where's your horse?"

The old man arched his eyebrows and smiled. "I left it on the hill behind the cave," he said. "We still need to talk, remember?"

"Aren't you worried? That villain said …" Chakka Ri stopped in mid-sentence, wondering if he had just revealed more than was prudent.

The White Beard bent down and tended the bacon. "I warned you to watch who you trusted here on the mountain. It would have saved you all that gut wrenching yesterday. And for what? I suppose that spy told you he's working for the Council. Don't believe him. He's really in league with the Realm."

"The Realm! What does Equis have to do with all this?"

"The Realm's leaders also are looking for the Horse Stalker. The evil ones know that he is somehow part of the King's plans. And one day they will greatly fear his child, as well they should."

Chakka Ri took a moment to consider that the spy had deceived not only him but also the GrandElder. "The Council will not abide foreigners in our land. They have no business here."

"Keeping them out is easier said than done. And some of our own leaders do business with them. They sell our people to the evil ones."

"And you want to end slavery, don't you?"

"Yes, I do."

"Our leaders say that some people can't live free, especially in the Dry Lands. They lack self-control. Even my father believed that. He used to tell me that some men need chains to keep them from living in the gutter or robbing you blind."

"Your father was my friend, but he shouldn't have chained his kinsmen just for being poor. And no one should sell his brother to the Realm. Even your father agreed with me on that point. And yet some of our Elders are doing just that."

Chakka Ri sat down at a small table. Slowly he sipped the broth and nibbled on the bacon. The White Beard sat down opposite and stared intently at the young man. "You are so much different from your father. You're a cautious fellow. He was a wild one. If not, I suppose I never would have met him."

"Mother said you met my father before her. How did that happen?"

The White Beard cocked his head. "Are you asking me how two men from such different stations in life ever met? Yes, it's a good question. Your father was the child of an Elder. I was the son of a horse hunter. But as a young man I was selected by the Elders to be a seeker of the great treasure. You know the one I mean. Your grandfather was so exasperated with your father that he sent him to join my company, and he threatened him with a lifetime of solitude should he fail to restrain himself.

"We became fast friends, and your father introduced me to your mother. She was so beautiful. Being with her made my heart soar. But she was also the child of an Elder. Her parents wanted her to attract a good suitor. And a seeker cannot marry. His life must be devoted to finding the great treasure for the MuKierin.

"But I admit that I loved your mother, and I thought she had feelings for me. My heart was torn. Should I do my duty and become a seeker? Or should I steal away this beautiful young woman at night and take her back to my own people? I couldn't decide, and it caused me great worry.

"A few months before our company was to graduate, I went and visited my people near Orres. It was then that I spoke to an old horse hunter, and he changed my life. One night by the fire he joined us. This man I had known for years. But that night he told me a strange, new tale. He spoke of meeting the King's servants in high mountains. He told me of the great songs they sang. They were songs of a King so great that he ruled everywhere, even here in the Dry Lands. He ruled not by the hand of the Elders, and certainly not by the power of the evil ones who terrorize the rest of the desert clans. But still he ruled and he feared no one. Then the man looked at me and said, 'Young one, what would you rather be: a seeker of a great treasure or a friend of the King.' I was astonished. I had told no one of my coming appointment. No, I had guarded well that secret. How did this old man know about it? So I asked him, 'Which are you?'

"'Come and see,' he replied. It may seem foolish to you, but I agreed. I was at a crossroads in my life. I needed to know the way I should go, and I hoped the time in the mountains would help me decide. So I went with the old man up to the high places. And I met the King's servants, heard their songs for myself and never went home. Instead, I answered the call of my King.

"A few years later, I learned of the marriage of your father to your mother. I was told that your father had been released from becoming a seeker and that he had agreed to your grandfather's demands to settle down and take a wife. And so he did, and in time he also became an Elder."

"That explains my mother's reaction when you sent for me," said Chakka Ri. "She still loves you. I saw it in her face. What a strange tale. You could have married her. You could have been my father."

"Perhaps. As a man, you will make many choices, and you must live with the consequences. I have made my choices, and I would not change them now, even if I could."

"So why did you bring me up to the high country? Did you want me to hear the King's music and to come under its mythic spell?"

"No, I told you that I brought you up here to meet someone. And so you did. Now you have met the child. And you will meet him again when he has grown to manhood. Then you will be a witness that he is the son of Horse Stalker. He is the one promised to us by the Stone Woman. He is the one the Dark Brood fears."

"Are you saying that baby will become the Champion? Is that what this is all about?"

The White Beard solemnly nodded. "One day he will stand before you as a sign that I have told you the truth. And on that day he will give you the black stone that he received here yesterday. From boyhood, he will wear it around his neck. But on the day he stands before you, he will remove it and say, 'Chakka Ri, this stone testifies of me.' And he will give it to you."

"I do not wish it! I will not take it. And I will not be his witness."

"Perhaps, but willing or not, these things will happen. You cannot stop them."

"How can you be so sure? Many babes die young. And you yourself said that the spy is in league with the

Realm. He may lead the bad warriors up here and kill the child."

"Those evil ones cannot overcome the forces gathered in these mountains to protect the Horse Stalker's son. No, Chakka Ri, you will not escape your destiny. Remember this: you will meet the child again one day."

Pibbibib and Weakling halted at the rim of a deep canyon in the high desert mountains above Kierinswell. A tangle of brambles and stunted trees filled the slope beneath them. Across the chasm they could see a dirt path that wove through boulders and emerged onto open ground.

"Look where the trail is," said Weakling. "Rakmah's going to bellyache that you've brought us this way. His pretty she-archers are going to get all scratched up passing through that prickly brush down there."

"We came the right way," said Pibbibib, the larger warrior whose name meant Backstabber. "You yourself said you could sense that the enemy is waiting for us up on the mountain. I'm not going to walk straight into an ambush. We'll go another way, one that isn't well guarded. Who cares if those females get a little scratched?"

Weakling shrugged. "I keep thinking about those she-devils and all the beautiful arrows they're carrying. How I wish I had my old bow back. It must be five hundred summers since I shot something."

"If you wanted arrows, you should have stayed in the old country. Think of all the vast forests we left behind. Now we live in a stinking desert where it's easier to find jewels than good wood for arrows. Do you know what that means? It means our leaders aren't going to let you or me have a bow. They have bigger plans for the arrows they have left."

"Well, I don't like it."

"Fine. Would you rather be a she-archer?"

"Hah! At least we can go kill a horse dog and gnaw on his bones every now and then. I hear those she-ones only get a meal when their minders like Rakmah let 'em take off their iron collars."

It had been a year since the two warriors had last encountered Roj. They remained the only rebels who knew the young MuKierin's face. Weakling's leg continued to ooze a little from the wound that Roj had given him—a knifing that had created in him the strange ability to sense the presence of his enemies, the King's servants. Weakling kept this a great secret and suggested that it was Pibbibib and not he who had gained The Powers, the mysterious ability to detect the approach of their enemies.

At the canyon's rim, Pibbibib looked back and spotted a line of warriors approaching single file: six males and two females. Like him, the males wore the black leather armor of the Realm; most had beards and braids that flowed long beneath their leather helms. But the females were dressed in sleeveless beige tunics that extended barely to their knees. The two were tall and thin, not quite emaciated, but without an ounce of fat to spare. The left half of their skulls had been shaved clean and scalded to prevent the re-growth of any hair that might hinder their aim. The thin, blond strands on the right half were gathered and tied with a single leather thong. Each female had the brand of the Broken Star burned into the middle of her forehead, but no marks adorned their cheeks as with the male warriors. And around their necks each female wore a close-fitting iron collar that kept them from eating all but the daintiest of morsels.

"Those two aren't too ugly," Weakling observed. "Do you think either one of them would like to get acquainted with me?"

"Hah, they're not exactly what you'd call tame. That's why they've got three warriors each to keep 'em in line. You wouldn't want to be alone with one of them, especially if she wasn't wearing that collar."

Weakling frowned at the thought. Slowly he turned toward the canyon. A moment later, he jumped up and hissed.

"What is it?" asked Pibbibib.

"She's over there."

"Who?"

"You know who?"

"What! Is our MuKierin vermin with her?"

"How should I know? But I can sense that she's coming this way. She's somewhere near the top of the canyon, somewhere over there on the other side."

"Good. That means she's going to come down that trail and cross that open ground over there. Rakmah's she-devils will get their shot at the Horse Stalker after all."

"But that's too far. That trail has got to be two hundred paces away."

"I don't care if they can hit him. But if we get them a shot, that'll be praise for me. Just let me do the talking to Rakmah. We're about to get ourselves a commendation."

Rakmah led the warriors up the hill. He stood as tall as Backstabber, taller than the other warriors with him, but he wasn't quite as handsome. Both warriors kept their dark beards neatly trimmed, unlike Weakling and the others who let their facial growth turn into long, unruly tangles. But Rakmah was pug faced with cropped, short hair and no helm. Pibbibib had deep-set eyes and his dark brown hair fell from his helm and rested upon his armor.

Rakmah belonged to an order of the Realm called Cleavers; his cheeks were branded with images of knives cleaving hearts in two. Pibbibib and Weakling were of a different order called Slinkers. It was another reason Rakmah and Backstabber disliked each other.

"We shouldn't have come this way," Rakmah growled. "We need to get up the mountain. We can't rely on the human spy or even the first wave of our troops. We need to be ready in case they fail. I want to get a shot at the Horse Stalker."

"Get your archers ready," replied Backstabber. "You're about to get your shot. The human vermin will soon be riding down that trail across the canyon."

Weakling interrupted with a lie. "You said that you only sensed She who holds the little light of fire. You can't be sure if he's over there, too."

"Shut up," snapped Pibbibib. "He came up here with her. He's always with her. But can your archers kill him at this distance?"

Rakmah gazed across the gorge. "Of course," he said. To his troop, he bellowed, "Take the archers down to that promontory beneath us." The warriors scrambled over the crest with the archers following. When passing through brush and over boulders, the males hoisted the females onto their shoulders.

On the other side of the canyon, Healdin halted her gray mare. The infant Blaze was strapped to her back. Beside her stood Dash, the golden-haired hound. She called out to Roj, "Weakling and Pibbibib are waiting for us on the other side of the canyon. I can sense them. Now you must take this and hold it for me." She unstrapped a sheath from her leg and handed him Mara, the Vine, her light of great power.

"I don't understand, Healdin," said Roj. Why would you give this to me? You may need it against those cutthroats."

"I must let go of it for now. I am too tempted to use it to protect our son. The curse is strong now, Roj. It's much worse than what I used to feel when you were in danger. If I kept the Vine, I might be unable to stop myself from killing those two today. That must not happen. Their time has not yet come."

"When will this curse leave us?"

"There is no escaping it, Roj. I fear it will be even worse for our son. Much worse. He's going to suffer every time he helps your people. But that is still many years away. Today we must keep him alive and escape our enemies. Now pay attention. I want you to ride close behind me down this trail. When I say the word, you must follow me off the path and up the slope. We must do this quickly. Do you understand?"

"No," said Roj as he put Mara in his leather shoulder pouch. "But I'll do what you say. And I'll make sure to stay close behind you." He pointed to the hound. "But what about Dash. Will he be safe?"

"Yes, Dash knows what to do. He's going to stay behind us. I want him to spend some time following Weakling."

"Weakling? But how is he going to recognize him?"

"Dash can sense the power flowing from the wound you gave him. It's important that he become familiar with our enemy."

On the promontory, the archers strung their bows and surveyed the distance. When ready, the first picked a thin tree on the far side and fired a test shot. It barely missed to the right. The second archer adjusted for wind and drove her arrow into the bark.

Rakmah grinned derisively at Pibbibib. "Could you make that shot?"

"Of course, if you starved me and gave me five thousand arrows for target practice."

"No, these two have a deft touch that you could never develop. Just watch their slender arms draw back and fire. It's the most graceful form of violence."

"Fine, but the Horse Stalker's not going to stand over there and wave while you shoot at him."

"Let him gallop as fast as he can. My beauties have made this shot hundreds of times. Oh, yes, they've been practicing on these human vermin for generations. From this distance you can see the arrow and the prey collide with each other. The victims never understand how the act of flight actually contributes to their deaths. They rush blindly into the arrows."

Rakmah ordered his warriors, "Take off the collars." He turned to Backstabber. "A word of warning. After the archers slay the Horse Stalker, don't get in their way. They become quite touchy at suppertime. We never ask them to share. The kill is theirs alone."

Weakling spotted movement on the other side. "Here they come!" he yelled.

The warriors could see Healdin ride among a series of boulders as her mare descended a stone staircase. Roj followed, trailed by a packhorse. Soon the two would reach the open ground. Already Healdin had urged her mare into a trot. Weakling began to wince and clutch at his wounded leg. Even Pibbibib felt his scalp tingle, recalling the day on the mountain when the lady had raised Mara in her hand, and its piercing light had blocked his way. *Yes, I can still sense you, lady,* he thought. You've *got a power to make your enemies take notice, to force them all to bow at your feet. I'm going to hold that kind of power some day. And no one will be able to stand against me.*

Rakmah got an idea. "There's your old mistress," he told the archers. "Let's show off your skills. One of you shall take down her gray mare, while the other shoots the Horse Stalker's mount. Then you can both kill the human with your second shots. On my order." The archers drew their bows and stood ready.

Healdin broke into the open and urged her mare into a gallop. A moment later she yelled to Roj, "Now!"

"Now," Rakmah ordered.

The archers let loose, their arrows soaring with awesome speed above the canyon. A moment earlier the aim had looked perfect. But then the horses had changed direction. Already they were climbing above the trail. Healdin leveled out about ten feet above the path, with Roj following. The arrows sank deep into the hillside, slightly in front of and well below each rider. "Down!" yelled Healdin. Her mare swung back to the trail. Roj's stallion and the packhorse slid down behind her.

"Fire again!" screamed Rakmah. The archers drew arrows and took aim, but the riders already had reached the cover of another set of boulders. The two females began to curse and grind their teeth. Rakmah turned on Pibbibib. "How did she know we were here?"

"How should I know? You were so sure you could shoot their mounts from here. Maybe she saw us from across the gorge. Maybe this looked like dangerous ground. Wasn't she the one who taught your playthings here? Maybe the old mistress still knows her pupils well."

The archers started to wail and scratch their faces, drawing blood with their fingernails. There would be no meal tonight. Rakmah stared with contempt at Pibbibib. "I think you know more than you're letting on. It seems a little too convenient that you led us to this canyon just as she was passing by. Oh, yes, we get to see them over there, but we can't get close enough to get a second shot or to pursue them. So I end up looking like a fool while you win a commendation as the wise scout. Are you really so wise? Lord Mackadoo doesn't think so, and his sergeant thinks you're a lying sack of manure."

"Look!" interrupted Weakling. "There's a great hound staring at us over there. What's he doing?"

Even the archers stopped cursing and hissing long enough to stare at Dash. The hound held still, his brown eyes fixed on the rebels. "I don't like him," said Rakmah. "Put an arrow in him." The archers made ready, but before they could fire the great dog bounded down the slope and into a great mass of prickly brush.

"That's not good," said Pibbibib. "Not if he comes over here and gets our scent."

"We'll be leaving soon," said Rakmah. "My archers can handle one hound. Now you two vermin move out. Don't get in the way while we persuade our beauties here to put down their bows and don their neck jewelry again. They're already upset enough." He motioned to his warriors to close in on the archers. The females glared fiercely at the approach of their iron collars.

Pibbibib and Weakling began their climb back out of the canyon. "She got inside me back there," said Weakling. "It scared me."

"What are you talking about? She was on the other side of the canyon."

"She might have been over there but somehow she was also in my head. It's like she was using my eyes to watch Rakmah give the order to fire. Then she rode up off the trail and dodged the arrows."

"Are you sure?"

"Yes."

"Incredible. So that's how she knew we were here. She was using The Powers from your wound. I can't wait to get power like that. Then watch Rakmah bow down to me."

"You're crazy. I'll tell you something else. I don't like that hound. I've got a bad feeling about him."

"Well, yes, I don't like him either. The enemy hasn't brought hounds to the Dry Lands before, not that we know of anyway. We'll have to keep an eye out for him."

"We wouldn't need to do that if we could go back and join one of the regular divisions. Let's ask Mackadoo to send us over to Zhaggee and the Red Brigade. Those chums don't have to worry about anything except where to find their next meal, and they usually have plenty of little human vermin around to choose from."

"We're not going back to the old ways. Mackadoo won't let us. We're the only ones who know the Horse Stalker's face. We're too valuable."

"Hah. Mackadoo thinks we're scum. And his sergeant's even worse. You know it. You just want to stay with them because you think they can help you get your hands on the Great Valuable. Well, Mackadoo said he'd gladly let you hold it, because you would burn up if you ever touched it. I say you're crazy, and I want out."

"Who cares what Mackadoo says? He doesn't know for sure what will happen when I take hold of the Great Valuable. No one knows. Anyway, he won't let you go, and neither will I. Listen, I'm the best hope to keep you alive. Who else is going to watch out for you? Do you think Zhaggee will risk his sorry carcass for you? Hah, he won't lift a finger to save you when the fighting starts. But I will, and we both know why. I need your gift. Without even trying, you can tell me when the enemy is near us. That gives us an edge, and it may be just the beginning. Who knows what else you might be able to do if you really put your mind to it? Why, one day you might lead me right to where the Great Valuable is hidden. Now do you know what Mackadoo will do if he ever finds out about your little secret? He'll put an iron collar on you just like those she-archers wear. Then he'll drag you around like his pet hound." Backstabber waited a moment for his ally to ponder that thought. "That's right. You'll never have another free moment to yourself. You won't ever be able to nibble a strip of human flesh without his leave. Is that what you want? Of course not! And I'm going to see that that never happens. That's why we've got to make everyone think that I have The Powers. I need to be the cocky one out front, bragging about my abilities. And you need to keep your mouth shut and follow my lead. Understand?"

Weakling lowered his gaze. "Yeah, but I still don't like it. And I don't want her in my head again."

"Agreed. If she can sense your presence like you can sense hers, we want to stay as far away from her as possible. But I do need to figure out a mystery. Did you see what was on her back? I think it was some pitiful offspring of that horse dog?"

"What of it?" asked Weakling.

"Well, where was the mother?"

"Who cares? Maybe she stole the child. Maybe they bred the Horse Stalker to some wench and then abandoned her."

"No, stupid. Stealing children and breeding wenches is the sort of thing we'd do. She's too weak for that. Try using The Powers to imagine how they came by that child."

"All I can imagine right now is how hungry I am."

"Ah, you're worthless. I'll have to figure it out myself. No matter, I think we'll have plenty of time. I've got a feeling she's going to go into hiding again. It looks like she's now got two sniveling vermin to watch over. No doubt she's going to try to protect that young whelp. If I'm right, we might not see any sign of them for quite a while."

Pibbibib guessed well about Healdin's plans (though he remained puzzled over the mystery of the child's mother). After the days on the mountain, Roj and his son did vanish, even as rumors spread that a special child had been born among the MuKierin. In the days that followed, no one could find the Horse Stalker or his offspring. Years passed, and in time Roj's people forgot about the young man who had won the Challenge of Orres. However, far to the west, a child grew to manhood along the shores of the Great Lake of the Pappi. And his mother told him stories of a people whose hearts were pierced with a strange longing, and of a champion who must pass through fire.

PART ONE:

THE COMING OF THE CHAMPION

Chapter One

A New Horse Hunter

"Mama! Mama! Three riders have come to camp."

Remy opened the tent flap and stepped outside, her eyes wide and searching. With one quick turn she scanned the beige tents of her husband's kinsmen. Up ran her seven-year-old son, the youngest of her three children. Barefoot, bare-chested and ponytailed, he sprang and jumped around her like a puppy chasing butterflies.

"It's two men and a lady. They're waiting by the horse herd!" he chirped as his hands latched onto dirty breeches. "Is it them, Mama? Is it?"

Remy's eyes seemed to glaze over at the words. "Go get your father," she said softly. "Hurry, child. It must be them. Let's not keep them waiting."

Once Noli heard the news, he trotted directly to his wife. He knew she'd want him beside her. Remy, meanwhile, went inside to comb her hair, the strands of which had grown prematurely gray. She pulled it back and tied it with a leather string as her husband entered the tent. She turned, and he saw her forehead wrinkled in frustration. "Tell me I don't look so old," she said. "Tell me he won't cringe when he sees me."

"You're the best-looking woman in this camp," Noli replied. "Why, Roj will gaze at his big sister and wonder how she could stay so young."

"It's been nineteen years, Noli, such a long time. Oh, well, it can't be helped. Just take me to him."

Arm in arm, they walked through the sprawling encampment near Orres. Nearly two hundred of Noli's kinsmen were gathered for the annual summer week of festivities. Most of them lived in the South Lands. Each year, Noli and his family traveled from Kierinswell—nearly a week's journey, the longest of any of the relatives.

Outside the collection of tents, near a herd of horses that outnumbered the people, Remy saw the three riders.

They sat relaxed atop their mounts, talking with a small gathering of herders. A young man—Remy knew it was Blaze—let his right leg hang easily over the pommel of his saddle. At the sight of her brother, Remy froze and a lump bulged in her throat. Roj turned and saw her. "Remy!" he cried. He sprang off his horse and ran to her. Embracing her, he lifted his sister off the ground. Together they smiled and wept.

Noli, meanwhile, looked in awe at Healdin. She didn't look a day older than that night when Roj and he had first met her on the mountain, and that was twenty years ago. At least his brother-in-law looked like two decades had passed since their last meeting. His hair and beard were streaked with gray, as with most men his age. Noli ambled up to Healdin and gently touched her hand as a sign that he had mellowed toward her. "Hello, sister-in-law," he said. "It's good to see you."

"It is so good to see you, Noli. Now my husband is a happy man."

Noli turned to Blaze. At nineteen, the young man was tall and lean, with shoulder-length brown hair that was gathered in a ponytail. Beneath a thick beard, his face had the same sculpted features of his mother. "Welcome, Blaze," he said. "We're glad to meet you. We'll get you and your folks settled in, and then we can talk over dinner. That's when you'll get to meet my oldest boy, Roffie. He's a bull of a MuKierin and a good horse hunter, too. He's much better than your papa and me, if you can believe it. You two will get along fine. Just fine."

The newcomers led two pack animals into the camp and pitched their tent in a spot beside their relatives. Noli's two younger children scurried around as Blaze unpacked gear and spread it out on tarps. "Where have you been, cousin Blaze?" asked Noli's daughter, who was eleven. "Why haven't we ever met you before?"

"I've lived far away," said Blaze, "among the Pappi, the people of the Lake."

"Did you live in boats?"

"No, we lived in a home near the lake's shore. But we used boats to catch fish and to gather reeds. The Pappi taught us how to weave the reeds into beautiful baskets. Let me show you." He stooped over a canvas pannier and brought forth a small round basket, about the size of his hand, complete with a woven cover. The girl's eyes widened with curiosity. "This is for you," he said, handing it to her.

"Mama! Look, Mama! Look at my gift from cousin Blaze." Remy tenderly placed a hand on her daughter's shoulder and gazed admiringly at the basket.

At dinnertime, the two families gathered beneath Noli's canopy, one of many set up around a large dirt patch that served as a contest field. Other families also began to sit down on cushions beneath their canvas overhangs. Remy's cook from Kierinswell prepared a stew of young goat and desert roots. As the women ladled the stew into clay bowls, a stout young man strolled up to the canopy.

"Here he is!" Noli proclaimed, standing up and putting his arm around the newcomer. The young man was tall and full chested and his bearded face featured rounded cheeks that made him look almost cherubic. At once he locked eyes on Blaze and gave him a warm smile. Noli continued, "Roj, this is my oldest boy, Roffie, probably the best horse hunter you're ever going to meet. Roffie, this is your uncle and your cousin Blaze."

"It's good to meet you, Roff," said Roj, shaking his nephew's hand. "Tell me, has your mother tried to turn you into a candle maker like your papa?"

"No, uncle, I get too cramped in Kierinswell. Horse hunting suits me better."

"He's just like his father," said Remy, taking her place on a cushion. "Noli has brought him down here every summer since he was twelve. I don't try to fight it anymore. I need all my strength just to worry about one old horse hunter."

"Now darlin'," said Noli, "You know we don't need another candle maker in the family right now. That's because I'm so talented."

The two families sat on cushions in a circle and began to eat. The cook brought forth a wineskin and poured its red contents into clay mugs. "I haven't had a stew like this in ages," Roj said. "Noli, my sister spoils you."

Healdin touched Remy's hand. "You must know how much Roj has missed you. He's been waiting for this day for nineteen years."

"But it must be a hard day for you," said Remy. "Your only child is about to leave you."

Healdin's face turned sober. "Yes, until now I didn't know how hard it was going to be."

"Well, don't you fear," said Noli. "My Roff will look out for Blaze, just like he does for all his cousins."

After dinner, men from the camp began to gather in the open field beside Noli's canopy. One called out in a great baritone voice: "The time has come to send out the young horse hunters. The fathers must join them out here."

Another man stepped forward and beckoned Roff and Blaze. "Come, young ones," he said. "And you, too, Noli, you old aristocrat. Even wealthy candle makers must take part in sending out their sons."

Noli grinned and stood up. "They like to tease me here about being from the capital. My kin think that Orres is too crowded, let alone Kierinswell. Come on, Roj, you've got to come out with us, too."

Four bearded young men gathered around Roff and Blaze at one end of the clearing. "This is my cousin Blaze," Roff announced. Blaze clenched his right fist and bumped it against each of the young men's own right fists, in turn, just as his father had taught him. In this way, the newcomer was formally introduced to Roff's cousins from Noli's side of the family.

"Let's do this job one-handed," Roff announced. "I'll take the front." On the ground near them lay a thick rope spread between them and their fathers. Roff picked up the rope in his right hand and put his left down on his thigh. The others lined up behind him and grabbed the rope with their right hands. Blaze was instructed to grab the end of the line.

"Now put your left hand on the shoulder of the man in front of you," Roff said. "That will steady us."

The fathers picked up the other end of the rope. "They're going to try it one-handed," said Noli. He stepped to the head of the men and grabbed the rope. "Well, fathers, I guess they think they can take us. We'll have to show them that we're still the real men of the clan."

The two sides began slowly to pull the rope taut. A woman came forward and began to sing a bouncy verse: "Keep him home, Papa; now don't let him go." The other women and young girls of the camp joined in the melody, singing it over and over. The master of ceremonies sang a different verse in his deep baritone, "Going horse hunting, Mama; don't make me stay home." The men and boys around the field joined in with him, singing in time with the women. As the chant/singing grew louder, the young men and their fathers began to tug on either end of the rope. Soon each side was straining hard to pull their opponents across a line in the dirt. "Keep him home, Papa, now don't let him go." The young men's left arms quivered as they pushed against one another's shoulders. At the head of their line, Roff leaned back and squatted low, his legs slowly churning for the traction that would bring victory.

Neither side, however, seemed able to budge the other. After more than a minute of heavy straining, Noli called to the other fathers: "Brothers, this is too much work. We shall give them the rope—on three. One, two, three!"

The older men released the line. Their sons fell backwards in a heap on Blaze. One skinny cousin nicknamed Kick pushed himself off the newcomer. "Sorry about that," he said, offering a hand. "We should have warned you. The old men like to do that when they get tired." Blaze grinned and took the proffered hand.

With the contest over, the men of the camp huddled around the victors. "This Roffie's a stout one," proclaimed a man who was missing front teeth. "You shouldn't be going horse hunting, boy. You ought to be finding a wife. Let's take you down to Orres tonight, and you can pick yourself out a bride. We'll help you grab her, and then you can ride for the hills."

The other men guffawed at the idea and slapped each other on the backs. Roff, however, stood unfazed at their frivolity. "No, sir. My mama would skin me alive if I took a woman without paying for her. She says I need to pay a righteous dowry when I take a wife."

"That's for city folk," another man said. "Out here you pay the father only if he catches you. That's why you need a fast horse."

An old man with leathered hands stood before Roj, rubbing his white beard and staring at the stranger. At length he stepped forward. "You be the one," he said. "Here at Orres, long years ago. Noli brought you to my cousin Char. You climbed aboard the stallion and rode him for fifty drumbeats. Do I not recall rightly, Noli?"

"Yes, uncle," said Noli. "He was that man. This is Roj, my woman's brother."

"I still remember," the old man said as he stepped up to shake Roj's hand. "And you have a special son. So says the White Beard."

Roj pointed to Blaze. "Yes, uncle. That's him there. That's my son."

The old man froze, his head cocked and mouth agape. He turned back to Noli for confirmation. Noli nodded and said softly, "Yes, that's him, uncle. He's the one."

The kinsman walked slowly to Blaze. Haltingly he put a hand on the young man's shoulder. Blaze turned and the two gazed silently at one another. The old man spoke, "Remember me, horse stalker, when you ride beside the shining waters."

"Those words were once spoken of my father," Blaze said.

"Yes, boy, but now it be your day." He hugged Blaze and turned to Roff and the other cousins. "Listen to this one. For the sake of your people, listen to him." With that, the old MuKierin turned and shuffled slowly away.

The young men soon left the field and went to gather their gear. Blaze, however, returned to the canopy to say goodbye to his parents. Healdin was crying. "The time has come," she said. "And yet I seem so unprepared for it."

"It's the curse," Roj told his son. "She once feared for my safety. But now I think you're going to cause her even more grief than I did."

"I know," said Blaze.

Healdin reached into a bag and removed a small leather pouch. From it she grabbed a clear, jewel-like stone that hung on a flat leather thong. Quickly she tucked it back inside the brown pouch. "The time has come to give you the White Gem," she said. "Remember that I may use it without effect, but you must take care. Unlike the people of the Dry Lands, you can touch this gem without falling unconscious because my blood runs through you. But you also have your father's blood in you, which means when you use the gem, it will bring you low. It will hurt you. Use it sparingly but use it when you must. Remember the curse."

"I will, Mother. I'll also remember the fear that you feel whenever I'm in danger."

"Yes, the curse will continue to plague both of us. But the worst will fall on you, my son. The curse will fill you with fear, much greater than the fear of men. But you can prevail. You are the King's grandchild."

Blaze took the gem in its pouch. He kissed his mother, hugged his father and set out to join Roff.

Healdin wept as he departed. "How I wish the time was right to give him my power," she told Roj. "One day I will give it to him. I must."

Blaze, meanwhile, felt the anxiety rise up in his gut. *You really are your mother's son, aren't you?* he thought. *So afraid. So gripped by terror. Well, don't give in to it. Hang tough. Be like your grandfather. And please don't get these other boys here killed.*

He found Roff, and they set out for the horses. Both carried a loaded, canvas pannier for their packhorse. The two joined Roff's cousins at a camp near the herd of horses.

As Roff started a fire, Noli came to the young men. "Gather round for a minute, boys," he told his nephews. "I need to say something. The truth is I've been waiting a long time to say it. It's a story about Blaze's papa and me. I was just a few years older than all of you are here when the two of us went up into the high country above Kierinswell. Roff knows some of the story. I'm not sure exactly how much Blaze knows. Anyway, Roj and I went up into the mountains chasing a Spotted Stallion. We never caught that horse up there, but we did get ourselves into some trouble. Some enemies of Blaze's mother ambushed us in that high country. She ended up rescuing both of us, which was a little embarrassing, to tell you the truth. I wasn't very grateful to her back then. All I could see was that she had some powerful foes, and I didn't want those brutes coming after Roj and me. Well, the next thing I knew, my little brother-in-law was falling in love with her."

"Suffice it to say that Roj and I found ourselves in more tight places, including one night where I thought we were both goners. But in the end, Roj saved me. So I owe him. And I owe Healdin. I don't know Blaze's plans, but I've got a feeling that one day he's also going to go up the mountain, if you get my meaning. He well may find himself in some tight places, too. And should that happen, I hope some of my kin will be standing there with him. And if he calls on me, I'll try my best to help him, too.

"Blaze can speak for himself. All I ask is that you give him a little time. Don't be too quick to judge him, like I judged his mother. Just remember I'm in debt to his family, and I'll be grateful for any help that you can give him."

One cousin, the tallest among them, lowered his green eyes, giving a studied look like he was gauging the soundness of a wild one. "So," he asked, "exactly what is it you mean to do here, Blaze?"

"Please tell me your name," said Blaze.

"I'm Stannis."

"Well, Stannis, the first thing I need to do is to get acquainted with my people. I've got a lot to learn about the

MuKierin, and I'm grateful to have the chance to join you on this horse hunt. I'll try hard to do my part."

"Aren't you going to go find the lost power? You're the Champion, right? Isn't that what you're supposed to do?"

"Not now. I'm not ready. The King is still preparing me for that day. He'll know when I'm ready."

"What about these bad ones that Uncle mentioned? Are they looking for you now?"

"Yes, they're out there. You've heard of the Realm, the giant warriors who come from Equis, far to the south on the Red River. They're the evil ones Uncle Noli is talking about. The good news is they don't yet know that I'm here."

"How can you be so sure?"

"You might not believe me."

Roff interrupted: "He knows it because he's the grandson of the King, the king of the Stone Woman. Isn't that right, Papa?"

"That's right," said Noli. "And the King's people are keeping an eye on both Blaze and his enemies. I know this sounds crazy, but Blaze is descended from the same King who knew and helped the Stone Woman. His mother Healdin is the King's daughter. If you were to spend enough time with her, you'd know that she's different from us. I first saw her twenty years ago and I swear she doesn't look a minute older now. I know all this sounds strange. I don't expect you to believe me. I didn't believe it either, not until I met the King's people. All I ask is that you give Blaze a chance. If you do, in time you'll see that I'm telling you the truth."

That night the six cousins slept near their horses. Before dawn, while the rest of the encampment slumbered, they loaded their gear atop three packhorses and set out north. Behind them lay a vast rolling land of sagebrush on the western plains. But they were traveling east for the brush-covered foothills of the Powder Mountains.

Blaze had donned a straw-colored hat from the lake country. It was made of reeds with a curved brim in the back that draped below his neck, while in front the brim was short

like a cap. He had fastened it to his chin with two long leather
braids strung though a braided round knot.

"Is that what the fish boys wear?" asked Stannis.

"Yes," said Blaze. "It keeps the sun off us when we're
on the boats."

"What exactly is fish?" Kick asked.

"Nothing you've ever seen," said Roff. "My papa says
they're like little birds that live under the water."

"Really? Do you pluck 'em?"

Stannis pointed to the rope tied to Blaze's saddle and
asked, "Is that your papa's rope?"

"Yes. He gave it to me. I throw it left handed, just like
he does."

"Good for you. Now, listen up, fish boy. You can
wear that funny hat, but you're not on the lake any more.
And these wild horses we're chasing won't swim into your
net. Sometimes we'll race after them like madmen. But it's
real easy to get killed if you don't know what you're doing. So
go slow for now and don't take too many chances. A lot of
new horse hunters push their luck and end up going down
and getting crushed beneath their horses. Don't be one of
them."

"Good advice. Thanks."

Stannis spurred his horse to the front of the line.
"Don't worry, Blaze," said Kick. "Roffie here will take care
of you. He's a tactical genius. He can catch horses in the
flatlands and on the hilltops, by the springs and in the
canyons. You watch him and you'll learn plenty."

"Thanks, Kick. Tell me, how'd you get that name?"

"My Pap said I was a real rascal as a boy. I loved to
ride behind him, hanging on to him and jabbing my heels into
his horse. I never knew when to stop."

"He still doesn't," said Roff.

Blaze grinned. "Tell me about the other cousins."

"Well, that's Quirt up there riding on the sorrel.
Stannis and he are our point riders. They rope pretty well and
they love to ride close to the edge of disaster. Stannis is better
at giving advice than taking it when it comes to danger. Now,

Harney there behind us is a quiet one. You get ten words out of him after dinner and you'll think you've gone to the theater. But he's the best one here to work with the wild ones. You catch a nice young colt and Harney will spend all night leaning on his rope, working his way closer and closer. Pretty soon he'll have a hackamore on him. He talks with the horses and they seem to like him, better than the girls do, anyway."

"And what about you, Kick?"

"Well, I'm the cook. And none of these boys ever complain about my food. No, sir, they will eat what I cook and smile or they'll be eating their own grub, of that you may be sure."

"Well," said Blaze, "if they eat it, I will, too."

In the early morning light, the riders crested a small hill. Below them in a dusty bowl of a valley lay the residue of battle. At least five corpses were scattered there. Nearby, half a dozen soldiers in tan uniforms huddled near what appeared to be a wounded comrade lying in the dirt. When the soldiers spotted the horse hunters, they sprang for their mounts. "Hold still," said Roff. "If we run, they'll chase us down."

Seeing that the strangers didn't bolt, three soldiers cautiously rode forward. Stannis noted the insignias on their sleeves. "They're from the Elder's guard in Orres," he said. "They're hard men. Don't give them any lip."

A muscular, bearded corporal with a dented helm rode up and pointed his spear at them. "What are you doing here?" he demanded.

"Riding north," said Roff. "We're horse hunters."

"Where'd you camp last night?"

"With a few hundred of our kin at a big encampment near the North Springs, just like we do every year."

"Get off your horses and sit by that rock. I'll let my captain decide what to do with you when he returns."

"Excuse me," said Blaze. "Is that man wounded over there?"

"What of it, boy?"

"I can help him. Please let me have a look at him."

"You can go down and ask the sergeant there. But don't try anything stupid. We'll be watching you."

The horse hunters dismounted and stepped away from their animals. Two soldiers stayed near them while Blaze took a leather pouch off his saddle and walked briskly down the hill. The corporal rode behind him with his lance at the ready. "Sergeant," he said, "this scared-looking boy here claims to be a healer. Should I kill him or let him come down to you?"

"Let him come," said the sergeant, a bald man with a big belly and gray whiskers. "This man of mine needs help bad." The sergeant kept staring at Blaze's head. "Where'd you get that hat, boy?"

"From the Pappi, the lake people."

"Really? Never been there. Well, you may have a look at Pens here, boy. I'd be grateful if you can do anything to help him."

Blaze knelt beside the wounded man, who seemed barely conscious. From his saddlebag Blaze removed a small clay vial, from which he placed a drop of liquid on his finger. "Open your mouth," he said, holding up the man's head. "This will help ease your pain." When the wetted finger touched the soldier's tongue, he gasped, shut his eyes and fell limp onto a blanket.

Blaze uncovered the bloody cloths over the man's wound, a deep slash along his midsection edged with a few dark red clots. Blaze opened a small jar of gooey, dark salve. Dipping in two fingers, he gasped for breath as a man might do when stepping barefoot into a snow bank. His hand trembled as he took the ointment and rubbed it along a fresh dressing, pressing it gently over the wound. Immediately the bleeding stopped. The sergeant's eyes popped. "How'd you do that, boy?"

Blaze winced and wiped the salve off his fingers "It's the medicine," he said. "My mother makes it." From his pouch, he pulled out new bandages. "If you lift him, sergeant, I'll wrap his wound." The sergeant grabbed the patient by the shoulders and Blaze made fast the bandages. Gently they laid the sleeping man back on his blanket.

"Who are you?" the sergeant asked.

"I'm MuKierin, like you. But I'm new to this land. I'm going horse hunting with my cousins up there. Sergeant, will you tell me what happened here?"

"I'll tell you what I can. We caught up with some rebels. These dead boys are all troublemakers from Orres. We have one of their friends locked in the town prison for insurrection. These boys had planned to break him out. Of course, we had a snitch among them, so we learned all about it and the Elder ordered us to go after them. I'm a jailer, so I was picked with three of my men to come along. The Elder's own guard and his captain came with us. Some of them are out there now taking a look around. The captain's sure that some of them got away. That's why we jumped a bit when you boys showed up."

Blaze pointed to one of the corpses. "There are ropes on that man's hands. Did any of them surrender?"

"Yes, a few did. But by that time they had split open my man here. So we didn't show them any mercy. It gets ugly when you're fighting insurrection. But we know these rebels wouldn't have spared any of us, either. That's just the way it is."

Blaze studied the face of the wounded soldier. He was young, about his own age. "I think Pens here will survive if you let him rest the night here. If you move him, it could kill him."

"The others aren't going to want to spend the night here. But I'll stay with him and so will my two men, if that's what we need to do. But tell me, boy. How do you know so much about tending the wounded?"

"My mother's a healer. She taught me."

From the east came six soldiers atop lathered mounts. Their captain, a square-jawed, mustached man in his forties, shook his head and called out, "We lost any sign of the rest of them, sergeant. But what's this? Did you catch us some more troublemakers?"

"No, sir, these boys are horse hunters who stumbled upon us. This young lad here is one of them. He's a healer, honest he is, sir. He saved my Pens, stopped the bleeding of that nasty wound and put him to sleep like a baby. It left me speechless, is what it did."

"Well, we'll have to tell the Elder about that," the captain replied. He turned to Blaze and eyed him skeptically. "Why are you shaking boy? Is there something you're hiding from us?"

"I get scared easily," said Blaze.

"Well, sergeant, did you hear that? He's an honest one, even if he is a coward. Now listen to me, healer boy. I want you to take one last look at these dead ones. Remember it well. This is what happens to those who break the law."

The soldiers released the horse hunters. As the young men rode away, Stannis lamented, "They'll be watching us every time we step foot in Orres. We'll be suspects from now on."

"But what did we do?" protested Roff. "How were we supposed to know they were out here killing troublemakers?"

"They won't care about that. You didn't grow up around Orres. I know that captain. He's put a lot of people in prison, including some of our kin."

"Blaze," said Quirt, "we heard them say that you saved that wounded soldier's life. Is that true?

"Yes, he's going to survive," said Blaze. "He would have died without the medicine I gave him. So I'm glad we came this way, no matter what else comes of it."

Roff led them for a few more hours to a familiar place where there was a spot of shade from the midday sun. Along the way, Kick occasionally noticed flashes of light from hills to the east. He saw that Blaze observed them, too. "There's something out there, cousin," Kick said. Blaze smiled at the way he said "cousin."

They reached a resting spot by the base of a cliff with great slabs of chocolate-colored rock that rose straight up for nearly one hundred feet. Near the rock grew high brush that offered a bit of shade. The men began unpacking their horses for a three-hour nap during the worst heat of the day.

Blaze came to Roff, holding his hand to his side. "I'm not well, cousin," he said.

"What's wrong?" asked Roff.

"It's the medicine I used to save that guard back there. It can bring me low when I touch it."

Kick asked, "What kind of medicine is it?"

"My mother makes it. It doesn't bother her, but it can hurt me because I'm part-MuKierin. I'll feel better after I get some rest."

Stannis said, "Next time just leave the medicine in your saddlebag. There's no point in you getting sick just to save a stranger."

"I can't do that," said Blaze. "It's even worse if I just leave people to bleed to death. Then I'd really suffer. It's part of the curse of my family. I just need to rest for a few hours. I'll get better. There's one more thing. This afternoon, I think we're going to have visitors."

The cousins all turned to scan the horizon. They couldn't see any movement. "Are you sure?" Roff asked. "Maybe that strange medicine is making you see things."

"No, on the way here I saw flashes of light out to the east. Kick noticed them, too. It was from friends signaling me that riders are coming our way."

The six men lay down for the afternoon rest. Roff and Blaze quickly nodded off. The others closed their eyes and waited for the sun to swing west. The summer heat seemed to slither off the land and hills in shimmering undulations. Kick watched a small lizard scamper up onto the front of a canvas pannier. For a moment it froze there as if turned into stone.

After two hours, Stannis spotted movement far across the desert. Eventually he could see a man on a sorrel horse and two women riding together on a paint mare. They apparently had sighted the horse hunters and were riding toward them. Stannis took a pebble and hit Kick with it in the ear. "Company's coming," he said. "Give 'ol Roffie a kick for me, will you?"

"With pleasure," said Kick, who obliged.

The women rode without leggings, their long skirts hitched up and tucked beneath them. They stopped their horse in the flats while the man rode closer to the cousins. He carried a sword. "Brothers," he called. "Can we join you? We're traveling north."

Roff turned to Stannis. "Do you know him?" he asked.

Stannis nodded. "His name's Sunny. He's from Orres, and he's trouble. They say he once stole another man's horse."

Roff called back, "We don't need any trouble. Maybe you better go back to Orres."

"I can't go back to Orres," said Sunny. "And I didn't steal that horse. I just borrowed it temporarily for justice. Listen, I need your help. I've got to get these daughters of the Stone Woman safely to Kierinswell. You can't turn your back on two kinswomen. I'm asking you as true MuKierin to place them under your wings."

Roff asked Stannis, "Who are the girls?"

"They're Sunny's sisters. That one with the short black hair is Lowi. The other with the brown hair is Darnelle. They're not what you'd call innocents, especially Lowi. My guess is that they all had dealings with those dead rebels back up the road."

Blaze rose up from his blanket. His face looked pale and his speech was labored. "Roff, if they go back to Orres, they'll be executed."

"If that captain finds us traveling with them, we'll all be hanged." said Roff. "You saw how he operates."

"The captain's headed back to Orres. These three can't make it north through the desert without supplies and water. What if we take them with us and swing west to reach the main road to Kierinswell? They'd be with us only four or five days."

Roff drew near Blaze. "Let me ask you something. Would it make you sick if these three died of thirst out there?"

"I don't know. And I don't want to find out. Listen, I'm willing to take a turn standing guard at night to make sure that they don't run off with our horses."

"You're too sick to stand watch," Roff said as he turned toward his cousins. "Well, what do the rest of you say?"

"I suppose I can stand them for five days," said Stannis. "I don't much trust Sunny, but I can't see us letting a woman get hanged, even Lowi."

Sunny leaned forward and extended his arm, "Thank you, brothers. I give you my word, the word of Sunny, that I won't harm you."

"You'll give me that sword of yours, too, and your knives," Roff answered. "I'm not taking any chances with you."

Sunny nodded and signaled for the women to come forward. As they did, Blaze called out, "Sunny, you ought to know something. This morning we came upon some soldiers who'd been in a battle. They had attacked some young men from Orres."

"Did they spare anyone?" asked Darnelle.

"No, they killed them all. And there was a soldier there with a bad wound. I stopped the bleeding and saved his life. I thought you'd want to know that before you decide whether or not to come along with us."

Darnelle wept at the news, but Sunny and Lowi tightened their jaws and tried to look unfazed. "We're coming with you anyway," said Sunny. "Say, where'd you get that funny hat?"

"The Pappi, the Lake People."

"Really? Never been there. Say, did those stinking soldiers hurt you, healer boy? You don't look so good."

"I'll get better once we start moving again."

The horse hunters set off walking their horses that afternoon because Sunny and the women already had ridden their animals hard that day. They climbed slowly into the foothills above Orres. Atop one ridge they got their first glimpse of Mt. Fama, the highest peak in the Powder

Mountains, still crowned in summer with small patches of snow. Blaze's strength seemed to return as he looked upon it. "I want to climb that mountain some day," he told Stannis. "It reminds me of one I climbed in the land of the Pappi."

"It's not safe up there," said Stannis. "They say some evil haunts these southern mountains. If you climb up there, you might not come back down for breakfast."

"It won't be that way much longer. The King's warriors are coming. They'll soon drive that evil far away. It's all part of a new day."

That night the horse hunters camped in a long gully with poor feed and no water. Roff and Harney took the water skins and poured a ration for each horse into a collapsible leather bucket. While the animals drank, the two men examined their legs and hooves. Meanwhile, Kick got a fire going and Stannis helped him count out the pieces of dried meat and roots for the evening meal. When all was ready, the horse hunters flopped down beside the fire and ate. The two women sat across from the men. Sunny brought over their portions.

"What a miserable land this is," Sunny declared as he sat down beside his sisters. "It's a land filled with injustice. Tell me, horse boys, wouldn't you like to do something about that?"

"What'd you have in mind?" asked Roff. "Do you want us to end up like those dead boys back there today?"

"No, but I want your life to matter, like their lives did. Those brave boys were trying to stop injustice. They hated how our Elders chain up the poor and sell them into slavery for their debts. Yes, they died today, but they died fighting for The Cause. Do you know what that is? It's the liberation of our people. Wouldn't you rather die for such a cause than live like slaves under those tyrannical aristocrats?"

The other cousins looked at Roff, who stayed silent. Blaze asked, "What would the White Beard say about all this?"

Sunny's eyes opened in surprise. "Well, listen to the newcomer," he said. "Perhaps I've underestimated you. Tell me, fish boy, have you ever met the White Beard?"

"He held me once when I was a baby."

"Did he? How precious. I'll grant you that you've asked a good question. Personally I'm partial to the White Beard. I've heard him speak a few times, and I wish that more MuKierin outside of Orres knew about him. We still see things a bit differently, but I'm grateful for him. He's opened many eyes to the injustice of the debtors' chains. And he's not afraid to take on the Elders. He's earned my respect, and I can't say that about many men. I still wish he'd pick up a sword and fight, because I know that many MuKierin would join him if he did. Even some of the Elders who oppose slavery might find the backbone to stand with him if he pushed them. But I still have hope for him. I think he won't stay out of this fight forever. Eventually he'll join us."

"You're wrong," said Blaze. "You don't know the White Beard. He knows our story, even if you don't."

"Our story? What's that supposed to mean?"

"Long ago our ancestors stole a great power from the King of the Stone Woman. It wounded our people and left them with a great longing, and they passed that longing down to all their descendants. Now you're trying to heal that wound, but you don't know how."

"And you do?"

"The King does. And the White Beard is the King's steward. That's why he won't join you. He knows our story."

Sunny shook his head. "You're too much of a mystic for me, fish boy. I don't care about stories. I care about building an army. And all of you could be part of it. You could make a difference."

Lowi added, "We don't need a king. What we need is to get rid of the tyrants we already have."

Roff stood up. "What we need is to get some sleep. Kick, you take the first watch. Sunny, I want your sisters and you to stay away from the horses until morning. We'll all be getting up before the sun."

As the others made ready to sleep, Roff took Blaze aside and asked, "How's that story end, the one you were telling Sunny about?"

"Time will tell. But I'm part of that story, Roff, and now you are, too. I've known all my life that a big day is coming. When I was little, I started to have bad dreams. They always included a huge warrior from the Dark Brood named Pibbibib. Years ago he chased our fathers."

"Yes, I've heard his name. My papa said he's a scary giant."

"Well, he certainly was scary to me as a little boy. I started to dream about him before I even knew his name. And I always dreamed the same thing. Pibbibib and I would be fighting for the Root of Glory. Each of us always had a hand on it and together we tumbled round and round on the ground near a great castle. I was always so scared. All I could do was hang on. I figured if I ever let go, Pibbibib would kill me with it.

"The first time I had the dream, my mother came and comforted me. I was maybe five or six years old. She knew why I was afraid. She even told me my dream without me ever saying a word about it. After that, whenever I had the dream, she would come in to hold me. But as I got older, she came in less often. Instead, I would go find her. Once when I was fourteen, I got up and went looking for her. We lived beside the great lake in a compound with a high stone wall. That night I found her on the rampart staring over the wall toward the waters. She couldn't stop crying. It made me cry to see her like that. All we could do was hug each other.

"So I know I fit into the story, Roff. One day I'm going to meet up with Pibbibib. I know it's going to happen. And I know that right now I'm not ready to meet him. I'm at a disadvantage. My family was cursed the day the Root of Glory was stolen. Now my mother becomes so afraid and frenzied when I'm in danger that she could kill everything in sight, including you and your cousins. And I've got some of that fear inside me, too, fear for my life and fear for the others who might get hurt, like you. I can get unnaturally scared.

And I get sick when I'm around hurt and dying people. You saw that today. So one day I've got to go to the King, my grandfather. Only he can help me get ready for that meeting with Pibbibib. Don't ask me what he has in mind, because I don't know the answer. But I do know it won't be easy and I may lack the courage to persevere. If I turn and run, then I'll be ruined and so will all the people who put their hope in me. Here's the truth about the story, Roff. There's nobody else among our people who can save us from these bad ones. Those aren't just my words. They come from my grandfather the King, who knows the Root of Glory. The White Beard will tell you the same thing." Blaze stopped and bit his lip. "Do you ever wonder if you might be a coward, Roff? I worry about it a lot. Pretty soon we're going to find out one way or the other."

Roff shrugged and put a hand on his cousin's shoulder. "You're about the strangest person I've ever met. Sorry, Blaze, what I mean is, I've never met anybody like you. I'm not very good with words. But my papa told me to stick by you, no matter what. And that's what I intend to do."

The night passed without event. Blaze took the last watch and awoke everyone before dawn so they could start their journey in the coolness of the morn. The party moved steadily northeast into the foothills toward a spring that was widely known among the horse hunters. Roff and his cousins rode stern-faced and silent. Blaze trailed at the end of the line behind the two women.

The group again rested in the heat of the day, although they had almost reached the spring. Roff lay down beside Blaze. "Cousin," he said, "we're hoping to find a few horses up ahead. We often surprise the wild ones hanging around the water. Even so, it can be tricky because we need to get everyone in the right places before they catch our smell. I think our best chance will be to keep our three troublemakers far back from the spring."

"I can stay with them and the pack animals," Blaze said. "Maybe you can put us where we might have a chance to throw a rope if some horses break our way."

Roff nodded. "I know a good spot, if you can get those three to drop The Cause for a few minutes. But I'm going to take two of the three packhorses with me, especially the ones with the swords and the water bags. I don't want Sunny to get any crazy ideas while you're alone with him and the women."

After the midday rest, Stannis, Quirt and Harney set off first, swinging wide through steep foothills to reach the far side of the spring. Roff and Kick led the rest of the group to the base of a slope. "The spring is just over this hill," Roff told Sunny and the women. "The horses often bolt back this way to escape. If you three get up there on that right side, you can push the horses through that chute of rocks there. Then Blaze may have a chance of roping one."

"If we help," said Lowi, "we get half the profits."

Roff climbed aboard his horse. "Lady," he said, "that's between Blaze and you." Thinking more about it, he took all three packhorses with him as he set out for his place overlooking the spring.

"There are four of us," said Blaze, "so each one will get an equal portion of whatever we catch. Does anyone else want a rope? I have an extra one."

"Just show us where to stand," said Lowi. Sunny, however, took a rope.

Blaze spread them out in hiding places near the top of the ridge. Sunny and Lowi kept the two horses. Blaze took Darnelle to a place in the rocks just over the ridge, but out of sight of the spring. "If the horses come this way, wait until they reach you, here," he said. "Then after the first horse passes by, call out to your brother and sister."

Blaze took his place at the bottom of the slope. They didn't have to wait long. From over the ridge Darnelle called, "Horses! Horses! Get ready!" Then nearly a dozen wild ones galloped over the ridge and rushed down the ravine. The first horses tried to veer left, but Sunny and Lowi rode out from behind boulders and cut them off. The animals then bounded right, galloping down the chute. At the bottom, Blaze and his stallion bolted after them, splitting the terrified herd. The rider lifted his left arm and twirled his rope above him. The loop landed cleanly around the neck of a sorrel filly. Blaze pulled up his stallion while the filly swirled excitedly in a circle at the end of the rope. Sunny rode up and threw his lariat. It missed the frantic horse. Roff rode over the slope in time to watch Sunny throw and miss a second time. Sunny looked up to see the stout horse hunter above him watching from the hillside. Gripping the rope tightly and swinging it feverishly, he forced the filly up against an immense boulder. Sunny drew close, slowed the rope's twirling and let it drop down over the filly's head.

"Yes!" he yelled in celebration.

Roff rode down the hill. "Sunny, we're going to make a respectable MuKierin out of you, yet. Blaze, it's a good thing the four of you waited here. They bolted early. We couldn't stop them."

"You mean you failed to catch a single one of them?" Sunny asked. "Hah! The great horse hunters get skunked and the fish boy and the troublemakers rope a wild one. Wait until I tell my people!"

That night they camped by the spring. After the men got in their bedrolls, Darnelle went to Blaze as he sat on a stone ledge keeping watch near the horses. "I want to thank you for the kindness you've shown us," she said.

"You're welcome, Darnelle. I can see these have been hard days for you."

She lowered her head and nodded. "Yes, hard days. The night before we met you we were all out on the desert with our comrades, preparing to free one of our men from prison. Before daylight another member of our band rode out to warn us that the soldiers were coming after us. He told us we had been betrayed.

"There was no way we could all escape. The man who warned us knew that we had only Sunny's horse with us. That's why he rode out on the paint. He had feelings for Lowi, though he was too shy to ever tell her. He wanted to save her by bringing her the extra horse.

"Even so, Lowi became infuriated that the men wanted to send her away just because she was a woman. Poor Sunny was ashamed that he would have to run away because he was our brother and would have to take care of us. And me, I felt guilty because I didn't want to die.

"So we got on the two horses and Sunny and Lowi promised them that we would spread the story of how they died bravely, how they had sacrificed themselves for The Cause. They looked back at us so grim and forlorn. Then the man who had ridden out to us started to cry. And Lowi turned her back on him. I wanted her to go and thank him for what he had done, for saving us. He deserved that much. But I was too shaken and Lowi was too angry for having been deemed inferior to men. So we rode off without saying goodbye."

When morning came, the horse hunters turned northwest for the main road to Kierinswell. They dropped down out of the foothills and rode across rolling flatlands of sagebrush. They stopped for the midday rest at a tight circle of boulders, an island-like group of rock that rose above a flat expanse of desert. The men strung a picket line for their horses and tied the wild filly between two boulders. For shade they set up a canvas canopy among the rocks and rested underneath it during the afternoon's heat. Blaze, however, grabbed his pouch and climbed atop one of the great rocks. From his perch he looked out over a vast valley of sagebrush. Off on the eastern horizon lay the curved ridges and saddles of the last line of foothills before the Powder Mountains.

After an hour, Blaze saw a large band of riders coming out of the north. Turning east, he soon spotted several quick flashes of light from the distant hills. From his pouch, he pulled out a small mirror but carefully kept it hidden until he was sure the approaching riders wouldn't see its light. Then he uncovered it and flashed signals eastward. A moment later a reply came from the hills.

Blaze put the mirror away. From his pouch, he removed the White Gem and its leather thong. Tying it loosely around his neck, he slid off the rock and went to Roff.

"There's a group of riders coming toward us," he said. "I think they're bandits."

Immediately Roff and Sunny scrambled up the nearby rocks. Lowi arose, too, but Blaze warned her, "Lowi, our one hope may be in preventing the bandits from seeing Darnelle and you. If they discover two women are with us, they'll likely attack us and not stop fighting until they've taken you as their prisoners. For everyone's sake, please hide behind these rocks and let me cover you with a canvas tarp." Reluctantly Lowi complied. Darnelle crawled underneath the canvas with her sister.

Sunny knelt beside Roff atop the rocks. "Are they bandits?" he asked.

"We'll know soon enough," Roff answered. "They're coming this way. They must have seen us."

Stannis called from below, "How many of them are there?"

"Close to twenty," Roff answered. "The closer they come, the less they look like horse hunters."

"Then give me my sword," Sunny demanded. "If there's going to be a fight, I'm the best one here with a blade."

"You'll get your sword if you need it. Don't be in such a rush to get killed."

Kick started to unfasten the picket line from a boulder. "Roff," he asked, "shouldn't we bring the horses in behind these rocks?"

"Wait," said Blaze, swallowing hard. His voice had a squeak to it, and he wheezed when he caught his breath. "We can't stop them from taking the horses. There are too many of them."

"What does that mean?" Sunny asked. "Do you want to give up without a fight?"

Blaze wheezed again and pointed to Lowi and Darnelle. "Your sisters are hiding behind those rocks. The bandits haven't seen them. Right now all they can see are our horses. If we refuse to give up the animals, they'll attack us. If we give them up, they may leave without a fight."

"Listen, coward, we need those horses to go north!"
Sunny insisted. "Without them, we'll have to walk back to
Orres. We'll still end up dead, only over there it will be from
an executioner."

"Let's deal with one problem at a time," said Blaze.
He looked at Roff. "Please, cousin. Let me take the horses out
to them. That's our best hope."

"Well, it might work," said Roff. "We certainly can't
fight so many bandits. But maybe I should take out the
horses, Blaze. You can stay back here safe with the others."

"No, Roff, please. I need to do it. I've got a plan if
they won't leave us alone. Trust me."

Roff frowned. "Alright, we'll do it your way. Just let
me help you start driving the horses out to them."

The outlaws halted on the flats beyond the rocks,
taking time to size up the strength of their opponents. Blaze
and Roff quickly removed the ropes from their horses and
herded them toward the bandits. Kick led the wild filly behind
them. Roff told Blaze, "You better stop shaking or they're
going to see it."

"I'll try. If I can't handle this, how will I cope when
things get really dangerous?"

"This looks plenty dangerous to me."

Blaze cracked a smile. "Thanks, Roff. I just need you
to trust that I can make my way back to you."

"Just don't get yourself killed or my papa is going to
be mighty disappointed in me."

Kick handed Blaze the filly's rope and retreated with
Roff to the rocks. The outlaws began to jeer and guffaw when
they realized that their victims were handing over their horses
without a fight. The bandit leader, a man of thin beard and
narrow face, took two riders and rode forward. The filly
reared and tried to run off. To keep her under control, Blaze
swung the rope behind his hips and grabbed fast, leaning hard
against the taut line. He bounded forward a few steps with the
wild horse, then leaned back on the rope and braced himself.
One of the bandits rode alongside him. Blaze tossed the man
the filly's rope. The bandit took it and went back to his

comrades, who already were roping and collecting the rest of the horses.

Their leader, meanwhile, rode slowly forward, pointing his lance at Blaze. "Boy," he said, "do you cowards really think we'll simply take your horses and leave here without a fight?"

"We don't have much else. It seems like a pretty hot day to fight over ropes and cooking pots."

"You seem to be forgetting about yourselves," the leader said. "A half-dozen boys might bring a fair price in the slave trade."

"I don't think my friends would go peaceably with you. There wouldn't be a half-dozen of us alive when the fighting was done. And some of your men might fall down and not get back up, either."

The bandit shook his head. "You don't look like you're going to put up much of a fight, boy. You look plenty scared."

"I am, for both of us."

The leader chuckled. "You're funny, you know that? Now tell your friends to throw down their weapons and come out here. If not, I'm going to climb down off this horse and slit your throat."

Blaze reached beneath his shirt and removed the large gem hanging on the thong. "First there is something I need to tell you," he said. "This gem belongs to The Great King Over the Mountain. It came from his home in the Green Lands, from his castle at River's End. It is a sign that you should leave us alone."

The leader stretched out his hand. "Is that so, my little mystic. No wonder you're so brave. You have a king's protection. I'm impressed. Now hand me the gem."

"The King doesn't want you to have it."

"Blast your King into the dung heap! Give me the gem!"

Blaze nodded and raised it toward the outlaw. What happened next shocked all those watching. The moment the leader's hand touched the gem, he gasped and fell from his horse as a dead man. Blaze caught the bandit's lance as the man toppled to the ground. Quickly the young man grabbed the gem's thong and secured it around the butt end of the lance shaft. The other bandits watched stunned for a few seconds. Then they came to their senses and galloped forward. Blaze stepped back a few paces from their fallen leader and grasped the lance in both hands, pointing the tip to the ground. The outlaws formed a semi-circle around Blaze as their second-in-command jumped down and knelt beside his fallen leader. They could see the young horse hunter before them was shaking.

"He's not dead," Blaze told the outlaws. "But he won't wake up for a day or two. And he's going to have some bad nightmares."

"What did you do to him?" growled the second-in-command, rising and drawing his sword.

"He cursed the King and then he fell over. He should not have cursed the King."

"I piss on your king!" the bandit roared. "Now give me the lance."

Blaze nodded and pointed the butt end to the approaching outlaw. As the man reached for it, Blaze twisted the shaft so the gem caught the man's left palm. Immediately the bandit's head jerked, he dropped to his knees and tumbled down unconscious. The other outlaws looked dumbfounded at one another. Before them, both their leader and his second-in-command lay face down in the dust.

Blaze's voice became labored: "That is the second man to curse the King and fall down. He also will awaken in a day or so. His nightmares also will be terrible to bear. I must warn you that more of you will end up just like them if you stay here. If you are wise, you will take these two with you and leave. And it would please the King if you would give us back our horses."

Blaze began to retreat to the rocks. The perplexed outlaws made no attempt to stop him. Several of them dismounted, hoisted their two unconscious leaders onto their horses and tied them in place. But the bandits wouldn't give up the stolen horses. "I may not curse your king," one shouted, "but I won't please him, either." With that they galloped south with all the horses, leaving a cloud of dust behind them.

The horse hunters cautiously emerged from the rocks. The two women threw back the canvas tarp and stood tall. Lowi was clutching a knife, ready for battle "What did you do to them?" she demanded.

"I touched them with the King's White Gem," he answered. "The children of the Dry Lands can't touch it without falling into a deep sleep. Those two won't wake up for a few days. They'll soon be dreaming horrible nightmares. I doubt either of them will ever want to rob another soul."

"But Blaze," said Darnelle, "you touched the gem. It didn't affect you."

"My father's from the Dry Lands, but not my mother. So I can touch it, but it still affects me. It makes me ill when I use it."

"So that's another thing that makes you sick," Stannis said. "You've got some strange playthings, you know that?"

"I can fight off the illness better if I move around. I want to go now and try to get our horses back."

"And how do you mean to do that?" Sunny demanded. "I thought you said there were too many of them."

"I know some friends who can help us. They're out there in the eastern foothills. I just need to find them."

Roff turned and looked east. "You're not thinking of going out there all by yourself. That sounds risky, especially when you look so poorly."

"I don't need to go alone," Blaze said. "I'll take the fastest cousin with me."

The horse hunters all looked at Stannis. He shrugged. "This is what I get for winning footraces all my life," he said. "Alright, Blaze, let's go find your friends."

Blaze smiled and grabbed a water pouch. He slung its strap over his shoulder and set out east, still clutching the bandit's lance. Stannis grabbed Sunny's sword and followed him. The two men jogged through the sagebrush with the sun still high in the southwest sky. Eventually they crossed the flatlands to rolling hills and began climbing upwards through thickets of prickly brush. The pair walked for another hour, took a rest and walked again. Stannis was beginning to think they would walk all night. But Blaze stopped when they reached the top of the next rise. "I can't go any farther," he said, dropping to his knees and throwing down the lance. "The illness has caught up with me. I need to lay low here for a little while."

Stannis knelt beside him. "Blaze, why'd you come here?" he asked. "You don't seem to do too well in this land."

"This is where I've been sent. This is where the next part of the story is going to take place."

"Is that the story you were telling Sunny about a few days ago?

"Yes. You know how you've got to walk before you can run? Well, I need to learn to walk among the MuKierin. Don't ask exactly what that means. I'm not sure yet."

"I'm glad it doesn't mean you're going to join up with Sunny."

"No, I'm not here to spill blood. But the King does hate slavery. The White Beard's been telling the Elders that for years. The Council remains divided between Slavers and Anti-Slavers, but all of them seem too comfortable with the status quo. They won't listen to the White Beard. So maybe one day the King will use us to get their attention. But first I need to get my bearings, to live for a time as a horse hunter. I need to learn more about my people. And today we need to get back our horses."

"How are we going to do that when you're feeling so ill?"

Blaze pointed east. "There's your answer."

On a distant slope, Stannis spotted a single rider on a dark horse, trailed by a spare mount. The rider and the horses descended the hill and disappeared from sight. "Is he a friend?" Stannis asked.

"Yes. My enemies usually travel in packs."

"Now that's a comforting thought."

"It's good that you're going to meet my people, Stannis. They can help you decide whether I'm crazy or telling the truth."

"I never said you were crazy. Okay, I may have thought it, but I never said it."

The horseman crested the ridge. His stallion trotted up the slope toward the two MuKierin. Stannis tried to determine the height of the rider in comparison to the sage he was passing through. The dark mount seemed larger than most of the horses that the MuKierin rode. But that meant the rider was taller, too. Indeed, Stannis soon realized he'd never seen such a huge man. On the stranger came, holding a great lance in his right hand. His long dark hair flowed from beneath a golden helm and a golden breastplate covered his beige tunic. Stannis later had trouble explaining whether the man looked young or old. The rider reined in near the two horse hunters.

"My lord," he said in MuKierin, bowing in his saddle.

"Fidden Gadaeyo, Captain," Blaze said. "Thank you for coming. My kinsman Stannis and I will gladly ride double for now."

"We'll soon provide you another horse, lord. Commander Tor suggested that we ride south from here and join the main company."

Blaze grabbed the lance and slowly approached the spare mount, a gray stallion. He put his foot in the stirrup, swung aboard and offered Stannis his arm.

"Are all the other warriors his size, too?" Stannis asked.

Blaze smiled. "Yes. We're in good hands."

The next morning Roff and the others had little to do but wait and watch the empty wastelands around camp. Sunny passed the time by betting the horse hunters on who could hit a clay mug with a pebble. Lowi sharpened her knife. But Darnelle sat on the highest rock and looked south.

"I'm not going back to Orres," said Sunny.

"Well, you can't go north," said Kick. "You'll never make it to the next well."

"Then I'll go back south to the last spring where we caught the filly. Sooner or later someone will stop there."

"What about us, Roff," asked Kick. "If Stannis were here, he'd be wondering aloud whether we shouldn't start walking south, too."

"Stannis isn't here," said Roff. "We're waiting for him to return with Blaze."

"And what if they don't come back?" asked Sunny. "What if the bandits kill them?"

"You can leave whenever you feel like it," said Roff. "But don't you dare come back. As for my cousins and me, we're staying put."

"I'll stay until evening, horse boy. I don't want to walk in the heat of the day. But I'm not going to stay here forever."

Darnelle called out, "I see somebody. There are horses coming our way." Roff and Sunny sprang up and climbed onto her rock. "Yes, they're coming," Darnelle called to the others. "I can see two horsemen. They're bringing back all our animals."

Slowly the riders made their way to the camp, each man leading a string of horses. Roff dropped off the rock, as his other cousins stood up. They could see Blaze was smiling, but Stannis was clenching his jaw.

"Well," Kick yelled at them when they drew near. "Start talking. I want to know what happened."

"You're not going to believe me," said Stannis.

"Why's that?"

"Because I'm not sure I believe it, and I was there. It's like Uncle Noli said. We're in strange company with Blaze. But I'll tell you my story. We met up with twenty giant warriors. See, I told you it sounds crazy. Anyway, they helped us find the bandits late at night. Nobody got hurt. When the outlaws saw what they were up against, they ran off like scared rabbits. And we got our horses back."

Sunny asked, "What do you mean, 'gigantic warriors'? Who were they?"

Blaze replied, "They serve the King of the Green Lands, the King who long ago protected the Stone Woman."

Lowi said, "There's no such King."

"Then how did we get our horses back?"

"I don't know. Perhaps you're in league with those outlaws. Perhaps you're all trying to trick us and play games with our minds."

"Alright," interrupted Roff. "We've sat around here long enough. We're almost out of water. We need to pack up and make for the next spring. Let's get moving." As the others moved off, he drew close to Blaze and Stannis. "We need to talk tonight," Roff said. "Just the cousins. We don't need those other three around."

"I'll say," said Stannis. "Blaze has more explaining to do. And the rest of you need to see those warriors. I don't want you all thinking I'm crazy."

"We'll talk," said Blaze. "I'll tell you what I can. The King already has set things in motion. Those warriors that Stannis met are headed next for Mt. Fama. The King's enemies have long held that ground for generations, but the Greenlanders are about to take it from them. A battle is about to begin."

Weakling took the lead, tramping at night down a dark mountain trail east of Orres. Before him the moonlight illuminated a troop of dead warriors sprawled along the rocky slope. Some bodies had fallen atop one another. Weakling stopped to examine a hand from one corpse dangling over the armored torso of another.

Pibbibib approached from the rear, his sword in his hand. It was just the two of them traveling together that night. The larger warrior paused and scanned the darkened hill for any movement. "Ours or theirs?" he whispered of the dead.

"Ours," Weakling replied in a hushed voice. "All Cleavers. All I've seen so far are dead Cleavers."

"Good. Maybe these poor suckers died a long time ago. But keep alert as we pass by them."

"Do we have to go this way? There are so many of
them. What if the enemy is hiding among all the bodies?"

"No. You could sense them if the enemy were near.
Anyone still breathing here is one of ours."

"Which still doesn't make it safe."

None of the fallen so much as twitched as the two
crept past. Weakling again set out ahead of his partner. His
dark leather armor had only a few metal buckles and some
bleached human bones to catch the moonlight. But there were
still far too few places where he could altogether escape the
light and blend into shadow. He was forced to trust his senses
and hope that he really could detect any enemy warriors that
might be hiding out there in the darkness. He sensed nothing
in his wounded leg, but still his heart kept pounding. He
heard his foot dislodge a few rocks, and he cursed under his
breath. Stopping, he strained to hear any movement around
him. The night was still.

Farther down the trail, the two warriors reached a
waist-high boulder. There a hand darted out and grabbed
Weakling's ankle, tripping him. As the hulk fell, a second
attacker sprang up nearby and hobbled forward. The wobbly
Cleaver dragged a crippled leg, but he nonetheless advanced,
raising a sword and making ready to plunge it into his victim.
The first, the one who had tripped Weakling, also crawled
forward on his belly, clutching a double-edged dagger.
Weakling landed on his back and wasted no time squirming
away from his assailants. However, sliding along the earth he
failed to avoid a sharp rock that caught his shoulder and
brought him to an abrupt stop. The standing warrior limped
on and made ready to swing his blade. But he didn't notice
Pibbibib, who caught him from behind and plunged a sword
through him, sending him toppling down the hill. The
crawling warrior turned and vainly swung his dagger at
Backstabber. He missed, and Pibbibib stabbed him in the
shoulder, making him howl in agony and drop the dagger.
Backstabber picked up the weapon and placed it against the
warrior's throat.

"Don't you know who I am?" he asked with all the menace he could muster. "I am the Great One. Ekdonuk. And no one harms my Number Two." With that he slit the warrior's throat.

Weakling picked himself up, unharmed but hissing: "Stinking Cleavers. Can't they just die quietly?"

From down the trail came the sound of advancing feet. Weakling's eyes bulged. Silently he drew his sword and whispered, "More trouble."

"Step back to that boulder," Pibbibib ordered. The larger warrior also retreated a few steps, dropped to the ground and began to crawl up the slope above Weakling.

Six warriors trotted up the trail. Even in darkness, Weakling felt certain that these were fellow rebels. The only question was whether they also wanted his blood. The lead warrior advanced a few steps ahead of his comrades, who spread out and began to climb the slope above him. A moment later the leader froze and called out, "Weakwi? Is that you? It's me, Zhaggee."

"Zhaggee? What's the Red Brigade doing out here? Don't you know the enemy's on the move?"

"Of course, we do," said Zhaggee, brushing back his tangled locks of yellow hair. "We're running as fast as we can to get out of these blasted hills. There's a large company of our chums out in front of us. We're rushing to catch up with them. We were just taking a breather when we heard you raising a ruckus. I guess you just couldn't let the dying go in peace."

"They picked on us first. We just put them out of their misery."

Zhaggee noticed Pibbibib stand up on the slope above him. "That's far enough, Backstabber," he called. "I've got six swords here to keep you in line, so don't try to mess with me."

"Just let us pass, coward," Pibbibib replied. "We don't need you."

"Oh, really? Out here there's safety in numbers. That's why we passed by this spot unmolested and you two got bushwhacked. Look, these wounded buggers are the least of your problems. In the past few days we've come across massacres of our troops. We're talking dead Cleavers everywhere, not that we care much for them. But it's a sign of the trouble that's out there. There are rumors that the enemy commander himself is leading the assault."

"Tor?" gasped Weakling. "What's his game?"

"Who knows? The enemy seems to be cleaning Cleavers out of these southern mountains, just like they did years ago in your old stomping grounds in the north. Makes me glad that I'm a Slinker. Anyway, we wouldn't be here but we got a tip about the Great Valuable being somewhere up here. Our captain just had to have a look. What great timing, huh? Say, what brings you two here?"

"None of your business," said Pibbibib.

Weakling interjected, "We're on assignment for Lord Mackadoo. No big fish, Zhaggee, but we can't say more. We've also come across a few battlefields. Seems like this fight has gone on for days, and our side has gotten the worst of it."

"No argument there. Well, you both better come with us for now. We could use two extra swords."

"No," said Pibbibib. "We're going our own way."

"Hold on," said Weakling. "I want to save my skin, especially after nearly getting throttled here by those Cleavers. If Zhaggee can help us get out of these hills, then I want to join up with him."

"That's the stuff," said Zhaggee. "If your gasbag wants to come along, he can join us, as long as he plays nice. But we'll be watching him, just the same."

Together the warriors began a quick tramp downhill. The moon was still high, and they made good time rushing along the trail. Eventually they passed into a canyon and faded into the shadows.

Pibbibib stayed in the rear with Weakling. Backstabber didn't like following Zhaggee. He worried that the fool could lead them smack into disaster. But it was true that there might be some safety in numbers, especially if they had to fight their way out.

Soon Weakling halted. He grew still and closed his eyes. "I sense something."

"Where?" Pibbibib hissed. "In front or in back?"

"I can't tell. But it's getting stronger. If we hold still a minute, maybe I can tell if we're coming up on them or if they're overtaking us."

Zhaggee noticed that the two warriors had fallen behind. He strode back up the trail. "What's holding you two up?" he demanded.

"Just go on without us," said Pibbibib.

Weakling whispered, "Give us a moment, Zhaggee. Something's wrong."

"Shut up!" snapped Pibbibib. He turned to Zhaggee, "We're tired. We've gone far enough. You go and rejoin your company. We don't need you anymore."

"Something smells funny," said Zhaggee. "You two better tell me what you're up to right now."

Neither warrior gave an answer. Both seemed to be sniffing the cool night air. The other stragglers from the Red Brigade came back to see about the holdup. Zhaggee could do little but glare at the two silent allies. After a minute, Weakling whispered into Pibbibib's ear: "They're coming up from behind, and fast. I'm sure of it. And there are far too many of them for us to handle."

Pibbibib looked for an escape route and quickly made his decision. "Listen to me, you miscreants. We're going up to hide on that hillside. A big troop of the enemy is going to swoop through here soon. We've got no time for talk. You're all coming with us because if I leave any of you here, they'll catch you and then you'll squeal on the rest of us. But I'm in charge and I'll slit the throat of anyone who tries to make a false move on me. Now start running up that hill. I'll be right behind you."

Weakling rushed up the slope. The others scrambled after him. Hurriedly they climbed through brush and boulders, often slipping on loose soil, but never stopping.

They were still far from the crest when they began to hear noises from the direction they had come. It sounded like horses moving across rocky ground. "Get down!" Pibbibib ordered. "Lie flat and don't so much as scratch your nose. Don't get up until I give the signal or none of us will ever get up again!"

The members of the Red Brigade hastily complied, flopping onto the rocky ground and holding still in the darkness. A minute later, Pibbibib spotted the intruders. It was a company of cavalry riding single file down the trail. Pibbibib couldn't distinguish the features or garb of the riders, but he was sure that these soldiers belonged to the King. He began to count them: One hundred, two hundred, three hundred and still more followed. It took many minutes for them to pass beneath him, and he waited several more before he crawled on his belly to Weakling. "Are they all gone?" he asked.

"Yes, but their scent's still strong. Let's wait a while before we try to find a safe route out of here."

"Agreed. We don't need to be hasty. The night will soon be over anyway. Let's climb up to the top of this hill and find a hiding place." Pibbibib rose up and said to Zhaggee, "We're leaving. We've got to find a safe place to rest before daylight."

"How did you know that those riders were coming up from behind us?"

"Haven't you ever heard of The Powers? I can sense the enemy, just like our most malevolent Master. I can tell when Tor and his warriors are drawing near."

"You? Are you sure it's you that has The Powers?"

Pibbibib drew his knife. "If I ever hear you ask that question again, I'll give you my answer. You had better think long and hard before you ever dare ask it. Now you and these other losers have two choices. You can run down that hill and find the corpses of your old company after Tor's troops have crushed them. Or you can come with us and sneak through the enemy lines. Scatter if you want to. I don't need any of you. But if you come with us, you won't leave my side until we're out of this."

Zhaggee looked at his allies and nodded with them. "We're with you," he told Backstabber. "Just get us out of here."

Chapter Two

Going Forth

In the summer of his seventieth year, the White Beard rode east from Orres. With him came six old horse hunters, including two who had been there two decades earlier when he anointed a baby boy high up in the Powder Mountains. By now the White Beard took a little more time climbing aboard his piebald mare, and he cut each day's journey a little shorter than he had as a younger man. Even so, he still rode tall, his body aligned from ear to heel and his knees supporting his aged frame when he stood in his stirrups riding up steep ascents.

For this journey, the White Beard brought along Dash, the golden-haired hound that had been present with Roj and Healdin at the birth of their son. As they traveled, the hound usually was content to trot beside the old man. But occasionally it bounded far ahead to survey the land beyond the next hilltop. At night, it lay down among the old horse hunters but seldom seemed to sleep. It rarely growled, never barked and never begged for food.

Early one morning, the party reached a ridge that looked out on a great bowl-shape valley. In the distance the White Beard spied a small band of horses racing through the sagebrush. Four horse hunters galloped after them. Mares, colts and fillies kicked up faint plumes of dust in the flats. The riders fanned out and dashed wildly after them. The men bent low in the saddle and began to twirl their horsehair ropes. Their mounts extended their necks forward as the wind whipped through long, wavy manes.

Instinctively the old horse hunters looked ahead to a group of boulders strewn across the far end of the valley. What would happen when the horses drew near? Would they pass among those towering rocks or swing around them? On ran the herd, desperate to escape its pursuers. At the last possible moment, the lead horse broke right to avoid the boulders. The others followed. Immediately a rider on a dark mount galloped forth from that side of the rocks. Another rider on a pale horse sprang into the open from the other end. A new jolt of fear impelled the wild horses to swerve further right. Even so, the closest horseman caught up to the animals and twirled his lariat. He picked out a paint colt and took aim. The rope's loop darted swiftly and fell cleanly onto the colt's neck. The hunter's mount slid to a halt, spraying a stream of dust before it. The rope tightened and the paint's head snapped. Its body careened and swerved out from the herd. Regaining its balance, the colt bounded and bucked as it circled its captor. The second rider came alongside and quickly dropped a second loop around the paint, drawing it taut. Caught between the two unyielding lines, the creature surrendered.

The old timers trotted down the hill and across the valley. They now could see six horse hunters gather around their catch. The White Beard called back to his companions, "I can see Blaze among them. We have found him." The old men pushed their horses and pack animals into a slow canter. The morning air felt cool on their faces, with a hint of dust still present in the air.

When they reached the band of hunters, the White Beard stopped his mount and raised his staff in his right hand. "Oh, to be young again," he said.

"What would you do if you had another chance?" asked Roff.

"I would ride with your kinsmen. I would fight the good fight."

"You've already done that," said Blaze.

The White Beard smiled. "The King has sent me to find you. Your time has come. There's a young man who needs to be rescued. He will leave Orres in chains tomorrow."

"Then I'll go and free him," said Blaze. He dismounted and walked up to the White Beard.

Still mounted, the Steward of the MuKierin took a small vial of oil and shook a few drops on his fingers. He leaned down from his saddle and anointed Blaze's head with the oil. "As I did when you were a babe, I do so again this day for you. The time has come for the King's champion to go forth."

"Thank you, White Beard. I'm ready."

"Take this with you," said the old man, handing over his wooden staff. "Keep it until you give it to the next steward of our people." He pointed to the great hound. "Your mother sent Dash here to stay with you as long as you need him. He'll keep watch over you and your cousins. I hope each one of them will choose to follow you."

That evening the young and old horsemen camped together in a small canyon with a good spring. After the evening meal, Roff sat beside the White Beard as the old man drank his desert tea. "Why is Blaze going to rescue some slave?" Roff asked confidentially. "I know he's not ready to find the Root of Glory. But why put him in danger? He gets the shakes pretty bad whenever someone threatens him. Aren't there going to be armed guards with this slave?"

"You think he'll get scared?"

"I know he'll get scared. It's the curse."

"Yes, Blaze is cursed. But so are all of us. And still he wants to help us."

"What's that mean?"

"Blaze knows that he gets scared easily. But he also knows that our people are terrified of the Root of Glory. Our ancestors saw it burn red, and it cursed us. Now we both want it and are terrified of it. Every one of us would steal it if we could grasp it in our hands and feel its power flowing through us. But when someone else holds it, we become gripped by fear. As long as it burns red, we can't help but fall down and hide our faces from it. If Blaze is going to prevail, he's got to do more than simply hold the Root of Glory and defeat the Realm. He's got to make that great power burn white, the way it used to shine for the King before it was stolen. The red flame brings fear, but the white flame would bring comfort and hope. It would satisfy the longing that we all have inside us. Undoubtedly some of the desert people still wouldn't trust

Blaze. No, they would still run from him. But many others would follow him back to the Green Lands. That can't happen as long as the power burns red."

"But why doesn't the King just come here and take back the Root of Glory for himself? Why not have him hold it, instead of Blaze? He could come with his army and take the power and crush his enemies. Wouldn't that fix everything?"

The White Beard took a sip of his tea. "No, Roff, it wouldn't. The King certainly could take back what is rightfully his, but we'd still be doomed. Now that the power burns red, even he can't make it burn white again. Only his champion can. Only Blaze can set things right."

"But how? How can Blaze make it burn white?"

"I don't exactly know how he'll do it. The King knows, and one day he's going to help his grandson get ready to hold that power. But first Blaze has to learn about us. And that means he must learn that there are all kinds of curses, including the curse of the debtors' chains. Tomorrow he's going to learn about the curse of being a slave."

"It's not fair. He's my cousin. I don't want to see him go through all this."

"You're right. It's not fair. But the desert people are in trouble, Roff, and he's our only hope. And this is where you come in. Blaze needs your help. I'm an old man, and my time in this land is growing short. But you and your cousins can make a difference. He needs you. He may fail without you."

"I won't leave him, White Beard. I promised my papa. I may not understand much. But my papa told me to go with Blaze, and that's what I intend to do. But let me ask you one last thing. Where is this Root of Glory? Does anybody know?"

The old man motioned him closer. "Yes, the King knows. Please don't share that news with anybody now. Let Blaze tell the others when the time's right. And don't ask me where it is. I don't know and I don't want to know. If our enemies ever capture me, I don't want to be carrying such a secret."

The next day the sun baked the heads of fifty slaves climbing up to the South Pass between Orres and Pylan. Six guards rode alongside the prisoners as the line curled back and forth along a series of switchbacks that passed among boulders and prickly brush. Each slave wore wrist shackles, and they were all linked together by a single rope that was held by a rider at the front of the column. Midway to the summit, the slaves rested briefly, but soon the guards were prodding them to get up and move on.

Near the top, the trail traversed a long, sandy slope marked with occasional boulders. From behind one of those large rocks, Blaze emerged and leaned on the staff that the White Beard had given him. The guards halted and surveyed the hillside. They saw only the one man with a strange hat blocking their way. He didn't appear to have a sword. Two guards rode forward while the others stayed back with the slaves. One of the guards who advanced was the chief, a man with a salt-and-pepper beard covering a round face. He wore a small sword. The other carried a lance. The two men stopped side by side before Blaze. The chief said gruffly, "You're in my way, boy."

Blaze closed his eyes and bit his lower lip. It took a moment for him to wheeze out a reply: "You have some of my kinsmen with you."

"Is that so?" The bearded one turned back to see if any of the slaves seemed to recognize the stranger. "Which ones?"

"All of them."

"That's funny, boy. Say, where'd you get that hat."

"The Lake Clan. Release the slaves."

"Excuse me? Am I supposed to be scared of a little wimp like you? Even if I were, which I'm not, these slaves don't belong to me, boy. I just transport them. If I were to let them go, I'd have to pay for every one of them."

Blaze gripped the staff harder to control his shaking hands. He took a step closer to the chief. "Your contract with the slave owners says that you don't have to pay anything if you lose your prisoners to bandits or other unforeseen circumstances."

The leader's eyes widened. "You've read my contract?" he asked. Blaze nodded. The leader frowned and once more scanned the hillside for any sign of danger. He saw nothing. "Boy, you are the sorriest bandit that I've ever seen."

"No, I'm not a bandit," said Blaze, taking a step closer. "I'm more what you'd call unforeseen circumstances."

"Whatever you are, you're about to be a dead man." The bearded man reached for his sword. But before the blade cleared the scabbard, Blaze stepped forward and swung his staff, with the White Gem lashed to its tip. The stone tapped the slaver chief's bare hand and he collapsed unconscious. Blaze pushed him onto the guard beside him. As the rider tried to fend off the limp body, Blaze reached over the leader's saddle and tapped the guard's bare arm. Both men toppled over senseless. Blaze grabbed the reins of the leader's horse, swung aboard and gave two loud whoops. From atop the ridge, Roff and his cousins charged into view. So did Dash, racing with bared teeth down the hillside. When the remaining guards saw their fallen comrades and the charging hound, they galloped away. The rider holding the rope with the slaves dropped it, turned his horse and spurred it back down the narrow trail. The prisoners had to jump away to avoid getting trampled. To escape, one young man scaled a boulder, pulling those closest on the rope along with him.

Blaze whistled and yelled, "Dash, come back!" The golden dog already had run far beyond the slaves. But he immediately stopped and trotted back up the trail, his tongue flopping out one side of his mouth.

Roff rode up to the slave on the boulder. "I like this one," he said. "He's a regular spider."

Blaze dismounted near the slaves. "Friends," he said, "we've come to take those chains off you."

"What do you mean to do with us?" a slave asked.

"I mean to set you free."

"Why?"

Blaze smiled. "It's what I do."

"Who are you?"

"I'm a man with a hammer and a chisel. And I have
friends who can help you get a new start in life."

Blaze pulled his tools from a pouch and broke the first
man's chains. Next, he passed the hammer and chisel to Kick,
who began removing the shackles from the other slaves.
Blaze, meanwhile, turned to Roff. "Bring me the young
fellow who climbed the boulder. I need to speak to him."

"Are you about to get ill?"

"Yes, I need to start walking to fight it off. I'll climb
back up the pass. Bring him to me there. And please move
those two sleeping guards off the trail."

Blaze barely had reached the top of the pass when
Roff and the young slave came to him on horseback. Blaze
clutched his side and leaned against a small boulder. "Your
name is Tustin, isn't it?" he called to the slave.

"How did you know that? We've never met, have
we?"

"The White Beard told me about you. He told me that
I'd find you here. I need your help, Tustin. Will you help
me?"

"Doing what?"

"Taking chains off people. This land has so many
people in chains. Some day even our Elders may find
themselves threatened with chains. People need our help. Will
you help me?"

"Who are you?"

Blaze winced with pain. Roff interrupted, "Cousin,
you need to rest. Lie down for a while."

"In a minute," said Blaze. "Tustin, I'm the man the
White Beard told you would come to help our people."

"How can I be sure of that?"

"You can't, unless you come with me. But here is the
White Beard's staff. He gave it to me yesterday and he asked
me to come here to free you. He wants you to help me."
Blaze winced again. "I've got to walk over to those rocks and
lie down for a while. Roff will look after you."

Tustin watched him slowly walk away. "What's the
matter with him?" he asked.

"He'll get better after he takes a rest, Spider. I just hope he didn't get sick for nothing here."

"What's that supposed to mean?"

"It means he risked his life for you."

"I didn't ask him to."

"Fine. Then let's put the chains back on you, tie you up to a rock and leave you here for the next gang of slavers to come along."

"Alright, sorry. I didn't mean it. It's just that I'm not used to getting rescued. Put yourself in my place. I don't know anything about your gang, except what the White Beard told me a long time ago, and that was right after I was put in chains. I don't recall much, just something about a champion. At the time, my mind was fixed on my own problems."

"Well, now you've got a choice. You can come with us or go your own way. I don't know why he wants you. All I know is that you're never going to get another chance like this. He's willing to let you come with him and watch what he does. What's better than that?"

"You make him sound pretty special."

"Have you ever met anybody who's freed fifty slaves? And this is only the beginning."

"Alright," said Tustin. "I guess I'll stick around long enough to see what he does next."

It was early one morning about three months later when the square-jawed captain of the Guard entered the Elder's residence at Orres. He passed the compound's stout wooden gates—a rare sight in the nearly treeless expanses of the Dry Lands—and then strode briskly to the entrance of the main meeting room. A guard opened the door, but the captain found the space empty. He crossed to the other end of a hall and exited. He reached a covered patio and looked out to a fountain beside a garden. He listened and heard the inviting trickle of water. Orres had two spring-fed wells, one in its public square, and the second here. The Elder's water collected in a stone tank, then bubbled and gurgled across a surface of well-worn rock to a small pond. Few people but the wealthy of the village had ever beheld that pool.

There by the pond stood Shutoo, the Elder's counselor, a man who looked much younger than his forty years. He dipped his fingers into the refreshing liquid and ran it through his shoulder-length hair. He wore a navy blue cape and pantaloons. Glancing at the captain, he motioned him to draw near. Then he nodded toward a man sitting in the shade beneath the end of the covered patio.

"We've had more trouble, captain," the counselor said. He motioned to the man. "Come and tell the captain."

The man rose hurriedly but hesitated to step out of the shadows. "I won't transport any more slaves," he mumbled. "Not after what he did to me."

"Come, come," Shutoo replied gently. "Step up and tell the captain what happened."

Reluctantly the man shuffled into the morning sunlight. He had a round face and jowls that trembled as he spoke. "He caught us near sundown, all tired and weary. You know the man. I drew my sword and refused to give up the slaves, so he poked me with his magic stick. I passed out and then the nightmares overwhelmed me. I dreamed I was chained up and digging in a mine. It was a mine like the ones where I've delivered slaves. And the guards beat me and wouldn't give me water. It nearly drove me crazy. I couldn't wake up. I thought I was never going to wake up. But at last I came to, and then I promised myself that I wouldn't have anything more to do with the slave business."

"How could he get the best of you?" asked Shutoo. "He didn't kill any of your guards, did he? This outlaw sounds like a bit of a pansy, all scared and shaking. He's too dainty to even spill blood. Why, I bet he would have run away if you had only shaken your fist at him."

"He may have looked scared, but he didn't run. And he knows how to use that magic stick. I never want to meet him again. I'm through, I tell you."

Shutoo shook his head. "Of course, there is the little matter of how much you owe our Elder for the slaves you lost. I believe it must be five hundred pieces of silver."

"Hah. You know my contract. It says I'm not responsible for bandits or such as this man. All the slave transporters agree on that point. Even the man with the magic stick has said it to us. We all know that I am not the first to lose a shipment of slaves to him. If you cheat the transporters, who will do your dirty work?"

"You have a point," the counselor agreed. He reached down and slowly dipped his hand again in the cool water. He lightly swept the drips across his forehead. "Indeed, you do have a contract, but what really matters is how we interpret it. Think about it. What kind of lawyer would I be if my Elder were the only one to suffer in this affair? I would be a very poor lawyer, wouldn't I? Do you think I'm a poor lawyer? Do you? No, my friend, you'll pay something for your failure to deliver your cargo. Maybe not all you owe, but something. If you don't, those nightmares of yours might well come true. The captain here might actually lock you in chains and take you to the mines."

The man's knees gave way, but he regained his balance by leaning against a post. "I hope some day he pokes you with that magic stick. Then you'll know what it feels like. You'll get something from me. But then I'm done with you." He stormed out of the courtyard.

The smile vanished from Shutoo's face as he turned to the captain. "This makes the fifth group of slaves stolen from us in three months. Both the Elder and the slave transporters blame you for failing to catch this man."

"My lord, I'm doing the best I can."

"Then, blast it all, why is it taking so long? You ought to be able to catch one pansy."

"This outlaw is no fool, lord. I've sent men out to watch the road and the caravans. But we can't be everywhere at once. Eventually we'll catch him. But it takes time."

"Who is he?"

"No one knows. If he were allied with the insurrectionists, our spies would know about him. But they seem to know even less about him than we do."

"It's bad enough that this man has the slave transporters terrorized. But he also has taken slaves that were promised to Equis. The agents of the Realm hate it when we don't make good on our shipments. They demand an extra slave for every two that we fail to deliver on time. If this outlaw keeps it up, he will cost our Elder a fortune. You must stop him."

"I will, my lord."

"I don't care how you do it. Find the man and put an end to this madness."

In the night, Lowi heard a voice, but in her exhaustion she refused to wake. The ground beneath her felt unmercifully hard, and still she slept. Her feet ached from miles of walking and yet she ignored them. What finally grabbed her attention was the sensation that the voice she was hearing wasn't directed at her but instead toward Darnelle, her sister lying beside her. Immediately Lowi opened her eyes and turned to see a man kneeling over Darnelle. Lowi's hands were shackled, but she brought them together and slowly pushed herself up. "What do you think you're doing?" she demanded.

"We've come to free you. I've been trying to wake this woman, but she won't open her eyes," the young man said.

"She's sick," Lowi replied, and she brushed back her matted hair. "She's my sister. Tell me, stranger, are you from my people? Do you know the passwords? Do you fly with the hawk or the sparrow?"

"Neither. But my people say I climb like a spider. Now we need to get these chains off you and the others. Please wake your sister."

"Wait. Who are you? And why are you helping us?"

"My name is Tustin, and I'm with him," he said pointing behind her.

Lowi turned to find herself face to face with Roff .

"Lowi," said Roff. "Let me guess. You're still playing with fire."

"Hah! So you're the fools I've been hearing about. You free slaves but are too delicate to spill a drop of your enemy's blood. I suspected that your cousin might be the one who has the slave transporters in an uproar around Orres. Where is he? Take me to him at once. And don't tell me that you and this fool here overpowered the guards all by yourselves."

Tustin's mouth dropped at the slight. Roff put a hand on his shoulder. "Relax, Spider. She's like that to everybody."

"Are you sure? I think she's mad because I'm not a sparrow or a hawk."

Lowi stood up, tightening the rope that held her shackles to those of Darnelle and the other slaves. Roff took his knife and began to cut the line. When it snapped, he led the woman past the other slaves who were rousing one another from sleep. Walking with her arms still shackled, Lowi noted that her former guards lay sprawled unconscious on the edge of camp. Kick and Quirt guarded them. And beyond them stood Blaze.

"Fish boy, I need your help," Lowi said.

"Where have you been, Lowi?"

"We've been fighting for our people. We were captured outside Kierinswell and placed in these chains. They didn't kill us because we are women. They mean to sell us to foreigners."

"You said you need my help."

"I need a horse. I can't tell you the reason, but I need to get back to Kierinswell as fast as I can. Lives may be at stake."

"What about your sister?" Roff asked.

"I think she's dying. The slavers and their thugs have done unspeakable things to us. If you were real MuKierin, you would let me take a rock and bash in the heads of each and every one. If you can't abide that, will you at least let me take a horse and leave Darnelle in your care? If you can save her, we have a great-aunt in Orres who will take her in. Tatti Oom is her name. Your cousins know her."

Blaze searched Lowi's eyes. "I will take the shackles off you and give you a horse," he said. "But you must let Roff and Harney go with you as far as the edge of Kierinswell. From there you'll be on your own."

"Fine, fish boy. You know, I thought it was you. Who else could be the man with the funny hat, the shaking hands and the magic stick that makes slavers collapse asleep in the dust? What do you think you're doing out here? Will freeing a few slaves bring the Elders to their knees? Wouldn't you rather make a real difference? Come and join us. We could put you to good use."

"No, Lowi, I'll stay with the King. I know his story."

"Very well. I'm in your debt. When we get rid of the aristocracy, I'll repay you for your help. Now I need to take one last look at my sister and get on my way."

As she departed, Roff drew close to Blaze. "Cousin," he said, "I've got a bad feeling about this. Lowi's going to tell all the rebels that you're the man attacking the slave caravans. And those folks couldn't keep a secret to save their lives. The Elders' spies will know about you before her tongue gets dry. You might as well hire a town crier to spread the news."

"It's alright, Roff. Sooner or later the news must spread. We can't stop it. At least it gets me closer to the day when I must stand before the GrandElder. Now please go find Harney and take Lowi to Kierinswell. But be careful."

"Don't worry about us. Lowi will kill anybody who gets in our way. Harney and I just need to make sure we don't make her angry."

Blaze went looking for Darnelle. Already his followers had started to break the prisoners' chains with hammers and chisels. Blaze found Tustin kneeling beside the sickly woman. "Darnelle," he said softly. "It's me, Blaze. Wake up. I've come to help you."

Slowly the young woman opened her eyes. Tears began to flow down her cheeks when she recognized Blaze. He took out a small vial and put a drop of its liquid on the tip of his finger. "Open your mouth," he said. He touched her tongue and put her into a deep sleep. "Choose to live, Darnelle. Choose to live."

"She's beautiful," said Tustin. "Will she live?"

Blaze smiled. "Take her hand. Hold it as much as you can. I want you to take her back to Orres."

Tustin's eyes lit up. "Thank you, Blaze. I'll be happy to watch over her. But how will I get her to Orres?"

"I'll send a wagon for you. Until it arrives, I want Stannis and you to wait with her up in those rocks on the hill behind us. Keep watch for a wagon with six mules and a driver with a gray beard. Expect him the day after tomorrow.

A group of men gently lifted Darnelle on a stretcher and took her to a hiding place on a nearby hilltop. Before dawn, Blaze and his men departed with the freed prisoners. They left the guards sleeping by the road. Stannis and Tustin, meanwhile, began their wait with Darnelle. They strung up a canvas tarp in the rocks to shade their patient, who slept soundly all morning. Tustin rarely let go of her hand. "Tell me about her, Stannis," he said. "I hear you both grew up around Orres."

"She used to be a nice-enough girl. Her brother and sister are natural-born killers. Not her. She's not so hard. But she goes along with them. They're all insurrectionists, and they don't think much of us."

"Well, I like her. And I hope she'll like me, too. Do you think she can hear me?"

Stannis smirked. "Maybe so. If she starts laughing at you, then we'll both know that she hears you loud and clear."

Tustin slept beside her that night. Darnelle awoke at dawn and found her hand in a stranger's grasp. Quickly she yanked it away and rose to lean on an elbow. "Who are you?" she demanded. "Where's my sister?"

"I'm a friend of Blaze. Remember, we rescued you early yesterday from the slavers. Your sister left you with us and rode for Kierinswell. Blaze asked Stannis and me to see that you make it safely back to your great-aunt in Orres.

There's a wagon coming for us. Until it arrives, you can just rest easy."

"Why were you holding my hand?"

"Blaze told me to. I wouldn't have done it otherwise. Honest. I'd be too scared."

"Why's that? Do you think I bite?"

"No, it's just that I was a slave myself for a long time, and I'm still not used to doing things without permission. And I'm a bit of an outsider. I'm not full MuKierin. My father was MuKierin but my mother was Barsk. I haven't even told Blaze about her. At first, I was afraid he might send me away if he knew the truth. And now I think he probably wouldn't do that, but I still haven't worked up the nerve to tell him."

"So you thought you'd tell me first?"

"Well, yes, I figured I'd try it out on you and see how it works out. I'll understand if you don't want anything to do with me."

Darnelle eased herself back down with her head on a folded cloth. "What's your name?" she asked.

"Tustin. But they call me Spider."

"Well, Tustin, I don't care if you're a half-breed."

"Good. Then will you be my friend?"

"I don't have many friends left. Too many of them keep getting killed. So it's nothing personal, but let's wait a while on friendship."

Stannis called out from a lookout above them, "There's a wagon coming with six mules. I'm going down the ridge to flag the driver."

Tustin told Darnelle, "You just rest a little longer. Blaze told me that this driver makes a pot of soup that can revive the dying. He's going to help us get you safely home."

Chapter Three

The Freedom Fighters

Shutoo, counsel of Orres, wore a broad smile as he strode into the Elder's study. He bowed to Morros, his lord, who sat in a cushioned chair beside flames leaping high in a great stone fireplace. A nearby window looked out on the courtyard garden, which on this winter morning was barren except for an occasional green cactus growing on the edges. Along one wall of the study stood a tapestry that reached from ceiling to floor—an intricate weaving of red and purple, the Elder's family colors.

"Good news, my lord," Shutoo announced. "It has taken months, but we have come a step closer to catching our troublemaker."

Morros, a red-bearded man with thinning hair and a large paunch in his midsection, turned and squinted. He gently set down a clay mug that held a steaming tea. "That sounds too good to be true. Tell me more."

"Our man is a follower of the White Beard. It turns out that some of the insurrectionists are acquainted with him. He freed a few of them a couple months back. You can thank the Stone Woman that he rescued them. Those traitors never could keep a secret. Our spies soon caught wind of the news."

"What else did you learn about him?"

"They call him Blaze. They say he is something of a magician—able to heal people or put them to sleep or some such nonsense. It is the same rubbish the slave transporters have told us. He seems to be a coward when it comes to spilling blood. Our people have tried as delicately as possible to learn his whereabouts. But it appears that the insurrectionists have no idea how to find him. The man apparently is too smart to let them get too close to him. It seems the best way to apprehend him may be through the White Beard."

The Elder thought for a moment, rubbing his beard and staring into the fire. He was nearly fifty, the son, grandson and great-grandson of Elders. He didn't easily flinch from conflict, and he had a reputation for calculating each move that he made against his enemies.

"We need to know more about this man, especially what plans the White Beard has for him," Morros said. "That old fool already is telling some people that a hero has risen among the Clan of the Horse. He's even proclaimed such nonsense to some of the anti-slavers on the Council. Until now, I couldn't fathom what he was talking about. But this might explain it. This outlaw might be his champion. If he is, we are dealing with a greater threat than the loss of all these slaves. The White Beard might be planning to use this false hero to launch a civil war. If that were to happen, many might follow him. And even some Elders who oppose slavery could be tempted to join him."

"What would you have me do, lord?"

"I need a plan, Shutoo. We must find a way to bring down this outlaw and the White Beard, too, if possible. Don't think it will be easy. If it were, I would have hanged that old goat long ago. But he has the protection of our GrandElder Chakka Ri, even though he's a fellow slaver. The old man once loved his mother, or so they say. No, even our allies on the Council will flinch once they hear that the White Beard is tied up with this troublemaker."

"Very good, lord. We don't need to tell them until it suits your needs. The good news is that this outlaw has moved north. He's no longer hijacking your slave caravans. He's now taking slaves from other Elders on the Council. Our allies know little about him, but they've already started to complain about their financial losses. Give this rebel a few more months. In time our allies may become angry enough that they'll agree to do anything to get rid of him, even if it means moving against the White Beard."

"Perhaps they will. But I suspect that they'll still be afraid of the anti-slavers. We need a way to assure them that we can stop the White Beard and still keep our seats on the Council."

Shutoo lowered his eyes and grew quiet. "I see. You want to get rid of the old man and yet do it in a way where you can't be blamed for his downfall."

"Yes, if that's possible. At least I need to be able to say that I did nothing improper."

"May I suggest that our contacts in Equis might assist us in this matter?"

"The Realm? What are you thinking?"

"Equis hates the White Beard as much as you do, lord. Its agents might agree to help in a way where you could plausibly deny that you had any involvement with the old man's downfall."

"Now you're talking, Shutoo. Keep scheming. I like it. You give me an alibi, and I will happily give the White Beard a swift kick in the head."

Dusk was washing over the desert when a long line of slaves began to trudge up the narrow trail of a great copper pit three days north of Kierinswell. The men left shovels and picks at the bottom, but even without the extra weight they shuffled wearily in ragged clothes and leg shackles. The guards kept them separated into crews of twenty. Four crews climbed out of the pit.

A half-mile away, Roff and Kick lay on their stomachs in gritty soil atop a high hill. Keeping their heads down, they watched the prisoners return to their hovels. Behind them the desert appeared empty for miles, an immense plain of sagebrush and rock where daylight was fading. In the distance rose a large hill and cliff overlooking the copper pit. Below the cliff, a few lights shone in squat adobe buildings that housed the guards and the kitchen. Nearby a row of work buildings sat dark and silent.

"Look at them," said Kick. "Those boys will be dead before spring."

"That's why we'll have wagons to carry them away," Roff said. "Blaze doesn't want to make them walk after all they've gone through."

"Doesn't this scare you, Roffie? If we get caught, we'll be the ones down there with shackles on our legs and our eyes sunk deep into our skulls. They have a lot of guards and dogs. This is different than ambushing a slave train with a few soldiers in tow. This is getting dangerous."

"I know. But what scares me more is what comes next. Four Elders own this copper mine. Do you think they're going to sit still when the work stops here because all their slaves escaped? No, they're going to scream bloody murder. This time Blaze is really going to stir up a whirlwind."

The two waited until night descended and all the lights had gone black in the compound. Then they slung on packs and coiled ropes and set off down the hill and across the next slope. Roff led the way, carefully picking a path through the rocky ground. Kick stopped often to scan the land behind him. Overhead a great cloud enveloped a half moon, smothering its light, then sliding along to let a faint, silvery glow seep into the night sky,

An hour later the two men rested on a boulder-strewn ledge on the edge of the cliff overlooking the compound. Dawn was four hours away. Kick touched Roff's shoulder and pointed below. Far off a single torchlight passed through the work sheds near the edge of the copper pit. Roff nodded at the sight of the night watchman. "Let's get started," he whispered.

They dropped down through a cut in the ledge, clinging to any handhold they could find among the eroding face of rock. When they could go no farther, Roff climbed back up until he located a boulder he could get a rope around. He tied the line fast and let the other end fall slowly along the sharp wall. "Get ready," he whispered. He wrapped his palms with strips of rags, then grabbed the rope and began his descent.

One hundred feet beneath Roff lay the compound's dog enclosure. It was built along the rock wall, with a small cave that was carved into the side of the cliff. Inside slept eight large hounds, penned in by a wall that stood eight feet tall. The animals were kept far from the guardhouses and the prisoners. By now the dogs had settled down for the night. As Roff descended the rope, his sandals kicked loose a handful of pebbles. Still, the animals rested. Roff proceeded down until he heard the first low grumble. Immediately he pulled in and found a place to set his feet. He reached into the pouch hanging at his waist and his hands touched gooey pieces of jerky. He clutched a handful, took aim at the sound of the awakened hound and heaved the dried meat. The pieces plopped onto the ground. The animal pounced on one, causing the other dogs around him to swing their heads up simultaneously.

For the next minute the sky rained jerky. The hounds bounded to catch it as it fell through the air. They sniffed it as it landed around them. They licked it. They took it between their teeth and crunched it. And then, one by one, they snuggled down and fell into the deepest sleep of their dog lives.

Roff dropped a little lower along the rope to take advantage of a better resting spot. When he was sure that all the hounds were properly drugged, he grabbed the rope and tugged three times, three times again, then once more. On the upper end, Kick felt the signal and returned one of his own. He climbed back to the top of the cliff, moved to a rock that lay a bit back from the edge and coaxed just enough of a fire to light a candle. He looked out to make sure he couldn't be seen from the work sheds or the guardhouses and quickly revealed the light once, twice, three times, and then with one puff from puckered lips he plunged himself back into darkness. A few moments later, a light shone twice from the other side of the copper pit. Kick smiled and dropped back down the cliff. He found the rope and started his climb down to Roff.

Roff already had tied a second rope onto the first. Once Kick reached him, the two quickly slithered down the last section of rope and reached the bottom. Kick touched the ground, but at first he didn't let go of the rope. He remained ready to jump back up it at the slightest twitch of the hounds. The animals, however, didn't budge. Satisfied, Kick joined Roff in picking his way through the dog droppings and the gnawed bones scattered around the enclosure.

"Are these people bones?" Kick whispered.

"I don't want to know," Roff said.

The wall before them was so high that Roff had to climb atop Kick's shoulders in order to reach the top. From there he could see a platform and steps attached to the other side of the wall. Atop the platform a man could climb up and look over the wall to observe the hounds. Roff dropped back down and whispered, "It's clear for now. Let's wait a few minutes."

"I never liked dogs," Kick hissed. "I never knew how much I disliked dogs until this very minute."

"Then be glad that they can't chase you down later."

From the other side of the wall came the sound of footsteps. Roff climbed aboard Kick again and slowly pulled himself up so that he could peek over the wall. A moment later he dropped down again. "It's the watchman, torch and all."

Kick's eyes bulged. "What do we do now? Climb back up the rope?"

"No. Brace yourself against the wall again. I'll climb up on you. When I give the word, pull away and let me fall. Got it?"

Kick frowned but nodded slowly and once more placed his hands on the wall. Roff waited a few moments— there was no telling how long Kick might have to hold all that extra weight on his shoulders. At last he climbed up, keeping his hands and head below the top of the wall. His heart began throbbing. He repositioned his weight so only one hand leaned against the wall.

A long minute later the torch light gleamed over the wall as the watchman climbed onto the platform. He raised his torch and shook it, but none of the hounds as much as turned a head. "Pssssst! Dogs!" he growled. "Lookit! Dogs!"

Over the wall sprang two hands, clutching the watchman's arm that held the torch. "Now," Roff hissed. Kick dropped to the ground and rolled. Roff fell, too, pulling the stunned watchman over the wall with him. The guard fell on Roff and they tumbled to earth. Kick was there at once with his knife at the watchman's throat. "Not a word," he said, "or I'll feed you to these beasts."

Roff grimaced in pain, but he smothered the torch with the watchman's cloak. Next, he helped Kick tie and gag their prisoner. Standing up again, Roff tried to walk but had to lean on the wall. "My right leg," Roff moaned. "I didn't break it but I can't seem to put much weight on it."

"I know what you did. You broke his fall so he wouldn't break his neck. You big fool, what do we do now? Want me to leave you here and go for help."

"No. Blaze said to go down into the copper pit if we get into any trouble. Let's try for that."

Kick grabbed Roff's waist and lifted him until he could grab the top of the wall, then he got beneath his cousin so that Roff could push off him with his good leg. While Roff rested on the top ledge, Kick scrambled over the wall so that he could catch his cousin coming down the other side. Once down the platform steps, they hobbled arm in arm across the empty yard, making their way toward the work sheds. They made no attempt to hide, but reached the first work shed without being spotted. From there they tried to use the buildings to stay hidden from the guards' huts. The two listened for any sign of alarm. Each expected at any moment that the compound would erupt with shouts and the thunder of running feet. Cautiously they passed to the second work shed, then the third. There Kick pulled up. "I thought I heard something," he whispered. Leaning Roff against the shed, he dropped on his belly and crawled around the corner.

Roff listened and fretted. Where were the others? Were they going to be able to free all the slaves without rousing anybody? For once he hoped somebody would make some noise, if only to attract attention away from him. He turned to see Kick crawl back into view, then rise and rush toward him.

"Somebody is heading around the other side of the sheds toward the dogs," he whispered. "In a minute he's sure to find the watchman over there. Stand up. I'm going to carry you to that pit while there's still time."

Kick latched his arms around Roff just below the hips and lifted him up. Roff clenched his teeth at the pain, and then doubled over his cousin's shoulder. Kick turned and began to waddle as fast as he could toward the last shed. From there he ventured into the open. He was starting to wonder how far he could carry his stout kinsman when he heard a shout, "You there. Halt! Halt, I say!" Kick was too scared to even glance toward the voice. Instead, he quickened his pace for the pit.

"Captain of the guard!" the voice cried. "Captain of the guard! Bring the dogs!" A moment later a bell began to ring near the guards' quarters.

Kick reached the trail leading into the pit. It was a narrow path that cut and curled down one slope of the pit. "Lean back, Roffie!" Kick shouted. "Lean back!"

"No. Put me down! Put me down! You are going to get us both killed."

Kick skidded to a halt and Roff slid cautiously back to earth. Once more the two shuffled arm in arm, doing an awkward wiggle-waggle down the steep and twisting path. Kick turned back toward the top. "No one's arrived yet."

"They will soon enough."

A few moments later they could hear the sound of men and metal. Above them, the first guards hustled into the pit. Kick stopped. "I am carrying you again," he said, lifting Roff over his shoulder. Once more he waddled beneath the prodigious weight of his cousin.

In all, nine guards followed Roff and Kick into the pit. The last one had advanced about thirty paces when he heard footsteps behind him. He guessed it was another guard, but he slowed his pace and turned back to be sure. To his surprise, it wasn't a guard but a stranger closing in with his staff at the ready. "Trap! We're trapped!" the guard yelled.

The stranger was Blaze, who raised his staff to his shoulders. He closed in quickly and caught his opponent on the hand with the White Stone. The first man fell. As he did, two more guards turned and crouched at the ready. "Hold on!" one of them yelled to the others. "We're in some kind of trap!" The remaining guards turned to face Blaze.

"It is not much of a trap," another man grunted from behind. "He looks like he's alone."

Two guards advanced side by side toward Blaze with their spears aimed at their opponent. The others followed, but they soon found themselves hemmed in by the narrow path. Two guards tried to climb uphill off the path to get around Blaze, but the footing was precarious.

The first two guards attacked with their spears. Blaze parried and fought off their jabs, retreating a step or two, and then attacking again. "Stick him good!" a guard yelled from behind. One of the men in front lunged forward at Blaze's midsection. Blaze sidestepped and caught him on the hand, dropping him into the other guard's feet. The second man stumbled and Blaze caught him with a smack to the neck.

Other guards quickly took the place of those who had fallen. But Blaze showed himself too skilled to be overwhelmed on the narrow trail. His staff slapped out a lively beat against the two spears. His feet danced to the rhythm of the blows. Again the men came at him. Again he turned their spears aside and thrust back at them. Soon only four guards remained.

At first Kick and Roff kept retreating down the trail but then they stopped and listened to the sounds above them. They couldn't see the fight but they could here the rat-a-tat-tat of staff and spears. Kick gathered his courage and ventured back up the trail. "Stay here, Roffie. I'm going to have a look." A minute later he rounded a bend and could make out silhouettes in battle. Blaze stood alone, fighting as three guards crowded at him and a fourth tried to climb the slope above him. Blaze whirled his staff to the left and right, giving way but never allowing a blow to reach him. Kick found himself caught up in the spectacle. "Get 'em, Blaze! Give it to them. You can do it!"

Again the three guards on the trail attacked. The fourth moved above, finding at last a solid piece of ground and bounding across it in hopes of flanking his opponent. In response, Blaze retreated quickly to the next bend in the trail. When the guards approached, he stopped, switched direction and attacked. Quickly he forced two back and caught one with the stone. As that guard fell, Blaze attacked and took another down.

"Get them, Blaze!" Kick yelled, running forward to join the fray. "We have them now!"

Only two guards remained. Seeing they were caught between Blaze above and Kick below, they leaped off the trail and slid down the steep bank of the pit. Kick turned and ran back down the path. "Roffie!" he yelled. "Watch out! Trouble is coming your way." However, he soon found that Roff had crawled up the trail on his hands and knees—safe from the guards as they descended far into the pit. Kick stooped down and lifted his cousin up. "Wait until you see what Blaze did."

Blaze trotted down the path to his kinsmen. "Stay just below the top of the pit," he said. "I'll send men with horses for you. I've got to keep moving before the illness overtakes me." He turned and hurried up the trail.

Kick helped his cousin hobble past the sleeping guards. Roff slumped to the ground and propped his aching leg onto one of the fallen men. Kick, meanwhile, went back to examine the downed men. "There are seven of them here and two more hiding at the bottom of this pit. Wait until I tell Stannis! Who says Blaze is a coward? How many other men can take on nine guards?"

Roff smiled and rubbed his aching leg. "Yeah, he did alright."

On a late spring afternoon, as bands of white clouds drifted over the eastern foothills, an old woman opened the door and entered her hut in the village of Orres. "Darnelle," she said, "that nice young man is here again."

Darnelle sat inside working at a weaver's loom. She didn't look up but replied, "Tatti Oom, what does that boy want?" She made no effort to suppress a frown.

Darnelle's great-aunt opened her mouth in surprise at the question. She started to answer, but then stopped and pondered her response. A smile came to her wrinkled face, and the wrinkles only served to make her look more impish. She walked up behind her grandniece and gently rubbed the young woman's shoulders. "Why, child, I expect he has ridden so far because he wants to see me, only he's too shy to say so. I cannot imagine why he would want to see a pretty young thing like you."

"Tatti Oom, do you encourage him?"

"Of course not. If you want to spend your whole life inside this hut, that just means that I shall get to keep you all to myself. And when I die, you can just prop my bony carcass over there in that corner and we shall have the grandest chats together. Why, think how lonely I'd be if you weren't here to sit by my side and watch me decay."

"Enough! Tell him I'll be out in a few minutes. Anything to escape your sarcasm."

"That's why I'm here, child. A little sarcasm is good if it helps get you out into the fresh air."

Tatti Oom turned and exited the hut. Outside Tustin sat on his horse, watching with anxious eyes. The old woman's impish smile appeared again, as if she might jest with the young man, too. But then she saw how worried he looked. "Calm down, boy," she said. "My grandniece said she would see you. Just give her a moment."

Tustin's face lit up. "Thank you, Tatti Oom! Thank you. You've made me the happiest man in Orres."

"You poor boy. You're about to spend time with the saddest woman in Orres."

A few minutes later the door opened. Darnelle squinted as she stepped into the afternoon sun.

"Hello, Darnelle," Tustin said. "You're looking better."

"I think she looks terrible," said Tatti Oom, stepping past her niece and shutting the hut's door.

Darnelle's eyes swirled darkly after her great-aunt. "Hello, Spider," she said as plainly as she could muster. "What brings you to Orres?"

"I had to visit my patient. I need to watch over you. How will I ever get a reputation as a healer if you don't fully recover?"

She shrugged and looked away. "Should we sit or walk?"

"Oh, let's walk. I need to get your blood moving."

They set off lazily up a village lane toward the north edge of Orres. Tustin led his horse. Darnelle walked alongside, but not too close. "So are you still rescuing slaves?" she asked.

"Oh, yes. I wish you could have been there with us a few weeks ago at a copper mine north of Kierinswell. Roff sprained his ankle and Kick had to carry him while a squad of guards chased them into the copper pit. Roff complained that Kick was slower than a tortoise. And Kick complained that Roff weighed more than a horse and next time he could fend for himself. In the end, Blaze rescued them both.

"Blaze surprises me. He doesn't seem like the kind of man who could rescue anybody."

"There's more to him than meets the eye. I like that about him. He's fighting a curse. That's why he gets so scared and ill. But I've never seen him run, no matter how scared he feels inside. At the copper mine, he faced down a whole squad of guards so that he could rescue Roff and Kick. He doesn't take the easy way out, that's for sure."

They walked in silence to the top of the lane. Once there, Tustin asked her, "Tell me, Darnelle, why did you choose to join the insurrectionists?"

"It wasn't really a choice, at least not for me." She pointed over to the next hilltop. "See those homes over there. My uncle used to live up there. My mother died when I was a baby, and my father was put in the debtors' chains while I was still a child. Other kinsmen raised us. When I was eleven, we went to live with my uncle, a bachelor who raised goats and tended a little garden. Sunny and Lowi and I would help him by filling up water jars at the town well and carrying them back here.

"One day while we were getting water, two of the Elder's guard showed up to arrest my uncle for his debts. By the time we returned, they already had his hands in shackles. Lowi was the first back. One of the guardsmen saw her and chased after her. He didn't see Sunny or me. Sunny caught the man from behind and tackled him. When he did, the guardsman dropped the hammer he was carrying in his hand. The two of them began to wrestle, but Sunny was no match for the guard. My brother then was only seventeen. That guard seemed so huge. He rolled on top of Sunny and began beating him. All I could do was scream. When I did, two things happened. The other guard turned away from my uncle, who took a hidden knife and stabbed the man. And Lowi, who was maybe fifteen, picked up the guard's hammer off the ground and hit him hard in temple. The blow knocked the man senseless for a moment. He fell off Sunny and slumped onto the ground. My brother jumped on the guard and held him down, and then my sister hit the man again and again until his skull caved in.

Afterward, we were so terrified at what we'd done. My uncle told us to flee to my great-aunt's home. He wouldn't even let us try to get the shackles off him. He took the dead guard's horses and rode off. And we ran off to Tatti Om, and she took us in.

"Of course, the Elder's guard caught my uncle. Lowi said she thinks he rode off alone because he wanted everyone to think that he had killed the two guardsmen by himself. In any case, they brought him back to Orres and hanged him in the town square. When we heard about it, we went over that evening at sunset and saw him still hanging there. I cried and cried. That's when a stranger approached us. 'Don't do something foolish, children,' he told us.

"Lowi was seething with anger. She told the man, 'Someone's gonna pay for this.' The man replied, 'Someone should pay for this. But we must make sure that they die and you live. I have friends who can help you. Come with me and I'll tell you how we can make sure that your uncle's death is properly avenged.'

"So that's how we became insurrectionists. We joined their secret society and trained for revenge. In time, we learned the names of the two guardsmen who had hanged my uncle. And we waited for an opportunity. As time passed, our leaders learned I wasn't a very good fighter. They said I was too young to take part in any of their missions. But one day they sent word that the two guardsmen had been sent out alone to arrest another family for their debts. Our comrades already had gone out after them. Sunny and Lowi knew this was what they had been waiting for, so they borrowed a villager's horse and rode out to the place. When they got there, our allies already had captured the two guardsmen. They kept them alive for my brother and sister. Sunny stabbed one of them. Lowi killed the other. I'm told the man and woman who would have been arrested screamed in horror. They cursed Sunny and Lowi and refused to join The Cause. Instead, they ran off with their family. Of course, the Elder's guard found them and hanged them. The couple had two young daughters, and the guard hanged them, too."

"I'm sorry, Darnelle," said Tustin. "What a wretched world. You've seen far too much bloodshed."

They walked back to Tatti Oom's hut. As they drew near, Darnelle asked, "Do you still feel like you don't belong with Blaze's gang?"

"I don't know. Roff and his cousins treat me well enough. But they're all related by blood. I'm not exactly one of them."

"Do they know that your mother was Barsk?"

"No. I'll tell them some day."

"Are you a coward?"

"Maybe. Are you?"

"Yes. That's why I'm through with fighting. You're right. I have watched too many people die. But you say you believe in Blaze. Do you think he still would have rescued you even if he had known that your mother were Barsk?"

"Yes, I really do."

"Then tell him."

"You know, Darnelle, for a woman who sits at a loom all day, you're pretty feisty."

"Is that all you have to say to me? I think you really are a coward."

"Do you? Well, maybe there are some more things I'd like say to you. Maybe someday I'll say them."

They returned to the hut as the sun was fading. Tustin climbed onto his horse. "You know where to find me, if you need to get a message to me," he said. "I'll be back as soon as I can, Darnelle. I'm not giving up on you."

Chapter Four

Eyes on the White Beard

Zhaggee stood stiff and scared beside the red coals of a night fire in a canyon far to the south of Orres. Around him lounged warriors from each of the two orders, both Cleavers and Slinkers. This gang in black armor seemed uncharacteristically at ease with one another. Not Zhaggee. He had never stood so close to a Cleaver without his hand on a blade. But his sword and knife had been taken from him. Thus, all he could do was hold still and try to keep the fear from exploding in his gut.

His old captain had handed him over to this strange band of warriors almost a week earlier. "What'd I do wrong?" Zhaggee cried in desperation. His captain just gave him a grim look and turned away. The warriors put him on a horse and rode hard until they reached this barren stretch of land. No one had said even a word about the trouble he was in. Whenever he asked about it, they punched him in the mouth. He soon stopped asking.

After standing for hours, Zhaggee heard a horse approach. The other warriors jumped to attention. Zhaggee turned and beheld a great warrior approaching. He had the brands of Cleavers upon his cheeks. It was Lord Mackadoo's sergeant, and he drew dangerously close to Zhaggee.

"Do you know who I am?" he growled.

"No, lord," Zhaggee replied softly.

"Don't call me lord! I'm the one who's going to brand your arm or burn your corpse here tonight. Which will it be?"

"I'll take the brand, lord, if it's all the same to you."

"I told you not to call me 'lord.' Let me ask you something. You came out of the mountains with Backstabber, didn't you? I'm talking about when Tor invaded the high places east of Orres. The enemy slaughtered my kind up there, but somehow you two got out alive. How'd you manage that?"

Zhaggee looked confused, as if he was being asked a trick question, one that could get him killed. "Well, I followed that old gasbag. There was a gang of us. And Weakling was with us, too. And he got all of us out alive."

"'That old gasbag.' I like that. That old gasbag sure is making a name for himself, isn't he? Some of our chums say he can sense the enemy's troops whenever they draw near, and he can find a way to slink through their lines. Is that so?"

"Well, yeah. That's what he did."

"Did he?"

"Well, yes, lord. He had us hit the dirt and hide one night in a canyon right before a great company of cavalry rode past us. And later he did find a way through the enemy lines."

"You know what I think. I think the enemy let him get away. I think Tor made it look like he was saving you."

Zhaggee swallowed hard. "You mean the gasbag's in league with the enemy?"

"That's what I think. And here's what I want to know: Are you in league with the enemy, too?"

"No, lord. I'm loyal to our one true Malevolent Master. You've got to believe me. I don't know anything about Backstabber's schemes."

The sergeant drew close. "Well, I'm going to give you a chance to prove your loyalty. Backstabber's been selected for a mission to kidnap the White Beard. You've heard of the old dog, haven't you? Well, you're going to go along with him. In order to kidnap the White Beard, you've got to pass not once but twice through the enemy lines around the MuKierin. If our enemies don't get you going in, they'll be sure to get you coming back out. You might think I'm sending you to your death. But your old gasbag says he can go in and grab the White Beard without breaking a sweat. Oh, yes, Backstabber brags that Weakling and he are just the warriors for this job. So they're going in, and you're going with them. I'm also sending a special emissary by the name of Rakmah. So listen up. You're going to help me figure out how Backstabber does his little tricks. Do you understand?"

Zhaggee couldn't keep his mouth shut. "But what if he really has The Powers?"

"Are you trying to make me angry? That wouldn't be wise. A miscreant like you wouldn't know anything about The Powers. There are greater minds to test Backstabber about that, should it ever be needed. Your job is to tell me if you see anything suspicious, anything that looks like the enemy is helping him. If you fail our one true Master, I'm going to slice you into little bite-sized chunks for the coyotes to feast on. Do you understand me? Now roll up your sleeve. I'm branding you. You work for the Lord Mackadoo now. That's not me, so quit calling me 'lord.'"

It was a small mirror hanging on a whitewashed wall in a hall at the home of the Elder of the Stone Fences, a village located about a day's ride west of Kierinswell. Shutoo, counsel of Orres, stood before the mirror, as he had each time he visited the compound. A mirror was a rare thing in the Dry Lands. The counsel stared carefully into its reflection and studied the face of a man who looked much younger than his forty years. It was still a boyish face, lean and tan with a straight nose, a gentle "V" of a chin and a bottom lip seemingly made for pouting. Shutoo glanced left, then right and patted the hairs of his brown ponytail. Were there some strands of gray in it?

A voice called from the doorway to a nearby study: "You have a handsome face, sir, but I was hoping to see another one. Why has your Elder sent you instead of coming on his own?"

Shutoo smirked at being caught examining himself. He turned to see his host, the Elder Novi, who was staring soberly at him and rubbing a salt-and-pepper beard. The counsel replied, "My Elder Morros heard about the raid on the copper mine. He sent me to tell you he wants to help put an end to your troubles."

"Is he going to hang these outlaws? That's what we need. They're costing me a small fortune. And I'm just one of the owners of the mine."

"My Elder has learned that these outlaws have ties to the White Beard. He's behind their villainy. We're sure of it."

"The White Beard. That sounds dangerous. He has important friends, including Chakka Ri, the GrandElder. He's an old family friend, I'm told."

"Perhaps, but the White Beard is about to disappear. My Elder wanted you and our other allies to know this before it happens. Things may get a little tricky."

"Indeed things may. You may set off a civil war."

"Perhaps, but it's only a matter of time before the White Beard and his outlaws try to take us all down. We must go after them before it's too late. Best of all, my Elder will be able to plausibly deny that he had nothing to do with the old man's disappearance."

"Is that so? Who's going to take him?"

"I'm not at liberty to say. Believe me, it's best this way. When the day comes, you'll want to say with all the honesty you can muster that you knew nothing about the White Beard's kidnappers."

As evening descended in the hills above Orres, the White Beard slowed his horse. Nearly all the day's light had slipped into the west. Up ahead a few candles shone from the village windows. The old man gently tossed back his head and breathed in the night air.

He rode out of the hills and stopped his mare in the town square. Two young men emerged from the shadows. He smiled when he recognized them. "Greetings, children. Tonight at last I'm going to visit an old friend in that tavern," he said, pointing to a two-story block of adobe across the street. "It's been years."

"As you say, White Beard," one man answered. "We'll keep watch. All is ready."

"One more thing, boys. Keep my mare with you. Just in case."

When the old man stepped inside the dim tavern, the grey-haired innkeeper whooped and waved a towel over his head. "So you've finally come for that cup of wine," the host said. "I thought this day would never come."

"I suppose I should have come sooner," the White Beard replied as he shuffled toward an empty table. "So many things left undone. Such is a man's life."

The innkeeper smiled. "Such is a man's life. But tonight you're here. You shall have my very best."

The two sat at a table and talked of the old days when they had chased horses together. The other guests left them alone for a time, but eventually a few stopped by to place a hand on the White Beard's shoulder or pat his back. More drew near until every man in the tavern was standing around them. One of them asked, "White Beard, what do you know about the men freeing the slaves? Are they true MuKierin?"

"Yes, brothers. True MuKierin. And one day their leader will become our Champion, the very one that was promised to our people long ago. I know him. The King of the Stone Woman had me anoint him as a baby. And I sent him out as a young man. He'll stand up for us, brothers, but his task won't be easy. Indeed, the days ahead will be filled with many sorrows for our people. It breaks my heart to think about what lies ahead for all of you."

Even as the men pondered those words, the front door crashed open. In strode Pibbibib, followed by Weakling, Zhaggee and Rakmah. The MuKierin had never seen such giants, these hulks of Equis with brands on their faces and great swords in their hands. Men gasped and stepped back from the immense creatures. Some fell to their knees.

"I smell dinner," Weakling chortled in MuKierin. "I can't decide who to eat first."

More knees buckled. Zhaggee crowed at the cowering men, "They're going to worship us before we rip their hearts out. Let the feasting begin."

Back in the square, the village bell sounded, a sharp toll that all Orres could hear. Zhaggee ran outside with his sword raised high. Quickly he returned. "Whoever rang it has galloped off," he said.

"You can thank me for that," the White Beard
declared from his chair. "I've been expecting you. If you go
outside and gaze up to the eastern hills, you'll soon see a
signal fire burning in the darkness."

Weakling sneered, "What's your game? Do you think
anyone can stop us from snatching you tonight?"

"Of course not. But I do hope to persuade you to let
these others go, because the King has decreed a life for a life
this night. One of you four evil ones will die for each
MuKierin you kill here."

All eyes turned, first to the White Beard and next to
Pibbibib. "His warriors will have to find us before they can
kill us," said Backstabber. "We won't make that easy for
them."

"Perhaps. But what do you gain by putting my words
to the test? Each moment you tarry here brings your enemies
a few steps closer to killing you."

The intruders began to argue in their own tongue.
Rakmah shouted, "We have our orders. Let's take the old
man and leave at once."

Zhaggee chimed in, "Listen to Rakmah, Backstabber.
He's in charge."

"I'm in charge when it comes to our movements,"
Pibbibib snarled in reply. "We move when and where I say."

Weakling strode over to the White Beard and raised
him by an arm from his chair. "I'll be waiting outside while
you decide when to move," he cried. "I've suddenly lost my
appetite for vermin." With that, he dragged the old man out
the door.

Pibbibib hesitated. Rakmah roared at him, "We go
now! If not, I swear I'll tell Mackadoo and the sergeant how
you put us at risk, you useless pile of dung." He backed out
the door, followed by Zhaggee.

Backstabber alone glared at the trembling humans. In
MuKierin he growled, "We'll be back soon enough, me and
my chums. And when we return, we'll feast on your corpses."

Outside, five immense horses stood waiting. The
warriors hoisted the White Beard upon a black steed and

galloped off through the darkened streets. At the south end of the village they stopped and looked to the eastern hills. Sure enough, they could see a signal fire burning on a hilltop.

"How'd you know we'd be coming for you?" Backstabber demanded.

"I know who you are," the old man said.

"Then you know that your allies won't be able to catch me."

"You think The Powers will help you. You think that to have them is to be touched with greatness. You're a fool. The Powers aren't a blessing. They're a curse. Just wait and see."

"Shut up," said Pibbibib, "or I'll rip out your tongue."

"You're not to touch the prisoner," Rakmah warned. "Now let's get moving before the enemy shows up."

"Before we leave, I have one more thing to tell you," said the White Beard. "The time has come to tell all of you the true identity of Blaze, the champion. He is the grandson of the King."

"That's impossible," said Pibbibib. "Isn't he the child of the Horse Stalker?"

"Indeed, he is."

"Wait," said Rakmah. "Are you saying that a MuKierin dog had a child with She who holds the little light of power?"

Weakling cringed. "That's the most disgusting thing I've ever heard."

"It is nonetheless true," said the White Beard. "Ah, you proud rebels. You think yourselves so much better than us mere humans, don't you? But the King has chosen us and rejected you. And now he has a grandson with human blood in him."

"That's why we're rebels," said Pibbibib. "We won't be a party to such humiliation."

The warriors and their prisoner rode south through the night. Before dawn they veered east so they could find a hiding place in the foothills. They stopped and huddled in a low spot between two hills. Weakling climbed up a rise and kept watch on the trail back toward Orres. Zhaggee soon crawled over to join him. For a moment they both scanned the darkness. "Wish I were back with the Red Brigade," Zhaggee confided. "Or up high in the hills with you in cave country. This ain't my idea of fun, especially when we don't get to eat any vermin."

Weakling shrugged. "Well, I think we'll be okay. But it startled me that the old dog knew we'd be coming for him."

"Yeah, I guess we've got some loose lips somewhere, either with the horse dogs or with our own kind. I'm guessing it must have been with the MuKierin. So what now? Do you think we can still make it back through the enemy lines?"

"It looks like it. For now it's quiet all around us. Let's hope it stays that way."

"That old boy sure got my hair standing up on end when he talked about The Powers. How 'bout you? Do you think they're really a curse?"

Weakling winced. "I don't know, Zhaggee. I don't think we should discuss it."

"Why not?"

"Because someone here wouldn't like it. He'd kill us both if he heard us talking about it."

Zhaggee drew close and whispered, "You know what I think. I think your old gasbag would throttle me for sure if ever I learned your little secret. But I don't think he'd kill you, Weakwi. I don't think that for a moment."

"Don't talk like that, Zhaggee. Don't go looking for trouble."

Zhaggee leaned back and raised his arms. "Alright. Keep your secret to yourself. But I promise you one thing. I'm going to take good care of you over these next few days. Yes sir, Weakwi, until we get out of here, I'm going to keep a close watch out for you."

Chapter Five

Beyond the MuKierin

Equis Castle was the grandest edifice in all the Dry Lands. It rose high above a metropolis of stone and adobe that was home to ten thousand people. The city straddled the Red River, whose waters wound three hundred miles south from the Great Lake of the Pappi. And Equis fortress, with its massive front turret and three central towers, lay at the city's southern edge. No one in the Dry Lands, not even the leaders of the Realm, knew who had built its stone walls and high inner passages. The castle stood cold and vacant long before Zoirra had led his followers in retreat from the Green Lands. When the rebels explored their new country, they found the empty fortress and quickly made it their own.

One warm spring morning a rider in black entered the city from the north. The man had a cleft chin and a shaven head, and he rode straight and tall as he trotted his dark stallion along a street lined with two-story inns and shops. Soon the lanes became crowded, and he found himself stuck behind a line of ox carts passing among throngs of pedestrians. The rider veered onto a side street. It was choked with gangs of chained slaves, most likely from the northern lands. At last he reached another side road leading to Equis Bridge, the one man-made passage over the river in all the Dry Lands. The rider turned that way and soon paused atop the bridge. Resting on the middle of its three stone arches, he peered heavenward and spied the black flag of the Broken Star flying above the castle.

On the city's east bank, the rider found a stable for his horse and a tavern for his thirst. A grizzled man with a bulbous nose sat inside, waiting for him at a table.

"My, you're looking fit," said the grizzled one, rising and giving a handshake. "How's the arm?"

"No good," the rider replied. "Same as always." Both men spoke true. The rider did indeed look fit, having kept himself in fighting condition for three decades. Despite his forty-seven years, his physique was trim and muscular. However, he favored his left arm, keeping it tight and nearly motionless against his side. Having shaken the other's hand, the rider adjusted his sword and took his seat. "What's the news, Botti? One last campaign?"

"Yes, captain, one more. Not like Middle Brook, of course. We're too old for that, though you were grand that day, leading us to victory. You risked it all that day. And we still carry the wounds to prove it. The Cheyok won't soon forget your sacrifice."

"I'd have worse than a bum arm if it hadn't been for you. You saved my life that day."

Botti smiled. "It's the one good thing I ever did. And it wasn't wasted. Look at yourself, Aeres. You're the headmaster of the most important academy in all the Dry Lands. For twenty years you've taught boys how to become warriors and statesmen. And now nearly all the clans send their brightest and bravest sons to you. You've shown us all that bringing these young men together can help bring peace among the clans. No one doubts that now, not after your cadets helped end the long war between the Pappi and the Barsk. When those clans signed their peace treaty five years ago, everyone sat up and took notice."

Aeres tightened his lips. "I suppose they did," he said.

"I know they did. And now you're on another great campaign—the best ever. And it's all coming together. But I forget my manners. Let me get us a couple mugs of drub." He arose and went to the bar, returning a minute later with two tall cups of a potent alcoholic drink. It was brewed by fermenting a root that grew amid the salt marshes south of Equis. Botti returned and set the mugs on the table. "You know, you can't get a drink this fine in the north."

"I know," said Aeres. "I suspect that's why you stick around Equis."

Botti smiled again. "You may be right. Well, here's to you. Now tell me your news and I'll tell you mine. How's that chief cadet of yours?"

"Bo? He's as good as gold. The boys love him. They'd follow him anywhere."

"Just like Middle Brook."

"Oh, no, Botti, he's head and shoulders above me. Bo's got a true heart for the men under him. He carries their packs. He shares his water on the long marches. And he stirs them up when it's time to stare down their enemies. My only concern is that he's truly scary in battle. I once led the cadets on some small missions against the Quolli, payback for raids against the Barsk and the Pappi. I wanted the senior cadets to get a taste of battle. But when we caught up with the enemy, Bo slaughtered them. I mean all of them, even the women and children. It stunned me. He'd always seemed so kind, almost gentle. But he can be a madman on the battlefield. It happened again on our second engagement. I had to halt the mission and get us out of there before we had the whole Quolli nation on the warpath."

"War can do that to the best of us. We've all done things we regretted later. But he does sound like a good leader, and you'll need that for the man who holds the secret power. Didn't you say he has a brother?"

"Yes, his name is Sorenth. But he's no longer with us. He had a horse go down under him about six months ago. It made a mess of his left leg and left him crippled. I had to send him home. What a shame. Good swordsman. Good head on his shoulders."

Botti chugged his drink and wiped his lips with a dirty sleeve. "Well, a soldier takes his chances. Sometimes we overcome. Sometimes we fall. But always we reach for glory. And for these young ones, glory is now within their reach. When the time is right, they'll have the campaign of a lifetime. I envy them. They'll bring the clans together for a war to end all wars. And you'll be their general."

"Let me ask you something, Botti. Can it happen sooner rather than later?"

"I suppose so. But why?"

"The peace between the Pappi and Barsk is growing fragile. It all could come undone in the next few months.

Please keep that to yourself. I haven't said anything yet to the cadets. But it would take some of the shine off the Academy and the good work that we've done. If we could take hold of the power soon, the clans might still look favorably on joining us. And in so doing, we might stop a war between Northsford and South Shore."

"Well, that would be a noble goal. It's time we stopped fighting each other and focused on our real enemy, who's too near to be named, if you get my meaning. As for the secret power, it's there for the taking. We both know where to find it. You send in the cadets and it will be waiting there for them. Once Bo takes hold of it, we'll rally the clans behind your boys."

"Very good. I've sent a squad of cadets north to the Barsk to arrange for more arms. One more cache of swords and spears should take care of our needs. Then we can begin." He paused and looked around the other tables. No one seemed to pay them any attention, but still he lowered his voice. "Did you bring the jewel? I'd like to touch it one last time before we begin."

Slowly Botti reached inside his shirt and pulled out a red stone on a leather thong. Scanning the inn, he waited a moment before placing the gem on the table. Aeres took it into his left hand and gave a deep sigh. "What a sensation. I can feel tingles all up and down this bum arm of mine. I almost feel it coming back to life. One little stone, and yet it gives off such energy. It's proof that the great power exists, Botti. It's real. It's not some old wives tale. Just think what it must be like to hold the real treasure. Think what it could do for us, for all of us. Our people need it. We desperately need it."

"Keep the stone, Aeres."

"What? Are you sure? It's so valuable."

"Yes, I want you to have it. And when the time is right, let Bo touch it. It'll help prepare him for what lies ahead."

"I'll do that. I promise. Thank you, Botti. I won't forget all you've done for me."

"I know you won't. We're about to embark on a campaign for the ages. Here's to us, my old friend. I promise to do all I can for you. I just hope to live long enough to see you stand in this long-occupied city and raise a new flag over that big old castle. It will be the end of the Realm. What a grand day that will be."

The flashes of light came in rapid bursts from the eastern hills. It was an hour before sunset, and Tustin saw the signals while standing on a barren slope in the canyon lands south of Orres. Above him, Blaze sat cross-legged on a rock outcrop. He also watched the flashes, which lasted for several minutes. As they ended, Roff and Stannis came up the trail. The four men gathered together on the outcrop.

"We're here, cousin," said Roff. "What's on your mind?"

"It's time for a new chapter in the story," said Blaze. "So far, we've freed many slaves. We've challenged the Slavers on the Council. And one day soon I'll stand before the GrandElder. But now we need to make some preparations for what will happen after I leave the Dry Lands. This very well could be my last season among the MuKierin."

"How can you say that?" asked Stannis. "Our people need you here. You're a leader and you've started something big. Every day more and more kinsmen want to join us. You've given our people hope. But we can't keep all this alive without you. If you leave us, it's all going to fizzle out."

"I think you can, if you don't forget the story. Yes, I need to gather friends and followers for what lies ahead. But I've come here to take hold of a great power. And I can't do that without the King's help. I need him to help prepare me for that day. And that means I need to go to him."

Roff asked, "So what's the next chapter?"

"Tomorrow I need to ride west toward the Lake Country. The King wants me to find two people who can help us. I want Tustin and you to come with me. Stannis, I'd like you to lead the others while I'm away."

As they spoke, a sentry called from below, "Roff, somebody's found us! You better come quick!"

Roff rushed down the slope. "Come with me, Stannis!" he called back. "Spider, go get Kick and meet us down below."

The sentry called to Roff: "There's two strangers waiting down by the horses. They rode up the canyon with a white flag and asked to see Blaze. They said they have big news for him."

"Alright," Roff replied. "Go tell Blaze what you told me. I'm going down to meet our guests. Stannis, you come with me. No one is supposed to know about this camp. So how did these two fellows find us? Now we're going to have to abandon this place, and the sooner the better."

Roff and Stannis jogged through a score of tents and made their way to a rise beyond their encampment. Below them lay a small valley with a herd of horses grazing amid sagebrush. The far end of the valley was ringed by steep canyon walls, which now reflected the evening light. And amid the walls sat a narrow passageway, the entrance to the remote hideaway. Roff looked below the rise and saw his sentries surrounding two interlopers. The strangers stood beside their horses. One was Sunny, Darnelle's brother. When he saw Roff, he relaxed his shoulders and waved a hand.

"Fine evening, brother," Sunny called, leaning against his mount and looking over the top of his saddle.

"Maybe for you, Sunny."

"Yes, it is, Roff. But I think you're going to be glad that I found you. Aren't you going to invite me up for supper? I'm one hungry traveler."

"I imagine you are," said Roff. Tustin and Kick came hustling up. They stopped in their tracks when they recognized Sunny. Roff squatted and picked up a rock, just the right size to throw at an ornery goat. "So how did you find us?"

Sunny smiled triumphantly and shook out his baggy, tan overshirt. "Makes you wonder, doesn't it, Roff? Nobody else could find you all these years, not those stupid Elders or all their hired killers. But Ol' Sunny did. Yes, sir, and I did it in record time, too. You never knew I was so good, did you? Admit it, brother. You have too low an estimation of my abilities."

"Maybe I do. I'm still waiting to hear exactly how you did it."

"Well, Roff, you have yourself a lover boy here. He visits my little sister in Orres. I had a hunch she'd know how to get a message to her honey. And sure enough, I was right."

"Is that so?" Roff said, turning soberly to gaze at Tustin, whose cheeks began to burn red. "Is that so?"

"Oh, Darnelle played dumb at first. Can you believe it? She actually was trying to keep secrets from her big brother. But she confessed once she realized that I have news for Blaze, big news."

Blaze walked slowly over the rise, followed by half a dozen men, their spears and swords at the ready. Blaze stopped and gazed for a full minute at Sunny and the stranger. Sunny found it hard to stand still. "Hello, Blaze," he called, stepping forward and brushing back scraggily, shoulder-length hair. "I've brought you some big news, brother. They've kidnapped the White Beard. They took him from Orres."

"Who took him?" Stannis demanded.

"Gigantic warriors from the Realm. They came at night and scared the people bad. They were huge and they wore the bones of dead people on their armor. The villagers had never seen anything like them. But no one thinks they acted alone. We know Morros and the other slavers were in league with them. And our people certainly won't stand for it. Already they've rioted in Orres. More than fifty people stoned the Elder's compound the other night. The guards caught three of them and hanged them. But their deaths won't stop this rebellion. Pretty soon we'll have riots in every slaver's village up and down this land."

"And who'd you bring with you?" asked Blaze.

"Sunny smiled. "Who, him? He wants to introduce himself."

The stranger stepped forward, a man in his late twenties with cropped hair and a costly brown tunic. "I wish a private audience with you," he said in a deliberate voice.

"No," said Blaze. "My men can hear whatever you want to say to me."

The man frowned and took a step back. "Then for now I'll keep my name to myself. But I was sent here by a group of leaders who hate slavery as much as you do. They include Elders and commanders in the army. These men respected the White Beard. They owe him and they are true MuKierin. Now they want to avenge him. These leaders have power and they are offering to help you. Together we can put an end to the enslavement of our kinsmen."

Sunny nodded enthusiastically. "Blaze, my brother, there has never been a moment like this. There has never been such a coalition possible. My companion here has to watch his words in public. But in private he'll tell you that the men he represents won't lift a finger to help Morros or any of the other slavers. Not only that, they can provide you some help on the sly. We can start down in Orres and rid this land of tyrants. What do you say to that?"

"No," said Blaze.

"No? What do you mean, brother? Are you saying that we already have enough strength to take Orres without their help?"

"I mean that I've heard your plans, and my answer is 'No.'"

Sunny's mouth dropped. He turned awkwardly to the stranger for support, then back to Blaze. "Wait a moment! Don't you understand what we're saying? There are people fighting and dying today in Orres. And soon kinsmen up and down this land will risk everything they have to do their part in this struggle. That includes people like my sister Lowi, somebody you ought to care about since you saved her from those stinking slavers. Now maybe you horse boys don't like my traveling companion and me. That's fine. But our people are looking for a leader, one who can stop slavery and end the days of tyrants like Morros. Now whether you like it or not,

Blaze, you are that man. The people need you. Yes, we may have to spill some blood. But this may be the one chance in our generation for the MuKierin to get rid of these villains. You can't turn your back now on your people. You've got to step forward and be the leader they need. You can't let them down. Do it for the White Beard."

Blaze replied, "Sunny, you still don't know your own story. You've heard my answer."

The stranger stepped forward and reached out a hand toward Blaze. "But what am I to tell the men who sent me?"

"Tell them I am a man under orders. And my orders are not to lead MuKierin in a war to kill other MuKierin."

Sunny shouted angrily, "After all the White Beard has done for you, you're going to turn your back on him! Is that the way of the MuKierin? Certainly not! You dishonor the Clan with your cowardice. And what about the rest of you? Are all of you cowards, too? If not, break away and come with me to avenge the White Beard." The men shifted their feet and looked warily at one another. Sunny saw that he had struck a chord. "I can tell that some of you are true MuKierin. You know you owe the White Beard. His enemies are your enemies, and you want to avenge him. I will wait for you at the entrance of this canyon for one hour. As for the rest of you, your cowardice will bring you down. When our people hear about your lack of manhood, they will never follow you. And you can be sure that they're going to hear about it, because I'm going to be the one telling them. The people will spit in your faces before this is over. You'll be sorry that you ever turned your back on Sunny!"

Blaze's followers stood frozen as the two visitors mounted their horses and slapped them into a trot toward the far end of the valley. For a moment no one spoke. Stannis began pacing back and forth. "Go ahead," said Blaze. "Say what's on your mind."

"The White Beard was our kinsman," said Kick, not daring to look Blaze in the eye. "And we do owe him."

"It's the way of our clan to avenge him," said Stannis. "Sunny may be a fool but he knows our people. If we fail to strike, the MuKierin certainly will call us cowards. And they'll never follow us."

"The White Beard is bound for the castle of Equis," said Blaze. "I am bound for the Red River. I must leave in the morning."

A young man named Eppas stepped forward and announced, "Then I'm leaving. I owe a debt to the White Beard. I'm going home to avenge him. Who is with me?" A dozen young men, nearly a third of the camp, followed Eppas as he strode back to the tents.

Stannis turned away and resumed pacing. The remaining men stared at the ground. Roff broke the silence: "The rest of you had better start packing. Sunny has found us. In two days he'll be selling maps to this place. We need to leave by morning. I'll have assignments for each one of you. Come on, brothers. Let's get going."

The men began to return to camp. Blaze, however, touched Stannis on the arm. He told him, "I need you to take these men east to our hiding place near Mt. Fama and wait for us there. I know I'm asking a hard thing. But will you keep the men in camp for me?"

"Won't you change your mind now and stay with us?" Stannis asked.

"No. The King has ordered me to go west. I will obey him. Will you obey me?"

"Yes, Blaze. I'll obey you, but I don't understand any of this."

Blaze walked back to camp. As he left, Tustin whispered to Roff and Stannis, "Did you hear what Blaze said to us? He already seemed to know about the White Beard's capture."

"Yeah," asked Roff. "He said the old man was going to Equis Castle. Somehow he must have gotten word about the kidnapping."

"Well, he's been up on that hill for a week watching for flashes of light. I even spotted some signals out there this afternoon before the three of us went up to talk to him. They had to be messages about the White Beard."

"Yeah, and probably about Sunny, too," said Roff. "Blaze must have known that he would be coming this way. I bet he even delayed his trip west and waited for those two to show up here. That way he could give his answer to them. Otherwise, it might have been left to Stannis here to decide whether or not to join the rebellion in Orres."

"Do you really think so?" asked Stannis. "Wow, that never crossed my mind. I wouldn't have wanted to be in that position. I don't like this decision, but I'm glad Blaze made it. If it had been left to me, I would have led our boys back to Orres and thought that Blaze would have done the same thing. I still don't know what to think about all this. It feels wrong. I want vengeance. That's our way."

"Well, don't give up on Blaze yet," said Roff. "He needs you now, cousin. I'd like to stay, but I've got to go west with him. And lover boy here is coming with us."

"I am not her lover boy!" Tustin protested. "I wish I were. I wish she'd look at me."

Before dawn, Blaze, Roff and Tustin departed the camp. They brought along two packhorses and a spare mount. For two days they rode west across a land of sage and rolling desert. On the third day they looked west and beheld a chocolate-colored mountain with bands of lighter rock running in layers along the face. Nearby, the hills and mesas were pocked from erosion. Late in the day they crested a steep ridge and looked down into a deep gorge of the Red River, a dark, serpentine flow passing into evening's shadow. In the distance, a string of domed hills shimmered, backlit by a golden haze. Tustin looked into the gorge and longed to descend into it and dip his hand into the cool water.

Blaze pointed upstream and spoke: "The river comes from the northwest, from the Great Lake of the Pappi. That's where I grew up. Water leaves the lake at South Shore and crashes through a series of waterfalls and rapids to reach this canyon. From here it winds its way south all the way to Equis. After that, it spreads out into the dead marshes of the Salt Basin."

Tustin turned to Roff. "You win," he said. "I give up."

"What do you mean?" asked Blaze.

"Roff and I had a bet. We wanted to see which one of us could wait the longest to ask you why we came here. I can't stand it any more, not after looking at the river and hearing you talk about it. So, tell me, Blaze. Are we going on to the lake? If we are, Kick asked me to bring him back a fish so he could see whether or not you pluck it."

Blaze asked Roff, "What did you win in this bet?"

"I get to pick our places when the fighting starts. I think I'll put Spider at the front of the charge."

Blaze laughed and swung his mount to better face Tustin. "In that case, I guess I need to give you a good answer. No, we're not going to the lake. From here we're going to ride south along these cliffs to the land of the Barsk. I hope to meet a man there, a Pappi. He's part of a group of young men who will be stopping at a trading post up ahead."

"What do we need with a Pappi?" Roff asked.

"The King wants his help. Not everybody can be MuKierin, Roff."

Roff frowned. "You said we were going to meet two people. Who's the other person?"

"I believe there will be a woman at the trading post, too."

"And what do we want with a woman? Don't tell me. Not everybody can be a man. And I suppose the King wants her help, too."

"Yes, Roff, the King wants her help. She is MuKierin, though she hasn't lived in our land for many years. She's had a hard life. She's been sold several times from one man to another."

"And what about this Pappi? Does he own her?"

"No, Roff, he's a cadet in training at a school called the Academy. The school lies more than a hundred miles south of here. Its students include young men from all the clans, even the MuKierin. I need to tell you one more secret – something you're not to share with another soul for now.

These young men want to find the Root of Glory. They hope
to use it to defeat the Realm."

"Do they know where to find it?"

"No, but their headmaster seems to think he does.
These young men don't know the trouble that's waiting ahead
for them."

The three MuKierin turned south and camped that
night near the pass leading down to Northsford, the capitol of
the Barsk. The route was one of the few places in the Dry
Lands where wagons could cross the river. However, Blaze
was bound a different way. In the morning, he led his friends
on a trail that stayed east of the river. As the three traveled, a
strong wind began to blow from the north. Soon flecks of
sand stung the men's faces. Clumps of tumbleweeds whipped
around them. By noon they had reached their destination, an
outpost in the eastern lands of the Barsk. A high adobe wall
surrounded the compound. Blaze led his companions through
the main gate and up to a two-story tavern and inn. Nearby
sat a large, enclosed stable.

The wind howled as the three MuKierin tied up their
horses in the yard and entered the tavern. It was filled with
men, mostly Barsk and Pappi. Near its one fireplace, travelers
sat on the floor and played pebble dice. The players eyed the
newcomers for but a moment before turning back to their
wagering. Blaze led his friends to the bar. A bald innkeeper
nodded gruffly and pointed to their horsehair belts. "Brave
MuKierin," he said in their tongue, though to Roff he seemed
to say it with a purposely-bad accent. "No room here. Sleep in
stable. Three pieces of silver." Blaze nodded and paid him the
money. Looking at a booth in a side room, the three noticed a
woman in a red robe seated on a ledge filled with beige
pillows. The innkeeper watched their eyes and shook his
head. "The woman is MuKierin, but not for you. She belongs
to another man. No touch!"

Blaze and his friends returned into the wind-whipped
yard and found the stable nearly as crowded as the inn. Barsk
herders and packers were lying on blankets and trying to rest.
A number of them worked for a trader, the same man who

had brought the woman there. The MuKierin unloaded their gear in a corner and put their horses in the huge adobe corral near the high outer wall of the outpost. The wind was blowing so hard that it clouded the view between the stable and the inn. Once their horses were settled, Blaze led his friends back inside the stable to claim a place for their bedrolls.

"This places stinks of men and horses," said Tustin. "I can't tell which smells worse."

Roff looked around. "Blaze, is the man you want to meet here?"

"I think so. The horses inside this stable belong to the Academy men. They must have taken rooms upstairs in the inn. Let's rest here a while. This wind is going to blow most of the night. But I want to leave early in the morning."

At supper, Roff and Tustin went into the tavern and waited for a place to sit and eat a bowl of a watery chicken stew. Roff looked again upon the woman with the scarlet robe. She noticed him staring at her and turned her head away.

Upstairs, a small man with a crooked nose knocked on a bedroom door. When it opened, he entered, but not before he looked carefully to his right and left, noting each man in the room. Inside stood three cadets, all dressed in black uniforms. One of them addressed the newcomer in the Common Tongue, the speech used between the clans: "Welcome. We are at your service."

"Greetings," the man replied. "My master welcomes you all to the land of the Barsk. You boys seem to travel in packs."

"We're careful," said a MuKierin with cropped hair and a cleft chin. "We wouldn't want someone else to take the gold we've brought for you master."

"You've come here to buy two hundred swords and spears. Why does a boys' school need so many weapons?"

"The Academy is a military school," said the MuKierin. "We're planning an expansion. And so we're turning to your master for arms. Our headmaster knows that no one makes swords like the Barsk."

"Does the Realm know about your expansion?"

"Does the Realm know everything about your master's business?"

The small man smiled. "Give me the required down payment. We'll analyze your gold. I'm sure it's fine. How soon would you like us to deliver the weapons?"

"We'll send word when the time is right," the MuKierin said. "Just have the arms ready."

The first cadet spoke: "On another matter, I understand that your master is unbeatable in Earth and Sky."

The small man turned to consider the cadet. "He enjoys the game."

"So do I. I am always looking for a chance to advance in my abilities. Perhaps we might play a few rounds tonight."

"What's your name, boy?"

"Frissa."

"Very well, Frissa. I'll call you when my master's ready to teach you a few lessons. I trust you'll bring a large bag of coins."

"Of course."

The small man nodded and exited the room. Frissa shut the door. "That went well," he said. "Let's stay an extra day. Tonight I'm going to fleece this fat arms merchant at the gaming table and take his pretty courtesan from him. She'll make a nice plaything for a few days, don't you think? Who wants in?"

"I do," said Bar, the MuKierin. "No doubt the others will, too."

"Not me," said Lon, the third cadet, a tall, slim Pappi with curly blond hair and bright green eyes. "You know I never pay for women."

"That's because all those Pappi girls want to have your child," said Bar. "They still hope to catch you and tie you down."

After dinner, Roff and Tustin sat at their table and watched as the arms dealer emerged from his private room on the ground floor. He wore a brown robe, and he had used a

little oil on a great black beard and a gray-streaked ponytail.
He took his seat at an empty table reserved for him. From
atop the stairs came Frissa, followed by a half-dozen cadets in
black capes that shone like satin. Each of them wore a great
black belt with a fine sword on it. At the bottom of the stairs,
Frissa bowed and spoke to the trader in a language that
sounded strange to Roff and Tustin. The younger man took a
seat and both gamblers set their bags of coins on the table.
Frissa began to stack gold pieces in columns of ten. The trader
simply poured his coins on the table. From a second bag he
brought forth several small silver shapes and one flat object
that was colored black on one side and white on the other.
The two men each placed four coins in the center of the table.
Then they grabbed three silver shapes and held them beneath
the table.

Bar, the MuKierin cadet, approached Roff and spoke
in his native tongue: "Brothers of the Stone Woman, you are
far from home this night."

Roff formally bowed his head. "We are at your
service, sir. And are you also MuKierin?"

"Indeed I am. And like you I am far from home in the
middle of this blasted dust storm. And so tonight we have
little to do except watch my friend Frissa and the trader here
play Earth and Sky."

"The game is strange to us," said Roff.

"It's a betting game from the south. One side attacks
for five turns, then the other. Each man has three pieces, one
piece for Earth, one for Sky, one for Mountain. When you
attack, you try to pick the same piece as your opponent. If
you pick Earth or Sky and you are right, you win the bet. But
if you pick Sky and your opponent picks Earth, he gets the
bet. If you pick Earth or Sky and he picks Mountain, the in-
between piece, he gets half your bet."

"It sounds complicated," said Tustin.

"It is. Do you see that black coin beside the trader? Its
other side is white. When you attack, you take charge of it.
You can turn it over to white once during your turn. If you do

and you choose the right game piece, you collect ten times the bet."

"How long will they play?" asked Tustin.

"All night. My friend is good at this game and he wants to win the trader's courtesan. Look at her and you can see why. She's also MuKierin, a beautiful vision of the Stone Woman."

Blaze entered the tavern. Looking around, he spotted the curly blond hair of Lon, the Pappi cadet, at a table near the gamblers. Blaze made his way across the room, passing the men standing on the edge of the game. When he reached Lon, he pulled something from beneath his cloak and placed it on the table. "Excuse me," he said in the tongue of the Pappi, "I believe this belongs to you."

Lon looked down. On the table sat a little toy "soldier," actually a small rock painted red and blue in the rough form of a human. The cadet arched his eyebrows as he beheld it. Gently he took it into his hand and examined it. When he lifted his eyes back toward the stranger, Blaze already had retreated to the door and stepped outside. Immediately Lon rose and followed him.

The Pappi stepped out into the windstorm and crossed the yard to the stable. Inside, he found Blaze leaning on his staff in the shadows by the back wall. At a far corner, a few herders squatted at a game of dice. The cadet stepped forward, his left hand resting on the hilt of his sword. Unfolding his right hand, he displayed the rock "soldier." "How did you come by this?"

"I'm a friend of Bairn. He gave it to me. My father met him in your land even before I was born. Bairn told me that this figurine would serve as a sign to you. He gave it to me because he wanted me to give you a message. He's told me a great deal about you, Lon."

"Well, it's true that I gave this stone soldier to Bairn. But how do I know you're his friend? You appear to be MuKierin, though you wear a fisher's hat and speak Pappi as well as I do."

Blaze reached inside his blouse and removed a small scroll. Slowly he extended his hand to the cadet. Lon took the scroll, unrolled it and read these words:

"Lon, my friend, listen to the one who brings you this note. I trust this MuKierin. His name is Blaze. He grew up among us. You are in danger. The Barsk have put a price on your head. Come to me soon as planned, but be careful. Don't go through Northsford. I have much to say to you. Your everlasting friend, Bairn."

Lon rolled up the scroll and placed it inside his blouse. "Well, it's clear that Bairn wrote this note. I recognize his handwriting. I take it that you know what this message says. So why would the Barsk want me?"

"Two reasons. First, the Barsk and the Pappi stand on the brink of war."

"How can that be? Members from my school worked hard to forge a lasting peace between these clans."

"A lasting peace? If you believe that, you don't know your own story."

"What's that supposed to mean?"

"Ask Bairn. He'll tell you how fragile peace is between the clans. That's why I came to you. It wasn't safe for him to send a Pappi through Northsford with this message for you. So I came to you from another way."

"Alright, I will ask Bairn about all of this when I get home. You said the Barsk might have a second reason to put a price on my head. What is it?"

"I think Equis also is interested in you. They would pay the Barsk in order to get their hands on you."

"Why?"

"I don't think its leaders want you to go home. I could guess why, but would you believe me?"

"Probably not. Who are you anyway?"

"I'm Bairn's friend. And I'm the man who's meant to hold the great power."

"Really? Many people have never even heard of the great power. And some who have don't believe it exists."

"But you believe it exists, don't you Lon?"

"Perhaps. But that doesn't make you the man who's supposed to hold it."

"Talk to Bairn. But don't go through Northsford on the way home. Cut through the badlands. And leave tomorrow. In a few days the Barsk are going to cut off that route, too. They want you, Lon. Please take care."

During the night, the wind stopped howling. In the stable, filled with snoring herders, the three MuKierin slept restlessly. Blaze got up twice and walked over to the inn. Each time he took his staff with him and spent a few minutes in the dim candlelight watching the two gamblers at their betting game. A few of the Academy cadets slept uneasily at nearby tables. Frissa was winning, but it was proving an arduous process to overcome an adversary with so much wealth. Nonetheless, the young man wore a confident face. Nearby the woman slept in the booth, her red cloak pulled tight to her thin frame. The trader, meanwhile, frowned as he studied the cadet, seeking some inkling of his opponent's next move. After each visit, Blaze slipped back into the darkness.

At dawn, the three MuKierin rose and stepped outside. The air was calm and the sun was about to rise into a crystalline blue sky. The three breathed deep, at last free of the intense aroma of sweat and dung. After checking their horses, they walked across the yard to the inn. Inside a fat cook was stirring a kettle of porridge over the coals in the fireplace. At the betting table, the faces of Frissa and the trader appeared lifeless. The trader's stack was down to less than one hundred silver coins. His woman watched the gambling with a look of weary resignation. Nearby two cadets still slept with their heads on their table. Tustin and Roff pulled up to one of the many empty tables and waved to the cook. Blaze, however, turned and exited the inn.

By the time he returned, his two companions had finished their porridge. Blaze sat down beside them and leaned in. "I put our horses in the stable and loaded the packhorses," he said quietly. "All the herders have gone outside to tend their animals. We'll be leaving soon. Roff, I'd like you to saddle our horses. Put my saddle on the spare mount and just place a bridle on my own stallion."

Roff wiped his mouth on his sleeve. "Are you going to tell us what you're planning?"

"I'd like to bring a guest with us when we leave. There might be trouble. Let's be ready, just in case."

Roff stood and pushed his stool out of the way. "Remember our bet, Spider. I'm putting you out in front when the fighting starts."

After Roff left, Blaze whispered to Tustin, "Follow my lead."

"Are you taking the Pappi cadet with us?" Tustin asked. Blaze shook his head. Tustin smiled. "That's a relief. So who do you want to take back home?"

"The woman." Clutching his staff, Blaze rose from his stool. Stepping back, he leaned against a wall and turned to watch the betting game. At the table, Frissa had his hand to his mouth, a feeble attempt to conceal his glee. The trader sighed wearily every time he had to pick among the three game pieces.

They gambled so for a few more minutes. Frissa took over the attack. The two placed their bets, and then Frissa turned the black-and-white coin over so that its white side appeared — raising the bet ten times. The trader shook his head. "I have too few coins left to cover such an amount," he said wearily.

Frissa smiled and eyed the woman. "Doubtless you can find something else to wager."

"I thought you'd say that." The trader slowly turned his head in her direction.

Blaze stepped quietly to the gamblers' table. Perspiration now covered his face. From the sleeve of his tunic he pulled out a red jewel and set it on the table. In the trader's ear, he whispered in Barsk, "For the woman's freedom."

Frissa didn't hear him. "What is this? What's he doing?"

"Doubtless you can guess," the trader said. Immediately he called over the innkeeper. The bald man approached, wiping an earthen mug with a dirty rag. The trader placed the red stone in his hand. The innkeeper hurried back to his counter. First he pulled out a scale and weighed the stone. Next he passed it before a candle and tested its strength with a special mallet. The woman watched all this from her booth, her eyes following the stone as the innkeeper took it to the counter and later when he brought it back to the gaming table.

"Perhaps five hundred silver coins," the man said slowly in Barsk. "Perhaps more. I have never seen one this beautiful before so I must be careful. But I'll give you five hundred for it right now."

Frissa slapped his hand on the table. "We have a game here!" he barked in the Common Tongue, waking the two nearby cadets. He pointed fiercely at Blaze. "This frightened stable boy has no part in it."

The trader chuckled. "Maybe those are the rules where rich boys play. But we are in my land now. Here I do as I please. And this man is offering me five hundred silver coins for the woman. If you like, you can offer more."

"Five hundred coins! That's crazy! That's ten times what she's worth."

The trader leaned back in his chair. "This MuKierin thinks she's worth it." Turning to Blaze, he motioned toward the booth and said in Barsk, "Do as you please with the woman."

Drawn by Frissa's protestations, Lon and Bar appeared shirtless at the top of the stairs. Blaze watched them, but stood motionless at the table. To Tustin, he said, "Please escort the woman to the stable."

Tustin stood up. "Yes, Great One," he said, stepping slowly toward the woman.

"He's not going to leave here with my woman," Frissa said in the Common Tongue. "I stayed awake all night to win her. I'm certainly not going to let this scared MuKierin scum take her away from me now."

The trader chuckled and leaned forward. "I think maybe he should have played this game against you, boy. He may look frightened, but I think he can read your mind. I think he knows what you mean to do."

Frissa gave Blaze a blank stare and eyed the coins on the table. Without warning he grabbed the underside of the table, flung it at Blaze and stood to draw his sword. Blaze sidestepped the table and brought the jeweled tip of his staff onto Frissa's bare hand. Thunderstruck, the cadet toppled lifeless to the floor.

The two cadets nearby sprang to their feet and grabbed their swords. Lon shouted at them, "Cadets, stand down!" Immediately the front door opened and Roff barged in. Blaze's left arm sprang up and motioned him to freeze. Bar cautiously approached Frissa and knelt beside him.

"He lives," Blaze said in MuKierin. "He'll wake in a few days. In the meantime, he's going to have some very bad dreams. And he may never want to use a sword again."

Tustin whispered to the courtesan, "Hurry, woman. If you wish to escape these men and gain your freedom, come with me." Silently she obeyed. But passing by the bar, she grabbed a slender cook's knife. Tustin and Roff watched her tuck it beneath her shawl.

One of the cadets shouted in the Common Tongue, "Bar, the woman's getting away!"

"Silence!" said Bar. "You know our orders. No unnecessary violence. Get back to your rooms. Obey me!"

The two cadets reluctantly climbed the stairs. Bar, meanwhile, turned to Blaze and whispered, "Leave while you may." Blaze nodded and backed out of the room.

Bar turned to Lon and asked, "Who is that man?"

"I wish I knew."

"One of his companions called him 'Great One' in my tongue. That's a strange title for a horse hunter, especially one who looks so weak in the knees."

"Yes, it is. Listen, Bar, I'm going out there. Try to keep our boys inside."

"Hah, that's not going to happen. The only reason those two went upstairs was so they could wake the others. In a few minutes, they're all going to climb out the back window and down the wall. I can't stop them. They won't rest until they avenge Frissa."

Outside, Blaze ran to the compound's main gate. Tustin and Roff already had made it inside the stable with the courtesan. There Roff shut its two front doors and began to tie them shut with a rope. The woman turned on him. "Who are you fools?" she demanded.

"Just keep that knife in your shawl, woman. In a minute those foreigners are going to try to bust down this door. I need to slow them down, so go talk to my partner."

She whipped around and looked at Tustin. "So who is this Great One of yours?"

"He's the champion of our people. He rescued me from the debtors' chains. He's freed others, too. And he just purchased your freedom. You can stay here if you want and let those foreigners get their hands on you. Or you can come with us. If you do, he'll help you. And if you have others you care about, he'll help them, too. Now we've all got to get out of here. We have an extra horse if you want to come with us."

Lon, meanwhile, stepped outside the inn and spied Blaze at the main gate. He ran to him and demanded, "Who are you?"

"I told you. I'm the man who's going to hold the great power."

"We'll see about that. You've just bought yourself a load of trouble. My friends will soon be breaking down those stable doors."

Blaze motioned Lon closer. "Let's avoid a fight. Please step into the shadows with me."

Lon complied. A minute later five cadets climbed out a second-story window and ran for the stable. Lon pointed as they rushed into view. "I warned you."

"So you did," said Blaze. "Now we'll see if your men know that the stable also has a back door."

The cadets slammed into the front stable doors and tried to pry them apart. One managed to reach in and grab the rope that Roff had used to tie the doors shut. Tustin shouted, "Let's get out of here!"

The courtesan, however, stepped up to the double doors and plunged her knife into the exposed arm. The attacked cadet howled and withdrew his wounded limb. Furious, the other cadets crashed vainly into the doors. Still clutching the knife, the woman smiled at Roff as she mounted her horse. Tustin flung open the back door and rode out. The woman followed, with Roff in the rear leading the pack animals and Blaze's unsaddled horse. The cadets howled when they realized the MuKierin were getting away.

"Goodbye, Lon," called Blaze. He pushed open wide the main gates as his friends galloped toward him. Still gripping his staff, Blaze caught the neck of his horse and swung aboard. By the time the other cadets reached the gate, the MuKierin were far off, racing for the hills.

The riders kept their horses at a gallop until they reached the top of the first ridge. There they halted. Blaze climbed down and untied his mount from the string of packhorses.

"Do you think they'll come after us?" Roff asked.

"No," said Blaze. "I think they need to go back to their school."

"Maybe so, but that woman stabbed one of them."

"Did she?"

"Only in the arm," said the courtesan. "I thought we needed a little distraction."

"My name is Blaze. I'm told you are called Cisly."

"You know my name. What else do you know about me?"

"I know you have a son. He's about ten years old. I've heard he was taken from you a few years back. I'd like to help you get him back."

"And how do you mean to do that? Do you even know where he is?"

"Not yet. But friends are looking for him. We'll find him."

"Just like that?"

"Well, yes. Don't you believe me?"

"No, I don't believe you."

"Didn't I just free you?"

"I'm not sure what you just did. If I were really free, that would mean I could leave you now and go my own way."

"You are free and you can go wherever you please. But first I hope you'll hear what I have to say. I need your help, Cisly. A lot of people need your help."

"My help? Are you crazy? Nobody's needed my help in years."

"What about your son? He still needs your help. And I do, too. That's two people right there, and I haven't yet said what I need to say."

"Then say it. I'm listening."

"You speak Barsk and Pappi, as well as MuKierin. I need a representative to speak for my King to those people."

"Now I know you're crazy."

Roff interrupted, "Cousin, those cadets are still watching us back there. We need to get off this hilltop."

Blaze nodded. "Cisly, I need to find a place to lie down for a few hours. I get sick at times. You can leave us if you want, but I hope you'll stay and give me a chance to tell you more. I want to free a lot of people, and that includes your son. Now I've got to get back home. There are some people I need to free in Orres."

The three men rode east. Cisly waited, turning her head back to the inn. Two cadets stood by the gate, watching her. Frowning, she kicked her mount and followed after Blaze.

Chapter Six

Jailbreak

In the middle of the night, Darnelle awoke to a tapping at the shutters of the bedroom. "Darnelle! Open up. It's Sunny."

At the sound of her brother's voice, Darnelle lost all sense of sleepiness. "Sunny, are you crazy? Don't you know how risky it is for you to come here? The Elders have put a price on your head."

"Open the door! Lowi's hurt bad. She's dying."

Darnelle turned to see her great-aunt Tatti Oom, still asleep beside her in bed. The younger woman arose and rushed from the small bedroom to unbolt the front door. Sunny pushed past her, followed by three men carrying Lowi. Darnelle didn't recognize the others. "Put her in there," said Sunny, motioning toward the darkened bedroom. The men lugged the wounded woman to the other room.

"What is this?" Tatti Oom called anxiously from the bedroom. "What do you think you're doing? Who are you?"

"Shut up, woman," Sunny shouted. "This is your nephew talking. Lowi and I are spending the night with you. Now shut up and don't give us any trouble."

Darnelle went to the fireplace and stirred alive the embers in order to light a candle. She took it and went in to tend to her sister. On the bed Lowi lay unconscious, her gown marked with a great splotch of blood across her midsection. Darnelle went and fetched old cloths to use as bandages. "When did this happen?" she asked.

"Before dawn today," said Sunny. "We got attacked east of here. We beat them off but not before they killed a few of us and wounded Lowi. You can be sure I killed the man who did this to her."

"Will they be coming here to look for you?"

"No, you're safe. The Elder's guard left town this evening. They're tramping out among the hills after your lover boy and his friends. Nearly all of the guardsmen went out with the captain. I hear they got a tip. One of our boys was around to see them hustle off. So we're safe here until tomorrow, maybe longer."

"And did you provide the tip, Sunny? Did you set them after Blaze?"

Sunny pulled a bloody bandage from his left hand, revealing a wicked slash across his palm. "No, it wasn't me. I wish it had been. I would gladly sell the lot of them for two copper coins. Our people have been overwhelmed in every village from here to Kierinswell. The revolt has failed, and it's all because that stinking fish boy wouldn't lift a finger to help us."

Darnelle ripped open Lowi's blouse and began to wash her wound. Her sister didn't open her eyes. "I suppose you think I'm just as bad as them, don't you, Sunny? You wish it were me dying here on this bed instead of Lowi."

"Indeed, I do, little sister. Lowi was my right arm. I don't know how I'm going to make it without her. And you? You've turned your back on us. You're not worth my spit."

Sunny walked back to the main room. His comrades already had flopped down in the darkness. One sat with his back propped against the door. Darnelle, meanwhile, wrapped a bandage around Lowi. The wounded woman let out a few weak coughs and fell back to breathing in a slow, uneven pattern.

"She looks bad," said Tatti Oom.

"She's dying. I'm sorry, Auntie. I don't want you to get hanged. But I need to care for Lowi. She's my only sister."

"I know, child. Don't worry. We'll make her as comfortable as possible."

Early in the morning, the goat herders outside Orres rounded up their flocks and brought them in for another day's milking. As they were returning them to the fields, Blaze trotted his stallion up the main road toward the village. The sun had been up for an hour and the streets already had collected a few dozen people on the way to the market stands in the square. The grain and meat vendors already were haggling with their first customers.

Blaze stopped his horse on the edge of the square. Around it sat adobe taverns and near-windowless shops. For a moment, he looked on the passing scene: stout women in head scarves with children in hand; young men sitting idly by the town well after the hiring had ended for day workers; a toothless old man who sat nearby braiding a horsehair belt. Blaze surveyed it all and a thin smile broke across his face. He took a great bull's horn that hung off his shoulder and put it to his lips. When he blew, the blast sang wild and piercing, like a mad cow. It alarmed some and angered others, but no one in the square could ignore that high-pitched horn. Blaze dropped it to his side and once more scanned the crowd.

"I've come here looking for friends of the White Beard!" he shouted from atop his stallion. "I need your help. Are there any friends of the White Beard here in Orres?"

One of the young men took a step toward him. "There used to be," he said, "but most of them got hanged. Say, where'd you get that funny hat."

Blaze wheeled his horse a quarter turn toward the man. "The Lake People. Hear me, people! I promised the White Beard I would come to Orres and tear down the prison. Will anyone here help me tear down that jail?"

The young man laughed. "You're one crazy fool. You'd better ride out of here before somebody tells the captain of the guard. He likes to hang troublemakers."

"The captain's not here today. He's out in the hills looking for me."

The villagers began to whisper one to another. The young man cocked his head and pointed a finger at Blaze. "Who are you?"

"I'm the one the White Beard said would be coming. And today my friends and I are going to tear down that jail." Once more Blaze put the horn to his lips and winded it mightily. Then he rode slowly down the lane toward the prison.

A few villagers followed behind him, but others scattered in every direction. They ran and told their neighbors that a tall, lean stranger in a funny hat had come to stir things up. He must be the leader of that band that frees the slaves. Perhaps he really is the champion the White Beard spoke of. Perhaps he really can tear down the jail.

Blaze rode toward the prison to meet Roff and Tustin, who were waiting on their horses, their arms leaning onto the front of their saddles. "You seem to be drawing a crowd," Roff observed.

"Where's Cisly?" Blaze asked.

"She's around. I bet she doesn't know what to make of all this. She must think you're either a genius or an idiot."

"She'll be alright." Blaze climbed off his horse, took the horn's strap off his shoulder and handed it to Roff. "Wait for my signal, then blow it one more time."

"How are your nerves?"

"I'll be twitching soon enough. Just be ready. If the guards don't start trouble, the villagers may try to."

Back at Tatti Oom's hut, Lowi had died in the night. Sunny wouldn't remove her body—not until dark, he growled. He also refused to let the two women leave the hut. But that morning one of his men came rushing back through the door. "Something's up. There's talk of an attack on the jail. It sounds like it's your sister's friends. The whole town's going down there to watch."

"Well, isn't this sweet?" said Sunny. "Let's go see what's up. Darnelle, you're coming with us. Maybe we'll get a chance to settle a grudge with those jailers. Think how many of our boys they've tortured. I'd love to stick a blade in some of them." He grabbed his sister's arm and thrust her out the door. The others followed.

In the street, Blaze stepped up to the two-story adobe jail. A fence of iron bars with an iron gate protected its front entrance. Behind the bars stood a stiff-lipped guard. For the past few minutes the man had anxiously observed the gathering crowd. As Blaze drew near, he raised his spear and called fiercely, "That's far enough! What do you want?"

Blaze stopped and leaned on his staff. "Tell the sergeant that the horse hunter who saved Pens' life is here. Tell him my people and I have come to take over the jail. Tell him I don't want a fight. If you all will go in peace, I'll stand before you as a shield to help you get safely over to the Elder's compound."

"Tell him yourself if you can get past these metal bars," the guard replied. With his shield before him he backed up to two large doors of bundled sticks that stood on the other side of the bars. He kept his eyes on the crowd as he opened the doors, stepped inside and closed them tight. Blaze turned and signaled to Roff. Immediately his cousin took the horn and gave a blast that made up in volume what it lacked in clarity. The crowd once more froze, straining for some answer to the call. For a few moments the people noted only silence. But soon came the sounds of hooves and jingling harnesses, seemingly from every direction. A minute later a team of horses came into view, four stout, dark creatures harnessed two by two with a rider on the left lead animal. Another foursome trotted around a corner, then others. They kept coming until seven teams had assembled in the square in front of the jail. Quickly the teamsters joined the animals together—a formation of twenty-eight dark horses paired up with a single rider to guide them all. Two other horsemen rode forward with a huge chain. Blaze took it and wrapped the links around the iron gate at the jail's front entrance. Next he attached the chain to the back of the great team. Stepping back, he raised his arm and motioned to the teamster atop the lead animal. The man nudged the team of twenty-eight forward until the chain pulled taut. The gate came under strain and with a pop crashed off its hinges.

The crowd roared its approval as Blaze stepped forward and rapped his staff against the two front doors woven from willowy sticks. "Let me to talk to the sergeant!" he shouted. A moment later a bolt creaked and the doors opened. The sergeant stuck out his old gray head.

"Hello, boy," he said. "I thought it might be you. You're going to be one sad MuKierin when the Elders catch up with you."

"Good morning, sergeant. I want you to leave this place in peace. Give me the keys to the jail and you can walk away. Will you do that for me?"

"Will you guarantee us safe passage?"

"My men and I will serve as a shield to help you get past the crowd. From there you should be able to make it the rest of the way safely to the Elder's compound."

"Alright, give me a moment to gather up my men. They've heard how you touch guards with your magic stick and drive them crazy. You've got them plenty scared. That's kind of funny cause you still look like that frightened boy who turned all pale that day when you stood near all those corpses on that battlefield. Anyway, all I ask is that you help us get past this crowd. Hopefully the captain will send someone else after you." The sergeant nodded once for emphasis and shut the door.

Near the edge of the crowd, Sunny and his comrades arrived and began to hover and dart around like beasts of prey. "It looks like a jailbreak, alright," Sunny said to Darnelle. "And there's your lover boy." He pointed to Tustin, who was holding the crowd back at a place close to the jail. "Let's make that our point of attack, brothers. Now Darnelle, you listen to me. In a minute I'm going to send you over there to lover boy. I could not care less how you do it, but you get him out of there. I want him out of my way so I can kill a guard or two. If he stays put, I'll kill him and you and the ol' woman back at the hut, too. You know I will. Now get over there and move him. Quick!"

Out from the doors the sergeant and the guards began to emerge. The crowd roared twice, first with astonishment and then with derision, as the sergeant handed Roff the keys to the prison. Blaze recognized one of the guards passing by. "Pens, you've recovered well from your wound. May I borrow your shield?"

Pens squinted defiantly. "If I give it up, you must agree that I've repaid my debt to you."

"As you wish," said Blaze, taking the shield. "Just stay behind me, all of you. You may not be out of danger yet."

Darnelle ran sobbing to Tustin. Astonished, he planted his staff and put an arm around her. "Please!" she cried, "Sunny is coming this way. He and his friends will kill you if you stay here. Please run and save yourself."

Tustin looked up to see Sunny and three other men approaching. He pushed Darnelle away and lifted his staff to defend himself. "Go to Blaze! Warn him!"

"No! There's no time."

Even as she spoke, the first attacker crashed into Tustin, knocking him to the ground and wrestling with him for control of the staff. Darnelle stepped into the gap, hoping to prevent anyone else from attacking her friend. One of the other rebels pushed her away and flung a knife at the guards. Another conspirator stepped up and threw a second knife. But Blaze stood in their way. Lifting Pen's shield, he swung it so fast that it deflected first one blade, then the other. As the weapons crashed to the ground, Sunny howled in fury. He grabbed Darnelle by the arm and plunged his knife into his sister. "That's for leaving Lowi and me!" Darnelle collapsed as Sunny raced off. The man wrestling with Tustin broke away, too. Together, the four insurrectionists disappeared through an alley.

Tustin whirled around on the ground and lunged for Darnelle. She lay there clutching her wound. He took her in his arms as blood streamed from her side. "No!" he wailed. "Darnelle, Please hang on. Please!" She looked at him with tears in her eyes, gasping and unable to speak. Around them swirled chaos, but for a moment they saw only each other.

Then Blaze knelt beside them. Quickly he opened a vial and put a crystalline drop on his finger. He pressed it between her lips. "Sleep, Darnelle," he said. "Sleep and live." At once she closed her eyes and went limp. "Hold her, Tustin." Taking a knife, he sliced open her gown. From a small pouch on his belt he lifted a salve-filled bandage and gently placed it on the wound. Blaze grimaced as he pressed it against her. At once the bleeding stopped.

The sergeant walked up and peered over Blaze's shoulder. "What a wonder you are, boy," he said, shaking his head. "I've never seen such a healer. It makes me sad to think the Elders are going to track you down and hang you. What a waste."

Blaze doubled over in pain but then raised himself on his knees. "You'd better go, sergeant, while it's still safe. I need you to take care of Pens."

"Yes, I guess I better do so, son, since you saved his life a second time. Farewell, boy. I really do hope you feel better soon."

Immediately the sergeant and his guards reassembled in two columns and jogged off to the Elder's compound. As they departed, Stannis rigged up a blanket stretcher and Blaze's men placed Darnelle upon it. Tustin and three other men picked her up in order to carry her back to Tatti Oom's hut. Blaze called to Cisly, "Hold this bandage in place. It will help save Darnelle."

Cisly at once felt her hand tingle. "What's on the bandage?" she asked.

"My mother's medicine. It might make you a little dizzy. Go with the stretcher and watch over Darnelle. I'll come as soon as I can."

Back at the jail, Roff took the sergeant's keys and went inside, unlocking the huge cells that held scores of people. Soon dirty, gaunt-faced men and women emerged onto the street. They shuffled in ragged garb through the open doors and eyed the waiting crowd warily. Then one of the villagers recognized a prisoner and shouted, "Taff! Cousin!" Blaze's followers gave a cheer, and the crowd echoed it. A woman ran up to a freed sister and spirited her away. Other debtors poured forth from the prison. The square filled with the uproar of reunited kinsmen. Amid the hugs and tears, onlookers made wild gestures to explain to baffled newcomers what was happening. Nearly a thousand people had congregated outside the jail, including the freed prisoners.

Stannis brought Blaze his horse and said, "I'm glad we have wagons to help transport these folks. Most of them look too thin to walk very far."

"Yes," said Blaze. "The wagons will be easy to follow. But at least we'll have a good head start on the captain and his men. And he'll know that for now we outnumber his troops."

Upon Blaze's signal, Roff winded the horn one last time and called to the crowd: "The champion must leave soon. Anyone who wants to come along is welcome to join us. Follow Stannis here and we will take you to a safe place."

With that, the scene changed again. Most of the former prisoners shuffled after Stannis down the alley and over to a nearby street. There fifteen wagons rolled up. Six mules pulled each rig, and a gray-bearded driver held the reins of each team. The rescued ones boarded the wagons and so began a long journey east into the mountains.

Meanwhile, Roff and his men took sledgehammers and began to knock holes in the prison's adobe walls. They laced chains through the holes and hooked the chains to teams of horses. The horses heaved, the walls blew out and whole sections of the jail's second story came crashing to the ground. Quickly the wreckage grew. Roff soon wrapped a chain around a large portion of wall and beckoned to the crowd, "Come, MuKierin, come take the challenge!" He tied a long rope to the chain and nearly eighty kinsmen stepped forward to take hold of it. The crowd rallied around them as the men and women strained and tugged. They didn't stop until they had pulled down the section. As it toppled, a great cheer went up. More men and women stepped forward to take a turn with hammers and chisels.

In two hours, the jail was reduced to a great heap of broken adobe.

Kick turned to Roff and declared, "Roffie, this time the Elders are really going to come after Blaze."

"I know, cousin. He's pushed them into a corner. This time they're going to push back."

Blaze, meanwhile, rode up a lane of mud huts to Tatti Oom's home. Tustin already had made sure that Darnelle lay safely asleep in her bed. Other men had removed Lowi's corpse and taken it for burial in the village graveyard. When Blaze entered the hut, he found Tustin, Cisly and Tatti Oom huddled over the wounded woman. "Cisly," he said, "may I speak with you outside?" The two exited and walked to a space of open ground on the far side of the lane.

"Cisly, I have a hard thing to ask of you," he said. "Darnelle must stay here today and rest. She will live if we let her sleep and don't move her today. But when the captain and his guards come back to the village, my men and I must be far away. Otherwise, there will be a battle. I want to avoid that, but I don't want to leave Darnelle alone."

"You want me to stay with her."

"I do. When the captain returns, he'll likely arrest you both, especially if he learns that Darnelle's brother tried to kill some of the jailers. I want someone to stay with Darnelle. She's already been put in chains once. It was hard on her. I think she would draw comfort in having you with her."

A faint smile came to Cisly's lips. "It's been a long time since I was a comfort to anyone. Yes, Blaze, I'll stay with her. By the way, my hand still tingles from that medicine. That's what makes you sick, isn't it."

"Yes, it's part of the curse. But it saved Darnelle, thanks to my mother. I hope you'll meet her soon."

"Meet your mother? I don't know if I'm ready for that. I still don't know what to make of you. But I'll stay with this woman. I'd like to be a comfort to her. It would be nice to be needed by somebody who didn't own me."

"Thank you, Cisly. Whatever happens, I promise I'll do all I can to get you both to safety again."

Those at the hut waited until Roff and his crew finished demolishing the jail. When all came together, Blaze ordered his followers to mount up and ride away. Orres was still alive with wonder and joy over what had happened there that day. But Darnelle's wound had left Blaze ill and his men feeling somber. Tustin didn't want to leave her. "You go on without me," he told Roff. "I've got to stay here and make sure she gets better."

"She'll get better, Spider. Blaze has made sure of that. But you can't stay here. The Elder's guard will be back tonight, and they'll be looking for blood. You won't do Darnelle any good if you stay in Orres and get yourself hanged. Now come on. We're not leaving here without you."

Clenching his teeth, Tustin climbed aboard his horse and turned back to Darnelle's great-aunt. "Tatti Oom," he said, "you tell her I'm coming back for her. This isn't over. I love her, even if she doesn't love me. And I'm not going to lose her."

Chapter Seven

A Change in the Wind

At the Barsk inn, both Lon and Bar said farewell to the other cadets. Bar rode east to Kierinswell, summoned there to report to his MuKierin Elders. Lon, meanwhile, set out north for the Great Lake of the Pappi. The other cadets returned to the Academy with a still-unconscious Frissa, the young man touched by the White Gem. (When Frissa awoke two days later, he threw his sword into the Red River and shook with terror recalling the nightmares he had endured.)

Lon took Bairn's advice as delivered by Blaze and avoided the Barsk capital of Northsford. Instead, the young Pappi passed through barren hill country and around steep canyons east of the Red River. Beneath one ridge he caught sight of troops in the distance. He thought they were most likely Barsk cavalry. But the riders never spotted him, and he passed on safely to his homeland. On the afternoon of the third day he arrived at South Shore, the capital of his clan. He rode through the city and dismounted at a stone terrace that surrounded the stone walls and arched rotunda of the Pappi Council Chambers. The terrace stood atop a cliff overlooking the vast shimmering lake. Far to the right sat a row of expansive villas, many with stone fences that walled off private cliffside patios. Each villa had carved stone steps leading down to the water. It was there that the wealthy Pappi lived. Beneath both the council terrace and the great villas lay a deep blue cove.

Lon had timed his return to coincide with a summer festival known as Night of the Fishers. He hoped to see activity that day in the cove and he was not disappointed. Below the terrace, a dozen young women were wading in the shallows just off the beach. Together they had spread out a long net and were using it to trap a species of tiny fish, the trillus, a prized delicacy of the Pappi. "Yes!" Lon exulted.

"I've come in time. Now which one of those beauties is going to feed me tonight?"

He abandoned his horse and scooted down a steep trail to the rocky cove. There, in the afternoon sun, he pulled off his boots and unbuckled the wide, black belt that held his sword. He rolled up the legs of his black pantaloons and waded out. Sloshing awkwardly forward, he made his way to the young women, who had hitched up their skirts and formed a great arc in the cove.

"Lon, you're late," one female called to him.

"Yes, gentle lady, I am," he said. "Even so, I offer you all my humble service. Have pity on me, ladies. It's been nearly a year since I tasted a bowl of fish-eye soup, or nibbled on even a morsel of anything with fins or scales. Please let me join you. I promise to refrain from eating anything until it is cooked—if I can control myself."

The women giggled and made room so the curly-headed, young man could join them on the net. Lon wrapped a foot into one of the toeholds fastened to the bottom of the finely knitted mesh. Slowly the semi-circle of women moved toward shore. As they waded closer together, the blue-green waters roiled with hundreds of tiny, silver fish, each one vying for some means of escape. "Ah, sisters!" Lon exclaimed. "Behold the trillus. Only the Pappi know such delights. Let the other clans keep their rabbit feet and their bird wings and their roots and grubs. We have the blessings of the lake!"

Three women waded out and began to scoop the fish into a large reed basket. At the same time, a thin young man descended the terrace. He had a narrow but handsome face and a dark ponytail. He moved slowly down the steps, limping with a crutch and a bum left leg. When Lon spotted him, he left the net and splashed his way to the beach. "Sorenth!" he called and ran to his friend.

Sorenth halted. "I should have known you wouldn't miss a fish dinner," he said. "Who's going to cook it for you?"

"I haven't decided yet," said Lon, lowering his voice. "But she'll be very beautiful, I'm sure of it."

"You haven't changed."

"You're looking good, Sorenth. Look at those arms and hands. Can you still grip a sword?"

"There's little need for that around here. These days I'm a trader. At least, that's what Bairn says I am. I can't stand it, but he tells me to give it time."

"Oh, forget the trader's life. Your brother sent me to fetch you."

"Fetch me? Why? He knows the shape I'm in."

"Bo wants you back with him. I told him I would come get you. It's time, Sorenth. We're going soon to find the secret power. When your brother takes hold of it, he wants you there with us."

"And what about the headmaster? It was Aeres that sent me home. He didn't want a cripple on his hands."

"Bo got Aeres to say 'yes' to your return. We've heard strange things about the great power, Sorenth. It may be able to heal you. That's what both Bo and Aeres think, and Bo wants to give it a try. Aeres agreed and said it's a chance worth taking. After all, he's got a bum arm. He knows what you're going through, even if he felt he had to send you home. Look, nobody knows for sure what will happen, but it might work. It might help you. Anyway, we can leave in a few days, right after I get my fill of fish-eye soup."

Sorenth shook his head. "Did anyone ever tell you that your timing is terrible?"

"What do you mean?"

"I don't think you're going anywhere."

"Why is that?"

"Well, you need to talk with Bairn. But I think the Elders plan to keep you here in South Shore."

"What? Is this because there may be war with the Barsk?"

"Yes. How'd you know?"

"I met a strange friend of Bairn—a really strange friend. Anyway, you and I need to get back to the Academy. We can't let some silly dust-up between the clans stop us now. So where's Bairn? We need to talk to him."

"He'll meet us tonight at the festival."

The two men left the sunbaked shoreline for the shade of a nearby tavern. There they stayed until evening, when at last they wandered over to the summer feast. They found a field filled with large canvas pavilions and crowded with people. There were plump cooks grilling fish over coals and wizened women weaving reed baskets. Some baskets were as small as a man's hand, but others stood tall enough for concealing a small child. Lon stopped often to banter with passers-by in the spaces among the booths and canopies. Standing with a hand resting on his sword, he especially enjoyed chatting with the young women. Sorenth usually stood off to the side, leaning on his crutch and watching the bug-eyed girls josh with and quiz his handsome friend. Sorenth didn't think any less of the young women for their flirting. Life was hard, and Lon offered the prospect of a mate with a future, albeit one who seemed in no hurry to take a wife. Sorenth guessed that the girls understood that, too.

Eventually the sun drew low and campfires began to blaze around South Shore. As the first star appeared, a horn sounded, calling the people down to the crescent-shaped beach. A crowd moved down the stone steps, passing together by floating reed docks and woven reed boats lying along the gravel. Soon hundreds of Pappi had gathered around dozens of fishing boats. From the council terrace, a long line of men began to parade down the steps. Among them walked scores of fishermen, each wearing straw-colored hats with cap-like fronts and curved brims covering the backs of necks. The crowd parted to allow the fishers to reach their boats, two men to each long, narrow vessel. The people gathered round the boats, placing their hands upon the woven gunwales. For a few moments everyone grew silent, listening to the lapping of small waves that caressed the boats. Finally a voice sounded, "We bid you farewell, but we go with you!"

The crowd echoed the verse, "We go with you. We bid you farewell, but we go with you." A few moments later the first fishermen climbed into their reed vessels and shoved off, setting a course for the middle of the lake. The rest soon followed.

As the boats departed, Sorenth and Lon broke off from the crowd and made their way farther along the shore. Up ahead they spied Bairn, the trader and Pappi Elder. His bulky frame sat alone atop his beached reed boat. A single torch glowed beside him. The older man's silver hair was pulled back in a sleek ponytail, setting off his high forehead and big earlobes. From the side, it was hard to discern much definition of his features, save the gentle line of his angular cheekbones. But when he turned toward the young men, the triangular shape of his face came into view. Softened and rounded by age, his features still exuded a handsome ruggedness. Lon had long thought it was a face made for pondering weighty matters, a face able to withhold more than it displayed.

The trader arose and waved a greeting. "Welcome, boys. Care to do a little fishing?"

"I just hope I don't sink the boat," said Lon. "Bairn, I must have downed a whole pot of fish-eye soup. It was so succulent and savory that I could drink it for a thousand years and still not grow tired of it. And to top it off, I promised a certain lady that I would come around later for a second helping."

As he spoke, the men prepared the slender boat and pushed out into the lake. The reed vessel was over twenty feet in length, with a removal mast and sail that for the night was stored beneath the fishing nets. Sorenth leaned on his crutch and swung aboard, taking his place in the bow. Bairn stepped into the middle and Lon took the stern. The elder let the younger men paddle.

They ventured into deep water as darkness came over the lake. In ten minutes, the lights of South Shore had grown small behind them. Lon set his paddle across the gunwales and spoke: "Bairn, I met your MuKierin friend. He spoke excellent Pappi, and he had quite a strange encounter with one of my fellow cadets. Please tell me exactly who is he?"

"He's like a son to me, even as you and Sorenth and Bo are all my adopted sons. His name is Blaze. He grew up among us, over on the north side of the lake."

"Wait a minute," said Sorenth. "How did Lon meet this friend of yours?"

"I arranged it," said Bairn. "I needed to warn Lon not to pass through Northsford. I couldn't send a Pappi with the message. The Barsk would have followed the messenger straight to Lon. So my friend Blaze took the message for me. And in so doing he kept you from harm."

"I suppose I should thank you for that," said Lon. "But what's his game? He certainly seems a strange one."

"Does he? Perhaps, but I hope that you'll get better acquainted with him and his mother. She is a most extraordinary creature, believe me. And his father is a good man, even for a MuKierin."

"And do you believe that he's the one meant to hold a secret, great power?"

"What?" exclaimed Sorenth. "Is that what he thinks?"

"Indeed, he does," said Bairn. "And I find it refreshing to see that both of you admit knowing something about this secret power. It confirms my suspicions about Aeres and his Academy. But I'm not sure how much you really know about it. The story really belongs to the MuKierin. Their Elders still believe that a champion will arise from their people and take hold of the power. I believe Blaze is that champion, not just for the MuKierin, but for all the desert people, including the Pappi. His mother was sent here from a distant country to help all the Seven Clans. She is the daughter of a great King, and her son has chosen to carry on her work. One day he will step forward to challenge the Realm."

"So you're one of this man's followers," said Sorenth. "Does the Council know that?"

"Our leaders will know in time. There are many things they don't yet know, including the secret plans of certain cadets."

"How do you know about any secret plans?" asked Lon.

"My friend Blaze is no fool. He knows much of the Academy and the Realm.

"Perhaps he does, Bairn. But believe me when I tell you that the Academy means no harm to our clan. Indeed, we intend to help all the desert people. But to do that, I need to get back to the Academy, along with Sorenth here. That's right, Bo has sent me to bring back his brother. Will you help us?"

"I'm sorry, Lon. I can't. The Elders already have given me your orders. I've got the packet right here. You've been assigned to help in the upcoming negotiations with the Barsk."

"No, please listen, Bairn. I need to get back to the Academy. You've got to get that order changed."

"Your people also need you, Lon. The Barsk are threatening war. I suppose you can blame me. Last year I helped persuade the Council to stop sending slaves to Equis as tribute. In retaliation, the Realm has pressured Northsford, and now the Barsk are raising old claims to be given a portion of the lake. The situation looks even more desperate than it did before we signed the peace treaty. Back then the Barsk knew that the MuKierin were our allies and would come to our aid if war broke out. But now Kierinswell soon may face its own war with the Realm. If that happens, the Barsk might feel free to invade our land."

"Why would the Realm go to war against the MuKierin?" asked Lon.

"Equis fears my young friend Blaze. Its leaders have heard that the true champion has come to his people. The Realm wants to kill him before he can lay his hands on the great power. To find him, they wouldn't hesitate to attack the Horse Clan if they thought they could catch him. Until now, Blaze's grandfather the King has guarded the MuKierin. But that protection soon may end. Let's hope it doesn't, for all our sakes."

Stars in their multitude shone overhead when the three Pappi beached Bairn's boat on the sand at South Shore. The two younger men hopped out and said farewell to the trader. Lon quickly took the lead.

"Slow down," called Sorenth, as his crutch planted deep in sand with each stride. "I can't go any faster here."

"What am I going to do now?" asked Lon.

"You don't have much choice. You're going to stay here, as ordered."

"But I need to get back to the Academy."

"You can't. Think what would happen if you left South Shore. Our commander would order you chased down and hanged for desertion. And even if our troops didn't catch you, you would draw unwanted attention to Bo and all the other cadets. Why, the Realm's spies might even hear about your desertion and wonder what the Academy is up to. The mission might fail because of you. You can't leave here."

"This is crazy! I don't want to miss out on this great campaign. We're about to unleash an amazing power and overthrow all those tyrants of Equis. But I'm supposed to stay back here and guard the frontier. It's not fair."

"Is there any message you want me to give Bo?"

"What? You beast! Do you intend to go south without me?"

"Well, one of us should get back to the Academy so they know what happened to you. You said Bo wants to play the healer on me. I'm happy to give that a try. And I'm not under any orders to stay here. I'm a civilian. They still don't take cripples in our army."

That night Sorenth wasted no time. He grabbed his sword and a few items, and rode off with Lon's black stallion. He decided it was too dangerous to enter Northsford or even to retrace his friend's route east of the river. Both routes were likely now guarded. Instead, he chose to swing west through the land of the Quolli, the clan of robbers and nomads southwest of the lake. Such a journey would take a little more time, but it would allow him to avoid the Barsk lands. Even so, he realized that as a lone traveler he would be a temptation to the Quolli. The clan's young men were always looking for someone to rob or capture for the slave trade. Sorenth wanted to avoid these thieves, if possible, and yet he knew he might have to visit some Quolli villages for water.

He decided he would try to do so in the heat of the day when the men would be more prone to napping and less prepared for visitors.

From the lake, he crossed into a land of dry, rolling hills and desolate valleys. On the second day, he made for a former Barsk trading post in the hill country. It featured a good well set up against a cliff. Its very location beneath the hilltop made it difficult to defend, and the Barsk had abandoned it due to constant harassment by the Quolli. The thieves never openly attacked the place, but they would hide in the rocks beneath the cliff and steal every horse, blanket and tool that was left untended for even a few moments. Sorenth had passed by the abandoned post once before with Lon and his brother Bo. The three swordsmen had made it through that country unmolested. But now Sorenth was traveling alone, and he knew a single rider would appear a more inviting target.

As such, he approached the trading post with his crutch strapped to his back and his right hand free to grasp his sword. He rode slowly past the first broken-down outbuilding—now little more than two partially collapsed walls. The adobe trading post itself was hardly in better condition, with its roof caved in and all the doors and windows gone. Sorenth saw no movement and heard nothing but his stallion's hooves.

He rode toward the well, which lay hidden behind a clump of tall, dun boulders. Behind one such rock, he caught sight of a sheet of goatskins that had been set up as a makeshift wall. What was it for? He tugged firmly on the rein and brought the stallion to a halt. He expected silence. Instead, he heard a woman's song, a gentle hum, followed by words in a tongue he didn't understand. Next came a rising trill and a few more lyrics. The stallion advanced a few steps. Sorenth didn't notice. He was too perplexed.

Is the woman behind those skins? Is she alone? Doesn't she realize I'm here? How can she stay so calm with a stranger at hand?

The singer's voice drifted into a lullaby. Sorenth finally saw how close his horse had brought him to the boulders. Once more he pulled back on the reins. He glanced up to the towering cliff overhead and the layers of dun rock beneath it. Nothing stirred, but he didn't like it. The columns of stone and the rubble rising before him offered too many hiding places. He backed the stallion up a few more feet.

There was no way he could get to the well without encountering the woman. There was no way he could learn whether she was alone without dismounting and walking around the wall of skins. Many men would have been enticed to do just that, to satisfy their curiosity, to see if they really were alone with a sweet-sounding woman. But Sorenth had a bum leg, and he was not inclined to get off his horse. He chose to sit tight.

As he waited, trouble came silently at him. Men sprang forth from both sides of the boulders, a half dozen in all. Sorenth saw them and swung his stallion around to retreat. Even as he did, two of the men advanced twirling lassos. They hurled their ropes as the great horse sprang away. One loop caught the stallion's front right leg. Three men clamped onto the rope and slid to a stop, crouching and waiting. The rope went taut and the stallion buckled, crashing headfirst into the dust and rolling sideways. Sorenth flew overhead. His mind recalled visions of an earlier spill that had left him with a crushed left leg.

This time he landed free of his animal and generally unharmed. His attackers raced at him, hoping to pounce before their victim could rise up. But Sorenth had tucked his head and somersaulted upon impact. His crutch strap broke as he rolled sideways over both it and his sword. He raised himself onto his knees and drew his sword. The first robber coming at him saw the great blade but couldn't stop his own forward motion. Sorenth aimed and skewered the man's thigh. Quickly the young Pappi pulled the sword back as the robber fell, shrieking. His comrades collided into him as they pulled up.

The robbers stepped back and spread out. As they did, Sorenth slid on his knees over to his crutch. He counted five adversaries, two with swords. The rest held knives.

"Cripple!" a swordsman yelled in the Common Tongue. "We see your crutch. Give up, cripple, or you'll regret it. We'll castrate you. Then you'll really be less than a man."

Sorenth said nothing but grinned, making sure his teeth showed. The Quolli swordsman sneered. "Very well. Let's cut off his manhood!" Slowly the robbers circled. They made one whole revolution before the two swordsmen attacked, one on each side. The others held back, and Sorenth saw an opportunity. He feinted toward the swordsman on his right, forcing the man back. Then the former cadet turned left toward the robber leader, the loudmouth who'd berated him. The Quolli attacker raised his blade in preparation for the approaching sword. But Sorenth had a different attack in mind. With his left hand, he slammed his crutch low into the Quolli's shin. The loudmouth screamed and toppled over. As he did, the second swordsman resumed his advance. But he wasn't quick enough. Sorenth's sword blocked the thief's clumsy blow, and his crutch whirled round and tripped the man as he stepped back in too hasty a retreat. Down he went. Now Sorenth attacked. Sliding on his knees, he pierced the robber's right hand. The Quolli howled and released his sword. Sorenth advanced and set his blade against his enemy's throat. "Hold still or I'll slit your throat," he told his captive.

From outside his vision, Sorenth heard a woman's scream. He didn't dare look at her. Instead, he pressed his blade against his victim and glanced toward the other thieves. "Nobody move," he warned in the Common Tongue, "or this one dies." With a slight tilt of his head, he scanned from left to right. The man with the wounded leg was still down, leaning on an elbow. The loudmouth was sneering but standing at least five paces back. The others were staring with their mouths agape. Sorenth saw it as a good sign and made his first demand. "Throw me my crutch. Gently." One of the robbers obeyed. Sorenth grabbed the crutch and the captured sword and placed them beneath him. "Now bring me my horse."

"No," said the loudmouth. "We're not letting you get away."

"You boys may want to think this over. You've got a man over there bleeding to death. I've got two swords and this man's life in my hands. You come at me and I'll have to kill him. Is that what you want? Or will you trade me my horse for this man's life?"

The woman began to implore the men. Sorenth took his first look at her. She was young and pretty, with a simple brown dress and long blonde hair pulled in a ponytail. He didn't understand her words, and he couldn't tell if she was calling for an attack or a deal. A few robbers shouted back at her. Finally, the loudmouth barked in the Common Tongue: "You stinking Pappi. You will regret this day. I promise you."

"Oh, I already do regret it. Believe me, I do. But are we going to just sit here all day in this hot sun? If that's your plan, you might want to tie a rag around your friend's leg. Otherwise, his death is going to be on your head, not mine."

In response, the wounded man cried out to the woman. She ran to him and wrapped a shawl around his blood-soaked leg. After she tied it tight, she looked over at Sorenth. The two gazed stone-faced at one another. Sorenth called, "Tell the woman she can bring another rag for this man's hand. I won't hurt her."

The robbers debated the offer. The woman raised her voice, seemingly to demand an explanation. The loudmouth barked at her, but she dismissed him with a wave of her hand. She ran out of sight and returned a minute later with a great strip of cloth. With caution she approached Sorenth and slowly knelt beside him in order to wrap her kinsman's wounded hand. Sorenth kept his eyes and his blade on his prisoner. But when the woman again rose, he looked up and gave her an approving nod. She kept her own face blank.

She's the one here with the smarts and the guts, Sorenth thought. She'd be the best leader among them, if she were a man.

Once the woman returned to the shade of the rocks, the untouched robbers drew together and talked in low voices.

Sorenth could guess the dialogue. They were in a standoff, and nobody could see a way out. They had sought to catch a man and sell him to the slave trade. They had managed to capture his horse, but they couldn't see any way now to get the man. If they attacked, the stranger would kill their comrade. That would be bad, because as Quolli they then would be duty bound to never rest until they had killed him or died trying. There was no profit in such work. And right now those four didn't look like they really wanted to test whether they could kill one desperate Pappi swordsman.

Sorenth figured that three of the thieves might be willing to cut some face-saving deal, but not the loudmouth. *He's not going to let it go. He thinks too much of himself to let you get the better of him. You may have to kill him. Don't want to do that unless there's no other way. If you do, the others will never stop chasing you. Never.*

An hour passed. Sorenth figured he would wait perhaps another hour and then force his prisoner onto his feet and march him back toward South Shore. It wasn't much of a plan, but it was better than sticking around here until dark. At least he could hope the loudmouth might make a mistake and get close enough that he could be killed with the flick of a knife.

Something in the distance caught the robbers' attention. At first, two of them stood and pointed. Soon all of them began to jump and wave. Sorenth cautiously turned to look out on the sage flats. He caught sight of three riders on dark horses. Sure enough, they were headed this way. The four Quolli were smiling from ear to ear. "Look there, cripple," yelled the loudmouth. "We have friends coming. You'd better let our kinsman go now. Otherwise, you're a dead man."

Sorenth put up a brave front. "Maybe I am a dead man, but I still don't see how three more fellas can keep me from killing this boy here. Who knows? Maybe they can help talk some sense into your heads so that nobody has to die today."

The riders kept coming. After a minute, the expressions on the robbers' faces turned puzzled. They began to look at one another and whisper. One closed his eyes and shook his head. Sorenth again turned to his left. What he saw caused him to groan, "Oh, no!"

The riders weren't Quolli. They were of the Dark Brood, three giants from Equis. They caught sight of Sorenth and slapped their horses into a brisk trot, then a gentle canter. The robbers huddled together and tried not to stare at the approaching warriors. They didn't run, presumably because they feared that would be an invitation to an execution. Sorenth rose on his knee and shifted the extra sword closer to his captive, the better to hide it. "Stay still and live," he warned the man. "Don't make me kill you."

The riders halted their mounts about ten steps away from the Pappi and his prisoner. The biggest of the three, a hulk with flowing red hair and beard, waved his arm and declared, "What do we have here? A little combat? A little treachery? Very nice. I'm sorry to break up this fun." He dismounted but didn't advance. "Hello, Sorenth. That's your name, isn't it, boy? We were starting to think we might not find you."

"How do you know who I am?"

"Wouldn't you like to know, sonny boy? It'll all become clear soon enough."

"Great lords!" interrupted the loudmouth. "We found this stinking Pappi for you. Will you give us something for him?"

The red beard glared at the robber. "Give you something? That's rich. Listen, worm, I don't pay losers. I eat them." He looked back at the Pappi. "Sorenth, you go right ahead and kill that Quolli vermin that you've got a hold of. My chums and I haven't eaten all day and we're mighty starved. If you like, we'll even let you nibble on a finger or a toe. And then we'll leave this place with you."

The captive jerked his head up and cried, "No, please!"

Sorenth pushed him down. "Remember what I said. Don't make me kill you."

The red beard drew his sword. "Do you need some help, Sorenth?"

Sorenth thought, *This is bad. He knows you. You've got to make him kill you! For Bo and the others. Don't let them take you alive!* Aloud, he said as cool as possible, "Yeah, I could use a hand up. I'm a cripple, you know."

The hulking warrior strode forward while his comrades waited on their horses. Sorenth's left hand slowly grasped his sword by the blade as it lay across his captive's chest. When the red beard drew close, Sorenth flung his sword backhand at his adversary's leg. The warrior could see it coming and swatted it aside with his blade. What he couldn't see was the other sword, which Sorenth grabbed with his right hand and thrust forward with all the ferocity he could muster. Both swordsmen had little time but to take aim at one another. The red beard caught Sorenth in the left shoulder. But the young Pappi, so willing to take a mortal blow, managed a seemingly impossible feat. He drew the blood of a giant, driving his blade into his enemy just above the right knee. The warrior howled so loud that the Quolli robbers fell to the ground and covered their faces.

The scream also sent a shudder through the two mounted giants. "Don't kill him!" they yelled as they jumped down from their horses.

The red beard, however, was preparing to decapitate his opponent. Screaming and cursing, he raised his sword. But as he did, an arrow zipped down from a crevice in the cliff. The missile pierced the great warrior's armor and heart. He convulsed and collapsed at Sorenth's feet.

The two other warriors slid to a stop and turned toward the cliff. Both saw the torso of a distant figure. Another arrow shot forth. A second giant fell.

The third warrior managed to turn and race back to his stallion. But as he sprang into his saddle, an arrow struck him high in the back. He slumped onto his mount's neck and tumbled off as the creature galloped away.

The three warriors twitched in the dust and expired. The Quolli robbers, including Sorenth's former captive, rose and dashed for the old trading post. They left behind their kinsman with the wounded leg. The Quolli woman also began to flee. But she stopped when she caught sight of the archer. It was a tall woman with dark short hair and a simple beige gown. With quick short strides she raced toward Sorenth.

"Yawnna!" the archer called to the young woman in the Quolli tongue. "Help me save these wounded men."

"How do you know my name?" the Quolli woman asked.

"Silence, child. Come help me save this Pappi and your kinsman." The archer knelt beside Sorenth and pressed a cloth against his wound.

Yawnna knelt beside her. "It's bad, lady. He's lost so much blood."

"Hold this rag and press it against him." The archer took a small vial from a pouch. She splashed its contents on her finger and pressed her hand to Sorenth's lips. "Taste this, child, and live." Sorenth briefly resisted but once the liquid touched his tongue, he sighed and fell asleep.

The archer next pulled from her pouch a jar of dark salve. She had Yawnna exposed his shoulder, allowing her to smear the goopy cream across his wound. At once the bleeding stopped. The stranger retrieved a bandage and wrapped it around Sorenth's shoulder and chest.

"Who are you?" Yawnna asked.

"Not now, child. Listen to me. Your kinsmen have run off to get their donkey cart. Go find them. They won't leave without you. Tell them I don't want to hurt them, but they must come with the cart if we are to save the life of your kinsman. We must all leave this place before any more evil ones arrive."

Yawnna obeyed, running off while the archer went to the Quolli with the wounded leg. Once more she tipped her vial and placed its contents on the man's tongue, rendering him unconscious. Once more she spread dark salve and tied bandages around bloodied flesh. When finished, she returned to Sorenth and placed his head in the shadow of her own body.

Soon came the sound of jangling harnesses and creaking wheels. A team of two donkeys approached, pulling a cart. Yawnna drove it, as the male robbers trotted alongside. Even as they drew near, a new wonder appeared: A great, white mare trotted up the trail behind the Quolli. The riderless horse had a shining coat and a simple bridle and saddle. It brushed past the robbers and came to a stop by the archer.

"That's unnatural," one robber muttered.

The archer rose and stepped away from Sorenth. She lifted her bow but made no effort to set an arrow in the string as the robbers stopped before her.

"We've come for our kinsman," said the loudmouth. "We'll take him and be on our way."

The female warrior said nothing but gazed over the men. Only the loudmouth dared look her in the eye, and even his glance broke when she fixed her stare on him. At last, she spoke in Quolli, "Both of these wounded men are going to your village in that cart."

"No," the loudmouth protested. "We don't want that cripple. You take him. We'll go our own way."

"No. He must go with you. If he dies, you will die. If he lives, you will live. Today you have made yourselves enemies of the Realm. You will be blamed for the death of these three warriors here. When they fail to return to their masters, the evil ones will send more of their kind to look for them. They will find you and torture you and kill you for what happened here today. And they won't stop there. They'll kill everyone in your village. They won't care how much you profess your innocence. If you want to save yourselves and your kinsmen, you will do as I say. You will help me get both these wounded men to your village. And then I will remove these dead ones so that no one suspects that you played a role in their demise. Now, load these two wounded men into the cart and gather up the horses and put the bodies over their saddles."

That ended the negotiations. Without a word, the robbers obeyed. They caught the three warriors' horses and loaded the gigantic corpses onto the animals. At the woman warrior's direction, the men led those horses east toward the great lake in order to leave tracks away from the trading post. Once they found rocky ground, the Quolli circled back west toward home and caught up with the donkey cart, which by that time was bouncing slowly along with Sorenth and the wounded robber both sleeping inside.

The party traveled through the night, passing over a rough trace worn more by pack animals than wagons. Yawnna sat in the donkey cart beside the sleeping invalids. The loudmouth rode Sorenth's horse, while the other men walked and led the dead warriors' horses. The archer took up the rear on her white mare.

They made one brief halt that night. The robbers collapsed among sagebrush in a little basin, while the woman warrior put new salve on the wounds of the two men in the cart. Yawnna came to her and asked, "Lady, are you a kinswoman of this Pappi?"

"No, I am his protector."

"His protector? But why do you care for him?"

"He is my charge. I serve a great King. He wants this man to better know the Quolli."

"To better know us? But he hates us."

"Perhaps. And perhaps you hate him. And perhaps all of you have much to learn."

"Lady, please tell me your name."

"Call me Aidyn. Now get your men up. We need to get to your village by daybreak."

The robbers grumbled, but they rose and resumed the tramp through a starry night. As their neared the village, Aidyn gave Yawnna her horse and sent her ahead. "Go to your father," she said. "Bring him to me. We'll wait for him on the rise to the west of the large corrals.

Yawnna rode ahead, and the robbers brought the cart to a high point overlooking the village. There they halted as the eastern sky turned pale from the approaching dawn.

Before them sat a village of two hundred people. Its adobe homes and servant huts were nestled against a small mount. The Quolli used the hill as a natural fortress, with protected caves built into the rocky slopes.

When Yawnna returned on the white mare, a short, pudgy man strode beside her. The man had bulging cheeks, a scraggly black beard and dark eyes, through which he squinted to get a better look at the woman warrior on the hill.

"Give me the Pappi's horse," Aidyn told the loudmouth. "You don't want the Realm to find it here. Now stay here." Aidyn led Sorenth's stallion and the three horses carrying the corpses down to the pudgy man and his daughter. Yawnna dismounted, handed Aidyn the reins to the mare and walked back up the hill to the donkey cart. From there she and the young Quolli men watched silently as a strange parley began between the tall, slender archer and the short, stubby father. Aidyn lifted the head of one of the corpses. She pointed to the robbers and the village. And she reached out and placed something small in the older man's palm. When she was finished, she called the other Quolli down.

"We have reached an understanding," she announced. "You will take the Pappi to one of Ciga's huts. I have painted my hand on its door. Let me show you which one."

She fitted an arrow in her bow and drew back. For a few moments she stood frozen, holding her aim in confident expectation. When she released, the arrow soared more than two hundred paces toward the village. In the early morning light the Quolli couldn't see where it had landed. Aidyn lowered the bow and turned to the young men. "When someone asks you why you must not kill this Pappi or betray him to the Realm, you will show them that arrow. And you will tell them these words: 'The warrior who put the arrow in this door told us that if the Pappi lives, we will live. If he dies, we will die. If we value our lives, we will obey her. In time, we all will see that she spoke true."

Aidyn mounted the white mare and trotted away, leading off all the horses and the corpses on them.

Yawnna's father watched her for a minute before turning back to the village. The loudmouth called to him, "Wait, Ciga! Do you intend to take in this stinking Pappi?"

"Have you a better plan?"

"Yes, let's take him far away and dump him in the desert."

"Don't be stupid," said Ciga.

"But Equis wants him. You can't give him refuge here. If you do, you will put us all at risk."

"And whose fault is it that he's here? You're the fools that brought this ill fortune upon our village. I'm just trying to find a way to keep us all from getting killed. If this Pappi dies, how will you protect us from that woman? If we keep him alive, she has promised to take the dead giants' bodies far away so the Realm doesn't suspect your part in their deaths. And if he dies, our whole village will face destruction."

"There must be some other way. I hate this stinking Pappi."

"Fool! I hate him, too. What does that matter? You just make sure that no one here hurts him or tries to sell him to the Realm. If those giants ever show up here, they surely will find out that you all were there when the three warriors died. For that grievance alone, they would kill all of us. Make no mistake, they would slit your throats and eat your bodies for dinner. No, we will do as I promised the fierce woman. We will keep this Pappi alive, and she will take the three corpses far away."

The loudmouth drew a step closer. "What did she give you?"

"Wouldn't you like to know? That is between her and me. Now get this cart to my place. We will put the Pappi in one of my slave quarters."

The young men and the donkey cart proceeded into the village as the sun's orange rim pushed above the horizon. Ciga halted and touched his daughter's hand. "Child, if you are wrong about this woman, it will be the death of us."

"She will be true to her word, Father. I know she will. Isn't she a wonder? I don't believe that she would ever be the one to harm us. Even so, we must listen to her warning. If we kill the Pappi, I believe that somehow it would cause our destruction."

"I wish I could trust her like you do, shy one. However, I have my own reasons for obeying her. Look what she gave me." He reached into his pouch and pulled out a small blue gem. "Don't tell anyone about it. I've never seen one so beautiful. It must be worth one hundred slaves. She gave it to me in payment for the wounded one's care. And she promised another one just like it when she comes to claim him. What a strange woman. She obviously doesn't know the value of one Pappi."

They caught up with the donkey cart. After the night's journey, the young men's feet were dragging. Their shoulders slouched as they approached the slave quarters. But their hearts jumped when they drew near the door.

"Look at that!" one called.

At eye level on the face of the door, a green hand had been imprinted. It seemed to be traced from a woman's right hand, with long fingers and a narrow palm. And in the middle of that print sat the arrow that Aidyn had fired from outside the village.

"That's impossible," cried the loudmouth. "It's a trick. Nobody could shoot like that."

"Yes, I'm sure the three dead ones from Equis would agree," replied Ciga. "Just don't let anyone touch that arrow. Any time you young ones get some stupid idea about this stinking Pappi, you just come over here to look at it and remember what the fierce woman said. Let's not put her bow to the test."

Chapter Eight

Fire Mountain

Tustin rode with red eyes and a lathered horse. The mount was splattered with white sweat, but its rider didn't let up a swift pace until he had returned to Blaze's camp above Orres. Once there, Tustin jumped down and ran to the mess tent where Blaze and Roff were eating dinner. He handed Blaze a small parchment scroll. "They've arrested Darnelle and Cisly," he said. "They left this note with Tatti Oom."

Blaze took the scroll and broke its red seal. The message read:

"To the One called Blaze. You are hereby summoned to appear before the National Council of the Sovereign Commonwealth of the MuKierin and to answer charges of the inquisitor who accuses you, namely the Counsel Shutoo of Orres. This warrant summons you to appear on the first day of the next month, upon the place known as Fire Mountain in the magistracy of Kierinswell.

"At such time you will hear the accusations against you and be allowed to make your defense. The Council demands your presence.

"In order to gain your compliance with this order, be advised that the Council now holds in its charge two women believed to be your accomplices in treason. If you fail to appear, the Council stands ready to try them in your place.

"Witness my signature and the Seal of the National Council.

Joanus Sokkus, Sergeant At Arms"

Blaze handed the letter to Roff. He read it and sighed. "Well, at least we know the kind of men we are dealing with. They take women as hostages."

Tustin put both his hands on the table and leaned in to Blaze. "What are you going to do?"

"I'm going to go to Fire Mountain," said Blaze.

"What?" said Roff. "That sounds a little risky."

"It's time, Roff. Tustin, get a fresh horse and ride back to Orres. I'll give you a note to leave with Tatti Oom. It will assure the Council that I'll appear for trial. After you deliver it, Roff and I will meet up with you outside of Orres. The three of us will ride north together."

Lord Mackadoo exited a small meeting room and emerged into the still night air. He strode across the darkened yard of an outpost of the Realm in the eastern wild lands of the Barsk. A few torches lit the way. The lord smiled when he noticed his chief underling standing by their horses. "Sergeant," he said, "you've shaved your head."

The sergeant nodded and ran a palm across his bald top. "I took a vow."

"Did you? Something tells me it involves our old gasbag. Truly I look forward to the day you can fulfill such an oath. But now we have work to do. We need to assemble an assassination team."

"How many archers?"

"Four. We're going after a new target, the enemy's Champion. Somehow the archers have to get through the enemy lines and into the hills above Kierinswell. You can guess who's been selected to lead them there."

The sergeant cursed. "Do we have to send that scumbag on another mission?"

"I'm afraid so. After all, Backstabber did manage to bring in the White Beard."

"He did that with the enemy's help. I'm sure of it. And his head already is so big that it almost blocks out the sun. Do you really think he has The Powers?"

"Him? Of course not. But somehow he does manage to get through the enemy lines and back again. Don't worry. We'll send Rakmah along to keep an eye on him. And to be safe, we won't be relying on Backstabber alone to get this job done. Our leaders soon will mass our troops along the MuKierin border. We'll make the enemy stationed there turn their gaze our way and take us seriously. Moreover, if the assassination team fails, things may get interesting."

"How interesting?"

"We might just invade the Horse Clan. Keep that to yourself for now. But it does show how much our leaders want to end the threat of this so-called champion. We've heard he's got a weakness. Our spies say he gets sick at the sight of blood. We'll soon give him a river of it."

That same night Healdin woke her husband from a restless sleep. The two lay in a cave in the high country east of Kierinswell. "Roj," she said, stroking his shoulder, "the time has come. You must go to Blaze at Fire Mountain. He's going to need your help." She rose to a smoldering fire and lit a candle.

Roj rubbed sleepy eyes. "What about you?"

"I must stay here. I fear that Blaze is going to suffer much at the hands of your kinsmen. If I were there, I might not be able stop myself from destroying them all."

"Maybe you should destroy them all. Maybe they deserve it. We can't let them kill our son."

"I know. But you must trust me on this, for the sake of your people. My servant Mirri will take you in secret to the mount. You must leave now and travel in darkness. Much is now in motion. Pibbibib and Weakling are on the move, too. Yes, the evil ones are hoping to kill Blaze at his trial. Moreover, the Dark Brood is preparing to invade your land. Until now, the King's warriors have held them back. But your Elders now stand on a precipice. If they reject the champion, darkness will fall on the MuKierin. The King will remove his hand and the Realm will conquer your people. Let us hope the Elders choose another way. But now you must leave me. Together we must do what we can to help Blaze pass through the fire."

Roj dressed and wrapped his gear inside a canvas tarp. "I'm ready," he said.

"There is one last thing," said Healdin. "You must put these on me." She handed him a set of chains and shackles. He studied them and realized they had recently been attached to the cave's rock walls.

"What do you mean? I don't understand."

"I have removed Mara and placed it safely out of my reach. But when Blaze is threatened, I will still be too tempted to use it. Even from so far away I might do much destruction. You must help me, Roj. You must put these chains on me so that I cannot kill Blaze's opponents. Please."

"Is there no other way?"

"No, my love. It is only for a time. Once Blaze is safe, you will come back and free me. It would pain my people too much to place these chains on my hands and feet. Please do this for me."

Roj shook his head. "I'm so sorry, Healdin. I'm sorry for what my people have done to you, and I'm sorry for what they want to do to our son."

On a breathless afternoon at the end of summer, Bar MuBarishta rode alone to Fire Mountain. As he drew near, he noticed nearly one hundred cavalrymen camped about a half mile away along the road to Kierinswell. When he arrived at the mount, he passed several squads of soldiers lounging among tents at its base. Bar rode to a sentry and presented his papers. Soon the gray-haired prison sergeant from Orres trudged down the hill to meet him.

"This way, sir," the sergeant called out. "I was sent here to fetch you up the hill."

Bar dismounted, grabbed his sword's scabbard with his left hand and began to follow the old man. "Excuse me, sergeant," he said. "Is some trouble expected?"

The sergeant stopped and squinted back at him. "You haven't been around here lately, have you, son?"

"No, I've been living south beyond the Barsk. I'm not sure what this is all about. Can you tell me why I've been brought here?"

"No, son. That's for others to say. But we might see some trouble. The Elders certainly aren't taking any chances. They want to be ready if the guest of honor does show up tonight."

"And who is this guest of honor?"

"Well, that depends on who you ask. Some say he's a freedom fighter. Some say he's a traitor. And some say he's the great one, the champion. Maybe tonight we'll find out exactly who he is."

Bar's eyebrows rose. "Did you say 'champion'? Is he a young horse hunter?"

"Yes, he is. So have you heard of him?"

"Not exactly, but I may have briefly met him."

Together the two men climbed a path that circled halfway round the mount. From atop the plateau, Bar stood and looked south across the long valley. The sergeant noticed and pointed. "Tonight he'll most likely arrive from that direction, riding up from Orres, my hometown. Rest here, son. You can sit and contemplate what's to come."

Bar plopped down on a stone seat beneath a small canopy. For several minutes he watched servants hauling up leggy branches of scrub brush to a great fire ring. The workers eventually built up two large piles on either side. An hour later Shutoo arrived, adorned in a black tunic. The counsel of Orres made straight for the cadet. "Master Bar," he said, "how good to see you. I'm pleased that your headmaster Aeres allowed you to spend a few extra weeks in Kierinswell so that you could join us here tonight."

"Did Aeres have a choice?"

"No, not really. Neither did you. Now let's talk for a minute. I still have plenty to do before dark, and I expect that you want to know why you've been summoned. In short, you're here because I want your help in stopping a traitor. He'll be put on trial here tonight. If I were sure that I could get the council to condemn him, I wouldn't need your help. But I fear that even I may be unable to persuade our leaders to execute him."

"Why's that?"

"Surely you can guess. Our council is so divided that it can disagree on almost anything. I don't want to see it deadlocked tonight. Thus, I may need a solution that all the Elders can be persuaded to agree to. That's where you come in."

"I'm listening."

"The Elders may call for the traitor to be challenged in trial by combat. If so, I will ask you to represent our people. I doubt that this man will have the courage to accept your challenge. He's certainly not a warrior. He's never wielded a sword that we know of. I doubt he even knows how to use one. However, if he does accept, I have no doubt that you can kill him."

"If he's the Champion," said Bar, "he'll know how to use a sword."

"He is most definitely not the Champion. Please don't even joke like that. This man is a pansy and an impostor."

"And you want me to be his executioner. I'm not inclined for such work."

"Of course not. Few men are. But I think you will find it in your own interest to kill him, if it comes to that. You want to get back to your dear Academy, don't you? I know that your Master Aeres is most anxious for me to send you back as soon as this night ends. He makes you sound so very important. That's all fine and good, no matter that some of his reported endeavors seem a bit mysterious and perhaps even, dare I say, a little shady. But I will remind you that you are still bound by an oath to this Council and you will not be going anywhere unless the Elders release you. I was able to get the votes needed to keep you from returning to the Academy, and I have the votes to keep you here as long as it suits me. So take a little time and think things over. Your role here is crucial, and a lot of very important people will remember what you do here tonight. You don't want to disappoint them."

Shutoo turned and strode away. Bar stood and began to pace the hilltop, pondering the counsel's words. Occasionally he muttered something under his breath. All the while he kept looking around for the prison sergeant from Orres. He couldn't find him anywhere.

An hour later, Darnelle and Cisly were brought under guard up the hill. Darnelle's eyes were red, but she had stopped crying and was trying her best to look strong. The two sat down on a low boulder. Bar recognized Cisly and approached her.

"Woman, I know you," he said.

She dismissed him with a cynic's eye. "Sir, many men have known me."

"No, I mean I was there at the Barsk inn a few months back when the MuKierin horse hunter bought you."

"You mean when he set me free."

"Lady, go easy on me. I didn't ask to come here, and I'm still trying to understand what's going on.

"Then what are you doing here? This is no place for lost souls and little children."

"I've been brought here to challenge a man in mortal combat. I believe it may be your man."

"So you've come here to murder the innocent?" She nonchalantly reached down, grabbed a hefty chunk of rock and hid it beneath her skirt.

Bar failed to notice the rock. "It won't be murder," he said. "You can be sure of that. If it comes to it, he'll be given a sword and the chance to throttle me."

"And what if he doesn't want to kill his kinsman?"

"Then he shouldn't have been born a MuKierin. Listen, woman, I don't want to be here either, but I have no choice. That's the truth. And no one knows which one of us might die this night. They say this man claims to be the champion. If he is, I won't be able to overcome him. And if he is a faker, then he brought this upon himself."

Cisly stood, drew close and whispered in Bar's ear, "I assure you, he's no faker." As she spoke, she swung and smashed her rock into the young man's temple. Clobbered, Bar collapsed onto his face.

A guard rushed over and flung Cisly down. "You whore! How dare you strike a gentleman?!"

"Is that what he is?" asked Cisly.

The guard kicked her in the gut.

"Enough," said Bar, rolling onto his knees. "Let her be." *She's scary*, he thought. *She'd kill you if you gave her another chance.* Slowly he rose and walked away, holding his bleeding head.

Darnelle stared in awe at Cisly. "Aren't you scared of what they're going to do to us?" she asked.

"Of course, I am. But they're going to do it anyway. I just want to land a few good blows before it's over. That one there has never been hit by a woman before. You could tell by the way he let down his guard. Well, he won't soon forget me. If he hadn't flinched, I would have put his eye out."

That afternoon Blaze, Roff and Tustin rode into the spacious yard of a horse farm near Kierinswell. The three horsemen passed two stone barns and a corral holding at least twenty horses wearing empty packsaddles. The three halted on a wide drive beside a great house on a hill. Nearby lay a mound of items stacked high — cooking pots and wicker chairs, old lampstands, broken jugs and heaps of clothes and rags. The travelers spent a long minute scanning the mass of discarded goods.

"We seem to have come on a strange day," said Roff.

"Or come to a strange place," Tustin said. "Who throws away such things?"

A servant came down from the house. "Greetings, MuKierin," he said. "May I help you?"

Blaze answered, "Thank you. Please tell Arg Wevol that the son of Horse Stalker wishes to see him."

"Very good. He is expecting you," the servant replied. "He has left on a brief errand but will return soon. In the meantime, he has instructed me to bid you welcome and to see that you have a chance to wash and refresh yourselves. Please follow me."

The riders dismounted. "Did you say 'Arg Wevol?'" asked Roff. "Isn't that the old horse trader who kept the stallion that your father won at the challenge of Orres? My papa told me about him."

"Yes," said Blaze. "He met both our fathers long ago. I hope to rest here a few hours before riding on tonight to Fire

Mountain. I also want to ask Arg Wevol for the use of some horses."

Tustin motioned around him. "Look at all the barns and corrals," he said. "He does pretty well for a horse trader. He must need a score of people to care for all these animals."

The servant led them inside a large, adobe bathhouse. "Gentlemen, hot water is already on its way. If you will disrobe, I will direct you to the bathing room."

The three stripped from their clothes, then wrapped beige towels around their waists and proceeded to a room where three large copper tubs lay on a red tile floor. A half-dozen male servants entered a side door. Each carried two copper pails of steaming water, which they poured into the tubs. The head servant laid out soap, brushes and towels. "Gentlemen, I shall await you by the main house," he said. "If I can be of service, please call out to me."

Roff was first into his bath. "It's been a long time since I stepped into a tub," he said. "We had a tub when I was a boy in Kierinswell. But I was always one of the last ones in it. The water never looked this clear."

Tustin stepped into his tub and poured a pitcher of warm water over his hair and beard. "Of all the things I expected to encounter this day, I never thought I'd be taking a bath," he said. He turned to Blaze. "I'm going to be clean and fresh when I see Darnelle tonight. Blaze, I will get to see her tonight, won't I?"

"Yes, tonight."

After their baths, the three dressed and walked out into the summer evening, where a gentle breeze caressed their scrubbed skin. They sauntered across the main yard amidst lighted torches that already had been set in place for the coming night. Behind them they could see men leading packhorses back toward the servants' huts. And before them an old man came riding up the wide driveway on a spotted mare. It wasn't as regal a horse as the one Blaze's father had won that night long ago in Orres. But in all his years of horse hunting, Roff had rarely seen so fine an animal.

"Who is the son of Horse Stalker?" asked the old man. He raised his quirt while his eyes scanned the younger faces. He was a bear of a man with a gray beard and thinning hair.

"I am," said Blaze. "You rode with my father years ago."

"Yes, I did. Indeed, I did. Greetings, gentlemen. I am Arg Wevol, and you are all most welcome. I will gladly offer you what refreshment and board my modest home can provide. And I bring you news. Your aunt and uncle send you their greetings."

"You saw my mama and papa!" Roff exclaimed. "I'm Blaze's cousin, Roff, the son of Noli. Please, kinsman, tell me when you last saw them."

"They rode in here a little more than a week ago," Wevol said. "It was a most unexpected surprise, and a bittersweet reunion for me. And it seems even more bittersweet now that you young ones have arrived. But the day is slipping away from all of us. Come, MuKierin, and share with me my last meal in this old home. We have so much to say and so little time to say it."

Arg Wevol led them onto his veranda with a view of the sun sinking below the western sky. Inside the house sat a dozen leather panniers lined against a wall, plus various goods on the floor waiting to be wrapped in canvas tarps. Wevol led the young men into a dining room lit with candles. The host seated his guests on pillows around a low, main table. Then he reached for a golden carafe filled with wine. Slowly he poured four glasses.

"Blaze, before you were born your father told me that one day the great King might ask for my help," Wevol said. "I promised him I would be ready. I hoped that Roj himself might return here one day. I always kept my best wine ready for him. But now you've come in his place. So let me give this toast: To the Horse Stalker and his family, whose generosity to me has far exceeded any friendship that I might offer in return. May the son of Horse Stalker live a long life, and may he succeed in all that he attempts." The men saluted one another and drank. Roff thought the wine the most delicious he had ever tasted, as heady and fragrant as the reddest rose.

"Thank you for your kind wishes," said Blaze. "My father still speaks fondly of the days when he first met you. I believe for a time he considered you a rival for my mother's hand."

Wevol snickered and motioned with his glass. "He has been telling stories about my foolish heart, has he? Well, I forgive him. Your father befriended me. And don't think I'm just referring to the use of his stallion. Yes, that one animal's offspring has made me a wealthy man. But it almost got me killed, too. Not all you young ones may know the story, how Roj's enemies came here looking for him. I mean those of the Dark Brood, Equis, the Realm. Oh, their warriors were fierce and terrible. I had never seen anything like them. And they certainly would have killed me if your father had not arrived with some powerful allies. I never saw them, but I heard their war whoops and the warning horn of the evil ones. And your father raced away with the stallion and I was able to escape amid the chaos. I was never so grateful to see another human. You have no idea how those villains gave me a new outlook on life. I only hope to never meet their ilk again. And that explains all the mess that you see about you here tonight."

Servants brought in lamb and flat bread and an assortment of roots. As they left, Roff squinted at his host. "Excuse me, kinsman," he said. "I don't understand what you mean about the mess. What's going on here?"

Wevol looked surprised at the question. He turned to Blaze, who gave him a gentle nod to proceed. "I'm sorry, Roff. I thought you already knew. The evil ones are planning to invade our land. Your father told me so. It will be very bad for our people. But your father told me how to escape this danger. He said we could flee to the mountains and find refuge there with the King's people. I would have left the very day he visited me, but he asked me to stay until the son of Horse Stalker came to me here. Of course, I promised him I would wait. Tonight I have fulfilled that promise. And now I am at your service."

Wevol took a great bite from his leg of lamb. As he wiped his lips, he noticed his guests had stopped eating.

"Thank you, Arg Wevol," said Blaze. "I do have two requests."

"Name them, my friend. I'll do whatever I can for you."

"First, tonight I would like the use of five fresh horses. They must be the stallion's offspring and they must be animals that will return here if given free rein. It may be some time before I can return the horses. The animals may be damaged or lost."

"The horses are yours to do with as you see fit. You shall choose them, and my best trainer shall stand ready to assist you, though I doubt that you will require much help. And now please tell me your second request."

"Tonight I must ride to Fire Mountain. Our Elders will gather there, and they have taken prisoner two young women that I count dear. I hope to persuade the Elders to release the women, and I wish for my two friends here to escort the women away. I would like all four of them to come back here to your home. The King's people will meet them here."

"Of course, I shall provide them rest and provisions." The old man sat silent, frowning until his eyes became mere slits. "Isn't there anything else I can do?"

"No, thank you."

Wevol stood up. "Blaze, it saddens me to send you off to those shriveled old aristocrats this way. Let me at least clothe you in a fresh robe. I know it is a trifle, but allow a foolish friend this one request."

After dinner Blaze took from his host a gray robe with a red sash. He donned it and gave Wevol his old fisher's hat. "For friendship," he said. Wevol smiled and tucked the hat under his arm.

At the stables, Wevol's servants held torches along the stone walls as Blaze looked over the trader's finest horses. He greeted the stallions, tenderly stroking their manes and whispering secret words in their ears. As he did, Roff and

Wevol stood together by the stable doors. "Did my papa say where they were headed from here?" Roff asked.

"To your kinsman in the south. They wanted to hurry there because the evils ones may enter our land that way. Your father hopes to persuade them to flee with him to the mountains."

Blaze chose four spotted horses for his friends, plus a gray stallion for himself. When all was ready, the three young men embraced Wevol and made ready to ride into the night. "Farewell," said Blaze.

"Wait, child," Wevol said. "When you first arrived, I had gone out in the hills to bury my jewels, my little treasure from years gone by. I alone know where these valuables lie hidden. Let me whisper the location in your ear."

Blaze leaned over as Wevol drew close to tell his secret. He nodded and replied, "When the time is right, you may wish to share the location with Roff here, too. Someday your wealth might help sustain many lives. Farewell, my friend."

Leaving the horse farm, the three riders moved quickly north into the hills. They followed a well-traveled road as a new moon gleamed above them and star clusters shone among clouds spread across the night sky. Roff rode quietly beside his cousin, keeping silent until they stopped on a ridge overlooking a long valley. In the distance stood the mount, set off with the light of one hundred torches.

"Cousin," said Roff, "are you going to tell us what's going to happen tonight?"

Blaze replied, "Tustin and you will ride up a little closer, and then wait for Darnelle and Cisly. I hope to win their release. If they do show up, take them back to Wevol's home. I'll send the King's servants there to meet you."

"That's not what I mean. What's going to happen to you tonight?"

"That depends on the Elders. But this is the last step for me before I leave this land. After tonight, I'll have done what I set out to do here. I'll be ready to go to the King."

"Cousin, I can see how you're already sweating. Please let me go with you tonight. It's not right for me to stay behind. I should be there with you. You shouldn't be alone."

"We have to do it this way, Roff. I need you to stay with Tustin and the women. I promise I'll do my best to meet up with you again. Please wait for the women and go back to Wevol's home. Stay there until my people arrive to help you."

Roff relented and the three rode downhill, passing through thickets of prickly brush until they came to the edge of the valley. There, off the main road, Roff and Tustin dismounted. Blaze rode ahead, leading the extra horses for the women. The lights of Fire Mountain loomed against the night sky. Beneath the lights, two hundred sentries stood watch, while more soldiers hid in the darkness. The Elders, meanwhile, waited together in a large pavilion or in private tents pitched along the edge of the hilltop. Blaze rode forward until he heard a sentry's challenge. A squad of soldiers raced to surround him. Blaze dismounted and was taken quickly to the captain of the guard. Nearby stood the sergeant from Orres prison.

"That's him," the sergeant told the captain.

The guards quickly searched their prisoner. "No magic stone on him, sir," one announced.

"Hello, boy," the sergeant said to Blaze. "You look worse every time I see you. Can you make it up that hill?"

"I must," said Blaze.

"Here, take my arm, son. We don't want to keep the Elders waiting."

Blaze leaned on the sergeant and the two strode up a path lined with torches and sentries standing at attention, their spears pointing heavenward, their eyes watching the much-awaited newcomer. Upon reaching the hilltop, the prisoner was made to stand in front of a roaring fire next to a low stone dais. Behind the dais lay the Elders' main pavilion.

From the pavilion exited a man in black. His name was Whit and he was an Elder from Kierinswell and the leader of the anti-slaver faction. Slowly he made his way to the private tent where Chakka Ri, the GrandElder, sat with his feet propped on a stool by a small fire. Chakka Ri was no longer the young man who had ridden with the White Beard into the high country a quarter century before. He was now balding, and he carried a goodly paunch across his midsection. But his face still exuded its majesty, though lined with wrinkles and trimmed by the gray beard of late manhood.

Whit entered the tent and produced a small scroll from beneath his gown. "I have something for you from the White Beard," he said. "He wrote it before he was abducted."

The GrandElder frowned as he took the scroll. He broke its wax seal and began to read its message: "Chakka Ri, By the time you read this I will be in chains for my people. How many more MuKierin must be chained before slavery and oppression end? Must slavers themselves wear chains before that day comes? Must you yourself wear the debtors' chains?

"I loved your parents. I speak as one who cares about you. The time is short, Chakka Ri. The Champion has come. Soon you will meet him, just as I said you would more than two decades ago. For the sake of our people, think well what you will say to him."

Chakka Ri crumpled the scroll and tossed it on the fire. "Even in chains that old man torments me," he muttered.

"You can rest assured that his message to me was even more caustic," said Whit. "He blames me more than you for the failures of our Clan. His message reminded me that I am an anti-slaver and yet I have not ended the enslavement of our people. And now his Champion has come and he expects me to come to his aid."

"Do your members really think this scoundrel is the Champion?"

"What my members know is that you slavers have caused a great anger in the land. Our kinsmen are furious about what your faction did to the White Beard, how you let foreigners come here and take him off in chains."

"I never authorized the taking of that old man, and certainly not by Equis. That was done behind my back."

"So you say. But the people certainly believe that all you slavers had a hand in it. This foreign intervention is a slap in the face of every true MuKierin, even those who condone slavery. Who knows what will happen next? Indeed, such chaos could lead to the overthrow of all of us Elders. My supporters aren't going to stand by and let that happen. We know that the time has come for action. We see two paths before us. We can work with your faction to begin to end the slave trade. Or we can throw our support behind the White Beard's man, and force you slavers into a corner."

"Well, I thank you for your bluntness. Once more the anti-slavers show that they don't really care about the debtors, these wretched men and women who can't take care of themselves. You've certainly never done anything to truly help them. All you care about is staying in power. But someone has to keep order. Someone has to make the hard decisions. If we didn't take care of the destitute and the criminal, what would happen? One group would starve and the other would rob us blind."

"Spare me your self-righteousness, Chakka Ri. At least we're not getting rich off the chain gangs."

"No, you have your other ways of getting rich. And even those ways benefit indirectly from the chain gangs. But let us turn back to the matter at hand. Would you really put all your hopes on this imposter? What do you truly know of him? By all accounts he's no warrior. What kind of Champion is he? Beware, my old friend. You may be disappointed. Why, this young one might be executed before the night is over."

"Perhaps. But if you kill him, he might make an excellent martyr. Indeed, I don't think you'll execute him over our objections. You can't risk it. You might set off a rebellion, with all the anger directed at you slavers."

"So you would choose as your Champion a man who flouts our laws and tears down our prisons? He may prove as dangerous to your faction as he is to mine."

"Perhaps. Once my people hear him tonight, they may be persuaded to help you end his escapades so that slavers and anti-slavers can come together to begin the serious work of abolishing slavery. But you must give us some hope before we choose that path. For the sake of the White Beard and our people, we won't let this moment pass."

Chakka Ri nodded and turned back to the fire. "Very well. I will agree to appoint a committee to consider the slavery question. You can appoint three members. I will appoint four."

"A committee? That hardly seems adequate. You slavers can simply ignore any recommendations made from such a body."

Chakki Ri's voice grew grave: "I am a man of honor. We will give this question the serious thought that it deserves. It may well be time to find another way, if your people can find some backbone for the hard leadership that would inevitably be required if the debtors' chains were abolished. In any case, I can offer you nothing more tonight."

"Very well, GrandElder. We'll leave it there for now. Tonight my people will have to judge between the worthiness of the accused and the promise of a committee. If the young man reveals himself as the Champion, you can forget about your offer. On the other hand, if he proves himself a disappointment, we will swallow hard and accept your bargain."

A minute later the captain of the guard found Shutoo in the Elders' pavilion. Leaning in, he whispered in the counsel's ear, "The accused has come, my lord."

Shutoo smiled. "And have you searched him, captain?"

"Yes, my lord. We found no weapons and no magic stones, only the black stone upon his necklace."

"Excellent. Take me to him. I wish to take a look at him before we begin." The officer and the counsel exited the pavilion and made quickly for the fire. Once there, Shutoo stared silently at Blaze and lightly pressed an index finger against his lips. Blaze, pale and sweating, turned his body slowly and fixed his eyes on the inquisitor. Shutoo kept the accused waiting for a time, then dropped the finger from his lips and gave a signal to a servant.

A drum began to sound, slow and deep, reverberating across the hills. Two servants pulled back the pavilion's entrance flaps, and shaggy, gray-haired Joanus Sokus, Sergeant of Arms, declared in a raspy tenor: "This emergency session of the National Council of the Sovereign Commonwealth of the MuKierin shall come to order. The GrandElder Chakka Ri is presiding." Out onto the hilltop strode the twenty-one Elders, each attired in a black gown that skimmed over the hard ground. Each leader sat upon a small throne on a raised stone dais. Soldiers and torchbearers surrounded them. Overhead, the new moon and summer stars glowed amid great clouds.

Chakka Ri stood to speak, leaning on his wooden staff. Before him the fire leapt high. Beyond those flames, the accused stared motionless at the men on the dais. "If all the members are present, we may begin," he said.

"I have a request," said Blaze, breathing hard to project his voice. "To bring me here, you took into your custody two women. Now that I have arrived, I ask that you spare them from witnessing what is to come. I ask that you release the women."

Chakka Ri looked to Shutoo, who raised a hand and spoke. "GrandElder," the inquisitor began, "I will abide by the desire of the Council. If the members wish them released, I will obey."

Chakka Ri surveyed the faces of his colleagues, then turned back to the sergeant at arms. "Release the women."

A nearby tent flap opened and two soldiers brought forth Darnelle and Cisly. When the women caught sight of Blaze, Darnelle began to cry. Cisly, however, straightened her shoulders and stood taller.

"Darnelle. Cisly," Blaze called, reaching out and taking each by the hand. His voice dropped to the softest whisper: "My friends, I've left two spotted horses for you at the bottom of the hill. Take the spotted ones, not the gray. Turn them south and give them free rein. They will take you to safety. Roff and Tustin are waiting for you on the far side of the valley. Farewell, my friends."

Cisly squeezed his hand. She saw the paleness of his face but made no mention of it. Instead she said, "We knew you'd come."

The captain of the guard pulled her away and led both women down the hill. All eyes fixed once more on Blaze, who returned to his place by the leaping flames. Shutoo began the proceedings. "Gentlemen, tonight it is my duty to bring charges against the accused. This man has done great harm to our people. If necessary, I will review each and every one of his crimes. But it is enough, I hope, to prove that he is guilty of the destruction of the prison at Orres and the illegal removal of its prisoners. The sergeant of the prison is here tonight, and he is ready to testify that this man was responsible for the crime. If the accused denies this, I am prepared to bring as many witnesses as the council requires. Let me assure you, gentlemen, we have the proof needed to justify a death sentence."

Chakka Ri stood again. "We now will hear an opening statement from the accused. Blaze, what do you say in your defense?"

With a labored voice, Blaze spoke: "I have long waited for this night, Chakka Ri. Many years ago the White Beard told you this day would come. He said I would stand before you, and he told you what I would bring." He pulled off the necklace and held the circular black stone up in the firelight. "Chakka Ri, this stone testifies of me. I have brought it here to you."

A murmur arose among the Elders. Morros stood and demanded, "What is the meaning of this display?"

The GrandElder stared resolutely ahead. Into his mind came an image of the White Beard pointing out a herd of mountain goats scrambling along a sheer outcrop of crumbling brown rock. He also recalled a mountain cave, a babe in a woman's arms and a spy with a wretched drug. Blaze took a few steps around the fire toward the dais. "Will you take this stone, Chakka Ri?" he asked quietly.

"No, young man. Please make your opening statement or produce those who would testify on your behalf."

Blaze raised his voice: "The White Beard would have testified on my behalf, if members of this Council had not conspired with the Realm to abduct him."

The anti-slaver Elders clapped and roared in approval. "Where is the White Beard?" one called, and others echoed the words in a brief chant. The GrandElder raised his staff to silence them. It took a few moments to restore order.

Shutoo stepped around the fire and drew close to Blaze. "If the accused has a defense, let him give it now," he demanded. "If not, let him admit his guilt."

The GrandElder straightened and peered down with stern eyes. "State your defense, Blaze."

"I've said what I came to say," said Blaze.

The Elders began to murmur. One of the anti-slavers rose and spoke, "GrandElder, I would ask the accused to reconsider. He serves neither his cause nor this Council by his silence."

Blaze, however, said nothing. With sweat dripping off his brow, he stared steadfast at Chakka Ri. The GrandElder bowed his head in contemplation. A moment later he turned to his colleagues and announced, "The accused refuses to answer the charges against him. I now look to the council members to express how they wish to proceed."

The two factions — slaver and anti-slaver — began to caucus on separate corners of the dais. Chakka Ri turned toward the two groups and leaned heavily with both hands on his staff. Every minute or so he turned briefly to examine Blaze's face, then turned back to those officials pondering their next move. His bloated stomach began to churn from gas. His bowels had never been the same after that terrible night in the mountains. *Blast that spy!* he thought. *We never did catch him. And blast the White Beard for taking me up into the mountains and making a wreck of my intestines. And blast this young one, too. Who are you, boy? Certainly the White Beard has put you up to this. Perhaps you were that baby on the mountain.*

Eventually the slavers, who held a majority with thirteen members, sent Morros to speak with Whit from the anti-slaver caucus. Together approached Chakka Ri. "Remember your bargain," Whit said.

Chakka Ri smiled. "Indeed, I will. Does that mean you're a tad disappointed with the accused? He doesn't seem like much of a Champion, does he?"

"That is about to be put to the test."

The Elders once more took their seats. Morros rose and was recognized by the GrandElder. With bravado in his voice, he spoke: "Gentlemen, as the protector of Orres, it falls on me to see that justice is done here tonight. I accept that heavy duty. And yet I am well aware of the fact that this man is not an ordinary criminal. Too many of our people wrongly believe him to be a freedom fighter, a hero and, dare I say, even the Champion of the Stone Woman. I realize that there may be a backlash if our Great Council simply punishes this man, even though he deserves death. I wish to avoid any needless violence and harm, and I believe that all of our leaders do as well. Therefore, I propose that we seek another way. If it pleases the Council, let the guilt or innocence of the accused be determined in trial by combat. Since he will not defend himself with words, let him establish his honesty with a sword. That is the way of the MuKierin. I will abide by the outcome, and I believe our people will, too."

Chakka Ri turned to Shutoo, "Can the inquisitor offer a suitable champion to carry out such a challenge."

"I can, GrandElder," said Shutoo. He motioned and a soldier hurried away into the darkness. A few moments later the guard returned with Bar striding behind him, his left hand on his sword. The young cadet took his place to one side of the fire. He immediately recognized Blaze from the day with Cisly at the Barsk inn. Nonetheless, he kept his gaze calm and his face turned toward the Elders. Shutoo introduced him, "I offer Bar MuBarishta as the champion of our people."

"An honorable choice," said Chakka Ri. "Many here know both this young man and his family. Bar MuBarishta, will you be the people's champion and oppose, to the death if necessary, the claims of the accused?"

Bar turned to face Blaze and gave him as cold a stare as he could muster. "I will," he said.

"Well done," said the GrandElder. "Blaze, son of Roj, you have heard the offer. Do you accept our challenge to settle your guilt or innocence in trial by combat?"

Blaze straightened his back and turned to Chakka Ri. "No, I do not accept it."

The Elders muttered their disapproval. Chakka Ri turned and glared in exasperation at his colleagues. "He will not fight," he called to the anti-slavers. "Do you wish to caucus again on his behalf?" Perspiration rolled down Blaze's forehead. He grimaced often. Bar stared at him, unable to look away.

One of the anti-slavers, a thin man with a stern face, rose and stepped to the front of the dais near Chakka Ri. "Young man," he called out, "I ask you to explain yourself to us. Tonight I heard you speak the name of the White Beard. There are many here that admire that great leader. I am such a man. And we believe, as he did, that one day the promised Champion will arise from among our people. Are you that Champion? If you are, you have a duty to show yourself to the leaders of your clan. Many of us are willing to put the past behind us, if only you will show us that you are worthy. Take up the sword, young man. Take it up and win the honor that belongs to a true Champion. Here is your chance to set all things right. Show us you are worthy. It is our way, the way of the chosen clan. Step forth as a MuKierin and show us what you are made of."

The entire assembly hushed. Blaze took a deep breath, then another. "I have a word for you," he said. "The days of this Council are almost at an end. Very soon your enemies will rule over you."

The thin Elder looked crestfallen. Other leaders rose up, scowling and hurling curses at Blaze. Morros strode to the front of the dais and raised his arms. "Enough of this!" he cried. "I will not be insulted by a coward. This criminal deserves our scorn. I demand that he feel the glove."

The GrandElder nodded and motioned for silence. "Morros has demanded the glove. Bar MuBarishta, champion of the MuKierin, strike the accused in challenge of mortal combat."

Bar turned toward the dais. The Elders, both slaver and anti-slaver, now looked as one man, glaring in anticipation. Bar removed his gauntlet and walked reluctantly up to Blaze. The two stood face to face. Blaze spoke softly: "Bar MuBarishta, when you fail to find what you're looking for, I hope that you'll accept a small hand in friendship."

Bar clenched his teeth. "What does that mean?" he whispered. "What do you know about me?"

Shutoo drew near and hissed impatiently, "Strike him!" Bar sneered and hesitated. At last he swung his gauntlet. Blaze tried hard to hold firm. Even so, he flinched as the blow struck his left cheek. He grimaced at his inability to stand still. Bar, meanwhile, returned to his place on the other side of the fire.

Chakka Ri straightened his black robe. "Does the accused still refuse to fight?"

"I do," said Blaze.

Morros spoke up and addressed the Council: "GrandElder, not even such an indignity can stir any passion within this coward's soul. Gentlemen, I confess that after the villainy done in Orres, I was ready to scream for this man's blood. But now I see that this false MuKierin does us less harm alive than dead. For if we execute him, I fear his followers will claim that we killed a valiant warrior, and thus they may carry on a deception that already has caused too much harm to our land. I say we let him live, so that all the MuKierin can see what a gutless creature he really is. Brand a "C" on his forearm for "coward" and let those who adore him be forced to confront his lack of valor. Therefore, I ask for a judgment of guilt and a punishment of banishment. And should he ever be found again within the boundaries of the

Clan of the Horse, let any man slay him, as we would kill a mad dog. I call for a vote of banishment and a reward of one thousand pieces of silver for his head should he remain in our land."

Without further comment, the Elders came forward and voted by casting stones in a clay pot—white stones for innocence, black for guilt. Chakka Ri examined the pot, then announced, "It is unanimous. Blaze, this Council finds you guilty and condemned to flee our land or be slain by any man who would take your life. I thank the Council members for their grave consideration of this matter, and I now adjourn our good body. May the Stone Woman smile upon all of us. Good night." The Elders quickly departed the dais. Gathering their bodyguards and servants, they proceeded down the torch-lit path, their black robes blending into darkness. The soldiers also began to disperse from the hilltop. Bar hung his head and returned to his tent, trying to avoid the eyes of those who hurried around him. For a moment, Blaze stood alone by the fire, the flames of which were receding into red-hot coals.

From the far side of the hill sprang forward a new group of men, each adorned in ragged clothes, all sporting long, unkempt hair. Their leader, a man with a broken nose and a leathered face, nodded respectfully toward Shutoo. He turned a sly grin toward Blaze and bowed. "We have come to say goodbye to you, our noble Champion, before you leave this land. Be a good boy and we shall treat you ever so gently."

The man snapped his wrist and a black leather whip uncoiled at his feet. "Would you care to beg for mercy, Great One?" Blaze stayed silent, even as he started to tremble. The leader shrugged. "Boys, our friend looks a little scared. Perhaps he's tongue-tied. Let's help him find words to soothe us dirty rabble."

Immediately a man struck Blaze from behind and sent him to the dirt. Others jumped forward, kicking and stomping him, all the while shouting, "Coward! Gutless worm! You're no MuKierin! Death's too good for you!"

They stopped briefly and their leader drew near
Blaze's left ear, now scraped and bloody. "Mercy, precious?
Can you say 'Mercy'?" the man chortled. Blaze gave him no
answer. "No matter, Great One. We shall have you dancing
yet." To his men he snapped: "Strip him! Let his back taste a
little leather." The accomplices jumped forward and pulled
the gray robe off Blaze's torso. They tied leather thongs
around his wrists, and four men grabbed the thongs, two on
each side. Together they pulled Blaze's arms apart and
hoisted him to his knees. The whip cracked against their
victim's shoulder blades. The men holding the thongs flinched
as the leather tore into skin and flesh.

Bar emerged from a tent with his gear slung over his
back. When he saw the lashing, he strode up to Shutoo.
"What ugliness is this?" he demanded.

The man with the broken nose squinted at him. "Oh,
gentlemen," he called to his accomplices, "we should not
force this young aristocrat here to witness such untidiness. His
eyes were made for gentler things."

Bar implored Shutto, "By the Council's edict, this man
is to be given the chance to freely leave our land."

"Master Bar," replied the counsel, "I assure you this
man will receive everything he deserves. That includes a good
head start away from this hilltop. Of course, what happens to
him once he leaves here is hardly my concern."

The attackers laughed derisively. The men holding the
thongs let go and Blaze dropped to the ground. Upon his back
leaked the blood from thirty lashes. From the fire, the broken-
nosed man took a branding iron, its tip aflame in the night
with a red 'C.' The man turned to Bar and sneered, 'C' is for
'coward,' boy. That way we'll know his head is worth a
thousand pieces of silver. A rich boy like you could care less.
But me and the boys here know nothing of the fat life. We'll
take those silver coins, thank you kindly."

Disgusted, Bar turned and strode away. As he did,
they branded their prisoner's left forearm. Blaze let out an
anguished scream. His attackers, meanwhile, brought his gray
stallion up to the fire ring. They lifted Blaze up and heaved

him face down across the saddle. His arms and legs hung limp on either side. "Farewell, Great One," the leader whispered in Blaze's ear. "You're a marked man now. We shall soon meet again. Very soon." The leader slapped the stallion's rump, sending horse and rider down Fire Mountain into the still, dark night.

The new moon had drifted behind a patch of clouds, but the stallion had no trouble finding its way across the valley floor. The animal set an easy pace, its head nodding rhythmically to gentle hoof beats. The moon reappeared, bouncing amber beams off the horse's great mane and tail. So the offspring of the Spotted Stallion carried its wounded burden across the long valley east of Kierinswell.

In the darkness, Roj knelt amid the valley's sage, waiting for his son. Dressed in a charcoal cloak, he had spent the night staring quietly at the mount. But when his son had screamed from the touch of the branding iron, a tear had fallen from the father's eye.

A wisp of a woman hid with Roj, her head reaching only as high as his shoulder. As the grey stallion drew near, the woman scampered ahead to cut off the animal. "Lamonay," she said softly, and the stallion slowed his pace. "Lamonay." She stepped forward and gently stroked the great horse's neck, grabbing the reins and leading the animal back to Roj. Blaze still lay draped sideways over the saddle. The small woman went to the right side and pushed the young man's chest off the seat. Roj, meanwhile, slipped underneath his son's torso and carried him over to a blanket stretched out behind a small boulder. The father gently lay Blaze face down. He beheld the blackened eye and the lash stripes across his son's back.

"I'm here, son," said Roj. "I'm here for you."

The woman, meanwhile, climbed onto the great horse and waited in silence. Even the stallion seemed to sense the sadness of the scene. Slowly Roj rose and stepped forward to touch the hand of the King's servant. "Thank you, Tara," he told her. "Ride swiftly. Fidden Gadaeyo."

The small one nodded soberly. "Tonight we'll race the moon, Horse Stalker. They won't catch us. Fidden Gadaeyo." With that she turned the animal south and set out at a trot, then slipped her body sideways across the saddle in order to appear as if she were Blaze. Roj, meanwhile, knelt beside his son and made sure they remained well hidden behind a boulder and dense clumps of brush.

Back on the mount, a servant brought Shutoo his black stallion. The counsel rode over to the men who had beaten Blaze, each one holding a horse and waiting in a semicircle. "Make sure you find him," Shutoo warned. "He couldn't be killed here on the mount. But once he crosses this valley, I want him taken. I want his head delivered to me personally."

The Broken Nose nodded. "Not to worry, my lord. Friends are waiting for him at the far end of the valley. When that horse arrives, they shall certainly finish what we started." A horn sounded far to the south. "Ah, there's the signal," he proclaimed. "Noble friends, let us go forth and claim our reward."

Unexpectedly, the horn sounded three more times. "What is this?" Shutoo demanded as the horn kept blowing. "Is he getting away? Get out there, fools! Find him! If you fail to kill that man, I shall hang you all!" The assassins leaped upon their horses and galloped down the mount. They slapped their animals and rushed frantically across the darkened valley. They passed close to Blaze and his father, but never saw them.

After the riders galloped away, Roj took a cloth drenched with a special oil and squeezed it over his son's bare back, letting the contents drip gently onto the lash wounds. "The worst is over, son," he whispered. "Tara is leading them far away. You've done all you needed to do. I'm proud of you, Blaze."

"While they were beating me, I could hear Mother in my mind. She was sobbing and thrashing in chains. But even in her anguish, she told me to hold firm."

"What a mess we humans have made. And it's not over, is it?"

"No, Father. It's only beginning. The Dark Brood is coming."

In twilight, Weakling froze and sniffed the still air. Slowly he reached over and touched Pibbibib's forearm. "How close are we?" he asked.

The two had stopped amid fading light in a long canyon east of Fire Mountain. Behind them followed Rakmah's assassination team. It included four female archers with darkened faces and black tunics and tights. Around them strode a dozen warriors, including Zhaggee of the Red Brigade. It was nearly three hours before the MuKierin Council was set to begin its examination of Blaze.

Pibbibib replied: "We've still got at least three ridge lines to cross before we can get within range. Maybe more."

"Then we're in trouble. The enemy's coming our way. I think they're still far off, maybe two hills away."

"Well, I guess we should expect them. They likely were sent to protect the champion. Alright, let's move a little farther up the canyon and avoid them." Pibbibib turned back to the rest of the company. "I sense trouble out there," he announced. "Get ready to dodge the enemy."

Rakmah showed his displeasure. "We need to get in position. If we're not there soon, we'll miss the chance for the archers to take their shot. We need to kill this champion."

"There's still time. But first we've got to sneak through the enemy lines. Now follow me."

The warriors headed south and began to climb up and down a series of dry gullies. Soon Weakling picked up the pace. "They've changed course," he said to Pibbibib.

"What do you mean? Are they getting closer?"

"Yes, they're getting closer and they've turned south with us. They changed direction, just like we did."

"Do you think they can see us?"

"No, they're still too far away. They're somewhere on the other side of that hill."

"Okay," Backstabber called softly to the others. "Move it, maggots! Let's get going!"

With Weakling still out in front, the warriors began to jog briskly through the bottom of the canyon. Even as darkness descended, the new moon provided its light, and they took advantage of a smooth trail. Pibbibib recalled how dangerous it once had been to travel at night in such country, unable to know whether an ambush lay just around the corner, always holding on to fortune to stay alive. This night they meant to murder the King's grandson, the one called Blaze. Now they knew that the King's troops were also in the area. Perhaps the enemy feared an assassination attempt on the Champion. What of it? Pibbibib reminded himself that Weakling had repeatedly proven that he could detect and keep a step ahead of his enemies. He had helped Pibbibib safely pass through the enemy lines on several occasions and he would do so again tonight. The Powers wouldn't fail them.

They came to a bend in the canyon that would take them back west toward Fire Mountain. But Weakling changed course and bounded up a gravel slope on the eastern bank. All the warriors knew he was taking them away from their target. "Hold it!" Rakmah hissed at him. "Get back down here! We've wasted enough time."

Pibbibib climbed up to Weakling. "What are you doing?" he called.

"They're on to us," Weakling replied. "Now we've got two groups coming at us. One is off to our right and another is directly in front of us. Between them they must have fifty warriors. And they're both coming our way fast. We're trapped."

"That can't be. They can't know we're out here."

Rakmah and the others drew near. "Turn around," the leader told Pibbibib. "I'm tired of your games. We're going to head west now."

"Hold on," said Pibbibib. "We've got two separate forces between us and Fire Mountain. And they both seem to be headed this way."

"Are they on to us?" asked Zhaggee.

"No, of course not. But we've got to change course to get around them. There's too many of them for us."

"I think you're lying," said Rakmah and he drew his sword. "I think you two cowards are trying to run away from your duty. Now you'll turn west with me or I'll whack off a hand."

Weakling turned and sprang away. "They're coming!" he yelled.

Rakmah turned to the archers. "Shoot him," he ordered.

But as the female warriors put arrows to bowstrings, Zhaggee stepped in front and pleaded, "No, he's our only hope!"

"Shut up!" yelled Pibbibib.

"No!" said Zhaggee, retreating a step but determined to speak. "Shoot the Backstabber if you want, but not Weakwi. He's the real one who can sense the enemy. He's the one with The Powers! We need him! If you kill him, we'll never get out of here alive."

Rakmah's eyes flared at Pibbibib. "You stinking sack of manure. At last we get the truth. The sergeant was right. All this time you've been playing with us, thinking only about yourself and how you can get your hands on the Great Valuable. But now your little game is up. I think Zhaggee's right. You're the first one who should get an arrow in the gullet."

The four females turned their bows toward Pibbibib. But they didn't have time to aim. Behind the western ridge a horn sounded deep and clear. Rakmah and the other warriors froze. A second horn answered from perhaps a half mile away to the south. The warriors recognized the trumpets of their enemies. The King's troops apparently felt confident enough now to announce themselves. And the horns had their desired effect. Zhaggee croaked to the others, "Weakwi's right! We've got to run or they'll trap us in the bottom of this canyon."

"We can still escape them!" Pibbibib yelled. "Follow me to higher ground!"

"I'll follow you, alright," said Rakmah. "And I'll stick this blade in your back the first time you give me half a chance." He turned to the other male warriors. "Take the collars off the females. Get them ready for battle."

The company began to scale the hill. The loose soil easily gave way and the warriors found it all they could do to keep their footing. Even so, they climbed without stopping for nearly five minutes. By then they had reached a shelf halfway between the canyon floor and the top of the ridge. Weakling was still far ahead and hustling for all he was worth. The others, however, were worn from the steep ascent and stopped for a brief rest. From below they caught the sound of horses moving up the canyon. In the darkness, they strained in vain to see the enemy. "Maybe they'll pass by and not come looking for us," said one warrior.

Pibbibib doubted it. "Let's move on," he ordered. He set off at a jog along the rocky shelf, determined not to let Weakling get too far ahead of him. Soon the level stretch ended, and he was forced once more to climb the slope. As he did, a horn sounded from within the canyon. Another answered, and it caused Pibbibib to stop in his tracks. While still far off, the blast seemed to come from somewhere higher up the hillside. *They're flanking us!* he thought. *Now we've got to race for the top!*

Up the company scrambled. Soon they heard horses halting beneath them. Their enemies dismounted and began to scale the hillside. Occasionally a horn sounded. Whenever one did, the other would always answer. The King's troops seemed to be closing in quickly. Pibbibib now was scrambling straight up the slope, straining for the top. He wanted to find Weakling and then slip down over the other side and make for the backcountry. There was still time. His hands began to ache as he clutched any rock or shrub that could help him climb. His lungs burned. Pure fear propelled him heavenward.

At the top, Pibbibib caught a glimpse of a dark figure rushing into a cluster of rocks on the ridgeline. Immediately he raced after him. A few minutes later Zhaggee and the others followed. The four archers slowed their pace and began to search for a good set of boulders around which to make a last stand, if it should come to that. For his part, Rakmah tried to catch Pibbibib, but the other warrior seemed to have gotten his second wind.

From atop the ridge, a horn sounded. A moment later a horse whinnied. Pibbibib cursed the sounds. It meant that somehow the enemy had found a trail onto the hilltop. Soon the King's cavalrymen might swoop in and attack them all. Just then Weakling reappeared, making a hasty retreat back toward his ally. It appeared that the enemy had blocked his way. However, when Weakling saw Pibbibib, he veered away east and scampered for a raised promontory at the back of the hill. Backstabber changed course and bounded over the scarred crags to intercept his ally. He hoped they both could beat the enemy to the backside of the ridge and find a path down that would be too steep for warriors on horseback. He took a good angle in order to cut off his chum, who was aiming for the highest point of the cliff. Pibbibib sensed they were about to reach the edge and instinctively slowed down. But Weakling ran on at full speed, oblivious to the danger. At the precipice, he leaped forward into the black abyss. With a great howl, he plunged off the cliff.

The fool! Pibbibib thought as he pulled up short. *Let's hope he's still alive. I've got to find him!* Backstabber looked over the edge but could see no easy descent. The cliff's wall was too steep and slick. He couldn't even see the bottom. Quickly he jumped to the ground and slid partway over the edge. Zhaggee and Rakmah ran up behind him.

"Are you crazy?" Zhaggee called. "There's got to be a better way down."

Rakmah screamed, "Coward! Climb back up here and die like a warrior!"

Pibbibib taunted him. "Come with me and I'll show you real courage!" With that, he released his grip and slid down the wall.

The two warriors peered over the edge and listened to the sound of Backstabber's body as it crashed onto the rocks and brush below. "He might have survived the fall," said Zhaggee, "but he'll sure be busted up."

Rakmah opened his mouth but never answered. An arrow had found its mark, piercing the leader's back. He fell forward and tumbled lifeless over the edge. Zhaggee dropped to the ground as another arrow flew over him. He had only a moment to decide whether to run or jump. He slid his legs over the edge and lowered himself until only his head remained in view. For a moment, the promontory stood empty. Zhaggee held steady, hoping he could hide and somehow avoid detection. Then he saw two archers and a great hound moving toward him. He now knew that death was certain if he stayed put. The Slinker from the Red Brigade took a deep breath and released his grip. Down the great wall he plunged.

Pibbibib already was at the bottom, trying to regain his senses. The unyielding rock face had peeled a good deal of skin off his exposed arms and legs. Halfway down he had slammed into a rock outcrop and broken his left arm. From there he crashed and tumbled to the bottom. Even so, he ended his descent alive. Along with the broken arm, his legs were bruised and his ankles sprained. Soon he heard a second body crash into a nearby gully. A few moments later a third warrior came wailing and cursing down the rock wall. The last one landed with a crash and short bounce.

"Ooooh," gasped Zhaggee. "Somebody help me."

"Shut up," whispered Pibbibib, who lay less than ten feet away. "Do you want them to come down here and finish us off?"

"What difference does it make now? They're on to us. Or they're on to Weakwi, anyway."

"What's that supposed to mean?"

"Are you so stupid? Tonight they tracked us down. We changed course and they did, too. They came right after us. They must be able to track Weakwi and his blasted Powers. Think about it. He can sense the enemy's whereabouts. But they've got someone up there that can sense his movement, too. It's the curse that the White Beard told us about."

The thought punched Backstabber in the gut. Could it be true? The Powers had been his big advantage, his best hope for greatness. And yet, something indeed had gone terribly wrong this night. The enemy had seemed able to follow their every move through the canyon. Could Zhaggee be right? It was a terrible notion to ponder. If the enemy really could track Weakling, all hope of finding the Great Valuable might vanish into the night.

Pibbibib crawled close and answered Zhaggee with a grimness that lacked much conviction: "Maybe you're wrong. Maybe they had a sentry out here and he spotted us moving through the canyon. Or maybe some traitor betrayed our plans to the enemy."

"Yeah, and maybe I'll pick up my busted body and fly away from these cursed mountains."

Pibbibib drew his knife. "No, you're not going anywhere. Tonight you betrayed me. I told you what would happen if ever you did that." He plunged his blade deep into the other warrior's chest. Zhaggee twitched and gagged and went still.

Backstabber stumbled through the rocky debris at the base of the cliff. He was looking for Weakling, but first he found Rakmah. The arrow in the great warrior's back was a reminder that the enemy remained too close for comfort. Even so, Pibbibib took the time to slit the leader's throat, just to make sure he was dead. From there he crept within the moon's shadow of the cliff, softly padding over the dross and rubble that testified to an eon of erosion. He found Weakling nearby sprawled on a pile of gravel.

Pibbibib leaned down and whispered, "Did you think you could fly away like some black swan?"

"Curse you! Leave me alone. I want to die here."

"No. You're coming with me. Can you walk?

"Of course not. Just leave me here. Let the enemy finish me off. I've had enough of your dreams of glory."

"Listen, I'm still giving the orders. I'm no quitter, and you're coming with me. I've got a busted arm so I can't carry you. I'm going to get you up and then you can lean on me."

"Who's up there?" Weakling demanded.

"What do you mean?"

"Someone strange is up there. I can sense it. It's not her, not her of the little light of fire. I'd know if it was. But it's someone or something that's been touched by her power. And whoever it was, whatever it was, it seemed to come straight for me, no matter which way I turned."

Pibbibib gritted his teeth. So Zhaggee had been right. Even so, now was not the time to ponder such wretched news. Aloud he vowed, "Whoever it is, we'll find him and kill him one day. But first we've got to escape. Come on."

Both warriors howled and groaned as Weakling pulled himself up. Their crash landings would have been the death of any mere mortal. Indeed, here was proof that they were of a different race. Even so, Weakling's right leg and ankle were badly broken. He also had busted his right shoulder, cracked some ribs and bloodied and broken fingers on both hands. What seemed miraculous was the condition of his left leg, the one with the old wound from Roj's blade. It was only bruised, and he was able to stand firmly upon it.

"I can't breathe," he gasped, holding his ribs. As he leaned on his ally, his right leg hung useless.

"Don't pass out on me," hissed Pibbibib. "We won't go far, but we're going to find some cover. After we get to a good place, I'll set your busted bones and mine, too. Then we'll lie down and take a nice, long rest."

Up on the cliff, two of the King's archers heard the warriors' howls below them. "I can't see them in the shadows," said one, "but I think we could send down enough arrows over there to kill one or both of them."

"No, my friends," called a voice. It was Mirri, Healdin's chief servant. The wizened woman stepped forward with Dash the hound. "Our orders were to end the threat to the prince. You did that job well. But our Lady and our King do not want Pibbibib to die this night. He still has some role to play in the outcome of this great struggle."

A warrior trotted up from the slope below. "We've killed them all, Mirri," he announced. "We found four female archers among them. None of them survived."

"Dash did his work well," said Mirri. "He got Weakling's scent and never lost it. Gather up the corpses of our enemies and throw them over this cliff. We need to return to our Lady and make our report. One thing I know: Weakling still lives. I just heard him howl down there. That leads me to conclude that Pibbibib is still with him. The rest of the Dark Brood would have left that wretched creature behind to die. But Backstabber won't abandon him. He still has big plans for him."

PART TWO:

A WORLD PULLED APART

Chapter Nine

New Worlds

Morros, the Elder of Orres, turned onto his side but stayed soundly asleep in his plush, canopied bed. He was dreaming of riding a wild one. Once more he was a young man, free of duties and obligations and focused solely on staying atop a bucking stallion. Suddenly the black steed turned its head and bit him on the throat. Startled, Morros left the dream and opened his eyes. Despite the darkness, he realized that someone actually had grabbed him by the throat and yanked him from his bed. He tried to scream, but the clasping hands squeezed so tight that he nearly passed out. Out from his bedchamber he was dragged. His holder, obviously large and muscular, brought him down a hallway and into the study. There by candlelight, he took his first look at his assailant: a mammoth warrior of Equis. Five more giants stood nearby, each fixing their glares on the Elder. Each face was huge and branded with strange marks. By the warriors' feet sat Morros' counsel and captain of the guard. Both Shutoo and the soldier looked like men expecting the worst.

His assailant let loose his grip and flung Morros to the floor. The Elder, still used to being in control, demanded, "What is the meaning of this? Don't you know who I am?"

The warrior kicked him in the head. "Shut up, dog!"

Morros shrank into a ball. When he uncoiled, he looked over to Shutoo. The counsel averted his eyes.

Into the room strode Lord Mackadoo, standing in his black cape and armor, with the red jewel set upon his forehead. "Which one?" Mackadoo demanded.

An underling pointed to the counsel. Mackadoo turned to Shutoo. "You were told to bring us the head of the son of Horse Stalker. Where is it?"

Shutoo could barely get the words out. "P-p-pardon me, lord, but... somehow he escaped."

"Then you failed us." Mackadoo pointed to the counsel. "Hang his head in the town square. It will help us keep order. Our troops can feast on his corpse."

"No, please! I can help you. I can do whatever you want." Shutoo begged, even as two warriors picked him up and carried him off. He kept pleading as he was thrust out the door. From the courtyard came a brief shriek, then silence.

"Now this must be the Elder," Mackadoo said, pointing to Morros. "You now belong to me. We have invaded your land and made you all our property. I am about to decide your fate. Should I kill you now or hang you alive by your feet outside this compound?"

"Please, lord," said Morros, "if you wish to find the son of Horse Stalker, I can help you."

"Can you? I doubt it. However, just to be safe, we'll hang you upon the wall." He pointed to the captain. "Hang this one with him. Let's have a matching set out there to keep the masses in line."

The Elder and the captain begged for mercy. Mackadoo left them wailing. He exited the study, passed through the courtyard and strode out the compound's main gate. There a warrior met him. "Lord," he said, "the sergeant has returned."

"Good. Take me to him."

Mackadoo followed the warrior down the lane toward the darkened town square. Along the way they passed two corpses from the village guard, each about to be strapped to a spit and roasted by the conquering troops. A warrior stood up and called out, "Lord would you care for some eyeballs? They're still fresh."

"Just one. Throw it to me." The warrior chucked it high. Mackadoo raised a hand, caught it and popped it in his mouth without breaking stride. "That'll do nicely."

The side streets around the town square lay deserted. Near the village bell sat the sergeant resting atop his black charger. His head was still shaved clean. "Greetings, lord," he called. "It doesn't look like you met much resistance here."

"No, sergeant, we killed a few guards and the rest ran screaming to their huts. We'll leave them be tonight. In the morning we'll round them up and begin their education as our new subjects. We won't need to leave many troops here. Most of them can go north in the morning for the assault on Kierinswell, though I doubt they'll be much of a fight there either. Now then, have you found any sign of enemy troops? I mean our real enemies."

"No, lord. Tor and his kind seem to have vanished. Our forces have advanced to the very edge of Kierinswell without meeting any resistance. It seems the enemy has abandoned the MuKierin to us. However, I suspect they're still somewhere up in those mountains."

"Yes, Tor took all that high ground from us years ago. He usually doesn't give up what he takes away. Hopefully he'll be content to keep his troops up there and leave us alone here in the lowlands."

"There's one more thing, lord. Near Kierinswell I was able to make contact with one of the scout teams that had been at Fire Mountain. They said Rakmah and the archers never returned from their mission. Neither did Backstabber nor Weakling nor anyone else from the assassination team."

"That's disturbing. It's no surprise to me that our gasbag would turn up missing. But Rakmah is another matter. What happened to them?"

"I don't know, lord, but I want to find out. And if Backstabber betrayed them, I want to personally kill him."

"Of course, but first things first. Right now we have a people to conquer. After we've put the MuKierin under our feet, you can go looking for Backstabber. If that miscreant is still alive, I know he won't be able to hide from you."

At daybreak, Blaze and Roff stood high atop a cliff at the edge of the great wasteland north of Kierinswell. From the bluff, they looked out north to the horizon. Before them the sagebrush seemed to grow sparser with each passing mile. The morning was warming quickly.

"At last, I'm going to meet my grandfather," said Blaze. "I've waited my whole life for this day."

"I know, cousin," said Roff. "But first we need to cross that dry ground. None of our people have ever done that."

"My people have. Now it's our turn. Let's go."

Below them, Roff's cousins waited by the horses. Off to the side sat Tustin, still thinking of Darnelle. The two had met again that night in the valley south of Fire Mountain. But they had parted after just a few days. Now Tustin was bound for the Green Lands. Cisly and Darnelle, meanwhile, had gone east with Roj into the hill country above Kierinswell to meet Blaze's mother Healdin.

Before they said goodbye, Tustin took Darnelle aside. "I almost lost you that day in Orres," he told her. "I've never been so scared in all my life, Darnelle. I've never cared for anyone like I care for you."

She didn't look him in the eye. "Spider, things are happening too fast now. Blaze says the Realm is going to conquer our people. You're going away. I'm staying here. Who knows what's going to happen next. Don't you fall in love with me."

"It's too late, Darnelle. I love you."

"No. We don't even know if we'll both survive what's to come."

"You think it's better to hide your feelings. I won't do that. If I die, I die. But now at least you know that somebody once loved you. And now I've said it. From now on, nobody can take that away from me, not even you."

Sitting beneath the cliff, Tustin thought once more of their last words. And he wondered what more he might have said to her.

Blaze and Roff descended the cliff. "Are you ready?" Blaze asked the cousins.

Stannis replied, "I don't know. It feels wrong to leave now when Equis is coming to conquer this land."

"What can you do to stop the invasion?"

"Nothing, I suppose, but it still feels wrong."

"I understand, Stannis. But one day you will be able to overcome the evil ones. I promise."

Kicked asked, "How far are we going, Blaze?"

"Just to edge of the Green Lands. Then I'll go on alone to my grandfather. But it's important that you come with me."

Blaze and his kinsmen rode north, bringing along four extra packhorses that carried two days worth of water. The riders quickly left behind the familiar sage and entered a barren ground of salt flats and sand dunes. The land before them sloped gently up and down, seeming to stretch out forever without a butte or ridgeline in sight. They relied on their water skins when they camped the first night. But late on the second day they knew they would soon run dry. It was then that Blaze brought them to a hidden well. Roff and his cousins were riding ahead and would have passed by it without noticing. The well was covered and lacked any marker. It looked just like the rest of the sandy expanse. But Blaze called to his kinsmen and they stopped. Dismounting, their leader began to carefully scan the ground around him. He leaned over and picked up a flat, oval-shaped rock. "Here it is," he said. "Bring me the bucket with the rope." He reached down and pulled up a small square plate of iron.

"How did you ever find it?" Roff asked.

"My mother helped me."

"How?"

"This plate has been touched by my mother's power, Mara, the Vine. I can sense it."

"So that's how your people pass over this land," said Roff. "They can sense the markers for the wells, can't they? No wonder we can't find this water."

They camped there that night, and lit no fire. For two more days they journeyed through the wasteland. Late on the fourth afternoon of their journey, Blaze found the second well and they made camp by it. That same night they awoke to the sound of distant cries. From the darkness came sobs and wailing that faded in and out. The high-pitched cries seemed both plaintive and ethereal.

Stannis jumped up and stared into the night. "That's bad," he said. "What is it?"

"Maybe we better go find out," said Tustin. "Maybe somebody's in trouble."

Roff and the others began to rouse themselves. "Wait," said Blaze, still in his blanket. "Don't go out there. Those are our enemies. They're trying to trick you."

"What?" said Tustin. "Who are they?"

"They're rebels stuck out there in torment. Long ago their leaders chained them out there to punish them and to serve as a warning for the others. They're chained to one another and buried up to their hips. They've grown so weak that they can't escape. Over time they shriveled in place. Now there isn't much left of them because they've grown so dry."

"Don't they ever die?" asked Kick.

"Not from thirst. They're not like us. They just wither. But they can still be revived. That's why they're calling out to you. They could hear us passing by and they want our blood. If they were to get hold of one of us, they could regain their strength and rise up again."

"That notion gives me the chills," said Kick. "Let's get out of here."

"No, Kick. We're safer staying put tonight. Those evil ones can't move far. We just don't want to go riding over them. Don't worry. I'll take care of you."

The next morning they journeyed on, eventually passing by seven wells. Early on the morning of the fifteenth day, the party climbed a barren ridge and looked down upon a small lake with a mist rising above its green waters. Waterfowl glided over it—the birds taking refuge as they traveled far that autumn to winter nesting grounds. A few scrub trees clung to one edge of the lake, and green reeds grew there as tall as a man on horseback. A handful of huts and a larger meetinghouse sat in the flats beyond the reeds. On a nearby hill stood a grove of white aspen trees, their leaves shining golden in the early light of day. Tustin needed no one to tell him. This was the land of the King.

A few warriors by the lake saw the newcomers and waved to welcome them. Blaze and his kinsmen rode down to the outpost. More of the King's servants appeared, bringing baskets of food. On a long table by the lake they spread out breads, fruit and meat. The MuKierin soon sat down there upon benches, eating and gazing out on the waters while ducks and geese glided by.

After the meal, the warriors cleared the table and set upon it a large package wrapped in canvas. "Cousins," said Blaze, "gather round. I promised you that the King would help you battle the evil ones. Here is his first gift to you."

Blaze unwrapped the canvas and grabbed a bundle holding four short spears. When he stood them up beside himself, the spears barely reached his chest. Each tip was covered with a strange skin."

"What are they?" asked Kick.

"Weapons. They are a great secret, long hidden from our enemies. We must keep them concealed until the day of battle. When you return to the Dry Lands, the King's people will teach you how to use them. Just don't remove the covers from the tips until the last moment, for your own safety."

Stannis asked, "How are we going to conquer hundreds of warriors with a few spears?"

"Don't worry. You're going to have help. I promise."

Weary from the journey, most of the cousins that morning lay down by the lake and rested. But Blaze took Roff and hiked around the water's edge, stopping beside a great patch of reeds. "Cousin," said Blaze, "When you return, I need you to go for me to the Pappi."

"Why would I go there?"

"They need our help. The MuKierin and the Pappi have long been allies, helping each other to stand against the Barsk. But now our Clan has been conquered, and the Pappi stand by themselves. They need our help."

"How can we help them? And why should we?"

"Why should we? Roff, you know the answer. I've lived among the Pappi. They are dear to me, and dear to my mother and my grandfather. Now listen to me. The King has prepared a special place for my followers near the edge of this wasteland that we just crossed. It stands between the Pappi and the MuKierin. My father knows the place well. It can serve as a refuge from our enemies. But our people will need supplies, and the Pappi can provide them. So you see we can help one another. My mother has a plan. She'll send Cisly and Darnelle to go with you. They can pass along her orders to you."

"But how can we get our followers to this refuge? The bad ones now control our land. Won't those giant warriors be able to stop us?"

"When the time comes, you will be able to pass safely through the land. But first you must go to the Pappi. Take Kick with you. My father and your father will meet you along the way. Will you do this for me?"

"Yes, Blaze. But promise me that you're coming back to us one day."

"I promise. While my mother is helping you, my grandfather will be helping me prepare for that day. And when everything is ready, I'll come back to you."

Before dinner the young men gathered again at the long table by the lake. Blaze told them, "My friends, my kinsmen, thank you for joining me on this journey. I brought you here to help prepare you for what is coming. You now have crossed over and touched the King's Land. No one can take that away from you. Now we are all Green Landers. Tomorrow I must go on to my grandfather. While I continue north, most of you will return to the Dry Lands. When the time is right, you will need to take my followers to a place of safety, a refuge from our enemies."

"Where is this place?" asked Stannis.

"The King's people will take you there. My father has helped prepare it for you. He's gone there every spring since before I was born. When the time is right, my mother and father will help you take the first group of our people there."

"Wait a minute," said Kick. "Why did you say that most of us are going back? Won't we all return together?"

"No, I have a different mission for Tustin. He needs to go a different way. I want him to go on a separate journey with a muleskinner from this camp. His name is Burl. He's a simple, childlike man, but a true friend of the King."

Everyone looked at Tustin, whose face became taut and pale. "Where do you want me to go?" he asked.

"I can't tell you that now. It's a great secret and our enemies would take it from your kinsmen should they ever be captured. But after you leave us and reach a place of safety, I have appointed someone to tell you about your destination. For now all I can say is that the King himself has chosen you for this mission. Will you do this for me?"

"Will I be gone from Darnelle a long time?"

"Yes."

Tustin sighed. "You know I'd rather go back to her right away, Blaze. I worry about her. I almost lost her once. I don't want to go through that again."

"I know, Tustin. I know I'm asking a hard thing. But it is important. Will you do this for me?"

"Yes, I'll do it."

That night the King's servants prepared a banquet. Lining the main table were roasted goats and chickens, plus fruits and nuts never seen in the Dry Land. Wine skins hung together on a large post. Blaze's followers sat near him on pillows around low tables. Guardsmen and other servants sat and ate nearby.

After dinner Blaze introduced Tustin to a dark-skinned servant. "This is Burl," he said. "He's a muleskinner and a true servant of the King."

Tustin's eyes opened wide to behold a man of medium height with a great belly. He had a thin black beard and a bald head. On the bridge of his nose he wore wire and glass spectacles, something unseen in the Dry Lands. Burl slowly extended a hand with short, stubby fingers.

"Excuse me," said Tustin, who was slow to take the hand. "It's just that I've never met someone whose skin is ..." His voice trailed off when he noticed that Burl's eyes weren't upon him but on Blaze."

"Burl doesn't speak MuKierin," Blaze said.

"He doesn't? Then why am I supposed to go with him? How are we going to talk to one another?"

"You'll learn his language." Blaze turned to the muleskinner and said a few words in a strange tongue. Burl nodded and stepped away.

Is he shy or just a simpleton? Tustin wondered. Aloud, he asked Blaze, "Are there others like him, his skin color, I mean?"

"Yes, you'll find many colors in the Green Lands. Listen to me, Tustin. I'm pleased that you're going to get to know Burl. You must learn to trust him. Where you go, when you go and how you go are matters best left to his judgment, with your input, of course. Please know that Burl is dear to the King. That's why he chose him. This journey is as much for him as it is for you.

"There's one more thing I need to say. When you arrive at your final destination, please be careful. The King will have some servants there to help you. But Burl might not be with you and he probably won't be able to introduce our allies to you. So don't blindly trust anyone. Test all those who offer you help. The enemy will be near. Use your head, as well as your heart. The danger will be great, and your life will hang in the balance."

"What? Are you sure you want me for this mission? I'm not a fighter, Blaze. You know that."

"I know that you're the man that I want for this mission. Do you know something that you and I have in common, Tustin? We're both considered half-breeds."

Tustin was taken aback. "You know that about me?"

"Yes, I knew it even before I met you. Listen to me. My enemies think I'm going to fail because I'm a half-breed. They believe I'm weak because I have MuKierin blood in me. I want to prove them wrong. And I want you to help me."

The two men hugged and returned to the table. A quartet of warriors rose to sing, accompanied by stringed instruments. Their verse was in MuKierin:

Seven, seven
stars from heaven,
falling from the midnight sky;
Greet them, greet them,
go and meet them,
for it means the day is nigh.

Sorrow, sorrow,
on the morrow,
for it means the stars must part;
Tend them, tend them,
stand, defend them,
till once more when heart meets heart.

When the song ended, Stannis turned to his leader. "Blaze," he said, "I've still got so many questions. Remember when you told Sunny that he didn't understand our story? Well, I don't, either. Not really. I can't see how we're going to overcome our enemies without you. And Roff says we're about to get caught up in some bigger conflict with the Barsk and the Pappi. It all seems more than we can handle. Part of me wants to beg you to come back with us. And part of me wants to go north with you to the King. The one thing I don't want to do is to go back home without you, and that's the very thing you're asking me to do. Of course, I'll do it. I won't abandon my cousins. But right now I don't feel very brave. I never thought I'd admit something like that. It's not what a MuKierin is ever supposed to say out loud."

Blaze put a hand on Stannis' shoulder. "I knew we'd be friends that first day we set out horse hunting," he said. "I remember how you told me to take care when chasing the wild ones, not to take too many chances."

"I was always better at giving advice than taking it."

"You're still my Stannis, the man who rides the wind. And now I need your help like I've never needed it before."

Blaze went and embraced each kinsman. He said, "The time has come for me to say farewell. My kinsmen, my friends, I will come back to you. I promise I will. Until that day, please look out for one another." He lifted a golden carafe from a silver tray with tiny glasses upon it. Carefully he poured thimblefuls of the golden contents into each of the glasses. "This is Ta Elowynn, the Living Fire. It comes from the vines of my people, the same vine you will find waiting for you at your new home. They are vines of healing and hope. Drink, my friends. Taste the Living Fire and live."

The King's servants lifted glasses and toasted, "To the King and his Child!" Roff and his cousins lifted their tumblers and drank. The draught went down smooth but immediately the kinsmen felt it set their insides afire. They tried to look upon one another but instead what they saw were visions of the future, dark dreams it seemed. Roff felt himself in a valley near nightfall facing hundreds of evil ones on a hillside above him. Tustin felt himself riding across a great wasteland, chased at night by some deadly evil. Kick and Stannis each saw themselves in chains, advancing toward a great castle. All the visions seemed like they would end badly. Each man sought a way of escape. The darkness seemed to grow, devouring all light.

Then they heard Blaze call out, "Fidden Gadaeyo!" "Shine in the Darkness, my friends." And every man no longer felt alone. Each relaxed, and there they all fell asleep.

In the morning they awoke on the same ground, by the long table, each man covered by a blanket. Stannis rose first and roused the others. They found gifts sitting beside them. Blaze had given each man a brown cloak for the coming winter, plus a white stone on a necklace. The stones were engraved with a sketch of the vine Ta Elowynn. As well, Blaze had given Tustin a small guitar and a leather satchel in which to carry it.

"But I don't know how to play this instrument," Tustin said.

"No doubt you'll learn," said Roff.

"Look," said Kick. "Isn't that the dark fellow you're going with?"

There on the ground by a nearby hut, Burl the muleskinner sat cross-legged, wrapped in his own brown cloak to ward off the crisp morning air. Beside him four mules stood dumb and still. Burl didn't seem to see the MuKierin, or if he did, he took no notice.

"Come on, Spider," said Roff. "You can't keep your new partner waiting." Together the young men helped haul Tustin's gear over to Burl. The muleskinner rose, took the baggage and tied it atop the loads of the two pack mules.

"What about the rest of you?" Tustin asked.

"We're going to leave today, too," said Roff. "We're heading for that place of refuge. Blaze calls it Newell. After we get there, Kick and I will go on to the Pappi. I'll be seeing Darnelle there. Do you still want me to give her a written message?"

"Oh, yeah, please," said Tustin. He reached in his pouch and handed Roff a small scroll. "I wrote it yesterday. Thanks for taking it to her."

When all was ready, Burl handed Tustin the reins for one of the saddle mules.

"Chinahwa," he said.

"What?" said Tustin.

A nearby soldier stepped forward. "Tiny," he said. "He wants you to know the mule's name is 'Tiny.'"

Tustin looked over the chocolate-colored beast, with black ears reaching above those of its rider. "He doesn't look tiny to me. Why don't we ride horses?"

"Burl loves his mules," the soldier said. "And in the Dry Lands they can outlast any horse."

"I like it," said Roff. "Tiny, meet Spider. Please take care of each other."

Burl asked a question. The soldier responded and Burl said, "Woochee?"

The soldier nodded and replied "Spider."

"Spi-i-i-der," repeated Burl, his face beaming. "Spi-i-i-der. Spi-i-i-der." He seemed pleased to have mastered his first lesson in MuKierin.

"I was hoping to leave that name behind," Tustin said.

Roff hugged him. "I'm going to miss you, Spider. But I think you're going to be in good hands."

Tustin hugged his kinsmen and mounted his mule. Burl led the way, followed by the two pack mules. Tustin, astride a plodding Tiny, brought up the rear. Slowly, steadily, the mules climbed the dusty slope above the outpost. Tustin watched the hooves ahead of him trekking through the soft, dun earth. Already he felt heartsick. It seemed it would take forever to get anywhere. He looked back. To his surprise, the outpost already looked distant, more like a painting than a real place where he had rested with his friends.

The riders and their mules headed northwest over dry hills toward great mountains. Tustin felt like an ant on a rumpled blanket. The land seemed so large. And he had the nagging feeling that someone might be out there watching him, just waiting for him to draw near. In the afternoon Burl led them along the western side of a large valley. Golden aspen leaves fluttered on the slopes and ridges above them. The men seldom stopped, but Burl regularly dismounted and walked in order to give his mule a break. He would motion to Tustin to get off, too, and say, "Spi-i-ider, shasooey, shasooey."

"What's that mean, dismount or walk?" Tustin asked

Burl never understood. He just repeated, "Shasooey. Shasooey."

"Alright, already," said Tustin, stepping down. "I'm shasooeying."

They passed no water all day and at evening they made their camp in a dry gully. Burl watered and fed the mules from their supplies, then laid out a cold dinner on a blanket. Tustin felt the night growing cold. "What about a fire?" he asked. Burl stood blank-faced. Tustin grabbed a few handfuls of brush. "Fire. May we have a fire?"

Burl shook his head. He swept a hand at the southwestern hills, and put two fingers to his eyes. "Oek distar."

Tustin wrinkled his forehead. "I don't understand. What are you saying?"

Burl put his mouth to the young man's ear and whispered, "Zoirra!"

He might as well have poked Tustin with a hot iron. The MuKierin snapped his head and scanned the southwest hills, straining to see any sign of movement. Burl, meanwhile, sat back down to eat his dinner.

Tustin kept watch for a full minute and then bent down toward the muleskinner. "Burl," he said, "listen to me. Where are we going?" Burl bit into a biscuit and silently watched him. "You, me, Burl. Where?" Tustin pointed southwest. "You, me, there?"

Burl emphatically shook his head.

"No, you say. Good, we're not headed over toward the bad ones. How about east? How about there?"

Tustin pointed east. Burl started talking, but Tustin cut him off. "No, don't lecture me. Just say, 'Yes' or 'no.'"

Burl gave no answer. Instead, he stood up, brushed the biscuit crumbs off his tunic and motioned for Tustin to follow him. They climbed out of the gully as dusk was settling on the land. When they reached a small rise, Burl pointed to the great stony crags in the north, then at Tustin, then at the high places again.

"You're telling me we're going over those mountains," said Tustin. He pointed north and put his hands together as if to form the shape of a peak. "You, me, mountains."

"Mounnn-tains," said Burl, nodding. He looked pleased with himself, as if he had just explained how the high places were formed. He walked back to finish his dinner. Tustin, meanwhile, turned to study the great peaks before him, and to watch the southwestern hills, over which the dusk was fading into darkness.

Sometime before dawn, Tustin began to shiver on his right side in the bedroll. He tried to turn over and felt the warmth of another body. Startled, he opened his eyes and found Burl snoring beside him, his cloak and blanket placed over both men. Tustin set his head back down and fell back to sleep. All too soon Burl shook him awake. Together they rose and made ready. That day they rode toward the high places that Burl had pointed out the night before. The mules stuck to their slow, steady gait. Tustin shivered as he rocked on Tiny in the crisp autumn air. He pulled his cloak tight around himself and thought about Darnelle. Burl hummed softly.

Late that morning they passed a tall evergreen standing like a sentinel amid the sagebrush. It looked nearly the height of four men. A few more such trees rose in the distance. "Burl," said Tustin, "what kind of tree is it? What's it called?"

"Shulleamain," said Burl.

Tustin repeated the word to himself. It was small compared to the ones living on the other side of the mountain. But Tustin had never seen one this tall, since nearly all the trees that lived beneath the Powder Mountains had been cut down long before his birth. He considered its cone-like stature as they drew near and felt a moment of coolness in its shade. The riders soon approached more trees mixed among the sage. Near the noon hour they crested a rise and came upon a deep blue lake, with a steep granite slope as its backdrop. Debris from a great rockslide had spilled down the hillside into the lake. Sharp-edge boulders had come to rest with their tops just above the water. Trees surrounded the shore and on the far side there was a small green meadow and a creek fed by the lake. Burl led the way among the trees to a place in the shade where pine needles kept the ground dark and free of grass. There the muleskinner dismounted. He kept the animals saddled and packed, but removed his mount's bridle and let three of the mules wander free to graze in the meadow. Those beasts quickly put their noses to the ground and began nipping the tall grasses. Meanwhile, Burl tied the fourth animal, a pack mule called "Tatta," to a small tree, apparently to keep it from wandering off. He handed Tustin a sack of food and walked directly to the far end of the meadow, where he took up his watch.

Tustin sat down against a tree, smelling its sweet pitch and listening to songbirds overhead in the canopy. He gazed on the lake and the steep granite cliff. He had never seen anything like this place. He wondered what the land would look like in winter with snow falling on the trees. He tried to

imagine what it would be like to live by such a lake, to build a
home out of logs and stone and live there with Darnelle. He
could imagine her helping him lift the logs one atop the other
to form thick, sturdy walls.

All too soon Burl collected his saddle mule. He went
and untied Tatta, allowing the beast to gather a quick lunch.
He gave Tustin two water skins to fill in the creek and led the
mules to the lake to drink from the shore. At last, the two men
mounted and set off through the trees along the edge of the
water. Burl stuck near the shore until he recognized an old
trail, one heading north into the hills. He turned upon it and
began to climb a small rise. Tustin followed but twisted his
head back for one last look at the blue waters—now
shimmering in the noonday sun.

They passed through the shade of a deep forest. Tustin
became both fearful and fascinated. He had never seen such a
world of wood and glen, of green needles and yellow light
filtering down from above. Before him the dark earth lay
covered with downed trees and branches piled randomly atop
one another. The land seemed so beautiful, and yet it offered
a thousand places from which to be ambushed. If his enemies
were near, he would never know it until they were upon him.

That night they camped beneath the trees and off the
trail by a granite wall that stood stained and cracked from
eons of ice and sun. Once more Burl lit no fire. They slept
close to the mules, a small huddle in the forest. Burl seemed
to take no notice of the night sounds and soon was snoring
soundly beside him. But Tustin stayed awake and tried to take
it all in. *The Green Lands,* he thought. *I've come to the edge of a
new world.*

Blaze, meanwhile, also set out north to cross the
mountains. But he took a different path than Tustin. From the
outpost by the lake, Blaze rode swiftly with a small troop of
the King's warriors. His guides led him across rolling desert
hills to a series of relay stations. Each was little more than a
hut, a well and a corral filled with a collection of the finest

horses. At each stop, the riders traded spent animals for fresh mounts, refilled their water bags and set off again.

The guides made for the lowest crossing in the Granite Mountains, Lone Pine Pass. It was there long ago that Zoirra the rebel Master and his followers had passed as they fled south from the Green Lands into the desert. After their departure, the King had ordered a stone fortress built at the pass to guard against a return of his enemies. The fortification had never been challenged.

It was there, beside its great stone walls, that the Champion passed into a land whose waters flowed north from granite mountains into a golden valley and beyond to the sea.

That day, groups of warriors gathered along the trail to watch Blaze as he crested the pass and came to rest that night at the fortress. The next morning, as the Champion began his descent, more warriors turned out to take their first look at him. They silently watched as he rode down rocky canyons, forded rushing rivers and passed through forest glens. By the time Blaze had reached the foothills beneath the mountains, the road was regularly lined with soldiers, packers, lumberjacks and farmers. No one ever said a word, but all fixed their eyes on the young man. They knew his coming signaled a new day.

On a crisp autumn morning, Blaze and his party reached a long ridge in the lower foothills. They passed through a grove of great oaks and emerged from beneath the gnarled and twisted limbs to a grassy hilltop. As they rode into view, a horn sounded nearby. Soon a second one answered. Blaze looked to the bottom of the hill where he spotted a white pavilion and a score of tents. He could see distant figures seemingly frozen in place, their gazes all turned toward him. From the pavilion a figure came running. He was tall and his stride was great. He bounded forth for all he was worth, aiming for the hilltop. Blaze turned and looked at his companions. They all smiled broadly.

Soon the runner cried out, "Blaze! My child! My child!" On he came. Blaze dismounted and stepped down the hill. He couldn't take his eyes off the runner. Soon he realized he was running, too. And the other's voice began to boom.

"Blaze! My child! My child!"

The runner had broad shoulders, a head topped with a great mane of brown hair. His face was rugged, partially covered in a brown beard, and his eyes set deep, but his smile and countenance radiated joy. The hill before him was steep, but it didn't seem to lessen his pace. Now Blaze was hurtling downhill at him. It looked as if the collision of the two would break bones. But at the last moment the runner stuck out his right arm, caught Blaze's torso in it and began to twirl the young man wildly into his embrace. Together they whirled round and round.

"My child! My child."

"Grandfather," said Blaze. "My King."

"My grandson. At last. At last!"

When the two stopped spinning, Blaze looked downhill and beheld a woman approaching on a gray mare. In her auburn hair and knowing smile, he saw his mother.

"Grandmother," he said and bowed. "My Queen."

"Hello, child. How good to see you. I only wish Healdin were here to share in my joy."

"Begin the Feast!" said the King. "Strike up the instruments! Come, child. A banquet awaits you. This will be a day to remember!" With those words, he put his arm around Blaze and set off with him down the hill.

Chapter Ten

On the Mend

Sorenth lay weak in bed for days. His battle with the giant warrior from Equis had nearly killed him. And the trip from the old trading post had further weakened him. However, the woman warrior named Aidyn had saved him with her healing arts. In the end, Sorenth made it alive to the home of Yawnna, the young Quolli maiden who first had tried to rob him. There, in what had been a servant's hut, the former cadet slowly regained his strength. For the first two days, he rarely opened his eyes, but each day he drank a broth made from the medicinal herbs that the woman warrior had provided. Aidyn also had provided extra medicine for the young man's wounds. Yawnna made sure that Sorenth drank the broth, and she watched as her woman servant applied the medicine to the Pappi cadet's shoulder.

Gradually, Sorenth began to take notice of his surroundings—the small hut's white adobe walls, the scratchy wool blanket, the pungent smell of the salves. When Yawnna saw that he remained conscious for more than a minute or two, she stopped coming to see him. Instead, she sent her servant, a plain-faced woman about fifty years of age. The servant spoke the Common Tongue used among the clans.

"Where is the young woman?" Sorenth asked one day.

"She says it is better for now if you don't see her," the servant replied.

"Why is that?"

"She didn't say. Who knows why the Quolli are the Quolli? I have lived among them thirty years, and I still can't begin to explain their ways."

"What's your name, woman?"

"Call me, 'Kitar.'"

"Kitar, tell your mistress I wish to speak with her."

"As you wish. You must learn about the Quolli in your own way."

The next day Sorenth awoke from a brief nap and found a short, fat man seated on a stool beside him. The man looked about as old as the servant. He had bulging cheeks, a scraggly black beard and dark squinting eyes. "So, swashbuckler," he said in the Common Tongue, "at last, you open your peepers. Your strength returns. That's good. Soon all the women will sing of your great manhood."

"Who are you?" asked Sorenth.

"I am the man of the house, the rooster who rules this roost. You may call me Ciga. My daughter found you dying like a dog. She brought you home, and I have become your protector."

"Your daughter? Do you mean the one who tried to rob me?"

"Let us not dwell on the past. After all, she did help save your life."

"Did she? Then I suppose I should thank her. Where is she?"

"She told me you had asked to speak with her. I am her father, so I am the one you must speak with, swashbuckler. Yes, you and I must come to an understanding."

"Must we? And why's that?"

"I wish to keep you alive. Some of the young men in my village want to hang you by your manly neck. And some want to slit your manly throat. You and I must make sure that this does not happen."

"That's very kind of you. And why would a Quolli help a Pappi?"

"I told you. I have become your protector. But you must do your part. You must not tell anyone, not even me, why those three giants of Equis wanted to take you prisoner. Do you understand?"

Sorenth unconsciously touched his wounded shoulder. Once more he remembered the exchange of blows with his huge enemy. Immediately he thought of his brother and the other cadets. "Don't worry, I don't know why they came after me. And even if I did, I wouldn't tell you."

"Excellent. A few of the stupid ones here may be tempted to sell you to the Realm. We don't want that, do we? Of course not! Let's keep them guessing about whether Equis really wants you."

"Forgive me for asking this again, but why do you care about me? I know that you are my protector. But what's your game?"

"What, you think the Quolli have no honor?"

"I know the Quolli have no honor."

"Oh, swashbuckler, you insult me. That's not wise for a man in your position, is it? It's a good thing I am not easily offended. In any case, I think it is good to be frank with you. I intend to be well compensated for my kindness."

"By whom?"

"The woman who saved you."

"And who is that? I know you don't mean that young thief of a daughter of yours."

"No, I don't mean my shy dove. I mean the woman warrior, the one who killed the three giants."

"The woman warrior? And exactly who would that be?"

"You don't know her? You don't remember seeing her that day?"

"I don't remember much after I got pierced by the sword. I did see a vision of a woman, or at least a woman's face. But I thought I was dreaming."

"No, she is real. I believe she killed the great warriors. I wasn't there. But I have met her and I have beheld the dead warriors. Moreover, I have seen her accuracy with a bow. She hit her mark at two hundred paces. And she warned us that the whole village would die if we didn't take care of you." Ciga stopped and sneered, displaying stained teeth. "You don't believe me, do you, swashbuckler?"

"Who believes the Quolli?"

"Once more you insult me. I'm keeping track, swashbuckler. And let me say one more thing. I don't believe

you when you say you don't know the woman. That makes
no sense, does it?"

"Perhaps it doesn't. So why did this magical woman
save me?"

"I can't imagine. What she sees in you is beyond me.
But she has warned my people not to harm you. And she paid
me well to watch over you. Don't tell my kinsman that, by the
way. It can be our secret. But now I am your protector, and I
intend to watch over you. Together we must keep you alive.
Then the fierce woman will pay me again instead of taking
vengeance on my people. So I will see that your strength
returns and then you will leave me and never come near this
place again."

When Blaze and his friends rode north toward the
Green Lands, Roj took Cisly and Darnelle and journeyed east
into the Powder Mountains. With them rode Mirri, Healdin's
chief servant, who guided them through the foothills and up
to the high country above Kierinswell. For three days they
ascended vast canyons and crossed stony ridges. They rode
beneath peaks that soon would receive their first snowfall. At
the end of the third day, they passed along a dry streambed
where the slopes seemed to press together on each side.
Before them a woman emerged from a cave. The riders rode
forth to meet her.

Roj spoke. "Cisly and Darnelle, this is my wife
Healdin, Blaze's mother."

Cisly noted sadness in the woman's eyes. Her wrists,
meanwhile, bore deep scars from shackles. *What happened to
her?* Cisly thought.

"Welcome, friends," said Healdin. "Please come with
me and rest from your journey."

Roj dismounted and hugged his wife. "Blaze did
well," he said. "I was all torn up inside, but he did well."

"I know. Thank you, Roj, for watching over him.
Thank you for comforting our son."

The couple walked arm in arm, and the young women followed. They walked to a fire ring and took seats there on wooden benches.

Darnelle spoke first: "Lady, please tell me what's going to happen to my people? We've heard that the Realm has invaded our land. What will become of my great-aunt and my kinsmen in Orres?"

"That depends on us," said Healdin.

"I don't understand. How does it depend on us?"

"We can rescue them. Will you help Blaze and me do that?"

"How can we rescue them?"

"The King has established a safe haven in the wild lands west of Kierinswell. It will be a refuge where we can shelter all the MuKierin who will join us. We can bring them there and protect them. But we also must reach out to the other people of the Dry Lands. The first shall be the Pappi. That's where Cisly can help us."

"Me?" said Cisly. "I don't see how."

"You speak their tongue. You can convey my message to their leaders. I won't send you there alone. I will send you as part of a delegation that will include my husband and my nephew Roff. You can begin your journey and meet Roff on the way when he returns from the Green Lands. And I want Roff's father, Noli, to go with you, too. All of you will be my representatives."

"Lady," said Cisly, "I'm not well-suited to such a task. I get angry at times. More than angry, I get violent. I stab people or hit them with rocks. You might need to put shackles on me to keep me in check."

Healdin rubbed her scarred wrists. "No," she said, "you won't need shackles. I will help you. You and I both have sons. If we remember our sons, both yours and mine, we'll be able to do the right thing when the time comes. For them, we can help put things right.

"But the Pappi won't listen to a woman, much less a courtesan."

"Cisly, you are a former courtesan. More than that, you are a free woman. Perhaps the Pappi won't listen to you, but we must offer them our help. The stakes are high. If the Pappi reject us, the Barsk will conquer them. Indeed, the Barsk will try to stop you from sharing my message. But I will help you." Healdin stood. "Follow me, children."

Leaving Roj at the fire ring, the three women entered the cave. Twin silver candelabra lit the interior, which featured a drop-leaf writing desk and a straight-back chair sitting on a woven rug of many colors. From the desk Healdin took a vial on a necklace. "This is for you, Darnelle," she said. "It contains an elixir from the vine we call Ta Ellowyn, the Living Fire. A drop on the tongue will bring sleep and healing for many ill people. Take it and use it wisely."

Healdin next reached into the desk and picked up a stone blade. "This is for you, Cisly. Now I must prepare it for you. I wear a great power sheathed on my leg. I will give some of my power to this blade, and you will wear it sheathed on your leg. Think of our sons when you draw it. Cut a human of the Dry Lands with it and you will put him into a deep sleep, even as Blaze has put men to sleep with the White Gem. The blade will be powerful enough to also hurt those of the Dark Brood, though not in the same way as with humans. I hope you won't need to ever use it on one of those evil ones."

Healdin took the stone blade and poured a small amount of Ta Ellowyn upon it. "Close your eyes, children," she said. "I don't want you to be blinded."

Cisly and Darnelle obeyed, even as Blaze's mother reached down to the sheath on her leg for Mara, the Vine. Suddenly a great burst of light overwhelmed the two young women. Closed eyelids couldn't shut its power out completely. Cisly and Darnelle fell to their knees and covered their faces with their hands. Soon they smelled a sweet fragrance. The Vine met the stone blade and the elixir sizzled into vapor. Cisly began to cry. In her mind she saw her son calling to her. He seemed to have grown taller and older.

Outside, Roj saw the light pour forth from the cave. "Oh, Mirri," he said, "she's going to be sick again. She's used her power once more. When will this end, Mirri? When will she ever be free of this terrible curse?"

"Her work here is almost over, Roj," said Mirri. "Soon she will rest."

Pibbibib spent his days throwing rocks.

After escaping the King's servants, he had hidden for weeks in a cave with Weakling. Both warriors had broken many bones from their crash landings off the mountain cliff. Backstabber had done his best to set the snapped and shattered limbs. But Weakling's right leg and ankle had been so smashed up that they never properly healed. The smaller warrior's broken shoulder also remained grotesquely out of place. Weakling couldn't move without limping hunched over like a bent, old hag.

Pibbibib had rebounded better than his ally from the injuries. Even so, he couldn't shake a slight limp, and his left arm wasn't able to fully swing and rotate. What bothered him even more was his uncertainty about the future. It now seemed certain that the enemy could track Weakling, just as the smaller warrior was able to detect the movements of their adversaries. Pibbibib still hoped that one day Weakling could help him find the Great Valuable. But such a search might expose them once more to their enemies, and the next time they might not be able to escape by jumping off the edge of a mountain.

For his part, Weakling had no intention of leaving the cave. He didn't care that their food supply was almost gone. They had been able to live for weeks off the corpses of their dead comrades, who their enemies had tossed off the cliff. The female archers had been especially lean. But though they had little left to chew on, Weakling vowed that he was staying put.

"I don't care if I starve. I don't care what happens to me."

"We can't lie low here forever," Pibbibib had said.

"You can leave any time you want. But now I'm a cripple. I don't care if I live or die here. If you want to chase your crazy dreams, you'll have to go without me."

Pibbibib fumed, but he decided to keep quiet and bide his time. At the moment, he didn't know his next move, so there wasn't much point in trying to change Weakling's mind. He would wait for a sign and another chance to bounce back.

While he was waiting, he threw rocks. He preferred hefty, rounded ones that fit well into his big right paw of a hand. He spent hours practicing at targets, winding up and letting loose with deadly velocity. Sometimes he mixed it up by flinging one right after another. After a few weeks he got to where he could regularly hit a helmet at twenty strides. Within ten strides, he rarely missed.

One morning he looked out from the cave and caught sight of humans on the cliff above him. "Visitors," he whispered to Weakling. "Little vermin up there above us. I think they spotted Rakmah's armor. Good thing we left it out in plain sight. Let's see if they come down to take it."

The bait worked. Four riders soon passed by the cave and rode up the box canyon to the base of the cliff. Two dismounted and began to rummage among the abandoned swords, helmets and breastplates scattered there. The other two stayed on their horses and kept watch. The men on the ground scooped up some of the booty and began to tie it to their saddles. As they did, they laughed at their good fortune.

Pibbibib, meanwhile, went skulking among the boulders, his right hand clutching his favorite rock. He stayed low as he passed along the right side of the box canyon. The riders would have no choice but to retrace their path. The great warrior drew within fifteen strides. He took aim and flung a missile that caught one of the horsemen just above the right ear. Stunned, the rider tumbled senseless to earth. The other men saw their comrade fall and scanned the canyon. To their horror, Pibbibib was coming at them, limping but still faster than any human. The three men took to their horses and made a hasty retreat around the terrifying giant. They managed to avoid the great hulk and the stones he sent zipping past their heads. However, as they rode near the cave, Weakling jumped out from a clump of rocks. He slammed into one of the horses, knocking down both the mount and its rider. Weakling rolled over the top of them with his hands on the man's throat. The horse scrambled up and galloped away. But the rider didn't escape. With one motion Weakling snapped his victim's neck. Over near the cliff, Pibbibib did the same with the man he had beaned. Soon both warriors were dragging their victims back toward the cave.

"You're getting pretty good with those rocks," said Weakling.

"I'm learning," said Backstabber. "You and I don't move as fast as we used to. There was a day when we would have caught all four of those dogs. Now I'm a step slower and I need a way to compensate. Killing with a rock may not be as satisfying as with a blade, but it helps put meat on the table."

Newly nourished, Pibbibib set out alone a few nights later to explore the hills around Fire Mountain. At dawn he found a resting place in an outcrop facing Kierinswell. He had been there less than an hour when he spied a troop of cavalry riding south. As the riders drew closer, Pibbibib was stunned to see that these warriors were from Equis. *They're ours,* he thought. *Slinkers, by the look of them. What are they doing here in broad daylight? Something's changed.* He could have jumped up and caught their attention, but he chose to stay hidden and let them pass. He remained there until dark and then hurried back to Weakling.

"Something's up," he announced. "I saw a column of our cavalry in the low lands yesterday. They were riding tall and proud like they owned the place. Our chums must have invaded this land."

"That's impossible. Where's the enemy? Tor and his kind have guarded these vermin for generations."

"Well, maybe that's all changed. We must be in control here now. That's got to mean new opportunities. I'm going out again. I want to find out what's going on."

"Not me. I'm not going anywhere."

"Fine. Stay here. I won't be gone too long. I think I'll catch me a horse dog and do a little interrogation. In the meantime, you'd better get ready. I'm sensing a change in the wind. If our troops have conquered this land, it's only a matter of time until somebody stumbles across us. Our leaders won't let us stay here forever. We're going to find ourselves back in action, whether you like it or not."

Chapter Eleven

The Granite Mountains

On his first morning in the mountains, Tustin awoke to the scent of pine. He had slept through the night beneath a granite cliff, which at sunset had glowed golden but now before dawn had reverted to a dull gray monolith. The chill air pounced on him as soon as he threw back his blanket. He could see his breath. Quickly he pulled on his brown cloak.

Burl already was tending the mules. Tustin decided to venture into the forest to discover the murmuring water that had put him to sleep the night before. He passed a downed tree and came to a small brook where a boulder rested in a bubbly riffle. As he looked into it, slim fish darted for the deep shadows of nearby pools. Jays cawed in the evergreen limbs overhead. Tustin peered upstream. He could see only a sliver of the stream before it turned and disappeared among brush and stone. He looked back and was surprised to discover that he couldn't see the camp. The woods seemingly had closed in around him. He realized how quickly he could get lost in such a land.

"It's beautiful," he told Burl when he retraced his steps. "Do you live in these mountains?" In response he received a blank stare from the muleskinner. Tustin waved his arms and pointed around him, vainly trying to be understood. "I've never seen anything like this place. I wish we knew one another's tongues. I wish you could tell me if all the Green Lands are like this."

They saddled mules, packed their gear and continued their journey as early sunlight glinted off the pine needles far above them. The trail veered alongside the brook and turned onto a switchback that took them up the back of the imposing cliff. On the ascent, the mules stepped up their pace. They no longer seemed the plodding beasts of burden that Tustin had thought them in the desert. With a steady gait, they chugged uphill and easily pivoted the switchback's tight turns. Soon the animals were trotting up a stone staircase that opened onto a flat stretch of bare granite.

The riders descended a ridge and crossed a large stream that glistened with glassy waters running swiftly over tan and golden stones. Tustin held tight to his saddle, but Tiny passed through the stream steady and undaunted. They came to the top of the bank and Burl brought them to a halt. Tustin wondered why. A moment later, he saw the reason: Six archers in green buckskins had appeared and blocked their path. Hastily Tustin turned to check the route behind him. Across the stream more warriors had stepped out of the trees to cut off any retreat. Meanwhile, the first group of archers began to advance. Along with their green uniforms, all the warriors had their faces painted green and black. Their bows were fitted with arrows, though all were still pointed down.

Burl raised a hand in a sign of peace. "Fidden Gadaeyo," he said. To Tustin, the greeting sounded almost childlike. The young man watched tensely to see how it would be met.

"Fidden Gadaeyo, Burl," replied one of the archers. The warrior stepped up and shook the muleskinner's hand. His comrades drew near and patted Burl's arms. A few moments later they stepped aside to let the rider and pack mules pass. Tustin found himself frozen, his rein hand holding Tiny back. The archers looked warily at him.

"Spider. Hona, Spider," Burl called. "Hona."

Tustin relaxed the rein and an eager Tiny bounded forward. The warriors stood silent and solemn as the stranger passed by. Tustin tried not to look scared. He focused his gaze on the grassy parkway before him. The trail was bounded on either side by tall rows of willow bushes. At length they reached a passage between the wild hedges. Ahead, Tustin spied a great meadow. The stream circled to the left and a tall forest nestled up to the edges of the expansive pasture. Tustin had never seen such lush grasses. He guessed there must be at least fifty horses and mules grazing there.

It took him a few minutes to notice a camp. He reached a high spot in the meadow and far off spotted a few white tents pitched on dark soil amid pine trees. Smoke from three fires rose above the evergreen branches. There among the shadows, the King's people passed. Burl made for the tents. As they approached, a few warriors strode out into the sunlight to greet them.

One was dark skinned like Burl, but tall and thin, with a glistening rounded forehead and intense eyes. He called out in excellent MuKierin: "Are you the one called Tustin?"

"You can speak my language," said Tustin.

"Does that surprise you?"

"Well, yes. It's just that…" Tustin's voice trailed off.

"It's just that I'm dark like Burl?" The warrior watched as Tustin grimaced. He walked over and took the hand of the mounted muleskinner. "Do you think we're all like him? I assure you that we're not. Burl is special. You could say he's one of a kind."

"I'm sorry. I didn't mean anything. It's just that I haven't met anyone like Burl or you in all my life."

"No offense taken. Now climb down from that mule and come with me. I'm the captain here. I have some questions for you."

"For me? Why do you have questions for me?"

"Climb down. Follow me."

Tustin obeyed. Leaving Tiny with Burl, he followed the captain. The soft ground beneath him cushioned his steps in a way so different from the desert sands. As they passed beneath trees, the ground became thick with pine needles. They reached bare earth and came to a table and a log bench. The captain motioned for Tustin to sit and said, "Tell me why you've come to the Green Lands."

Tustin tested the bench, found it sturdy and sat down upon it. "Don't you know?" he asked.

"I need to hear you tell me what you can."

"Well, I guess I'm here because Blaze sent me. I don't know exactly where I'm going or what I'm supposed to do when I get there. But I've come because he asked me to, and now that I'm here I'm a little spellbound. I've never seen such country."

"Yes, this land is dear to us. But it is not an easy place to cross, especially for a child of Hannah."

"And why's that?"

"Your body isn't used to the high places. This land can wear you down. And now summer is past. The ice and snow are coming. We need to help you cross the mountains as soon as possible."

"Are you going with Burl and me? When will we leave?"

"No, I can't go with you. I've got to get my own people ready to leave the high country before the snow flies, too. But you won't go without help. I'm going to send my chief scout to lead you. You'll leave in the morning. He'll be back by evening. In the meantime, my people will show you to your tent. Today you can relax and explore. Just don't get lost. Keep close to the stream and you'll be fine."

The autumn sun blazed high in a bright azure sky as Tustin made ready to explore the meadow. Before doing so, he had feasted on a tasty venison stew, served in a large mess tent. He must have been early, because no else was there, but the cook happily served him and encouraged him to have an extra biscuit. "You need more strength up here," the cook told him.

When he left the mess tent, the rest of camp seemed empty. Even Burl had disappeared. So Tustin set off by himself through the meadow. Along the way he found Tiny and the other mules. They had been turned loose and were rolling on their backs, each one of them kicking legs heavenward as they tossed to and fro on the grass. Tustin passed the beasts and set off across the meadow for the stream. The sun warmed his face as he passed among the grazing livestock. On the far side of the meadow he came to a flat-topped boulder perched beside the stream. He sat down upon the rock and dipped his feet in the rushing waters. "Whoa!" he shouted, "That's cold!"

The boulder was warm and made the perfect resting spot for a nap. However, he still had much that he wanted to see. As such, he rested briefly before setting off upstream.

Soon he came to a narrow trail that passed into the shadowy forest beside a stony hill. Up Tustin climbed, resting often as he found himself breathing heavily. He passed a small thicket and sent a covey of quail scurrying off across the dark earth. He broke into sunlight and made for a summit with blue sky behind it. From atop it, he could see the high peaks and ridges that encompassed the meadow. One distant slope held no trees but lay covered with loose rock and shale. Striking off again, he hiked uphill until he came to an outcrop with a forest below. He looked down and spotted a cave with the half-eaten carcass of a deer beside it. His mind raced to consider what kind of creature had killed the animal. *Was it a panther? A wolf? Whatever it is, I don't want to meet up with it. It's time to head back to camp.*

He descended the hilltop and retraced his steps to the stream. He quickened his pace and concentrated on the sounds around him. For many minutes there was little but the gurgle of the nearby waters. But eventually he caught the sound of hoof beats on stone. Without thinking, he rushed into the forest and hid behind a fallen pine. Horses drew near. Tustin could hear them stop at the spot where he had left the trail. A moment later they moved past him. Tustin peered from his hiding place and caught sight of three riders trotting toward the meadow. Slowly he rose and followed them.

Sunset was fast approaching when he reached camp, which was now alive with activity. Warriors in green leather stood in line at the mess tent. Others in tan buckskin led horses and mules to a hitching rack on the meadow's edge. Burl was there, along with the captain. Tustin went to greet them.

"Ah, here is our guest," said the Captain, "Tustin, this is Yaig, my chief scout."

Yaig was short and stout, with a gray beard that set off his round cheeks. He wore tan buckskins and a round hat made of beaver's pelt. Beneath his hat flowed a wavy mane of gray hair. "I've seen this young fella," the scout said. "He was hiding in the brush as we rode passed."

"Sorry," said Tustin. "I heard horses coming and didn't know if you were friend or foe. So I ran off the trail."

"No offense taken, son. But you likely won't hear your foes coming. And you won't escape them unless you can do a better job of hiding yourself."

"That's why he's going with you," said the captain. "Come, friends, we'll talk at dinner."

As they approached the mess tent, the warriors waiting in line began a song. It shocked Tustin to realize that the verse was in his tongue:

"Yaig of the mountains, Yaig of the sea;
He swims with the dolphins, he sings to the trees.
He knows the high places where eagles soar free,
Yaig of the mountains, Yaig of the sea.

The captain said, "Tustin, That was for your benefit. My men want you to know that you'll be led by the best scout in all the high country."

"Don't listen to them, son," said Yaig. "They've just been living up in this thin air a little too long."

"They sang of the sea," said Tustin. "Will you be taking me there? I really want to see it."

"Wouldn't we all? As much as I love these mountains, my heart belongs to the King's home at River's End. We all get a tingle inside when we crest the last ridge of the West. There you can look out over the green trees below you. And the shepherds are tending their sheep on grassy hills that run down to the sea. And the ocean is pulsing to the horizon – green and glassy, or blue as a mountain lake or gray as a winter storm. And the waves are crashing all along the jagged shore. And there at the mouth of the river, where the brown otter swims and the white egret flies, you can see the Castle of River's End. And its turrets glisten white against blue sky. And its walls fade to gray when the fog nestles in against the hills. I tell you, son, that fog can form a vast cotton curtain that seems anchored to the tops of the trees. Yes, sir, there is no finer place for me than River's End. To think of it is to ache inside. To see it is to find your heart in your throat. But to be going there, to know it as your destination, that is to fill your soul with music and to lessen the burden of a great journey."

"Now I really want to go there."

"Perhaps you will someday. But first we've got to get you out of these mountains alive."

"I still don't understand the danger. Is it the Realm?"

"No, son, it's not the evil ones. It's a different sort of challenge. It's the thin air and the coming snow. Your people aren't made for these high mountains. Tell me, have you ever waded through snow?"

"No, sir. I did slide on a patch of snow with Blaze one summer in the Powder Mountains. I suppose that's poor preparation for what lies ahead."

After dinner, the warriors gathered around a great fire. They began to make music as a half moon rose above them across the southern sky. They sang of the high country and of their battles in the wild lands. "Tell me the words," Tustin said to the captain.

"It's a song about our enemies. I'll give you a rough translation:

> "They came looking for arrow shafts;
> Rebels seeking good wood for bad deeds.
> They slithered out of the Dry Lands, their knives
> sharpened, hungering for blood.
>
> "By the lake they hid among the willows;
> Traitors taking what did not belong to them.
> They darkened their faces and set about their thievery,
> their eyes darting to and fro.
>
> "They came looking for arrow shafts.
> We gave them ours;
> They will never fight again.
> Let others follow, our bows are ready."

Tustin shuddered. "I'm glad I'm on your side, Captain. But I still wonder what you're all doing up here."

"My troops guard the high passes. We keep the enemy out of the Green Lands. These mountains provide a wall of protection for our people. And we are the sentinels who watch over the high country. Each summer and fall we stand guard until the snow flies. Each winter we pull back west to the foot of the mountains and wait for spring. We have done so for generations. And we must keep doing so as long as our enemies threaten us."

The musicians began another song, a jig fit for a romp on the starlit meadow. A fiddler bowed a lively tune that slid up and down the musical scale. A lyre and guitars strummed along, and four warriors sang the chorus. Tustin clapped along with the rest of the company. Out of the corner of his eye he noticed Burl get up and walk away. *What a simpleton,* he thought. *Not even music seems to touch him.*

After a number of verses and choruses, the voices rose to a crescendo and then dropped soft and low. The fiddler paused, too, leaving the guitars and lyre to strum softly. So it went for a few measures, until a new melody called out from somewhere beyond the fire. A flute sounded clear and mellow in a simple strain. The fiddler smiled to hear it and joined in with his jig. The two melodies merged, and the listeners gave a cheer. Tustin turned to identify the flute player. It was Burl, stepping forward to stand beside the fiddler. Together they brought the song to a sparkling close. A great cheer resounded through the meadow and off the granite ledges: "Burl the piper! Burl the piper!"

Tustin shook his head and smiled. *I have misjudged my muleskinner.*

The high country journey began at dawn. Yaig joined Burl and Tustin and brought along two companions. One was a scout and guitar player named Pitherinn. The other was a warrior name Crester. Only Yaig spoke MuKierin. The men brought along three spare horses, which were tied together head to tail. Those horses in turn were tied off to Yaig's white pack mule. The company departed just after sunup. Yaig took the lead, followed by Burl with his two pack mules. Tustin came next, with Crester and Pitherinn bringing up the rear with the white mule and the spare horses.

They climbed the first hilltop and descended into deep forest. The morning sun filtered in here and there among the pine boughs, but much of the trail was shaded, and the soil was dark. Tustin found himself caught up in the subtleties of light and shade. Soon the party emerged from the trees into a glen of small ferns, then back to forests and eventually to granite ridge tops. Four times that first day they passed lakes so blue that Tustin thought the waters must be magic. Four times they crossed creeks that flowed from the lakes, where Tustin beheld clear water tumbling and frothing over golden riverbeds. They camped that evening in a meadow. At sunset they watched deer come down from the hills to graze near the stock. Pitherinn gave Tustin his first guitar lesson. The young MuKierin fell asleep to the sound of the water dancing in the brook.

Frost came with the dawn. The company set out in trees but soon they climbed uphill to a place where the pines gave way to a land of sheer granite. Great slabs littered their way and the very hills seemed beat from cold, gray stone. Even so, petite alpine flowers clung to rocky crevices, and a string of small lakes sparkled across a rocky plateau. Off to the west, great peaks rose up like snowcapped pyramids. The sun was bright in the morning, bouncing off the speckled granite. But by afternoon, clouds began to sail in from the north and a chill settled over the land.

The gray morning that followed stung like winter. The tarps covering the gear were partially frozen, and steam puffed from both man and beast as the party struggled to break camp. The riders descended the plateau and passed once more into forested slopes. An hour later the first snowflakes fluttered by. Soon white powder was coming down soft and steady. It lay on the branches and dusted the rocks. Tustin had seen snow before in winter, but nothing like this.

That night they slept in bearskin robes. Before turning in, Tustin noted that the soft powder already was over his ankles. By morning, it was up more than halfway to his knees. By then the wind started to pick up.

They set out quickly, urged on by the blowing snow. Yaig went first, followed by Pitherinn and the three spare horses to help break trail. The trace they took led past a gray, white-capped lake, now encircled by snowdrifts. Tustin looked at it and shivered.

They rested once that morning, and then only to allow Yaig to get a fresh horse. Tustin sensed the guides' determination to break out of the high country. Cold as he was, he knew he must do everything possible to help. In the early afternoon, they came to a fork in the trail. Yaig had stopped in a clearing there to wait for the others to catch up. His helpers and Burl huddled around him on horseback. In short, crisp diction the chief scout appeared to outline the two trails. The other two guides added their views; Burl only nodded. Then Pitherinn looked up at Tustin and nudged his black stallion back through the snow to him. He touched Tustin's deerskin slippers and breaches, which his hosts had provided. The clothing felt soaked and almost frozen. Tustin had gotten them wet while dismounting in the late morning and had not wanted to say anything because it might delay the journey.

Pitherinn spoke sharply and motioned to his companions. The others stared at Tustin. He shivered and rubbed his hands across his arms. All the scouts and Burl dismounted. Yaig said, "Son, we've got to get you out of those wet clothes." Quickly, they spread out a tent for a groundcover and pulled Tustin off his mule. They stripped off the wet clothes and put on a new pair of breeches, plus thick wool stockings and deerskin slippers. They helped him get back on his mule and draped a bearskin robe over his legs. Immediately Yaig set out, leading the spare horses down the western fork. The others stayed behind while Crester brewed hot water over a small fire built on a large flat rock. When the water boiled, fragrant leaves were crushed and dropped into

the old pot. Then Burl poured a cup and put the mixture to
Tustin's lips.

"Spider, Spi-i-i-der," he said. "Chulay, Spider.
Chulay."

Tustin drank the heady tea. It sent warmth throughout
his chilled trunk and limbs. Immediately the four riders set
out to catch up with Yaig. The company stopped earlier that
day and Crester soon had coaxed a roaring fire in front of
their one tent—the guides decided they would all sleep
together that night. They put Tustin close to the fire and
carefully checked his hands and toes for frostbite. Pitherinn
did everything he could to keep their young traveler
comfortable, even heating rocks in the fire, then wrapping
them and placing them beside him for extra warmth. The
scouts took turns through the night keeping the fire alive,
while Burl slept next to Tustin to keep him warm.

Even so, Tustin coughed and wheezed when he
awoke. The guides made him drink two brimming cups of tea.
They again wrapped him in a bear robe and set off. The snow
had stopped but the sky remained gray and overcast.
Everything was quiet but the sound of the horses tramping
through powder. The company soon descended a rock
canyon, its ledges draped in white and its gray walls marbled
with black streaks—the age-old signs of water and ice eating
into rock. Tustin no longer heard the birds or the squirrels,
nor did he notice the deer passing down among the trees.
What he did sense was how much his muscles and joints
ached. Burl rode behind him, presumably to keep a better eye
on him. Yaig and Pitherinn once more took the lead. Once in
the morning and once in the afternoon the two guides pushed
far ahead of the others, then stopped and started a cooking
fire. When the others arrived, they filled Tustin up with a hot
cup of tea and then passed the cooking pot around for each
man to take a swig of the steaming brew.

They pushed on throughout the afternoon and came to
the bank of a small river. The water there roared as it raced
white over gray rocks. Late that afternoon Yaig and Pitherinn
again disappeared. When Tustin saw them again, they had

already crossed the river. Pitherinn spotted Tustin and swung onto his stallion's back. At once he spurred the animal back across the ford. Tustin watched amazed as the great horse lunged and splashed through the rushing water. Pitherinn rode low in the saddle with his bent head just above his stallion's neck. The animal kept its footing and emerged with its black coat steaming and shimmering. Pitherinn firmly reined in his excited mount.

"Ta Alouwain, Spider," Pitherinn shouted, pointing up and downriver. "Ta Alouwain!" He waved, beckoning Tustin to ride alongside him. Tustin nodded and urged Tiny down the bank and up to the water's edge. Pitherinn took Tiny's reins and came along Tustin's left side. Crester came alongside him on the right. Then the riders urged their mounts into Ta Alouwain, the White Dancer. Tustin shrieked when the water soaked his legs. He had never known such cold. The two guides whooped and screamed, and the horses thrashed through the water as if rushing into battle. Even Tiny seemed momentarily transformed into a war charger. Before them the river gave way. The three crossed over and climbed up the opposite bank. Burl followed with the pack mules and spare horses.

Atop the bank, Yaig already had a fire going. He helped Tustin from his mule and pulled off the soaked breeches and slippers. The guides dried Tustin, clothed him and set him back upon Tiny. Yaig once more led the way with Tustin behind him. The two rode for another half hour until they came to a split-rail fence near a rocky outcrop. Yaig passed the corral and led Tiny to the mouth of a cave. Jumping down from his own mount, he pulled Tustin from the saddle and helped him make it inside. "We'll stay the night here," said Yaig. "There's grain and other goods stored here."

Soon Yaig had a roaring fire going inside. Tustin lay in his bedroll and noticed provisions stored on rough wood shelves along one of the cave's walls. He closed his eyes and drifted off to sleep.

When he awoke, Yaig was gone but the others had arrived. The guides gave Tustin medicine and supper, a meaty soup. Still, Tustin seemed barely conscious as he lay beneath his bearskin. Burl soon crawled under it to help warm his companion.

"How much longer?" Tustin cried weakly. Burl said nothing, but gently rubbed Tustin's temple.

Pitherinn heard his cry and came over. "Spider," he said kindly. "Fidden Gadaeyo, Spider. Fidden Gadaeyo." He took out Tustin's guitar, tuned it, and softly plucked a lullaby. Tustin soon fell back to sleep. But twice in the night he awoke burning with fever.

At dawn he felt both weak and chilled. It was now the morning of the sixth day since they had left the high country camp. They again set out, following a trail that descended steadily to the north. Pitherinn led Tiny by the reins. Tustin hung weakly to the saddle with both hands. The wind soon came up and the guides wrapped a second bearskin around the young MuKierin—one around his shoulders and one across his lap.

Tustin couldn't grasp how far the group had come from the high granite plateau of a few days earlier. He hadn't noticed that he was now moving through new kinds of trees. All he saw was snow hanging thick in the branches. In the late morning, snowflakes again started falling and the wind blew. Tustin's heart sank. Still, the company pushed on.

In the afternoon, Tustin fell asleep and almost fell off Tiny. Crester and Pitherinn came and rode on either side to keep him in the saddle. By then the trail had widened into a wagon road. The snow soon turned into a steady rain. The daylight gave way to dusk. Still they rode on. Tustin drifted in and out of sleep. He burned with fever and shook with chills. They rode through the storm as darkness fell upon the hills. At last they came to a clearing in the forest where a cabin stood with a single light burning in a window. With the rain still falling, the guides lifted Tustin off his mule and carried him sleepily inside. There, at last the young MuKierin found a much-needed rest.

That autumn, Blaze rode north with the King and Queen and nearly one hundred servants. They passed out of the oak-studded foothills beneath the Granite Mountains and came to the Golden Valley, a vast stretch of low lands shaped by a slow-moving river. There the riders first entered rolling grasslands, now dry and the color of straw after months without rain. Horned black cattle ranged freely in the vast countryside, and shepherds tended great flocks of white rams and ewes. Eventually, Blaze and company came to a wagon road that took them past orchards with hundreds of ripening apple trees. Farther along, they found farms with workers harvesting corn and beyond that paddies of ripening rice. Unlike the mountains, the vista here was open with little to block the sky but an occasional tree or barn.

Beyond the rice fields, the party climbed a levee and arrived at a ferry along a broad river. Blaze noted the brown water as it passed slowly by, unlike the Red River, which frothed and tumbled wildly in steep canyons. But this river had so much more water than the one in his homeland.

It took nearly a day for all of the entourage to cross the river, and one more day to reach the other side of the valley. As the party entered coastal hills, storm clouds blew in and a cold rain began to fall. It drenched everyone and everything, but the King's party rode on, determined not to be delayed in their journey. The rain continued the next day as the travelers navigated a steep and winding road among a forest of immense trees. The dripping glens and darkened sky made for a gray day, but still one filled with beauty.

In late afternoon, they crested the last ridge and looked down on a great white castle beside a river estuary. "It's magnificent," Blaze told his grandfather.

"It's home," said the King. "You've come at last, Blaze. I'm sure your mother told you, but if you wish, you may stay here and never go back to the Dry Lands. I certainly can't compel you to leave."

"I understand, Grandfather, but I'll be going back. I promised my friends that I would. However, I fear the longer

I stay here, the harder it will be to leave this place. When can we begin the preparations?"

"Be patient, child. We must await your mother's signal. Then we will begin."

Chapter Twelve

Intrigue on the Lake

It was now autumn in the Dry Lands, and clouds were gathering over the Great Lake of the Pappi. One morning the clouds spread above the remote hill country east of South Shore and beyond the no-man's land between the Pappi and the MuKierin. By midday, the clouds had moved far to the east.

"Will it rain?" Cisly asked Roj as they sat together on an outcrop above the surrounding hills. Beside them rested Darnelle and Noli.

"I think it might," said Roj. "You can ask Mirri when she returns. The good news is that we won't have to camp many days in the rain. We should be in South Shore tomorrow, if all goes as planned."

"Roj, when we get there, why don't you act as the interpreter? You speak Pappi as well as I do."

"That's not true. And even if it were, I'm not supposed to be part of the official delegation. Healdin wants me to stay in the background."

"But no one is going to listen to a courtesan."

"Former courtesan. Listen, you've already gone over all this with my wife. Healdin chose you, and she always has her reasons. Believe me, I've learned not to question her choices."

"I've learned that, too," said Noli. "And I'm even more thickheaded than my brother-in-law."

The foursome looked north to see Mirri, Healdin's chief servant, riding along the back side of the ridge. Six male riders followed her, including Roff, Kick and four of the King's warriors. Their horses chugged steadily up to the outcrop.

"Welcome, friends," said Roj. "I'm glad to see that Mirri found you."

Noli went over and hugged his son after he dismounted. "You look good, boy," he said. "Did you really cross over that big wasteland?"

"Yes, Papa. We went with Blaze all the way to the edge of the Green Lands. I sort of wish we could have gone on with him. I wanted to see more of that country. Anyway, we're here now. What's next? He didn't give us many clues."

"Don't worry," said Roj. "In time Cisly will give you all the details. Healdin gave her orders for all of us."

Darnelle broke in. "But where are the rest of the boys?"

"Well, most of them are still at Newell, our new home in the middle of nowhere," Roff said. "Uncle Roj knows the place. Anyway, Stannis, Quirt and Harney are looking the spot over and making plans to build a village there. But pretty soon they'll leave with the King's warriors to go back to our people near Orres. And as best I understand it, we're supposed to meet them there in a few weeks."

"But what about Tustin?" Darnelle asked. "You didn't mention him. Where is he?"

"Spider didn't come back with us," Roff said. "Blaze sent him on a separate mission."

"Alone?"

"No, not alone. He sent him off with a good, stout fellow, a muleskinner from the Green Lands."

"How long will he be gone?"

"We don't know. Blaze made it sound like he could be away for some time. Anyway, Tustin asked me to give you a note. I'll get it out for you tonight when we make camp."

Noli went up to Kick and slapped him on the shoulder. "Nephew," he said, "you must feel like this is your lucky day. You're finally going to get to see what fish look like."

"Don't play with me, Uncle," said Kick. "I'm not too sure about getting near that lake. I can't swim."

"Me neither, son. But we'll be fine. You and I just need to stay out of that water."

Together the combined party set out south through the hill country. With the clouds above them, they journeyed across treeless ridges and passed through barren canyons. They didn't stop until they were less than a two-hour journey from South Shore, the capital of the lake people. By that time a light rain had begun. The party made camp in a small ravine. The King's warriors erected three canopies for protection from the rain.

Roff unsaddled his horse and went to the women, who were resting beneath a canopy set against a great boulder. From a leather satchel, the young man removed Tustin's scroll and handed it to Darnelle. She took it and went out in the rain to read it. As she did, Roff turned to Cisly. "So, what's the plan, woman?"

"We're going down to South Shore to the home of a Pappi trader and Elder. His name is Bairn. He's a friend of both Healdin and your Uncle Roj. He'll help us get a hearing before the Pappi governing council. A delegation from the Barsk likely will attend this gathering, too. The Barsk apparently are threatening to conquer the Pappi."

"Blaze said something about that. So what are we going to say at this meeting?"

"We're going to offer the Pappi the King's protection. We'll ask them to form an alliance with us."

"That sounds a little funny. Why would they trust us? Right now we don't look like we can protect ourselves, let alone anybody else."

"I know. But those are our orders. Healdin says this trader will help arrange a secret meeting beforehand with the chief of the Pappi. Roj will go with you to meet him. And Healdin wrote out a message that she wants you to convey to their chief. Here it is. And there's one more thing you should know: She sent me to be our translator because she has given me a message to say to their leaders, should it be necessary. Believe me, Roff, I tried to get her to send someone else instead of me. I told her the Pappi wouldn't trust a woman, and the Barsk will call me a whore to my face. But Healdin wouldn't listen. She said you and I are the ones she has chosen for this mission. We are the appointed leaders of the Green Lands delegation. You and me, a concubine and a horse hunter?"

"Yeah, you and I make quite a combination. I feel like when I used to dance as a boy and be all out of step with the music. Right now I'm in way over my head. But I told Blaze I would do this for him. So I will." He raised the letter from Healdin. "I guess I'd better learn my lines."

"You've got time. First, tell me what's Newell like."

"Actually, it's surprisingly good ground. It's got as much water as Kierinswell, if you can believe that. And wait until you see the vine that's growing there."

"A vine?"

"Yes, it's from the Green Lands. Ta Ellowyn, they call it. They said Uncle Roj planted it there before Blaze was born. It's the most beautiful thing I've ever seen. And the Green Landers use it to make a medicine that heals people. It's what Blaze used to help Darnelle back in Orres. Before we said goodbye to Blaze, we tasted it. It's powerful stuff."

"I know a little about it. Healdin used it when we were with her. I can't wait to see the vine."

"You will. They say its leaves glow golden in the light of the moon."

While Roff and Cisly spoke, Darnelle walked alone in the rain and read the message from Tustin: "It pains me to write this to you, Darnelle. Blaze is sending me on a journey, and I don't know whether I'll ever see you again. But I promise I'm going to do my best to stay alive and find my way back to you."

Darnelle wiped the rain from her eyes. She put away the note and shared it with no one.

The next morning the delegation rode to a hilltop between two jagged crags. There Roff, Kick and Darnelle got their first look at the lake. The sun had broken through the last of the clouds, and the waters beneath them gleamed dark blue. The lake was so vast that they could barely see the northern shores.

"How can one place have so much water?" asked Darnelle.

"It's something, isn't it?" said Roj. "Wait until you stand on the shore."

"How deep is it?" asked Kick.

"Way over your head, boy," said Noli. "Just don't get wet and you'll be fine."

The King's people stayed behind at the summit. "I'll come to you tonight," Mirri promised. She waved goodbye as the six MuKierin rode on. Roj, Noli, Cisly, Darnelle, Roff and Kick descended the hill and emerged onto the plains near South Shore. An hour later they could see the city wall. They came to a wide gate where Roj presented the guardsmen with a letter of introduction from the trader Bairn. The captain of the guard soon appeared and escorted the newcomers into the city. Small adobe huts lined the avenue. They rode slowly past a market square with shops, taverns and trading houses made of stone. As they rounded a bend and climbed a hill, they came to a set of walls that enclosed a series of lakeside villas, the houses of wealthy Pappi. The flattop stone homes featured lower levels built into the side of the cliff. Most had outside stone stairways that extended down to the lake. The captain of the guard knocked on the gate of one such house. A moment later a middle-age man with gray hair and a beige cloak opened it.

"Tie!" shouted Roj. He jumped off his horse and hugged the man.

"Who's that?" asked Kick.

"Friend of the family," said Noli. "He's MuKierin, though he's lived among the Pappi for many years."

"Welcome, friends," said Tie. "Bairn sent me here to help you settle in. This is his home at South Shore. Please come in. He'll soon be here himself to greet you."

Tie led them across a courtyard as servants appeared and brought in the baggage. The party passed along a patio with tall bunches of lavender growing in stone planters. The villa had a single story at the hilltop level, but two more levels of living quarters were built into the hillside below, and at lake level an inner stairway led to a boathouse. The guests walked through a large entry hall into a great dining room with windows looking out on the lake. The room was lined with reed baskets on the floor and small ones filling a low table. Many of them featured dark, intricate patterns along their edges. The guests looked out the windows to the lake. They could see a large reed boat skimming over the water near shore. Its lone sail cupped the wind as the boat moved slowly out into the deep.

"Please rest here," said Tie. "We'll soon bring you food and refreshments."

"Excuse me, kinsman," said Roff. "Your name sounds familiar. Weren't you once a slave?"

"Yes, I was when Roj first met me. But I'm not anymore. It all changed when your cousin was born. After Blaze's birth, my owner Bairn asked Healdin what gift he could give her. He'd already given her a statue of a water dragon, but he wanted to give something more to the new mother. Healdin did an amazing thing. She asked him to set me free, and he did. For a time I lived with Roj's family. Later, he and I went into business with Bairn. We started by buying and training wild horses from MuKierin traders. But eventually Bairn made us partners in his trading company. He moved here to the capital, and we stayed on the east shore. Of course, Roj since has gone back to our homeland. But I still watch over Bairn's eastern estate. And our business has steadily grown."

"I guess it has," said Noli. "This is one fine home."

Servants soon brought fresh grilled fish, raisins, flatbread and wine. Kick looked carefully at the fish. "I guess you don't pluck them," he said to himself.

The MuKierin ate seated on the cushions around a low table. Sunlight was now gleaming on the blue waters. Soon the guests spotted a small boat approaching with two men in it. "There he is," said Roj, pointing down at the vessel. "That's Bairn, the older one."

Eventually the silver-haired trader emerged from a door leading from the boathouse stairs. Bairn smiled broadly and hugged Roj. Next he grabbed Noli. His voice rose with a greeting, but it was in Pappi. Roj translated, "He says he remembers you, Noli, from my wedding day. That was a long time ago."

"Yes," said Noli. "That was back in the days when we still were riding the wind. Tell him I'm pleased to see him again."

Behind Bairn stood Lon, the cadet from the Academy. The trader pulled the younger man forward beside him and spoke. Roj translated for Bairn: "This is Lon. Bairn says he's a trusted friend. And he's met Blaze. He's going to help us tonight and again at the peace conference."

Lon froze when he locked eyes on Cisly. She cocked her head and nodded. Bairn took note. "I see you two young people both remember one another," the trader said. "Blaze informed me about all of the events at the Barsk inn. Lon, this fair woman is named Cisly. Cisly, I have been waiting to meet you. And this is my dear friend, Lon."

"If he is dear to you, Bairn, then I will overlook the company he keeps," said Cisly.

"Indeed," said Lon. "I recall this woman. But how does she speak Pappi? The man who had her was Barsk."

"You don't think a Pappi ever had me?"

Bairn interrupted: "Cisly, we have much to discuss. I will speak, and you will translate for your people."

Bairn briefly set out his plan: That night all the men except Noli would take two boats and travel on the lake for a secret meeting with the chief of the Pappi.

"The chief especially wants to meet Roj and Roff," Cisly said in translation. "It's too sensitive to hold the meeting in the city, where you might be seen. Healdin wants Roj to remain in the background. So after dark, Bairn will take you by boat to meet the chief's vessel."

Bairn next explained that the peace conference would begin in three days. It would include a Barsk delegation from Northsford.

Cisly translated, "He says the Barsk are here to demand that the Pappi give up most of the northwest side of the lake. Of course, if his people did so, it would divide their land and leave them unable to properly defend themselves. In time, they would end up at the mercy of the Barsk."

Roff spoke up: "Ask Bairn whether the Barsk will believe that we speak for the King? Does he think we can persuade them not to attack the Pappi?"

Cisly translated and gave the trader's reply: "Bairn says it's not the Barsk we need to persuade. It's the Pappi. We're their last hope. If they don't trust us, they likely will agree to make peace with the Barsk, even though it would mean losing their freedom. That is why he begs us to do our very best."

The meeting ended. Roj advised the men to get some rest. Cisly stepped out to the patio. She took shade beneath a small tree planted in a raised bed and stood silent gazing out at the deep blue waters. After several minutes she turned and noticed Lon watching her. Catching her eye, he stepped forward."

"Woman," he said, "when last I looked upon you, you were adorned in scarlet."

"Yes, I was," she said. "I gave up that robe, along with many other things."

"That's what I've heard. Bairn speaks highly of you. He assures me that you are a new woman."

"Does he? He's very kind to say so, especially since we've never met before today."

"Exactly. I asked him how he could place so much trust in someone he doesn't know."

"And what did he say?"

"He said he knows the one who sent you. And that's good enough for him."

"But not for you?"

"Honestly, woman, I don't know what to make of all this. I'm still trying to understand exactly what's going on here. I keep hearing about a Champion and a distant kingdom. I have yet to see the power that either can muster. What I have seen are the Barsk, and I know their warriors could wreak havoc on my people. And what's going to stop them? I can never get a direct answer to this question. Whenever I ask Bairn, he just tells me that our future lies in the hands of a bunch of foreigners, including some horse hunters and a ...”

“Courtesan? Is that the word you’re looking for?”

“Isn’t that what the Barsk will be calling you?”

“Can a woman change?”

“You tell me.”

“I think she can. Let me offer one small example.” Remember my escape from the Barsk inn? Before I got away, some of your fellow cadets tried to stop me, so I stabbed one of them in the arm. No doubt you heard something about that. After that I met another one of your fellow cadets, a MuKierin who was home on leave and making ready to hurt a good friend of mine. He was talking to me ever so civilly, just like you are now, when I picked up a rock and bashed him in the head. Oh, yes, I did that to both those young men in the blink of an eye. And if I were still that same woman, I have no doubt that I would have already drawn myself close to you, smiled sweetly and then stabbed you with a knife that is concealed beneath my gown. I wouldn’t have thought twice about it, not after the way your fellow cadets have treated my friend and me. So I have changed, sir. And yet, it may still not be enough. I may yet fail to control myself. Indeed, I may yet stab someone here when I should refrain. All I can do now is remember that some people have put their trust in me. They are people I care about, and so I will try very hard not to disappoint them.”

“Well, you’ve certainly gotten my attention, woman,” said Lon. “Indeed, I can’t wait to see what you do when the Barsk meet you. Let’s hope I can remember to stay out of your way when the fighting starts.”

The two went inside to join the others. The men and women napped separately until the sun went down. As dusk settled over the lake, they ate a light meal of leftover fish and flatbread. The servants lit candles in other rooms, but kept the main room dark so the men’s night vision wouldn’t be disturbed. Roj and Bairn watched from the windows as the darkness deepened. Lon and Tie, meanwhile, went down to wait in the boathouse. Nearly three hours after sunset, all the men gathered by the vessels. Noli went with them and whispered to Kick, "Just remember what I told you. Stay in the boat, and you'll be fine."

"That's easy for you to say, Uncle," said Kick. "You're staying behind."

Bairn, Lon and Roff got into one boat; Roj, Tie and Kick took the other. In silence they opened the home's water gate and paddled from the boathouse into the cove. The boats soon rounded the eastern point, leaving behind the lights of South Shore. Lon and Bairn's vessel took the lead and set a steady pace on a northeast course toward the middle of the lake. The night felt cool with a soft breeze. The men heard little except the sound of their paddles softly dipping into the water. Stars shone overhead, but the moon had yet to rise. Before them, the dark water and the horizon blended into one.

Roff and Kick sat in the middle of their separate boats and held tight to the gunnels as their companions maintained a steady stroke on opposite sides of the vessels. Roj sat in the bow of the boat, with Tie in the stern and Kick in between them. "There's nothing quite like sitting in a boat, Kick," Roj said. It's like floating on a cloud."

"If you say so, Uncle. I'll admit that it's pretty out here tonight. Even so, I think I'd rather take my chances riding a wild one over stony ground. At least you know what to expect when you get thrown off."

On they paddled for nearly an hour. The men rested briefly and set out again. A few moments later, Tie whispered to Roj, "Hold still and look behind us."

Roj turned back and caught site of a small vessel far in the distance. "Whose boat is that?"

"I don't know. I think we'll soon find out. They're gaining on us." Tie gave three short, low whistles. "Let's catch up with Bairn."

Lon and Bairn heard the warning and came to a halt. The two boats pulled alongside one another. Tie whispered in

Pappi, "Someone's coming up from behind us. Could it be a friend?"

"That's unlikely," said Bairn, looking back. "It seems we're being followed. That's bad, especially if they have spears. We'll be at their mercy."

"Let's do something they won't expect," said Lon. From near his feet he lifted a sharp fisher's blade attached to a wooden shaft about the size of a man's forearm. "Let me get in the water here. You can dump over both sails and masts to help hide me. We can put Kick into the other boat with you, Bairn. You three can row slowly on. Meanwhile, Tie and Roj will stay here with me. They can help me surprise whoever is coming after us."

Lon leaned back in his seat until he flipped backwards silently into the water. Carefully Kick transferred into the bow of the other boat and took up Lon's paddle, doing his best to help Bairn row slowly ahead.

"I wish we spoke Pappi," Kick told Roff as their boat glided forward. "What's happening?"

"I don't know," said Roff, "and Bairn can't tell us. My guess is that we're in some kind of trouble. Let's hope Uncle Roj and these other fellows can deal with it."

From the other vessel, Tie whispered to Lon in the water, "I think I see a second boat. It's even farther back. Let the first one pass you by. If it's a friend, we'll call out to you. If it isn't, go after the second boat. But be careful. If I can surprise the first boat, the others in the second may start looking for swimmers like you."

Lon took the discarded masts and placed one atop another. Next, he got underneath a floating sail and treaded water with his head just above the surface. Tie and Roj paddled a short stone's throw away from him and turned their boat broadside to the floating masts. Tie grabbed another fisher's blade attached to a short shaft. He slipped over the far side from the approaching boat and grabbed the gunnel. As he clung hidden, he told Roj, "Give me a signal when they get close to us. I'll need a little time."

When the first strange boat drew near, Roj stood up and stretched his arms wide above him. He could see it contained three men. "MuKierin!" he called in his native tongue. "I'm MuKierin! They left me here. I don't speak Pappi. I can't swim. Do you understand?"

The three strangers looked around, apparently trying to figure out whether Roj was really alone. The man in the middle stood up and raised a spear. He motioned for Roj to get in the water.

"No, please," said Roj. "I can't swim. They left me here all alone. Please don't make me get in that water. I'll drown!"

The assailants' boat kept coming straight for Roj. The man with the spear began to curse, and it wasn't in Pappi. Roj said in MuKierin, "You're Barsk, aren't you? Okay, Tie. Can you hear me. Get ready. Go!"

Roj jumped feet first into the lake a few moments before the attackers bumped their vessel into his. At once the three confirmed that no one else was inside the MuKierin's vessel. Tie, meanwhile, dipped underwater and swam silently to the back of the enemy vessel. When he surfaced, he drove his fisher's blade up into the armpit of the paddler in the stern. The man gasped and slumped backward, severely wounded. The standing spearman turned but couldn't see who had attacked his comrade. Tie already had slipped back underwater. Roj, meanwhile, surfaced on the far side of his boat and let out a shriek. "Help me! Save me!"

Distracted, the spearman swung around toward the new sound. Tie surfaced by the middle of the boat. This time he plunged the fisher's blade deep into the spearman's thigh. The warrior spun and tumbled down, whacking his head on Roj's boat as he splashed into the water.

The third accomplice dropped his paddle and dove from the bow. He stayed underwater for nearly a minute, surfacing far from the vessels. At once he turned on his back and began a quick stroke, frog kicking for all he was worth. It was clear he was a good swimmer.

"Stinking, thieving Pappi," said Tie. "They must have been well paid to bring these Barsk out on the waters for the purpose of killing us."

The spear of the wounded Barsk had bounced off the two vessels and plopped into the water. Roj swam over and clutched it. As he climbed back into his boat, he noticed the Pappi swimming away. "Let him go, Tie," he called. "We've got another boat coming our way." Roj noted that the wounded Barsk spearman had somehow managed to grab onto his boat, which already was drifting away from the two MuKierin. The man's wounded paddler lay dying in the boat.

Tie climbed aboard with Roj. He quipped, "Your swimming has improved much from that first time we went boating."

"Hah!" said Roj. "This isn't a good time to remind me how you almost drowned me that day. Come on. Let's get ready for the second boat. These wounded fellows don't look like they're going to give us much trouble. Now let's deal with their friends."

Tie paddled the vessel slowly back toward Lon, who was still treading water and staying hidden among the floating sails and masts. The second boat by now had come alongside the floating debris. "That's far enough!" Tie yelled in Pappi.

The boat slowed. "Is that so?" came a reply. "And who's going to stop us?"

"We now outnumber you six to three. We've already beaten up your three friends here."

After Tie spoke, the wounded spearman called from the first boat, to which he was still clinging. His words to his allies conveyed more anger than surrender.

From the second boat, a man called out in Pappi, "You're going to regret this night, old man. We're still enough here to take the likes of you."

Lon heard the threat and submerged. He swam underwater until he reached the stern of the second vessel. Up he surfaced and stabbed the rear paddler in the shoulder. The boatman groaned and slumped forward. The passenger in the middle jumped up with a spear at the ready. But Lon had already sunk from view.

"Tell your friend to throw down his spear," Tie warned the man in the bow. "I know you're a Pappi and you understand me. Tell him."

Lon surfaced again near the rear of the vessel. The spearman saw him and sprang for the stern, but his sudden motion made the boat tip, and it was all the man could do to stay upright. Lon dipped underwater again before the spearman could steady himself. Tie, meanwhile, was paddling his boat forward to meet the enemy. Roj was with him, kneeling in the bow with a spear aimed directly at the Pappi paddling in the front of the other boat. The Pappi turned and saw that his own spearman was out of position and couldn't offer him any protection. At the last moment, the boatman dropped his paddle and dove from the boat. As soon as he surfaced, he swam furiously away. Left alone, the remaining spearman crouched in the boat and scanned the waters, trying to anticipate from which direction Lon might next attack.

Tie slowed his boat and began to back paddle. "Hold up, Lon!" he called. "Leave this Barsk alone. He can't hurt us now."

Lon heard the call and swam back to the floating sales. "Tie, are you sure?" he asked.

"Yes, we'll leave him out here. Maybe he'll help these wounded ones get back to shore."

Roj smiled. "Well, I'd say times have changed. I remember a day when you would have relished the chance to kill all these men."

"Yes, but that was back when I was a slave. Now I'm a free man and I'd rather not have all their deaths on my conscience."

Roj and Tie paddled slowly over to the floating sails and masts. They loaded them in their boat and then Lon pulled himself in over the gunnel. "There's still two able-bodied men swimming around out in those waters," said Lon. "What if they circle back around to these boats? They might still come after us."

"No," said Tie. "I think we've taken the fight out of them for tonight."

The three men sat still and watched their allies returning in the other vessel. Bairn called to them: "My friends, are you all well?"

"Yes," said Tie. "We met up with some Pappi and Barsk out here. But I don't think they'll give us any more trouble."

"Excellent. We also have some news. We've spotted some large boats coming our way. I hope they belong to our leader and his entourage."

As the two vessels came alongside one another, Roj noticed Kick was paddling in the bow. "Well," he said, "look here at our new boatman. Kick, I'd say you're a natural."

"Don't make fun of me, Uncle," said Kick. "You never told me how scary it is out here. Roff and I can't swim."

"Well, let's hope those are friends coming in those big boats out there. I doubt we can outrun them, and we certainly can't outfight them."

Three large vessels skimmed slowly into view, their triangular sails catching the night's gentle breeze. Each was more than twice as long as the small boats containing Bairn and his friends. The trader stood up and waved to catch their attention. To everyone's relief, the lead boat contained the chief of the Council. He called out, "Why so many boats, master Bairn?"

"We were attacked, my chieftain," said Bairn. "But my friends here have repelled them."

"My congratulations, gentlemen. Let us finish what you have begun. Captain, arrest these knaves."

Pappi soldiers in the other two ships quickly took the remaining assailants into custody. The chieftain, meanwhile, welcomed the six guests onto his craft. He smiled broadly when he shook Roj's hand. "So you are the one that Bairn calls the Horse Stalker. I am delighted to meet you, sir. Why do the Barsk fear you so much that they would send men here to kill you?"

"It's not me they worry about, sir. It's my son they fear, or at least Equis fears him. In any case, I think the Barsk also fear that your people will make an alliance with us. My nephew Roff has a message for you. I can translate."

"You speak Pappi well, Horse Stalker. Very well. I do want to hear this message. Indeed, I also want to know more about your son. But first I think we should change course and return to South Shore. We ought to make sure the rest of your delegation is safe at Bairn's home."

"Oh, thank you, sir. In all the excitement, I'd forgotten about them. My brother-in-law is back there, along with two young women from our party. Do you think they're all safe?"

"I hope so. We'll return as soon as we can. And on our way there we'll have time to talk. Our meeting may no longer be a secret, but we must make sure that all is well with your people."

Cisly and Darnelle stood on the terrace and watched the two boats disappear into the darkness. They could hear a dog barking, apparently down the lane at a nearby villa. A cool breeze reminded them that autumn would soon pass away.

"I have a question," said Cisly. "Do you wish that Tustin had come back with the others?"

Darnelle turned and leaned against the terrace's low outer wall. "Yes, I suppose so. But please don't tell any of the men. I still don't know how I feel about him. And now I can't stop worrying about what might happen to him. Isn't that crazy?"

Cisly smiled. "Come on. Let's go down to the water." They descended the stairway as Cisly counted aloud each of forty stone steps from the terrace to the shore. At bottom, she kicked off her sandals and waded into the lake. She hitched up her skirt and spun around, looking up at the stars overhead.

"Aren't you afraid of the water?" Darnelle asked.

"No, I love this lake. Truly it's the most beautiful place in all the Dry Lands. Besides, I can swim. I'll teach you if you want."

"No, thank you. Is it safe to come out to you?"

"Of course."

"Ah, Cisly! The water is so cold. I didn't know what to expect."

"It's refreshing. The Pappi take it for granted. But this lake is such a rare place, a world of water and fish and reeds. Before you leave, I'll have to get you out in a boat. We can't let the men have all the fun."

"I'm not sure Kick is having fun right now."

They stayed in the water until they could no longer stand the cold piercing their bones. Barefoot they climbed back up the steps. At the fire they lit a candle and retired to their bedroom. Soon they climbed into their beds and drifted off to sleep.

About an hour later, a woman servant rushed into Noli's room. "MuKierin!" she called, taking his hand. "MuKierin!" Noli rushed into the hall, which was lit only by the firelight. He heard no movement inside, but outside he caught the sound of some sort of tumult. Then there was pounding and pushing against the bolted main doors.

"The women!" Noli yelled. He raced to their room and flung open the door. "We're being attacked!" he called. "Hurry. We've got to hide." He slammed the door and pushed a bed up against it.

"Let's jump into the lake," said Cisly. She arose, ran to the window and threw it open. She could hear screams and shouts coming from the courtyard. "I can swim. After we hit the water, I can help you both make it to shore."

"No, wait, woman," said Noli. "Roj told me another way. There's a secret passage from this room down to the boathouse." He went to a rug in the corner and pulled it back, exposing a trap door. Lifting it up, he motioned to the women. Cisly went down first, followed by Darnelle. Noli draped the rug over the lid, climbed down into the passage, shutting the door behind him. He found a locking bolt fitted on the underside and slammed it into place.

The narrow passageway was too dark for their eyes, but Cisly slowly felt her way along the walls until she came to a brief set of stairs. They descended them and soon reached a wall at the end of the passage. "There seems to be a window of sorts here," Cisly said. "Yes, look here. There's a tapestry that covers up a hole in the wall. I believe we've reached the boathouse."

"There's supposed to be a rope ladder here somewhere," Noli said. "Roj said we could use it to get down to the dock."

"I've got it," said Darnelle. "Let me lift it up to the window. It feels like it's tied down at one end here."

Soon the three had set the rope ladder through the window and into the boathouse. Noli helped the women climb through the hole and descend the ladder. He followed them in and set his feet firmly upon the stone dock. The pavement was U-shaped, lining the three walls of the boathouse. Behind them was the closed water gate. The lake water in the boathouse looked too deep to stand in.

"What now?" asked Darnelle.

"Let's hope nobody comes down here," said Noli.

"Let's swim under the gate," said Cisly. "I can help you."

"Thanks, but I'd rather not," said Noli. "Not unless we have to."

As he spoke, the door to the villa crashed open. A strange man with a sword in one hand and a torch in the other strode into the boathouse. Noli reached down and grabbed a paddle for protection. The assailant smiled and pointed his sword at Noli's chest. Slowly he stepped along the pavement toward his victims.

"Can you swim?" he asked in MuKierin.

"No!" lied Cisly.

"Tonight you all must swim. My sword will teach you how."

Cisly turned and whispered to Darnelle, "Count to five and push me in." Cisly began to dodge and twist, seemingly looking for an escape. She turned and bumped into Darnelle, who caught her and spun her into the water.

After the splash, Cisly rose to the surface, flailing her arms. "Help me! Please, sir, spare me!"

The assailant smiled and took a few more steps forward. "Tonight, you all must swim." With the torch still in his left hand, he lunged at Noli, who used the paddle to knock aside the sword thrust and then retreated a few steps. The stranger pulled back a moment but swung three times in his next assault and grazed the MuKierin's left arm. Noli retreated once more. Behind him, Darnelle already had reached the end of the dock. With nowhere else to go, she jumped into the water and began thrashing helplessly.

Cisly submerged until she touched the bottom beneath her. There she found the knife hidden on her leg, the one Healdin had given her. Quickly she removed it from its scabbard. Up she popped alongside the assailant as he stepped forward again to attack Noli. With her left hand, Cisly grabbed the dock and sprang up as she plunged her blade into the back of the man's leg, just above the ankle. The attacker screamed and toppled lifeless to the dock. Noli rushed forward and grabbed their assailant's sword.

"Help Cisly!" sputtered Darnelle.

Cisly dropped the blade on the dock and shoved off. She grabbed Darnelle's arm and pulled her onto her back. "Just relax, Darnelle. I've got you." Kicking fiercely, Cisly brought her friend over to Noli, who lifted each woman back onto the dock.

"Is he dead?" asked Noli, picking up the torch and lifting it over their victim.

"No, he'll revive in the morning."

"How did you knock him out?"

"Healdin gave me the blade. She treated it with her powers. She said it would knock out humans. It apparently has a different effect on the Dark Brood."

"It certainly does, woman. I've seen that firsthand. Someday I'll have to tell you how my brother-in-law made that giant Weakling howl like he'd swallowed a hornet's nest."

"Cisly, you're quite an actress," said Darnelle. "For a few moments, even I was afraid you couldn't swim."

Cisly bent over and picked up her knife. "Serves him right for underestimating a woman. Now Noli, can we all get in the water, please? We should escape into the lake while we have the chance."

Another figure emerged from the stairway. Noli grabbed their assailant's torch and lifted it for a better look. At once he recognized Mirri.

"Children," she asked, "are you well?"

"Woman, where have you been?" growled Noli. "People have been trying to kill us."

"I know, Noli. I've met some of them. Most of your attackers have run away. However, a few of Bairn's servants were hurt in the fighting. My people are tending to their wounds. Come, children, let's return upstairs. It will be safer up there. You've done well this night. Now everyone will know how much the Barsk fear you. They have failed to eliminate you. And now they're going to have to look you in the eye."

A few hours later, the men returned to the cove in the chieftain's vessel. Roj and Lon untied one of their smaller boats and swiftly paddled into shore. After they landed, they raced up the outer stairway. Cisly was waiting for them at the top of the patio. "Is this my protector?" she called to Lon. "Have you come at last to save me?"

"Is everyone alright?" asked Roj.

"Noli had his arm slashed. And I stabbed the assassin who wounded him. The man is tied up and sleeping in the hall."

Lon shook his head. "Well, it's obvious that you don't need my help, woman," he said. "Even so, I feel badly. I should have warned the Barsk. It seems that all sorts of men underestimate you."

Chapter Thirteen

Female Encounters

Sorenth leaned on his crutch and called to the servant woman, "Kitar, how did the Quolli take you as a slave?"

It was an early fall morning, and Sorenth was standing in a dirt lane a few steps from the hut where he had spent most of the past three weeks. The middle-aged servant woman stood beside him and held a basket woven from long slender sticks. At the question, she squinted her eyes at the young Pappi. "Hah. You have been here less than a month and you expect me to tell you my secrets."

"Of course. Why not? Both you and I are held here against our will. We have much in common."

"Don't be a fool. One day you will leave this place. But I will stay here until I die."

"Maybe, maybe not. Perhaps I'll take you with me. But first I must get stronger. May I walk with you this morning to the marketplace? I could use the exercise."

"Yes, the master says that you may join me, if you don't pick a fight with the young men. He wants you to get out so the young ones can look you over. He says they are most curious about you. But no fighting."

"Agreed. We'll let them have a look, and I won't pick a fight."

Sorenth hobbled beside her down the lane, past adobe huts and larger homes. Soon they came to the village's main road. Sorenth had never ventured this far before. "It's been too long since I took a good walk," he said. "I do feel better in this fresh air. Now then, woman, since you won't tell me about your past, I will have to guess the details of your story. I say you are a Barsk princess. That explains how you learned the Common Tongue. And one day the Quolli stormed your citadel and brought you here. There's my story. Have I not guessed the truth?"

"Yes, except I was a queen, not a princess. Hah! Tell me, young one, what is your story? Why were you riding alone in this forsaken country? Surely you must have known about the Quolli."

"Oh yes, Kitar, I know about the Quolli. But I needed to get back to a brother. I still do. I must leave here as soon as possible."

"Well, that will depend on the woman warrior. She told my master that she would return for you at the proper time. Until then, you are not to leave this village. The bad ones from Equis might take you if you do."

Kitar and Sorenth came to an adobe tavern with a few canopies hanging along its north wall. There in the shade, a handful of merchants had set forth their wares: roots, raisins, dried meat and goat cheese. Villagers paused from their shopping and stared as Sorenth came into view. The Pappi halted and planted his crutch in the road. "Go on, Kitar," he said. "I'll wait for you over here."

The servant woman went forth and began to inspect the food and other merchandise. Sorenth looked around for shade but could find no place to his liking. He wanted to stay clear of the crowd. There it would be too easy for a hothead with a knife to come at him. At least in the middle of the road, he had room to swing his crutch and fight back.

A group of young men began to gather in front of the tavern. Their eyes fixed on him for a few minutes. One of the men pulled a knife and kissed it. Sorenth stared back silent, tight-lipped.

Soon a new young man entered the scene, a scrawny one with a beaked nose and a scraggly beard. He came walking up the lane, and his eyes locked on Sorenth. The man's dirty hair fell over his shoulders, which were draped with a blanket that concealed his right arm. He stopped safely back from Sorenth's crutch and bared his teeth. "Swashbuckler," he said in the Common Tongue, "at last you've crawled out of you hole. I thought I might have to kick down the door in order to speak with you."

"Why do you want to speak with me?"

"You wounded my kinsman. Do you know what that means?"

"I hope it means you're grateful that I didn't kill him. After all, he was the one who first attacked me."

"Hah! You're a funny one, swashbuckler. I like your style. You are a worthy opponent. Allow me to introduce myself. I am Naug. I am the man who drew the black mark."

"The black mark?"

"Yes, the black mark. I drew it, and that makes us opponents. You gave my kinsman a wound. Now I must give you a wound or die trying." Sorenth tilted his head from side to side, as if a new perspective might help him make sense of his newly announced enemy. Naug saw the perplexed look and frowned. "Don't you take me serious, swashbuckler? Hah! That would be your mistake. Don't think that I'm afraid to fight you. I would welcome the chance to attack you here and now. But Ciga has forbidden me from striking you down until the proper time. He told all the young men that we couldn't kill you now because we might somehow bring destruction upon the whole village. How frustrating you have made things for my kinsmen and me. It would be so much easier to attack you now and be done with it. All the young men want a piece of you. Look at them over there. They hate you so much, swashbuckler, and none of us can touch you. It's driving them crazy, I assure you. Perhaps you heard that our elders already have sent away all the men who tried to rob you. Those sad boys couldn't stand to be near you and leave you alone. So now they're all out tending goats in the countryside. Hah! I laughed when I heard that. But don't think you will find safety here. We still have plenty of kinsmen here who hate you. If I were to attack you now, all of them would rush in to help me. I would hardly need to lift a finger. You should be thankful that I am a patient man, and I have promised Ciga that I won't strike you in the village."

"That's very kind of you."

"Don't mock me. Don't think I'm afraid of you. It's just that I have a woman. I have something to lose if everyone here is slain. Do you have a woman, swashbuckler?"

“No, I have nothing to lose.”

“Too bad. No one will cry when I inflict great pain on you.”

Kitar came up with a basket of food. Naug frowned at her. “Woman, don’t look at me like that.”

“How am I looking at you, bird beak?”

“With disdain. I can see it. I’ll tell Ciga.”

“Yes, tell him, and I will tell him how you were trying to pick a fight.”

“What? Liar! I am merely sizing up my opponent. I am a patient man.”

“Patient, yes, but devious. You dare to offend a woman in front of this man. Surely you know that this man is a warrior dedicated to chivalry. He cannot abide the denigration of a woman in his presence. So even though you have been forbidden to fight, you deviously try to engage this man by belittling me in front of him. You know that he must defend my honor. You know that he now must fight you. You are an underhanded scoundrel, and Ciga will hear of it.”

Naug scrunched his face and shook his head. “No, I had no such intentions. Are you toying with me, woman? I assure you that I knew nothing about this man and any chivalry. I meant it when I said that I would not fight him today, and that is how it must be.”

“It may be too late,” Kitar said. “You may have crossed the line. He now may have to kill you.”

“What? Woman, you stay out of this! Don’t listen to her, swashbuckler. You must not fight me today. You would surely die.”

“Fool, it makes no difference to a man of chivalry whether he lives or dies. He must protect a woman’s honor. He is duty bound to defend me.”

“Silence, hag! Or I swear I’ll hit you so hard that your ears will ring.”

“Please, Naug, don’t do that,” said Sorenth, “or I will have to kill you.” Naug froze. His lips gaped and his eyes began to glaze. Sorenth turned and winked at Kitar, making sure that the Quolli couldn’t see their conspiracy. “Now, then, worthy opponent, let us talk no more of fighting today. I believe you when you say you knew nothing about my vow of chivalry. Therefore, let us both overlook these rash words. We need say nothing to Ciga. And when we meet again, please do not speak harshly to me of any woman."

"Thank you, swashbuckler," said Naug. "I knew you were a worthy opponent. I will leave you now, but we will meet again one day. Until then, we must both be patient."

Sorenth and Kitar began to walk back home. "Woman," said Sorenth, "do you always confound men like that. You had that boy shaking in his boots."

"I have learned well from the Quolli. Their right hand embraces you and their left picks your pocket. But you can rest assured that this fool Naug also is being played by others, who seem to be secretly working to keep you alive. Consider this: Ciga knew that someone would have to draw the black mark against you. It is their law. The Quolli must hold to the old ways: A wound for a wound, a killing for a killing. So what does that old fox do? First, he gets rid of all the young ones who tried to rob you. He knows that those hotheads wouldn't obey him, but would come after you at the first opportunity. Even if they didn't draw the black mark, they would goad and bully the one who did to fight you. You would end up dead, probably along with several Quolli. Ciga can't have that. It would cost him that second precious jewel he hopes to receive from your woman warrior. And, if she speaks true, it also would bring destruction on the whole village. So what does Ciga do? He persuades the village elders to send off all those angry young men to herd goats. Only when they are gone does he arrange for the drawing of the black mark. And who gets it? It goes to Naug, the most cowardly Quolli in the village. How convenient. Even I could thrash him. And he knows it, too."

"You think Ciga rigged the drawing?"

"I think Ciga got what he wanted. How he did it, I haven't a clue. The Quolli work in secret."

"Well, I guess I should be glad that he's trying to keep me alive. But still I'm going to keep my eyes on Naug."

"Indeed, the boy may be a coward, but he won't rest until he has wounded you. He'll wait until you don't see it coming. Make sure you never let him get up close and embrace you."

The next day Sorenth rose to the sound of a woman's song. He dressed and stepped outside the hut to see Kitar and Yawnna, Ciga's daughter. They sat in the shade of a hut and sorted roots. Kitar nodded to Sorenth and said, "My songbird has drawn you to her."

"She tried that once before," Sorenth said. "Thankfully I kept my distance."

Conversing in the Common Tongue, Kitar said, "I told her how you defended my honor yesterday. She thinks you must be a romantic. Young women like that in men."

"Even Quolli women? Aren't they the ones who embrace you and then pick your pocket?" Sorenth asked.

"Not my songbird. Here is a woman without guile. How she could have such a crafty father and be so true remains a great mystery to me. It gives me hope."

Yawnna spoke to Kitar, even as she glanced up to watch Sorenth. The servant translated, "My songbird wants to know why you are so special."

"Who says I'm special?"

"The woman warrior saved you. She paid a small fortune to keep you safe here. She must think you're special."

"Yeah, well, we'll all have to ask her about that one day. I want to hear what she says myself."

The two women confided and again Kitar spoke: "The bad ones of Equis also want you. They also think you are special. But my songbird wants to know why you tried to sacrifice your life. If the woman warrior had not spared you, your enemies would have killed you. Why were you so quick to die? To spare your brother?"

The questions were hitting too close to the mark. "Let's just say I didn't want to be caged up by those brutes," Sorenth replied. "I'd rather be dead."

"But now you're in the lady's debt."

"Am I?"

Again the females spoke. Yawnna said many things. Kitar translated, "She says you hold both the Quolli and the lady in low esteem."

"The Quolli are thieves."

"Yes, my songbird says, the Quolli are thieves. And they are the poorest clan, often set upon by the neighboring peoples. Every clan thinks nothing of attacking and killing Quolli, even the women and children. She says they are slain like jackals. They are deemed less than human."

Sorenth thought of his brother Bo and the other cadets who had gone on a training mission against the Quolli. Sorenth was already crippled, and Aeres wouldn't let him go along. But his brother had come here and killed women and children. Would Sorenth have done the same if allowed? He hoped not. All this he considered, but he gave the Quolli woman and her servant no reply.

Yawnna stood and fixed her gaze on Sorenth. She spoke and her servant translated: "My songbird says that you may be a proud one who can afford to despise such a great act of kindness from the woman warrior. But she says she cannot. A woman is deemed less than men and a Quolli woman is deemed the least of all the people of the Dry Lands. My songbird says she will not forget what was done to save you. The woman warrior is a mystery and a wonder. She appeared out of nowhere to rescue you. And she battled the bad ones from Equis. That makes her good. She is a woman worth knowing. And she is your protector. She must know why you are special."

"Perhaps I don't despise her kindness," said Sorenth. "Perhaps I just don't understand it. I've got a lot of questions for her."

"One day soon you will get to ask your questions," Kitar translated.

In the Pappi capital of South Shore, a large crowd gathered outside the council chambers on the morning of the special meeting. At the appointed time, the MuKierin delegation left Bairn's villa and walked in formation down the main street to the meeting place. Roff and Cisly led the way, followed by Darnelle, Kick and Bairn's partner Tie. Lon took up the rear with his hand on his sword. Bystanders pointed and whispered as the foreigners passed. The Pappi leaders had said nothing about the reason for these strangers' visit. But rumors had spread about the assault a few nights earlier at Bairn's villa. Now many wondered why the Barsk wanted these MuKierin assassinated.

Inside the chambers, Bairn greeted his houseguests beneath a small rotunda. "Welcome, friends,' he said, waving a hand to a nearby bench. "All of you will sit there, where you can face both my fellow leaders and the Barsk delegation. Lon, please take your place by the wall."

"Thank you," said Cisly, as Lon stepped away. "When will the Barsk arrive?"

"At any minute. Once they do, the chief will call us to order. He has placed your matter at the top of the agenda, so you'll be speaking shortly."

"What will happen after we leave?"

"Not much, I hope. Negotiations may begin. The Barsk have come to demand that we give them land along the lake. I'm hoping our leaders won't give in. But that likely will depend on your words."

"They're not my words. They're from Healdin."

Bairn lowered his voice. "I know, child. Let's hope that they grab my people's attention the way that woman captivated me so many years ago. On that first day when she came to my home on the lake, my head told me to send her away. But my heart said otherwise, and so it has always been. I never have been able to say 'no' to her."

A trumpet sounded outside. It signaled for the crowds to make way for the Barsk delegation. The MuKierin watched as the chamber's two main doors swung open and six men with swords strode in. They wore red capes and black pants with tall black boots. Leading them was an older man with a gray ponytail and a carefully crafted mustache and goatee. He took his seat behind a great table opposite the Pappi chief. Somehow he seemed able to make his solemn entrance without once looking directly at the MuKierin guests. His subordinates, however, sneered at Cisly and Roff. One of them strode over to the wall where Lon was standing. The two strangers silently eyed each other.

The Pappi chieftain rose and nodded at the foreign delegations, first the Barsk and then the MuKierin. "Welcome," he said in his own tongue. "I will now call to order this gathering. The Elders of the Pappi have come together today in the service of our clan. We now will consider the weighty matters before us. As we do, let us keep our oath to protect our people and our land."

Cisly translated to her friends, as did a member of the Barsk delegation. The Barsk ambassador rose and called out in the Common Tongue: "Chieftain, I am perplexed at this change in the agenda. May I ask about these MuKierin? Do they presume to speak for their clan? I would hope not. The Realm now rules the MuKierin. As such, this rabble has no standing. So why have they been allowed to distract us from the serious discussions that the Barsk and the Pappi need to begin? I am offended that the legitimate demands of my people are being pushed aside for some sideshow."

"Your repulsion is duly noted," the chief replied. "My Council deemed it important to hear from this delegation standing before us. We also deemed it worthwhile that you be given the chance to directly hear their words. They will speak and then we will consider your demands."

The Barsk leader rolled his eyes and ever so slowly sat down. The Chief turned to Cisly and nodded. "Greetings, young ones. You may begin."

Roff and Cisly stood. He spoke and she translated: "We thank the Pappi for their hospitality and for allowing us to address your council this day. We have not come as representatives of the MuKierin, but we do represent a people. We have allied ourselves with a great king, one who has long watched over us. It is true that the MuKierin have fallen to the Realm. But still the King watches over our people. He has given us a refuge in the no man's land between the MuKierin and the Pappi. We will soon go there and build a settlement.

But first he has sent us to offer the Pappi his protection. He wants to help you. If your people are willing, he will take you under his wing, just as he is protecting us."

As the translators spoke, the Barsk soldier took a step closer to Lon. "You're guarding a whore," he whispered in the Common Tongue. "You know that, don't you?"

"Actually she says she's a former courtesan," said Lon. "She tells me there's a difference."

"She's a whore. And what does that make you? What does that make your people for bringing her here? The whore's fools. She makes your people reek of filth and the gutter."

"Thank you for sharing that. I'll be sure to tell her."

"Listen to you. Someone said you were a great warrior. Hah! You're nothing but the whore's fool. What do you say to that?"

Lon responded snidely, "Listen, friend, if you want a fight, you can have one with that former courtesan over there. But I should warn you. She already has bested two of my friends and one of your associates. And I'll wager money that she can take you, too."

The Barsk cursed in his native tongue and stepped away. Lon turned to see Cisly glance at him from across the room. He smiled and nodded at her. She frowned at him.

The Barsk ambassador rose again and raised his hand. "Forgive me, Chieftain," he said. "Now that we have heard from your visitors, it seems I was mistaken. This isn't a sideshow. It's a farce. What King have these people imagined? What refuge? Did you really bring us here to listen to such fantasies? Do you really take them seriously? I have a suggestion. Send this delegation back to Kierinswell and let us see how long their King protects them. Let them go and gather their kinsmen and try to leave that land. Let them pass through the Realm's warriors. Then we will listen to them. Then both you and we can take them seriously. But until then, I demand that you dismiss these fools and allow us to get on with our negotiations."

The chamber grew quiet. A few of the Pappi leaders stared grimly at the floor, silent and stung, while the members of the Barsk delegation glared at Cisly. Slowly, she began to speak. "Good Chieftain, I have been instructed to tell you that we accept this challenge. We will go back to our land and do what this Barsk leader has demanded. We will gather our people and leave our homeland for a better place. Then you will see that the King we serve does indeed protect us from our enemies. All we ask is that you wait and watch. Don't give up your land today. Instead, send a representative that you trust along with us and wait for his report. If the Realm kills or captures us, then make your peace with the Barsk. But if we succeed, you will know that neither the Realm nor the Barsk can stand against our King. All we ask is that you delay any decision for four weeks. By then, you will have your answer."

Cisly quietly sat down. As she did, the chamber erupted with howls of protest. "Order!" the chieftain bellowed, banging his staff on the stone pavement.

Bairn rose and was recognized. "I move that the council adjourn to private session to consider the matter before us," he said.

"Objection!" yelled the Barsk ambassador. "I demand to respond to this foolishness! My people demand justice!"

"You're out of order," the chieftain said. "This is an internal matter. Is there a second to motion?"

"Second," called another Pappi Elder.

The motion passed unanimously. "I declare a recess," the Chieftain said. "The council alone must decide this matter. We will contact both visiting delegations once we have concluded our deliberations. For now we are adjourned. Good day."

The assembled jumped to their feet and began shouting at each other. The Barsk ambassador cursed anyone and everyone near him. Lon, however, pushed through the crowd to reach Cisly. "You seem to have stirred up a hornet's nest," he said. "Do you always get this kind of reaction when you speak in public?"

"I don't usually speak in public. But you seem most entertained by my words. Do you think this is a game?"

"I'm not sure, woman. I confess that I still don't know what to make of you. Do you really think that the warriors of Equis will simply stand aside and let you pass by unmolested?"

"No, I'm sure they will try to stop us."

"Yes, they will. But you're going to face them anyway. What makes you think you can beat them?"

"Weren't you listening?"

"You really believe what you said, don't you?"

"Does that surprise you? I think it's time to tell you something." She leaned in and lowered her voice. "You seem to think that I've lost touch with reality, but what about you? What about your own little plan to take on the Realm? Oh, yes, I know a bit about you cadets, and about the hidden power you think you can find. Tell me, what makes you so sure that you can succeed?"

Lon's eyes flashed. "Watch what you say here, woman. This room has too many spies. I won't let you put my friends in danger."

"Don't worry. I won't shout out your little secrets. But the truth is that you may be just as crazy as me, maybe even crazier. There's one way to find out about my sanity. Come with us. See what happens when we return to my homeland."

A Pappi guard came and touched Lon's arm, pointing toward the door. The cadet took Cisly's arm and joined the crowd now exiting the council chambers. Once outside, the MuKierin delegation retraced its steps to the villa. Roj was waiting for them. "Let's start packing," he said. "Whatever the Pappi decide, we should leave this place before dark. We need to get back to Orres."

The MuKierin began to assemble their gear. Lon, meanwhile, went and stood alone on the patio overlooking the lake. *How does she know about the mission? And who else knows?*

At noon, Bairn appeared at the villa. All the MuKierin gathered around him in the dining room. "You have prevailed," he said, with Cisly translating. "The Council has agreed to postpone the negotiations for four weeks. The Barsk, of course, are furious. No matter. Now it all depends on you. If you pass safely through your homeland and reach Newell, I believe that my people will forge an alliance with you and come under the protection of the King. My chieftain has bid me to add these words: 'If you fail, the Barsk will know that our land is theirs for the taking. Therefore, our fate now is tied to yours. If you survive, we survive. If you fail, the Pappi will be conquered.'

"However, I, Bairn, say this to you. I know you will not fail, not as long as the King's people are with you. I would go with you now, but the Council has refused my request to do so. Nonetheless, all my hopes go with you."

Roj stepped forward and hugged the trader. "Good-bye, old friend," he said. "My lady bids me to tell you, 'Fidden Gadaeyo.'"

Roff and the others hugged Bairn and began taking out gear for the packhorses. However, Lon touched his mentor's shoulder. "We need to talk," he said. "Let's go out to the patio."

The two men walked to the edge of the stone wall above the lake. Lon fixed his eyes on Bairn's. "That MuKierin lady seems to know about my comrades' plans, about our mission," he said. "That concerns me."

"I can understand that. I'm also worried about Bo. I fear he soon may set out on a quest that is doomed to fail."

"How does she know?"

"The King's people know many things. They have ways. They don't say how and I don't ask. But it appears that Equis knows, too."

"What? If that's true, I need to get back to Bo at once. Someone has to warn the cadets."

"You can't go. The council won't allow it. And even if you could go south, you would never make it back to the Academy."

"What do you mean?"

"The Realm is watching for you. They've put a price on your head. Perhaps they're afraid that you might warn your fellow cadets to abandon the mission. Or perhaps, they have other plans for you. But they intend to capture you."

"How do you know all his? Who told you?"

"As I said, the King's people know much. And the Realm already has tried to take Sorenth. They want him, too. Don't worry. He's safe. He was wounded, but a friend of mine rescued him and he is now hiding safely among the Quolli."

"Among the Quolli? That's terrible. Those jackals will sell him into slavery."

"No, my friend is watching over him. She'll keep an eye of him."

"She? Who is she?"

"A woman warrior, a servant of the King, like Mirri, the old woman staying here with the MuKierin. Believe me, Lon. Sorenth is safe for now. And you can't get back to Bo. Instead, the Council has selected you for another task. You will accompany Cisly and the MuKierin delegation back to their homeland."

"What? You're joking. Why would the Council pick me?"

"We need an observer to verify that the King's followers make it safely to their new home, the place they call Newell. The council members wanted a skeptic, so they refused to send me. Everyone agreed that you are the best skeptic for the job."

"But they're all going to get slaughtered. It's crazy. They don't have a chance. And how am I supposed to keep from getting slaughtered with them?"

"They won't get slaughtered, Lon. And the Council has taken extra steps to make sure that you won't be harmed. They have written papers giving you the highest diplomatic protection possible. They have temporarily made you an Elder of our people. It's a great honor. Listen, even the Realm would be slow to kill a leader of the Pappi. They don't want to do something that would infuriate us during our negotiations with the Barsk. So those are your orders. You will be our official observer. When the Realm's warriors show up, you are free to stay at a safe distance away from the King's followers. And once they reach Newell, you will return here and make your report."

Lon leaned back against the wall and moaned. "I can't believe this. I should have gone with Sorenth. This is what I get for sticking with you."

"Well, we can't change the past, can we? You still don't see the good I've done for you, do you? If you had gone with Sorenth, you never would have gotten to know the woman."

"The woman? Do you think you're doing me a great favor by sending me off with her? That woman is crazy."

"I've noticed the effect she has on you, Lon. I think she's noticed, too."

In the cool of autumn, Weakling left his cave solely to draw water. On such trips, he leaned on a staff and hunched over like an old woman. Limping slowly, he passed through the canyon to a small spring at the base of a great rock wall. With much effort, he would kneel down on his good knee and fill his water skins.

One morning, as he returned with the water, he looked up to the cliff and spied two female archers watching him. Rebel archers. One of them let loose an arrow that zipped past his head. Weakling planted his staff and raised himself up as straight as his broken body would allow. "You call yourselves archers!" he railed. "Can't you even hit a cripple!"

The other archer fired. Her arrow slammed into the top of Weakling's staff and bounced off it.

"Curse you!" Weakling called. "I defy you! Come close and I'll spit on you. Shoot again! Kill me, if you can!"

From inside the cave Pibbibib began to hear his ally's screams and curses. Running outside, he spied the archers taking aim from the cliff. He jumped forward and tackled the

Weakling. Down the two tumbled behind low boulders. "Fool, what do you think you're doing?" Pibbibib demanded.

"I'm not going to let them toy with me! If they want to kill me, let's get it over with."

"Don't get crazy on me! Just keep your head down. Stay here and let me find out what these she-ones are doing here. You know they aren't alone. They had to come with someone. The question is: Who?"

Pibbibib looked up and immediately saw the answer to his question. Up the canyon rode Lord Mackadoo's sergeant. Pibbibib recognized him even with his newly shaved head. A half-dozen mounted warriors followed him. "Get up!" the sergeant yelled at his quarry.

Weakling stood and screamed, "Come on, kill me!" He leaned on his staff and limped forward. "What? Are you scared of a cripple?"

"Push me a little more and I swear I'll yank that tongue right out of your mouth," the sergeant replied. He dismounted and turned to Pibbibib. "Where's Rakmah?"

"Dead."

"And the others?"

"All dead."

"And why aren't you dead?"

"We're smarter than them."

The sergeant let loose with a right hook and clobbered Backstabber, sending him flat on his back. "I can't yet kill you two cowards," the sergeant said. "Not yet. But I can break you in two if I have to. So don't tempt me. My orders are to bring you both back alive to Lord Mackadoo. Now you can get on these spare horses or we can tie you across the saddles like sacks of manure. What's it gonna be?"

Weakling shook his head and muttered, "I don't want to go. Just kill me here."

Pibbibib whispered, "Shut up. They're not going to kill you. We have to go with them. Now let me help you get on your horse."

When the time came for Weakling to mount, Backstabber got beneath his ally's butt and hoisted him up.

Weakling put his good leg in the stirrup and strained to pull his body and his bum leg over the saddle.

"What happened to him?" the sergeant demanded.

"He jumped off that cliff up there," Pibbibib said. "So did I. That's how we got away from the enemy."

"So that's why he's gone crazy. I liked him better when he was scared of me."

Together the gang of warriors rode to Fire Mountain. Mackadoo was waiting there, along with many cavalrymen. The sergeant made Weakling and Pibbibib stay mounted far back from the rest of the warriors, and he assigned four males to guard them. "Something's up," said Backstabber. "Look at all these warriors. This isn't Mackadoo's style. He likes to keep things small and sneaky. What's it all mean?"

"When are they going to kill us?" Weakling moaned.

"Will you shut up about that? They need us for something. The question is: What?"

Many minutes passed before Mackadoo mounted his black stallion and rode toward them. In their bedraggled armor, the two prisoners looked absolutely pitiful next to the lord, with his black cape as shiny as his horse's coat. "You two failed me," he said. "I knew you would. And you both know that there's a price for failing me."

"Yes, lord," said Pibbibib.

"Your lives are forfeit to me for Rakmah and all the others who didn't make it back. I'd like to kill you now but I can't. I'm not done with you yet. However, if you fail me on this mission, I'll let the sergeant over there slice and dice you. Believe me, he's been waiting a long time for such a treat."

"Yes, lord."

"Tell me, gasbag. Have you sensed the enemy anywhere near us?"

Pibbibib glanced at Weakling, whose eyes were closed. His ally didn't seem to be paying any attention to the conversation. Backstabber was left to guess. "No, lord," he said, "I haven't felt the enemy all day."

"If you sense as much as a she-one on a donkey, you had better tell me."

"Yes, lord."

"We're going down onto the plains to hunt some MuKierin vermin in a few days. Our spies say they'll be coming this way. It's going to be quite a party. But we don't want to get ambushed. Your job is to alert us at once if the enemy shows up. Otherwise, I don't want to look at your sorry faces."

Mackadoo rode back to the sergeant. "Keep your eye on them," he ordered.

"Lord," said the sergeant, "we're not really going to depend on those scum again, are we?"

"Those are my orders. We still don't know what we're up against. These MuKierin have boasted that the King will help them pass through us on the plains west of Kierinswell. We still don't know whether they're bluffing or just crazy. If the enemy does show up, we need to be ready. And that means we need our gasbag a little longer. Don't worry. We aren't relying solely on him. If there is a battle, we're going to have thirteen hundred troops with us out there."

Chapter Fourteen

Maneuvers

The delegation of five MuKierin left South Shore on the night of the Pappi council meeting. Under cover of darkness they rode east for Orres. Mirri and a small troop of the King's warriors accompanied them. As did Lon, who had accepted his orders to serve as an observer of what was to come. The party avoided MuKierin towns and villages, all of which had come under the control of the Realm. Instead, Mirri led them south across the desolate plains east of the Red River. In a week's time the riders reached the camp of Blaze's followers in the foothills east of Orres. Their arrival at sunset caused a stir. Blaze's followers wanted answers to so many questions. But Roff insisted on a meal before answering any of them. After dinner, the entire camp gathered and Roff told the story of all that had happened since Blaze had left for the Green Lands. It was a long story, including Blaze's appearance on Fire Mountain, the crossing of the northern wastelands and the intrigue with the Pappi. Then came the questions. Mostly they regarded the future.

After the final question, Roff declared, "I am bound for Newell. I need ninety-eight volunteers. Who will come with me?" Immediately, his four cousins rose and stood with him, as did Roj, Noli, Remy, Cisly and Darnelle.

"Why not take all of us now?" a man asked.

"Those are my orders. The King's servants can better protect a smaller group. And those who come now must be ready to face the Realm's warriors. However, once we prevail I will come back for the rest of you. I promise."

More followers rose and stood with those bound for Newell. Darnelle counted and announced, "We have ninety-eight, including Roff. We need one more."

Arg Wevol, the horse trader, stood and raised his hand. "I wish to go, if you will have me. I am old but I owe a

debt to the Horse Stalker and his family. And I still have a
score to settle with the evil ones."

"You'd be most welcome," said Roff. "Now we
number ninety-nine. That's just right. All of you need to get
ready. We'll leave tomorrow at sundown."

The next evening the group departed, with Lon as
their observer. They rode north, staying high in the foothills
beneath the Powder Mountains. They traveled until well past
midnight that first night and huddled together for warmth
while resting in the frosty darkness. They rose early the next
morning and set off again through a brush-covered canyon.
As the day went on they slowly began their descent from the
high country. They camped early that night and built fires
within their tents, both to contain the warmth and to hide the
light from unfriendly eyes. After four days they reached a
valley halfway between Orres and Kierinswell. Gray, billowy
clouds obscured much of the sky, especially in the west.
Winter was coming. "Rest a while," said Roff. "We'll stay
here until evening. If the weather stays like this, we will set
out after sunset."

That day Lon kept watch on Roj, the only MuKierin
besides Cisly who could speak his tongue. For days the Pappi
cadet had been waiting for the right time to talk to the Horse
Stalker. He noticed that the older man didn't eat anything at
the noon meal, and he wore an expression far sadder than at
any time in the past few weeks. When Roj went to check on
his horse, Lon approached him.

"Roj, why are you doing this?" Lon asked. "I can see
your agony. Why are all of you going to your deaths?"

No, Lon," said Roj, "I'm sad but not because we're
going to die."

"Then what's bothering you?"

"I can't tell you. I'm sorry, but I'm sworn to secrecy,
for all of our sakes. Here's what I can say. I've already
suffered much, Lon. My family has suffered much. And it's
not over. Our ancestors took something that didn't belong to
us. They made a mess of things. Maybe someday that will be
set right, maybe not. I don't know anymore. But a price is

going to be paid. And that greatly saddens me, because the ones I love are going to pay the most."

"I'm sorry, Roj. I don't understand."

"Maybe you will in time. When we leave tonight, you can stay here with Mirri. She'll watch over you until it's safe to rejoin us. Once we pass through the Dark Brood, she'll bring you to us and you can go on to Newell. From there, we'll make sure you get safely back to South Shore. We'll need you to take back the news to your people. I want the Pappi to know the truth. Believe me when I say that your people have been good to my family. Bairn took us in long ago and has remained a steadfast friend. And I know he holds you in high esteem. That's why I'm so glad that you're here with us now."

The two shook hands. Roj gave the younger man a hug.

At supper, Lon took his food and went off alone to eat atop a flat rock. Cisly found him. "Are you really staying behind here?" she asked.

"That's my job, isn't' it?"

"Don't you understand what these people have done for you?"

"What have they done, woman?"

"There are ninety-nine of us here. With you, it would make one hundred people to go out together to meet the enemy. It's a great honor that they're offering you. You can be one of us."

"Well, thanks for the honor, but I'm going to decline. What difference does it make whether the Realm slaughters ninety-nine or one hundred?"

"So you're going to play it safe?"

"That's my plan, yes."

"Well, I misjudged you."

"Really? How's that?"

"I thought you could change. I guess I was wrong."

"What do you mean? How was I supposed to change?"

"I thought you might realize that you're not as smart as you think you are."

"I don't even know what that's supposed to mean."

"You're still holding onto your dreams of greatness. You still think your friends are going to outsmart the Realm and take the great power."

"Oh, I don't know about that. You've splashed a bit of cold water on those plans. Maybe my friends can take the power. Maybe they can't, especially if people like you already know something about our plans. But did you ever consider that maybe nobody will ever beat these giants? I still can't understand why you think you have a chance. It looks to me like you're all throwing your lives away."

"Come down with us and you'll see the truth. You'll see us overcome. It's the only way."

"I'll come down afterwards. If you survive, you can tell me all about it."

"If you don't see it with your own eyes, you won't believe it. You won't understand what took place. For you, it will be like it never happened. And it won't change anything."

Cisly left him to his supper. The MuKierin soon packed their horses and set out, ninety-nine in all. The evening showers let up and the last light of day clung to the clouds. When the people rode past Lon, the young man fixed his eyes on Cisly. But she never looked back.

In the darkness, the sergeant awoke Pibbibib with a kick to the back. "Get up, idiot!" he growled. "We've spotted them. Let's get moving."

"Where are they?"

"Out on the plains. We've got a two-hour ride in front of us. Now wake up that worthless chum of yours and get him up on his mount. Move it!"

Around them, warriors were springing up and hustling to their horses. In contrast, Weakling rose slowly. Amid the chaos, he stood out for his awkward limp and labored pace. The sergeant soon shouted at Backstabber, "If your partner can't keep up, we'll kill him now and leave him behind us. We don't need him anymore!"

"No! No!" answered Pibbibib, grabbing Weakling by the arm. "He'll keep up. I promise."

As the troops mounted, Mackadoo trotted up on his black stallion. In the darkness, Pibbibib could only see little white teeth, yellow eyes and the red ruby on the lord's forehead. "Listen, gasbag," Mackadoo said to him, "the MuKierin are camped in a valley some distance south of the Stone Fences. We think there are only about one hundred of them. There's no sign of enemy troops. It seems too easy. Now get ready. If you two fail me, you'll be the first to die."

"It's a good day to die," said Weakling.

"What's this? Did the Weakling finally get a backbone?"

"Yes, lord," said Pibbibib. "We're both ready for battle."

"I hope you are. No doubt you both remember General Sloacum? He'll be leading our troops in battle. If I were you, I wouldn't do anything to antagonize him. He does so hate deserters. And he'll hate you two deserters even more because, like him, you're Slinkers. If I were to let him have you, he would take you both and roast you alive over hot coals. As delightful as that sounds, I'm going to keep you both alive, for now. We may be in for some trouble out there. As I said, it looks too easy. Now then, if you sense the enemy at any time, you tell the sergeant and me at once. Got it?"

"Yes, lord," said Backstabber. "We'll do just as you say. But if those horse dogs really don't have any protection, shouldn't we just ride over there and take 'em hostage? The enemy's weak, Lord. Tor won't attack us if you've got a knife pointed at the hearts of his playthings."

"Don't start telling me what to do, not if you want to stay alive."

Mackadoo rode off. Backstabber leaned in the saddle and whispered over to Weakling, "Look, we need to talk. I know things haven't turned out exactly like we hoped."

"Like you hoped."

"Okay, like I hoped. But don't give up on me. I'm going to get us out of this, I promise. I just need your help. You heard Mackadoo. The enemy is probably going to try to ambush us. But you and I won't be caught unaware. You'll sense Tor and his warriors long before they can get close to us. And when the fighting starts, we'll escape through all the mayhem. We'll take some unguarded road and hightail it for the backcountry, just like we've always done. That's right. We can go back to the high mountains. How about we return to our old cave above Kierinswell? You'd like that, wouldn't you? You always wanted to go back there. Or, if you like, we'll go someplace else, anywhere you want. We'll lay low and plan our comeback. And we'll eat plenty of horse dogs. Doesn't that sound sweet? What do you say?"

"It's a good day to die."

"Ugh! Listen, you are not going to die! You may be crazy, but you're all I've got. Nobody's going to kill you today. Nobody!"

Clouds shrouded the noonday sun when Mackadoo brought Pibbibib and Weakling to a rise overlooking a small but deep valley. The place lay in the sagebrush lands south of the Stone Fences. Backstabber could see the MuKierin camp at the other end of the valley. The humans appeared to be resting under a dozen canopies. No warriors of Equis could be seen blocking their escape, but more than one thousand foot soldiers and cavalrymen were packed behind Pibbibib on the rise. And more were coming. The Dark Brood seemed to be tempting the MuKierin to flee. *This doesn't make sense?* Pibbibib thought. *Why aren't the horse dogs running? And what are our troops waiting for? Any one of us could walk alone down this hill and kill the whole lot of those vermin?*

Mackadoo's sergeant kept his two hundred warriors mounted and lined up in two long columns. Their lord, meanwhile, rode to a great canopy where General Sloacum's headquarters were set up in the center of the rise. Mackadoo spoke with an assembly of officers and downed a mug of some dark intoxicant favored by Equis. Eventually he remounted and returned to his company. "Bring me Backstabber and Weakling," he called. "Listen, you two. We're going to ride around this valley and set out groups of sentries from my columns here. You're going to lead the way. We're going to make a great circle about a mile away from that camp."

The mounted company left the rise and trotted down onto a great sage plain. From the front of the line, Backstabber noted that the warriors behind him seemed on high alert. The sergeant set out scouts on either side, and ten riders trailed the column as a rear guard. Meanwhile, Weakling rode with his eyes closed and his hands free of the reins, allowing his horse to wander wherever it pleased. Pibbibib eventually reached over and took the reins in order to lead his ally's mount.

"You're a mess, do you know that?" Backstabber whispered. "You've got to shape up or that sergeant is going to come over and run you through with his sword."

"Let him. I just want this day to end."

"Quit that talk. Listen, I need you. We need each other. We're still masters of fortune, aren't we? You've still got to want something. Think about it. Maybe it's one of those skinny she-archers you like so much, or maybe it's one more meal of human flesh. Just let your mind think on it. Dream on it. Partner, you can have whatever you want. I'll help you get it, I promise. But you've got to tell me if the enemy shows up. That's how we'll survive this mess. It's how we'll help each other. We're chums, you and me. You can't give up on me now."

Mackadoo loped forward on his black stallion and caught up to the two guides. "Is the enemy near? Do you sense anything?"

"No, lord," said Backstabber, preparing his lie. "I was just telling Weakling that I don't feel anything. If they're coming, they're still a long ways away."

It took nearly two hours to make a complete circle around the valley. Along the way, the sergeant posted small groups of sentries at regular intervals. When the now-reduced columns returned to the rise, Mackadoo went once more to the canopy and conferred with the officers resting there. He later returned and ordered the sergeant to take the remaining fifty warriors and make a second lap without him, this time within a half mile of the MuKierin.

On that second pass, Weakling still showed not the slightest sign of danger. The sergeant began hectoring Backstabber. "What's wrong with you?" he demanded. "Where is the enemy, blast you? Have you lost The Powers? Or are you in league with Tor?"

"What's wrong with me? Hah! This whole army seems too scared to exhale. Look at all those troops back there, huddled together like cowards. You'd think Tor and ten thousand warriors were staring us in the eye. But the enemy's not within miles of this place."

"You are such an idiot. Things have changed since you jumped off that cliff. Those aren't just any MuKierin down there. They belong to the Champion, the same one that you were supposed to kill. And there's a rumor that these humans have some sort of special protection. We don't know what it is. But that's why our leaders are taking this slow and careful."

Pibbibib pondered the news. "So all of this caution is because of some rumor? Well, I may not be up on all the latest intelligence, but I can tell you one thing: None of those vermin down there have The Powers. And I can prove it. You let Weakling and me go down there and grab some hostages. We won't have the slightest trouble capturing them all. And we can use them as shields. That'll keep Tor and his troops back, if they ever show up."

"You're not going near them. I don't trust you two to do anything right. We're going to follow orders. Mackadoo will decide what you two do and when you do it."

The fifty riders finished their second circle and returned to the rise. The sergeant let the troops dismount but kept them standing beside their horses. Pibbibib and Weakling waited in formation with the others for nearly an hour. A stiff breeze began to blow and the sky grew even darker with clouds. More troops arrived. Backstabber watched as one hundred female archers came marching double time up the back of the rise. Each archer was clad in a sleeveless beige tunic, with a collar around her neck and the left half of her skull shaved clean and scalded. "Hey, look at all that she-flesh," he called to Weakling. "One of those beauties has got to want to get better acquainted with you. What do you say? Want me to introduce you, while she's still wearing her iron collar, of course."

Weakling sleepily squinted at the archers. "I sure wish I had my old bow back," he said. " It's been five hundred summers since I used it. I was a good shot."

"Well, yes, you were, one of the best. Listen, we could get you a bow. You just tell me when the enemy's near and I'll steal you one."

"You'd do that for me?"

"Of course. That's what chums are for. We need each other. Listen, all I need is a little distraction. You tell me when the enemy is near, and I'll steal you a bow as soon as the fighting starts."

"And arrows."

"Of course. What good is a bow without arrows?"

They looked up as Lord Mackadoo and a dozen officers approached them on horseback. Leading the group was a hulking figure with a black cape. Backstabber recognized the broad-chested giant by the scar on his left cheek. It was General Sloacum. The enemy commander Tor reportedly had given the general that cut in battle, and Sloacum had been lucky to escape with his life. Pibbibib had never seen the general so richly adorned. The dark cape he wore was covered with delicate, bleached human bones, no doubt the better to frighten the encamped MuKierin.

The general pulled up directly beside Backstabber and spat in his face. "Where is the enemy, curse you?" he demanded.

Pibbibib thought it best not to wipe off the spittle. "They're not here, General," he said. "They may be coming this way, but they aren't yet close to us. I'd sense them if they were."

The general turned in his saddle. "Mackadoo, am I correct that you're responsible for this excrement, this deserter? Nearly fifteen hundred of us gathered here, and you want me to depend on this coward. Is this the best you can do?"

"General," said Mackadoo, "our Great Master sent me here to give you what aid I can. If you no longer desire my help, I'll gladly leave and let you fend for yourself."

"Oh, no, comrade, you won't get off that easy. I won't release you. If we get ambushed, you're going to have to explain to the Master how you and this imposter here brought ruin upon us all."

"Very well, General. If you wish, I will stay. And may I suggest that you attack now and take those MuKierin hostages. The enemy won't attack us if we have the humans."

"Don't lecture me, oh great, dark lord. You're not as high and mighty as you used to be. We all recall the days when you were the Master's special emissary. Even the great commanders of the two orders feared you, or so some wags say. But you failed us. First, you didn't kill the Horse Stalker and now years later you failed to kill the enemy's Champion. It's true the Master still sends you out, but no one fears you as much anymore. You star is falling. It may yet crash to earth."

"Would you care to draw your sword and tell me more?"

"Hah! We'll save that discussion for another day. For now, we both must do our duty. Captains, get your troops ready for battle. We're not going to wait for dark and give the enemy a chance to swoop in unseen. We'll attack right after sundown."

As the general rode away, Mackadoo pulled his sergeant aside and said, "When the killing starts, I want you to put an end to our two fools. We no longer need them, and I'd rather not have the gasbag around afterward, especially if things go badly tonight."

The sergeant grinned. "Yes, lord. At last, it's time for a little revenge."

When morning came, Lon awoke to a light drizzle. He lay alone beneath a small canopy hidden amid boulders and scrub brush. He guessed it was only a few hours after dawn. Slowly he pushed back his blanket, pulled on his boots and went looking for Mirri. He found her nearby tending a small fire beneath another canopy. The rain kept falling lightly.

"Good morning, Mirri," he said. "Did you sleep well last night?"

"When you've lived as long as I have, sleep is rarely needed."

"That's funny. My grandmother was like that."

"Would you like some tea? I've set out some jerky and a biscuit for your breakfast. It's not fish-eye soup, but it will have to do."

"Indeed, you are a funny one. It seems forever since I thought about fish-eye soup. I'm surprised a foreigner like you would know about it."

"I've spent many years around the lake. I know all about the delicacies of the Pappi."

Lon bit into the biscuit. "So when do we leave?"

"There's no hurry. I want to wait a few hours before we move down closer to the plain. Until then, we'll stay here."

Late that morning the rain let up. Mirri fed Lon another meal at noontime, and then they saddled their horses and set off west from the foothills. They saw no one as they passed into a steep ravine and through a dry wash. Soon they came to an old wagon road. They followed it for several miles as it turned north and passed along the top of a long ridge. From there they climbed to a promontory that overlooked the last foothills between them and sagebrush plains.

"We won't go much farther," Mirri said. "Roj and the others are out there, perhaps five miles away. You can see the trail down below. That will take us to them. Now we'll drop down into that little basin below us and wait until nightfall."

They descended the slope and tied up their horses beside two great boulders. It was perhaps an hour before sundown.

"How much longer?" asked Lon.

"That depends on our enemies. But I think they'll attack before dark."

"Well, that still gives us a chance to chat. I've been watching you, Mirri. I can't quite figure you out. You sure get around well for an old woman, much better than my grandmother ever did. She blamed it on my grandfather. She said he'd made her old. What about you, did you ever have a husband?"

"No, child. I have a King. Among my kind, that's better than a husband."

"Really? That's kind of hard to imagine. You never wanted anything more?"

"No, but my enemies did. The ones you call the Realm once belonged to the King. Long ago they chose another way. But I chose joy. And I've never regretted it."

"You mean those brutes from Equis were once like you. That's hard to believe. Tell me more. It must be quite a story."

"It is quite a story, although I don't have time to tell it today. But now you're also part of the tale. My lady said you would be. She told me so when you were a little boy."

"Your lady?"

"Her name is Healdin. She is Roj's wife and the mother of Blaze, whom you've also met. For many years she lived among the Pappi. She saw you one day when you were just a boy visiting Bairn's estate. She blessed you and said to me, 'One day you must help him choose joy, Mirri.' That's what she told me. 'You must help him choose joy.'"

"That's funny, Mirri. I wouldn't know joy if it hit me like a rock."

"I know. That's why I brought you someone to hit you like a rock."

"What that's mean? Are you saying you brought that woman to me? Cisly? Do you really think she could bring me joy?"

"Don't you?"

"So far she hasn't brought me much joy. She has questioned my bravery. And she's suggested I'm blind and selfish, just because I don't see things like she does."

"Look again. I see a woman of strength and character."

"Maybe. I'll admit she's brave, even if she's about to get herself killed."

"She asked you to be there with her tonight, didn't she? She wants you to see wonders. That shows she cares for you. But you must decide. The hour is almost at hand. Will you go down to her?"

"Go down to her? Wait a minute. What about you, Mirri? Why aren't you down there with her?"

"Right now I can't be with the MuKierin. There's an enemy warrior nearby who can sense my people. He would know if I were there with Roj and the others. That's why I have to stay back here until the time is right."

"I'm not sure I follow you. When is the time right? What exactly do your people have planned for tonight?"

"Wonders. And Cisly wants you to see them. There's still time, Lon. You can still choose joy."

Lon arose but hesitated. "This is crazy. You want me to ride down there, just to make sure that she really cares for me."

"She cares for you. I know she does. But do you care for her? If you do, there's only one way for you to see what she wants you to see tonight."

"But it would mean riding to my death."

"Perhaps. Perhaps it would be riding to your death and beyond to a new life."

Chapter Fifteen

Skyfire

Above the little valley, clouds filled the evening sky and threatened rain. Dusk would soon give way to night. Cisly looked up and spied hundreds of warriors gathering on the rise. "They're forming ranks," she said. "It won't be long now."

Indeed, one hundred of the Realm's spearmen were stepping forward and lining up as the front battle rank. Companies of swordsmen fell in behind them, with the hundred female archers taking their place in the rear. Thirteen hundred troops congealed into an army of malice, a pack of brutes preparing to pounce on and devour their prey. Flag bearers unrolled two standards. One bore the image of the Broken Star; the other featured lightning bolts and skulls, the images of the Slinkers. Warriors lit long torches and lifted them high to give the banners an eerie glow.

Thum, Boom! Boom! The drums of Equis began to sound, deep and slow. The spearmen lifted high their weapons and shook them with expectation. Despite the day's unease, the drums renewed their spirits. Always before the thunderous beat had signaled the doom of any human opponent. Always the drums had announced the destruction of their victims. And always afterwards the assembled warriors had quite literally tasted victory.

Across the valley, Roj stood among his people and waited. He looked out to the rise and saw the banners flying. He heard the drums booming. The sights and sounds made him grimace.

At his feet he heard three taps, then three more, then another three. Roj turned and shouted to his nephew, "Roff, get ready! Lon is coming! It's time to get your people out there! Go!"

Roff jumped to his feet and called, "Come with me!" In response, twenty men and women rushed over to him.

"Grab your weapons," Roff ordered, pointing to leather bundles at his feet. "Line up in your formation. Remember all that I've told you."

Each squad member picked up a bundle containing four short lances that had been brought back from the Green Lands. Each was about half the size of a normal spear and each tip was covered with a strange skin. The people slung the bundles on their shoulders and lined up, forming two ranks of ten fighters each. The first rank included Roff, Stannis, Kick, Harney and Quirt. In the second stood Noli, Arg Wevol, Cisly and Roff's mother Remy. Darnelle took her position behind them, clutching a long banner on a tall pole. She unfurled the cloth and raised it high, revealing the image of a green stallion's head on a white field.

Roff took a lit torch and handed it to Cisly. "Stay back with Darnelle until we fight," he said. "Use this to signal Lon. Then give Darnelle the torch and take your spot in line." Next he turned to his mother. "Are you sure you want to come with us?"

"Yes, son," said Remy. "If you and your father are going out there, I want to go with you. I can't throw well, but I can hand you my spears."

"Alright," said Roff. He turned and addressed his troops: "Let's move out together! Follow me!"

His followers stepped forward in two ranks, the first about three steps ahead of the second. Soon they were jogging out toward the slope at their end of the valley. "Look at them go," Roj told the others in the camp. "It's a new day. Our kinsmen are going to face our worst enemies. They're going out to rescue a foreigner. They're going out as MuKierin. But if they come back, it will be as Green Landers."

Roff led his people two hundred paces south along a rutted wagon road. There he raised his hand and called a halt. On either side the land sloped gently upwards. "Let's wait here," he said. "They'll have sentries on either side of this road. Let's wait to see which side comes at us first."

The others dropped to their knees and waited, anxious for what was to come. At the other end of the valley, they could hear the enemy drums pounding. *Thum, Boom! Boom!*

Up on the rise, General Sloacum mounted his stallion and rode over to Mackadoo. "I'm about to give up the high ground and move into the valley. Do you still insist that the enemy isn't near?"

"Quite so," the lord said.

"If I die tonight, I hope the buzzards also feed on your carcass."

"My sentiments exactly. Now go and do our Great Master's bidding."

Thum, Boom! Boom! Behind the main body of troops, Weakling began to pick at the scar on his good leg. "I feel funny," he said.

"What's that supposed to mean?" asked Pibbibib. "Are you hungry?"

"No, I'm not hungry. But something's wrong."

"Well, is it something you ate?"

"I haven't eaten, blast you. What's wrong with me?"

"You're crazy. That's what's wrong with you. One minute you're begging to die and the next you're complaining about some tickle in your gut. What am I going to do with you?"

Thum, Boom! Boom! At the other end of the valley, Kick stood and grabbed Roff's arm. "There's a rider coming toward us," he said. "It's got to be Lon."

"Stand up!" shouted Roff. "Form ranks. Get ready. Let's move up the road."

The twenty-one set out at a walk toward the rider, who was still some distance away and approaching at a trot. Cisly raised her torch beside Darnelle in order to shine it brighter on the banner. As she did, a great roar sounded to her left. A dozen enemy warriors appeared charging down the slope. They evidently also had spotted the rider and were running to cut him off.

"Swing left!" Roff ordered. "Good. Now remove the cover of one spear, just one. Alright, let's go meet them. Stay in formation. March!" Roff's band set out, with ten each in two ranks and Darnelle behind them with the banner. As they advanced to meet the enemy, they saw a second group of the Realm's sentries spring forth off to their right. However, those warriors seemed much farther away and, for the present, less of a threat.

Thum, Boom! Boom! Lon was indeed the rider coming up the valley from the south. He quickly saw the first band of warriors running to block his path. He spurred his horse to a gallop and turned his mount to run to the left of the road. Soon he spotted the second band of sentries rushing out to take him. He moved back toward the road, hoping to shoot the gap between the two approaching bands. He looked into that space and his heart sank. There was a lit torch directly before him and creatures moving. On he rode, determined to somehow break through. He looked again and realized that it was a woman holding the torch. And nearby he spotted the banner. It was foreign to him, but clearly it didn't belong to Equis. Again he looked and cried for joy, "Cisly!"

On the rise, General Sloacum and his captain rode to the front of his army. "Follow me!" Sloacum bellowed. *Thum, Boom! Boom!* As the drums sounded the cadence, the first warriors stepped off the brow of the hill. Twelve ranks of male warriors marched forth, with the female archers following in the rear. The light of day was almost gone. Soon it would be night.

Roff, meanwhile, halted his people and scanned the battlefield at his end of the valley. "Remember your orders!" he yelled to his troops. "First rank, wait for my command and afterward kneel down low so the second rank can have a clean throw. Now wait for my signal."

"Look at them," said Arg Wevol. "Those evil ones have killed our kind for generations."

"They're pretty big and ugly," Kick replied.

"Yes, brother. There was a time I would have run from them. But tonight I will have my revenge on them."

Lon kept coming at a full gallop. He now could see that the first group of warriors had adjusted their course. They were no longer aiming for him but for the MuKierin who were standing together in two small ranks. The warriors began to shriek and howl and beat their swords against their shields. Darnelle cringed and turned away, unable to look. "Hold firm," she told herself. "Hold firm. Hold firm."

"Wait!" Roff yelled to his people. "Wait and make it count. Wait." In the back rank, Cisly turned again and beheld the rider. She now could see it was Lon. It looked like he now would safely pass by her. She handed the torch to Darnelle and took the cover off one of her spearheads.

Again Roff called to his people: "Wait … wait." Lon galloped past the MuKierin and skidded his horse to a stop in the flats behind them. He turned to scan the scene. One group of sentries still remained some distance away, but the other warriors were about to crash into Cisly and her kinsmen. Lon drew his sword and spurred his horse to charge to their aid.

Roff called, "First rank, get ready. Ready. Now!"

Roff, Stannis, Kick, Quirt, Harney and the other men in the first rank hurled their spears as the enemy rushed upon them. The two sides were less than seven paces apart as the MuKierin launched their weapons. The dozen warriors of Equis raised their shields to fend off the spears. But in flight the spear points flamed red and blasted through all armor. The spears traveled on until they reached flesh and blood, whereupon the tips exploded, tearing gaping holes in their victims.

Seven of twelve giants fell in the first wave. Roff and the rest of the first rank dropped to their knees. As they did, Noli, Cisly and the members of the second rank took aim. Cisly picked a howling red beard and flung her spear as the hulk raised his sword above her kneeling kinsmen. Her spearhead burned through her enemy's shield and flamed orange as it blew a hole in his chest. The great warrior shuddered and tumbled into the heap of dead comrades. Roff, meanwhile, grabbed an uncovered spear from his mother and advanced screaming at the last remaining giant. The towering black bearded enemy turned and raised his sword against the smaller human bearing down on him. In a few more steps, the

MuKierin would be in striking distance. But Roff drew back his spear and flung it with all his might. It pushed the shield against the warrior's chest and then exploded, a small orange bolt that jolted the dead hulk off his feet.

All twelve of the Realm's warriors had fallen. None of the MuKierin had been harmed.

Across the valley General Sloacum and his troops saw the explosions and immediately came to a halt. The drums of Equis grew silent. "What trickery is this?" the general demanded. "What were those flashes out there? What are we fighting?"

Pibbibib ran along the rise to Mackadoo's sergeant. "Something's wrong over there!" he shouted.

The sergeant turned and drew his sword. "Is that so?" he replied. "Now you're telling me! Idiot!"

At the other end of the valley, the second band of enemy sentries slammed to a halt when they saw their comrades die. A moment earlier they had been howling, but now they stood in silence, calculating their next move. Roff watched them and called to his fighters, "Stand and reform ranks. We need to shift around and face those warriors. They may still attack us."

The MuKierin obeyed and lined up against the remaining sentries. But the enemy didn't advance. Instead, they began a slow retreat back into the darkness.

Lon brought his horse beside Cisly and jumped down. "What did you just do?" he asked her in Pappi.

"We saved you from the evil ones. I told you we could protect you."

"But how did you do it?"

"With wonders! The King has wonders. He has craftsmen. He has deep knowledge from beyond the sea. I told you. But you had to see it to believe it."

"Is it the small spears?"

"Yes. They have a special point. I can't let you touch it. It would take your fingers off."

Roff called to his people: "We need to get back to camp. Stannis and Kick, I want you to trail behind us and keep watch. Call out if those bad ones start to come after us."

Roff's band formed two columns and strode back to camp. Cisly and Lon fell in behind them. "You came to me," she said. "I knew you liked me. I knew it."

"Alright, I like you. But this isn't over. You've still got to deal with that whole army over there. What's everybody going to do now?"

"I think you should kiss me."

"Kiss you? How's that going to help?"

"Ooh, men! You are so thick-headed."

Across the valley, General Sloacum raised himself in his saddle and called back to his troops: "We have come too far now to turn and run from human vermin. We are the warriors who will kill and devour them this night. There is no turning back. Follow me!" Once more the drums sounded. The ranks resumed their advance as the last light of day vanished. Night had fallen.

Roff brought his troops back to camp. There he called to all his kinsmen, "Everyone come together! Gather in a circle around Uncle Roj!"

The MuKierin formed a huddle four people deep around Roj. Roff, meanwhile, left them and strode out toward the approaching army.

"What are we doing?" Lon whispered to Cisly.

"We're making it easier for the enemy to find us," she replied.

"You are impossible. When will you tell me what's going to happen?"

"You will see for yourself in just a few minutes."

Roj spoke to his people, "Brothers and sisters, you must do exactly as I say. Now stand still and quiet."

To the beat of the drums, the enemy army advanced across the valley. Roff watched the warriors approach as a light drizzle began to fall. When General Sloacum drew within one hundred paces, Roff took a great horn and put it to his lips. He sounded a blast that for a moment drowned out the sound of the drums. The general raised an arm and the troops halted. The drums once more were silenced. Thirteen hundred warriors strained to listen. But they heard no answer to Roff's horn. The quiet of the night held sway. The general cursed and shouted, "Forward!"

Roj spoke, "Move back one step." As the MuKierin obeyed, the ground began to jiggle and shake. Within the circle, a door in the earth popped open. Lon peered down and beheld a darkened vault.

On the hill, Weakling let out a great howl: "Aieee! My leg! Stop it! No!" He collapsed in the dirt and rolled onto his back. Screaming, he jumped up and darted down the backside of the hill. He ran so fast that neither Pibbibib nor the sergeant could catch him. The sergeant turned and ran to a nearby canopy. There he uncovered a bow and quiver of arrows. Taking them, he made for a promontory on the backside of the hill.

Mackadoo also heard the screaming and turned to see Weakling deserting. *Is this a sign?* he asked himself. He jumped atop his horse and galloped after him.

The sergeant reached the promontory and caught sight of Weakling scampering through the sage. Slowly he drew back the bow and took aim.

But Backstabber had followed and was ready with his windup. Smack! A rock slammed into the sergeant's helm. Down he tumbled. Confused, he rose onto one knee but another rock nailed him in the back. A third caught him again in the helm.

"Nobody kills my Number Two!" Pibbibib roared. "Nobody!"

The sergeant rolled over and swung to his feet. He drew his sword and his dagger. "That's a nice trick," he said to Backstabber. "But now I have a score to settle with you."

Pibbibib also drew sword and knife. The sergeant closed in. Blades clashed as the two hulks heaved against each other.

In the valley, the general drew within fifty paces of Roff. The young MuKierin once more put the horn to his lips and gave a second blast. Behind him, Roj shouted, "Make way in front! And get ready to close your eyes."

Up from the earth rose Healdin. Clothed in white, she climbed a wooden ladder. In her hand she clutched a small sheath. Slowly she stepped among the men and women and out into the open. Roj called to his kinsmen, "Close your eyes and get down. Don't open them until I tell you it's safe."

The general saw Healdin and raised an arm. "Archers!" he called back. "Prepare to fire!"

Roff ran to his aunt and fell at her feet. As he did, Healdin called out to her enemies, "You know me! My name is Skyfire!" As she spoke, she removed the sheath and uncovered Mara, the Vine. It blazed intensely in her hand.

"Fire!" yelled the general. At his order, a wave of one hundred arrows shot forth high over the ranks of the warriors.

"Fidden Gadaeyo!" yelled Healdin. She swung Mara and a great curtain of light spread out overhead from her blade. The arrows reached the light but did not pass through it. All of the missiles were burned to ash amid that intense heat. Healdin flicked the Vine again and a wave of lightning crashed into the row of archers. In one terrible flash all the female warriors were incinerated.

The general's stallion reared up and went over backwards. Its rider barely managed to avoid being caught beneath his crazed mount. As Sloacum got back on his feet, Healdin waved Mara a third time and sent a burst of lightning bolts into the center of the ranks. Hundreds fell, burned to a crisp. The remaining warriors broke ranks and fled.

On the mount, Pibbibib pulled away from the sergeant. "Look, it's the Lady! She's going to kill us all!"

"No, she's not," the sergeant replied. "I'm going to kill you all by myself." He advanced with slashing blades. Backstabber gave way, retreating toward the edge of the promontory.

In the valley, the Realm's warriors tried in vain to escape. But Healdin called skyfire down upon them. It struck in bolts and sheets, first in the flats and then on the slopes. No one in the valley escaped. Only the general refused to retreat.

Slowly he approached the daughter of the King. "I won't run from the likes of you!" he yelled. "Curse both you and your father!"

From the heavens, a flashing bolt descended and struck his frame, jolting him high into the air. He burst into flames and sprawled lifeless in the dust.

Far off on the other side of the rise, Weakling had stopped and curled up in the dirt, holding his knees and rocking gently. Mackadoo galloped up to him. "Fool, what do you think you are doing?"

"I wanted to die. Truly I did. But she wouldn't let me. She drove me over here. And then she stopped me. She can make it hurt so bad. Look at me!" He pointed to his good leg. The old scar had reopened and light once more oozed forth.

"What? Is it you that truly holds The Powers inside you? Is that fool back there just an imposter?"

Weakling flopped on the ground and began wailing. He clawed at his leg and scratched at his eyes. "Let go of me! I don't want to look." He rolled in the dirt and sat up with his face turned once more to the hilltop. "Alright, there he is! Look! That's him. See. There he is!"

Confounded, Mackadoo turned toward the promontory. There, with the storm clouds as a backdrop, Pibbibib and the sergeant stood locked in combat. Their swords clashed above them as lightning crashed in the distance. The sky flashed amber with a series of bolts that swept across the valley. As the light faded, the sergeant pulled back for a moment, then charged with both blades slashing.

Pibbibib escaped the charge. Even so, he cursed the bum leg and the arm that had never fully recovered from his plunge off the cliff. He knew he was now too slow for the sergeant. He had to find another way, to try something unexpected. Retreating to the edge of the outcrop, he switched his sword into his left hand and his dagger in his right. When the sergeant followed, Backstabber turned and met him, taking a slash to his left arm even as he drove his dagger deep into his opponent's left thigh. The two warriors shuddered and spun off each other. Pibbibib lost his footing and tumbled over the edge, landing hard below amid the rocks.

The sergeant dropped wounded to his knee. Limping to the edge, he saw Backstabber lying dazed beneath him. "It's time to finish this!" he yelled. Reaching to his right, he picked up his fallen bow. Rising, he fitted an arrow into the bowstring. Backstabber, who lay below caught between two small boulders, could do nothing but watch his enemy draw back and take aim. But as the sergeant did so, a string of lightning bolts danced across the hilltop. Each one fried the few warriors still waiting there, and thunder roared behind each strike. The last bolt touched down directly on the sergeant's helm. He lit up like a torch, shot high in the air and fell into the abyss. His flaming corpse slammed onto the rocks near Backstabber.

Pibbibib froze, hoping to avoid a similar death. Moments passed and the last peals of thunder subsided. The night grew eerily quiet and dark. A smirk came to Backstabber's lips. He began to snicker, then to cackle and guffaw. A minute earlier, his adversary had taken aim for what would have been an easy kill shot. But the tide had turned. In a strange twist, Pibbibib had emerged the victor. Rising up, he looked first at the burned corpse beside him and then at the dark and quiet landscape beneath the hill. "Behold the master of fortune!" he bellowed. "Behold the survivor! Do you hear me, all you who ever doubted me? I have fallen as low as a creature can sink, but still I live. Despite all the cuts and wounds you have given me, I have risen again! And now, The Powers have fallen all around me. Yes, indeed, the very Skyfire has touched me. I can feel its power within me. I can sense it pulsing through me. Do you hear me, great lady? I can sense you clearly now! Why, I can even sense your cursed father, sitting contently deep in his castle in the old country. I can detect your distant armies moving and even hear the heartbeats of all those who seek me. Now where is the Great Valuable? You must know that it can't be hidden from me much longer. Let me near it and I will find it. Nothing can stop me now. Nothing!"

Not a warrior of Equis remained alive in the valley. A few of Mackadoo's sentries surrounding the edge of battle did manage to escape. All of them would keep running for hours. As a last act, Healdin had swung Mara at the hilltop, sending a series of lightning bolts and striking down the sergeant before he could slay Pibbibib. As the warrior had burst into flame, Healdin collapsed unconscious. The light vanished from Mara, even as it stayed clutched in the lady's grasp.

With eyes closed, Roj sensed the return of the darkness. He stood up and rushed to his wife. Carefully he took her sheath, covered the great power and returned it to her hand. Then he sat down and placed her head in his lap. As he did, a single tear rolled down his cheek.

The MuKierin rose and beheld Roj and his wife. Soon they and Lon encircled the fallen daughter of the King. "Is she alive, Uncle?" Roff asked.

"Yes, Roff. She's alive, but none of us can wake her. Only Blaze can do that now. She's passed beyond us. And she's passed her power on to him."

"What's that mean, Uncle?"

"She's given the Vine to Blaze. One day he'll come and claim it. I don't know when."

"So what do we do now?"

"We need to take advantage of this victory. Most of you must continue safely on to Newell. But not you, Roff. You need to take a few friends and go back to Orres. There you can collect both our followers and all the villagers who'll come with you."

"But won't the enemy still be in Orres?"

"Maybe so, but things changed tonight, Roff. The Realm's warriors in Orres and every other village in our land are going to hear about our victory here tonight. That'll put the fear in them. Nothing like this has ever happened before. And the King's people will go with you to make sure the enemy doesn't harm you. Mirri will show up soon with enough warriors to get you safely to Orres and back. And she'll bring another escort for those who go on to Newell."

Cisly knelt beside Roj. "And where will you go?"

"With Healdin. I'll go with a few of her people to take her back into the high country above Kierinswell. She won't wake for a long time, and never if Blaze doesn't prevail. The King's people will help me watch over her. I don't want to leave her now, not unless I absolutely have to."

Nightfall was spreading across the land when Backstabber made his way through the sage to Mackadoo and Weakling. The lord sat waiting atop his stallion, while Weakling remained curled up cross-legged on the ground. "Behold, the imposter returns!" Mackadoo exclaimed. "At last I've learned the truth about you, worm."

"Perhaps, Lord. But the truth keeps changing. I've just been showered with skyfire. Now I can feel The Powers surging through me. Maybe one day I'll even be able to sense the enemy as well as Weakling."

"Maybe. But I think you're still lying."

"Think what you wish, lord. But wasn't it good that we were here with you tonight? Otherwise, you would have been up on that hill when the skyfire struck down all the others."

"Do you expect my gratitude? Even I didn't think you were that stupid."

"Of course not, lord. But I hope that you can see how valuable Weakling and I remain to you."

"Valuable? You just got my sergeant killed."

"He was trying to shoot Weakling, lord. I knew you didn't want that. We still need him if we're going to get out of here alive."

"Is that so?"

"Oh, yes, lord. Weakling can help us escape through the enemy lines. He is still more experienced than me in sensing our enemies. And my job is to help keep Weakling calm and on his best behavior. Believe me, that's no easy task these days. Isn't that right, partner?"

"She got inside my head again," moaned Weakling. "She made me look at you when you were fighting on the hill.

She wouldn't let me turn my head away. She kept me looking your way until she sent down all that skyfire."

"What's that mean?" demanded Mackadoo. "What does she do to you?"

"She uses my eyes. She can see what I see. It's absolutely frightening when she gets ahold of me. I can't get rid of her."

"But why does she do that? Why does she care about Backstabber? Why is she always looking out for the both of you?"

"Looking out for us!" howled Pibbibib. "Are you joking? Her warriors drove us off a cliff! If Weakling and I hadn't jumped, we'd be dead now like that fool Rakmah. The enemy hunted us down and turned us into cripples. That's how she looked out for us."

Mackadoo reached for his sword.

"Kill me, if you dare, lord" said Backstabber. "But we can still help you make a comeback. I know that's what you really want. As the general said, you failed to catch both the Horse Stalker and the Champion. But with our help you still could find the Great Valuable. If you did, your star would rise again. And we can help you. Both Weakling and I can sense its power. But before that happens, you've got to get out of here. And we can help you pass safely through the enemy lines."

As Backstabber finished speaking, a horn sounded off to the east. A second one answered from the west. That meant only one thing: The King's troops were approaching from two sides. Mackadoo took his hand off his blade. "Do I still need you dogs? Perhaps I do. I wish it weren't so. But I don't want to be too hasty here, especially when the enemy is so close at hand. Very well, gasbag, I'm going to let you live another day. Indeed, you two are going to help me escape the enemy. And then I'm going to take you both to Equis. The Great Master himself will judge you. Perhaps someday you really will help me find the Great Valuable. But first we'll examine all your secret dreams of glory."

"Search my mind and my body, lord. You'll learn
only one thing, and that was proven tonight. My star is rising.
I am destined for greatness."

Postscript

Soon after the battle, Mirri rode into the valley with fifty male and female warriors. They grew solemn at the sight of Healdin lying so still, her eyes closed and her head cradled in Roj's lap. Silently six warriors brought a stretcher and lifted the King's daughter onto it. They placed her in a small wagon, where they covered her torso and legs with a white cloth.

"She's so beautiful," said Cisly.

"So are you, brave one," said Lon.

"Lon, I have to tell you something. I've got to leave you for a time. I'm sorry, but I need to go back to Orres with Roff and Darnelle."

"What? I thought you were all going on to Newell."

"No, not all of us. A few are going back to the village to get the rest of our followers, along with anyone else who'll join us. Darnelle is going back, and I promised that I'd go with her. Her brother Sunny may be in Orres, and the last time they saw each other, he stabbed her. She would have died if Blaze hadn't saved her. So I promised her I'd go there with her. We women have to stick together."

"Well, I feel sorry for her brother if he gets in your way. But what about me? I risked my neck to come to you, just like you wanted, and now you're telling me good-bye."

"No, not good-bye. This will be only a brief parting, and it would have happened anyway. You know you can't stay at Newell, not yet. You've got to return to South Shore. The Pappi need to know what happened here tonight. They need to know that we prevailed against our enemies. That means they don't need to surrender to the Barsk. You've got to go back and share that good news."

Lon's shoulders slouched. "I hate it when you're right. Very well, I'll leave you. But when will I see you again?"

She kissed him. "I'll be in Newell in less than three weeks. Waiting for you."

The sky was blue on the morning after the storm, when Tustin woke in a house of amber-colored logs. As he opened his eyes, the first thing that caught his attention was the log wall beside his bed. The spaces in between the round logs looked to be filled with mud or mortar. Tustin rolled over and beheld a great window with early sunlight streaming through it. At both ends of the window, colored images had been infused into corners of the glass. Still weak from his illness, Tustin pulled himself up and slid out of the bed. He shuffled straight for the glass. On the window's right side was an image of some great plant, both root and vine. He reached out and put his hand upon it. The window felt warm to his touch. Beneath the image were the words, "Fidden Gadaeyo."

"Light the darkness," Tustin said aloud. "And what's this atop the vine?"

A woman's voice answered from the darkened doorway: "It is a thorn, child. The Thorn of Glory."

Tustin turned and saw a stranger's silhouette. "Forgive me, lady. I shouldn't have touched the window. But it looked so beautiful."

"You may touch it, Tustin. I made it for you."

"For me? But why?"

"You were chosen to bring back the Root of Glory. It is why you have come to this place."

"Me? Are you sure?"

"Yes, child. The task has fallen to Burl and you. So says the King. Aren't you going to ask me about the other image?"

Tustin walked to the left end of the window. There he studied a second design of darker hues. "It looks like a dungeon," he said, "with bars and chains. What does it mean, lady?"

"It's part of your story, Tustin. That's where you're bound."

As his wounds healed, Sorenth found himself anxious to depart the Quolli village. One autumn evening he asked

Ciga, his keeper, "When is the mysterious woman coming for me?"

"Not soon enough for me, swashbuckler. And she had better pay me well when she arrives or I'm going to let Naug have you. He's been practicing with a sword. I'm told he's gotten a little better."

"Are you still going to send that poor boy after me?"

"Of course. He drew the black mark. He must avenge a wound for a wound. It is our way."

"Well, then, let's hope I don't have to kill him."

"Don't worry about him, swashbuckler. Worry about the twenty other men who will join him. Naug may be a fool, but he's also a coward. He'll bring plenty of friends with him when he attacks you."

Later that night Yawnna and her servant Kitar came to Sorenth. "My songbird said the woman warrior is on her way," said Kitar. "She sent word that she's coming for you."

"Good, I can't wait to get out of this place."

"What will you do after you leave us?"

"I've got to find some friends. I think they're in trouble."

"You mentioned a brother. Is he among them?"

"Yes, he's with them."

Kitar translated and spoke again to Sorenth. "My songbird says the woman warrior may help you find your friends. After all, she is your protector."

"Is she? I'm not so sure."

"Wait until you meet her. Then you will know that she is the one who saved your life. Perhaps she will say why she cares so much for you. Indeed, that is a question all the Quolli want answered."

"Me, too, Kitar. Me, too."

On a moonless night, a lone horseman galloped to the entrance of Equis Castle. In darkness he crossed its drawbridge and entered its inner grounds. There he delivered a dispatch to the captain of the guard, who took it straight to a special office that was manned by four officers: two Slinkers and two Cleavers. An officer from each order scurried down separate halls to the quarters of their executive officers. Ten minutes later, the Slinkers' General Suktoos and the Cleavers' General Mooschus met at the special office and proceeded side by side into an unlit chamber. Zoirra was waiting there for them. A guard lit a single candle and exited.

"Master," said Mooschus, "the cadets have set out to our trap. The one named Bo is leading them to the Barrel."

"Excellent. I will go at once to meet him there."

Suktoos asked, "Are you sure this human can prevail against the enemy's Champion?"

"Of course, as long as he has the Great Valuable. Almost any mortal could conquer with its power. After all, this Champion is weak. He's half mortal, isn't he?"

"Yes, Master, he's an abomination."

And you're going to find the great power for me, aren't you, Suktoos?"

"Yes, Master."

"If you don't, I'm sure Mackadoo will do my bidding. We must find it before the enemy does. Whoever has that power will surely prevail. Remember the inscription on its Golden Box. It says the Great Valuable can't kill the King, but he isn't coming to this fight. No, he's sending his grandson."

"And what about Bo, Master? Can he be persuaded to wield the power for us?"

"He's mortal. He won't be able to resist it. The desire to have it has been burned into all these creatures' hearts. Indeed, Bo has already set his mind to wield it. It's just that he now wants to use it against us. No matter. We can turn him to our purposes. And what of his brother Sorenth?"

"There's still no sign of him," said Mooschus, "and no sign of the three scouts who went looking for him. They seemed to have vanished. It must be the work of the enemy. But we'll keep looking for the young one."

"Yes, do so. Holding one brother by the throat might persuade the other to do our bidding, if needed. But it bothers me that our enemies seem to have interfered in this matter.

Have they learned of our schemes? Perhaps they have. I have long wondered whether we might have a spy in our midst. Now I suspect that we do. Nonetheless, we must stick with our plans. We will proceed to the Barrel. Bo goes there thinking he will find the great power. Instead, he will find me. And I will help him find his destiny."

On the night of the battle west of Kierinswell, Blaze couldn't sleep. In darkness he rose and climbed to the highest turret in the Castle of River's End. Waiting there for him was the Queen, wrapped in a robe of blue satin.

"It's happened, hasn't it, Grandmother?" said Blaze. "Mother has prevailed."

"Yes, Healdin triumphed over her enemies. In so doing she has ensured that the Vine will pass on to you. One day it will be yours to join with the other great powers."

"Then the time has come. When will we start?"

"Soon, child. The King already is making preparations. Soon we will touch your heart with a new power. Soon the Thorn will become part of you."